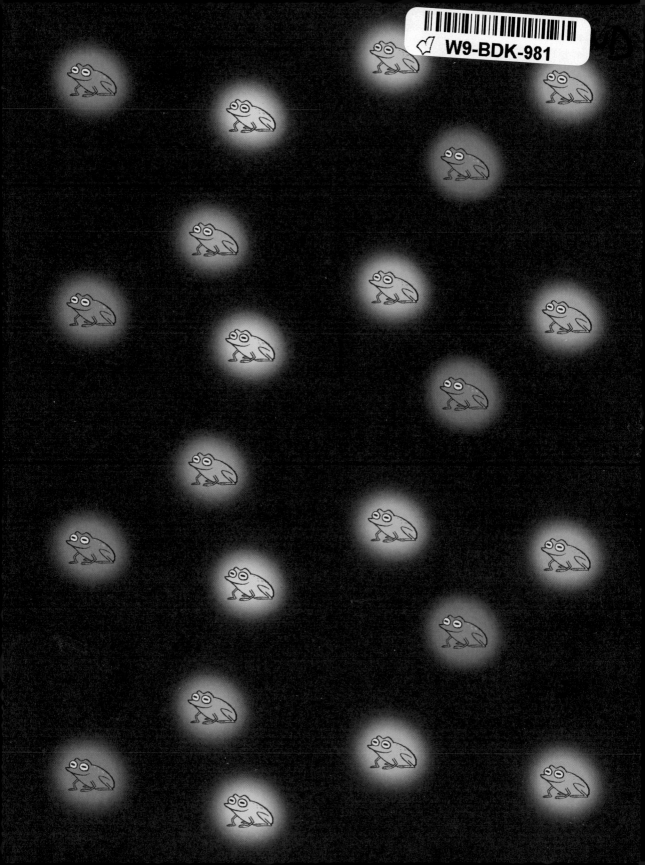

PETER & ERNESTO

SLOTHS in the NIGHT

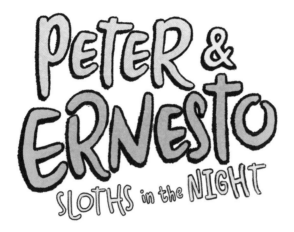

PETER & ERNESTO
SLOTHS in the NIGHT

graham ANNABLE

:01
First Second
New York

:01
First Second

Published by First Second
First Second is an imprint of Roaring Brook Press, a division of Holtzbrinck Publishing Holdings Limited Partnership
120 Broadway, New York, NY 10271

Don't miss your next favorite book from First Second!
For the latest updates go to firstsecondnewsletter.com and sign up for our enewsletter.

Library of Congress Control Number: 2019930672
ISBN: 978-1-250-21130-9

Our books may be purchased in bulk for promotional, educational, or business use.
Please contact your local bookseller or the Macmillan Corporate and Premium Sales Department
at (800) 221-7945 ext. 5442 or by email at MacmillanSpecialMarkets@macmillan.com.

FIRST EDITION

First edition, 2020
Edited by Calista Brill and Alex Lu
Book design by Molly Johanson
Printed in China by 1010 Printing International Limited, North Point, Hong Kong

This book was created entirely by drawing and coloring on a Cintiq monitor and using custom brushes in Photoshop.

1 3 5 7 9 10 8 6 4 2

BY ART WE LIVE

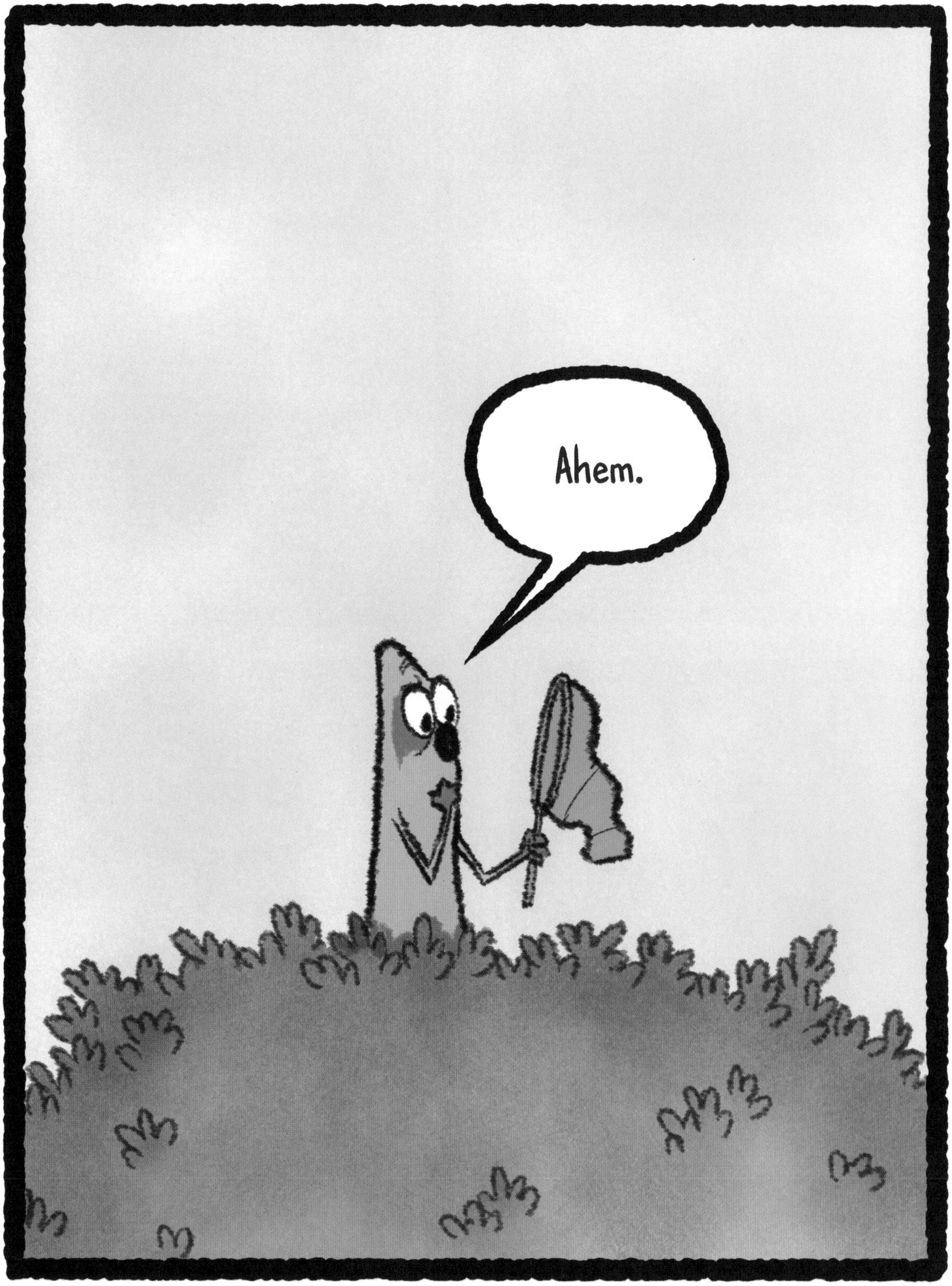
Ahem.

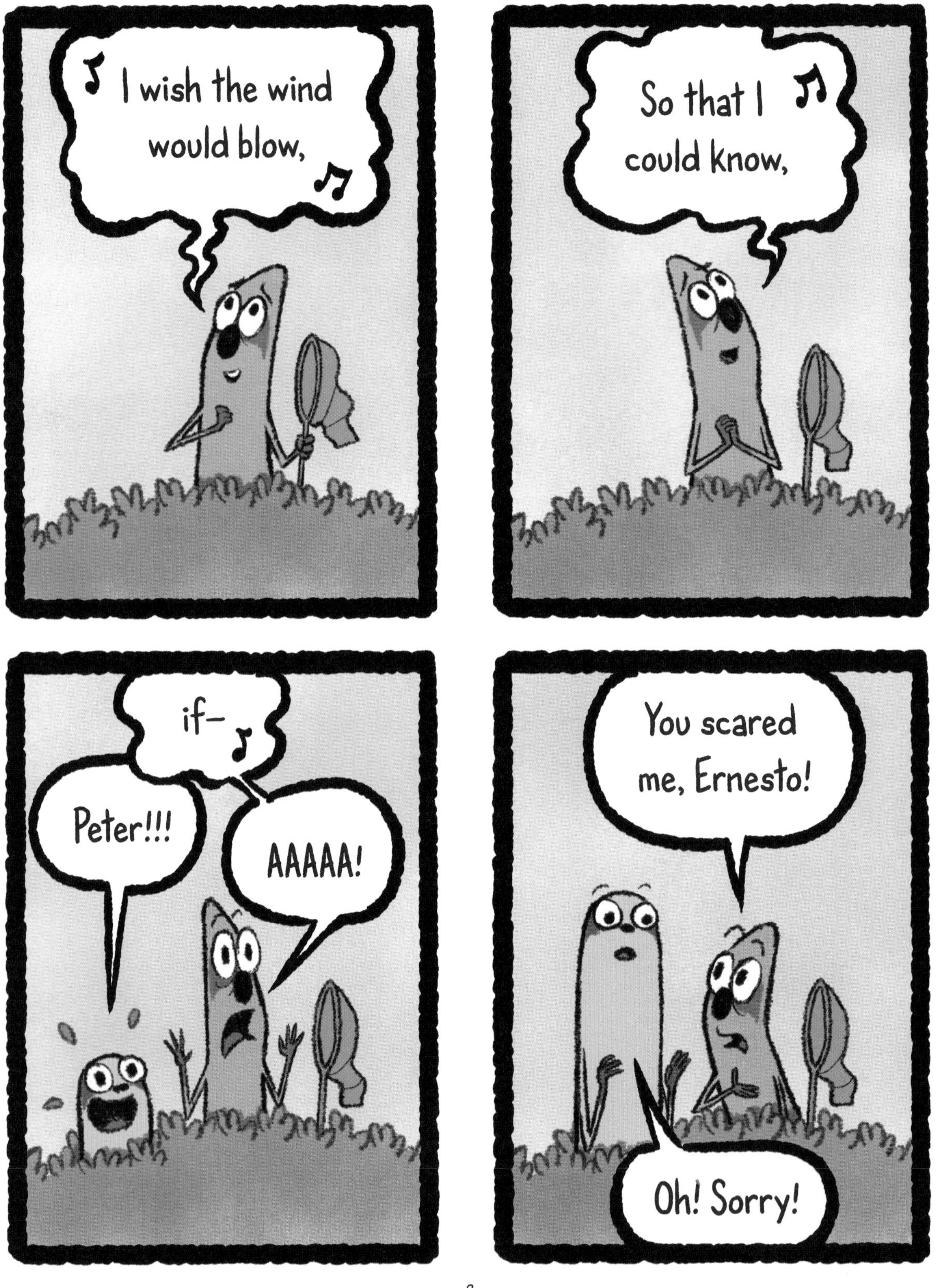
I wish the wind would blow,
So that I could know,
if–
Peter!!!
AAAAA!
You scared me, Ernesto!
Oh! Sorry!

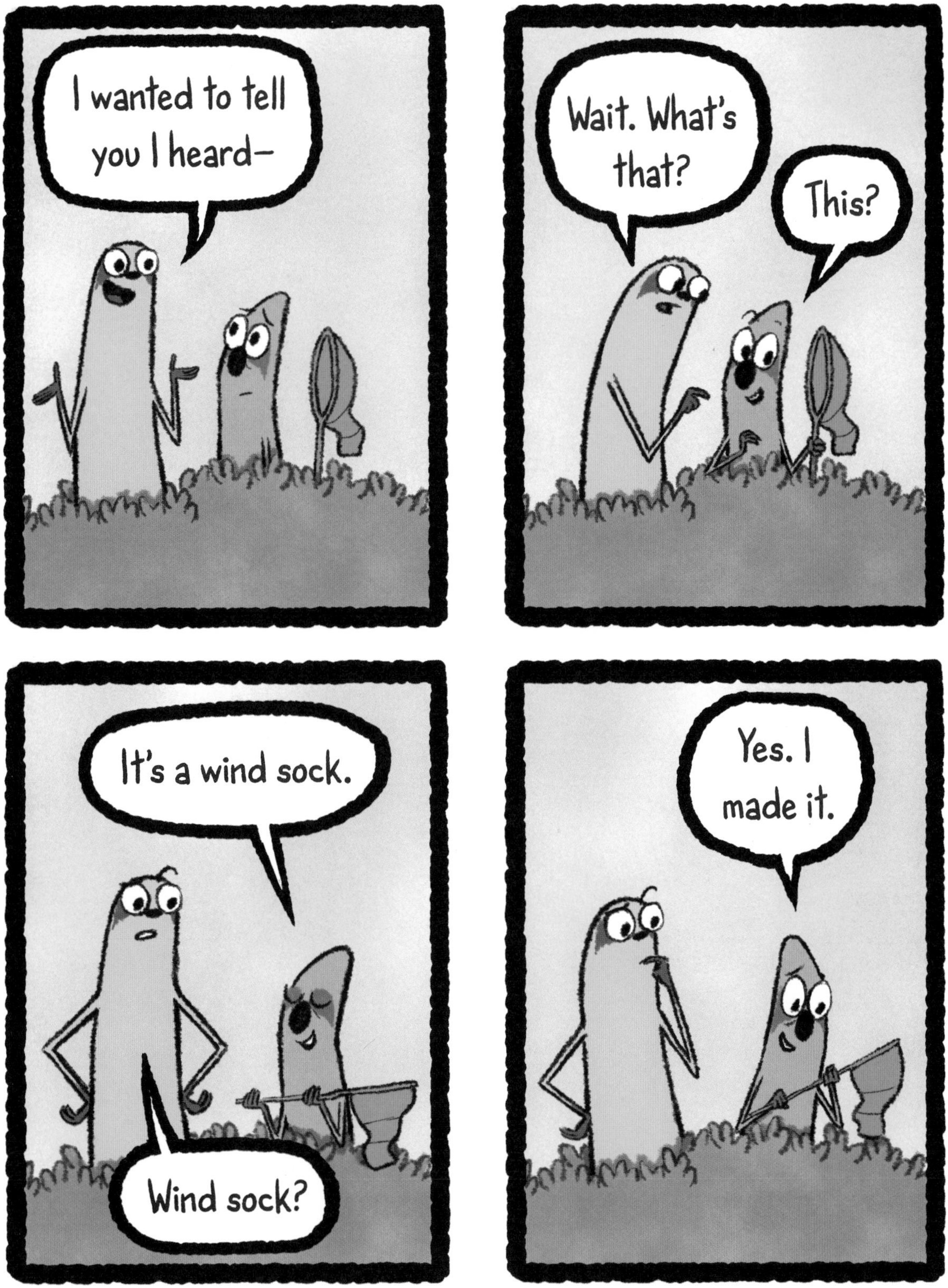
I wanted to tell you I heard–
Wait. What's that?
This?
It's a wind sock.
Wind sock?
Yes. I made it.

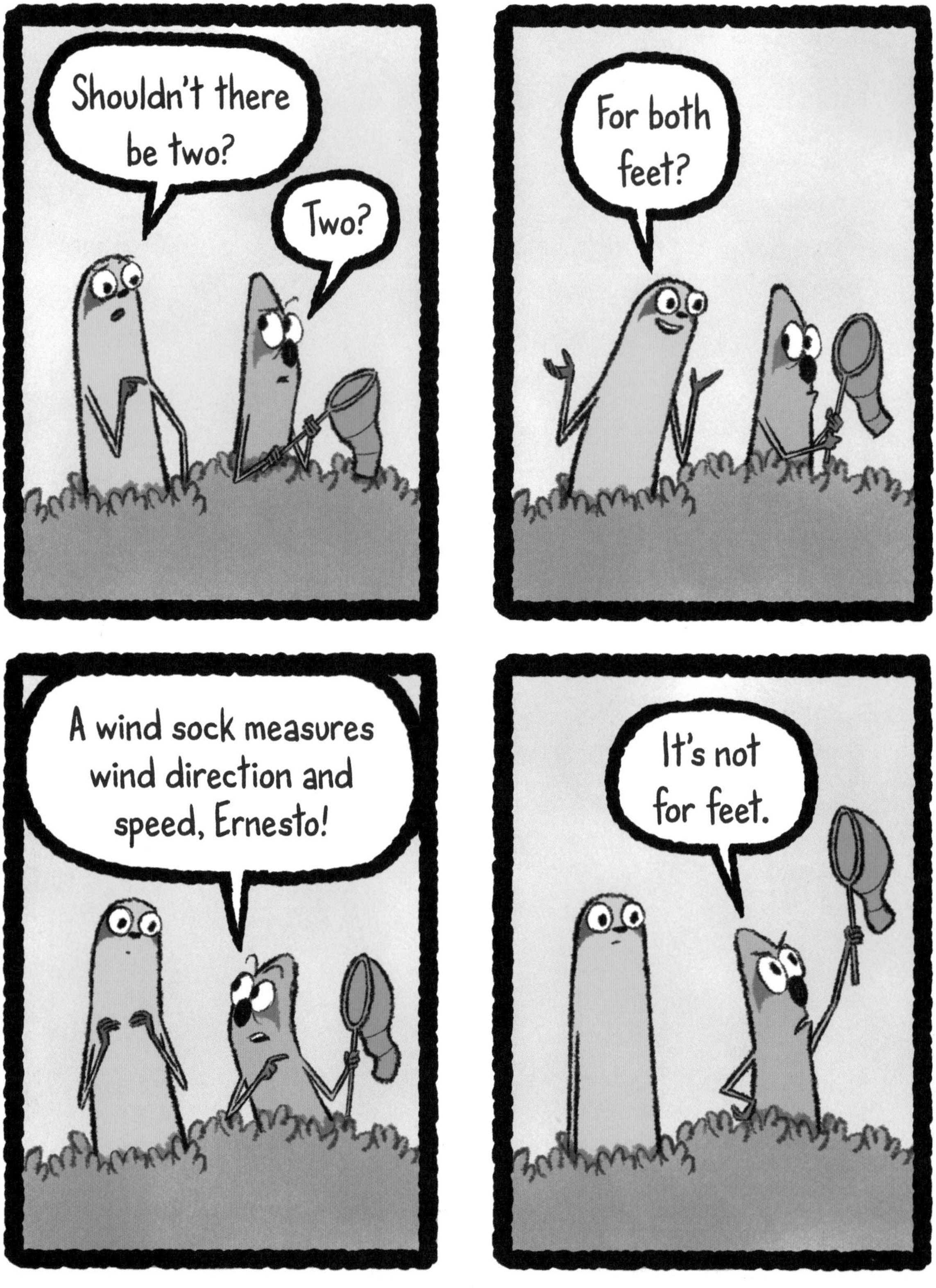
Shouldn't there be two?
Two?
For both feet?
A wind sock measures wind direction and speed, Ernesto!
It's not for feet.

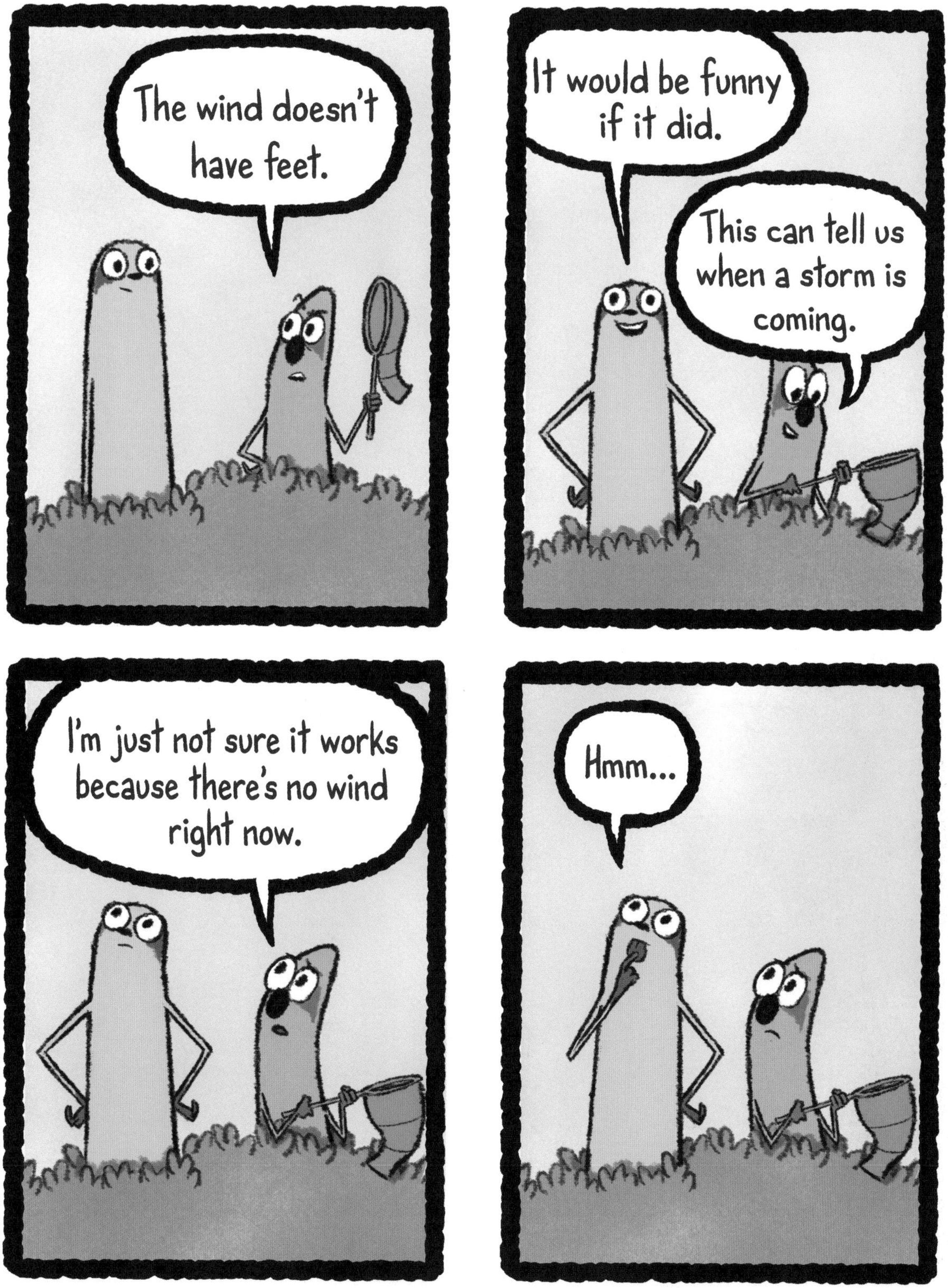
The wind doesn't have feet.
It would be funny if it did.
This can tell us when a storm is coming.
I'm just not sure it works because there's no wind right now.
Hmm...

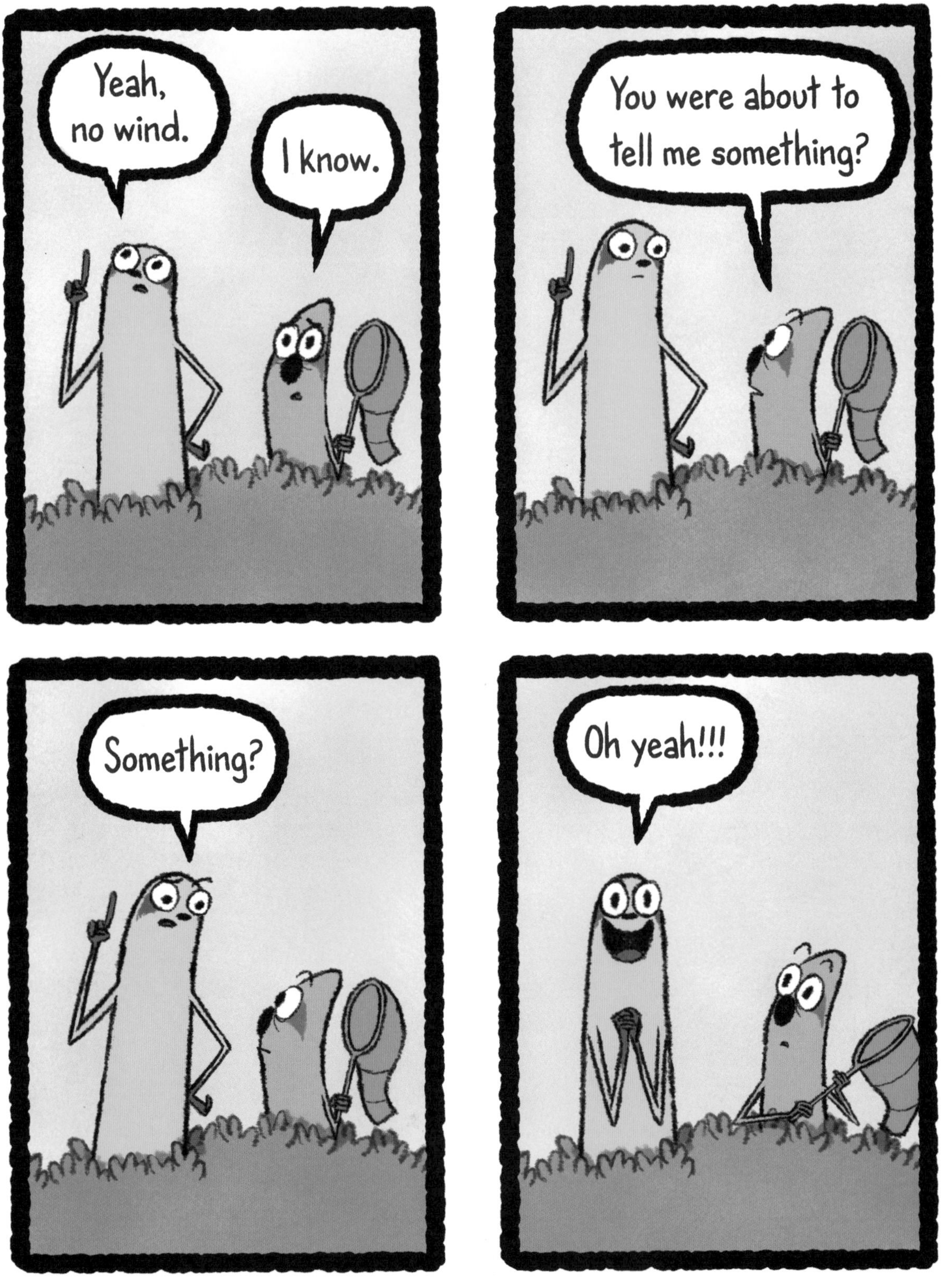
Yeah, no wind.
I know.
You were about to tell me something?
Something?
Oh yeah!!!

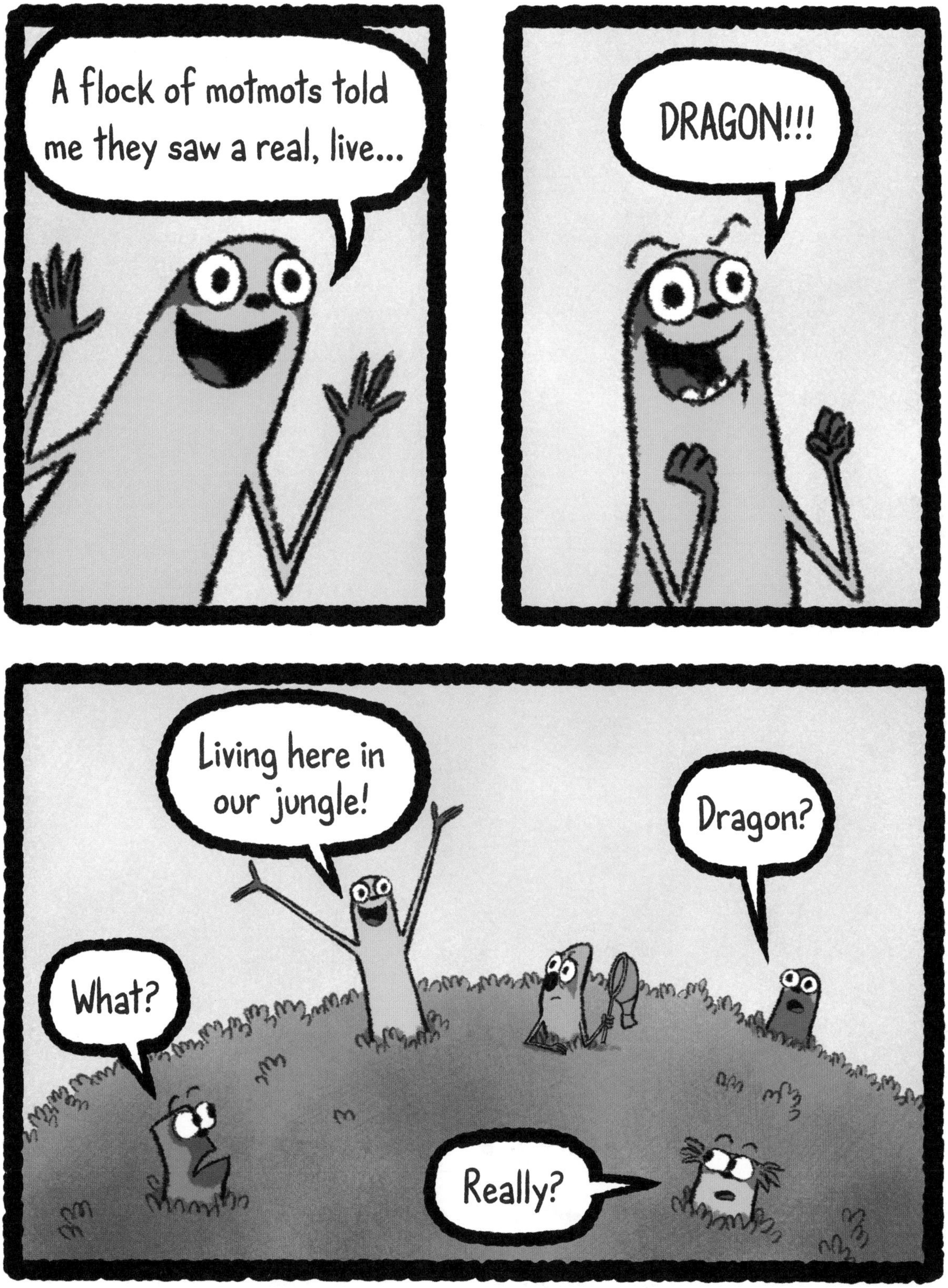
A flock of motmots told me they saw a real, live...
DRAGON!!!
Living here in our jungle!
What?
Dragon?
Really?

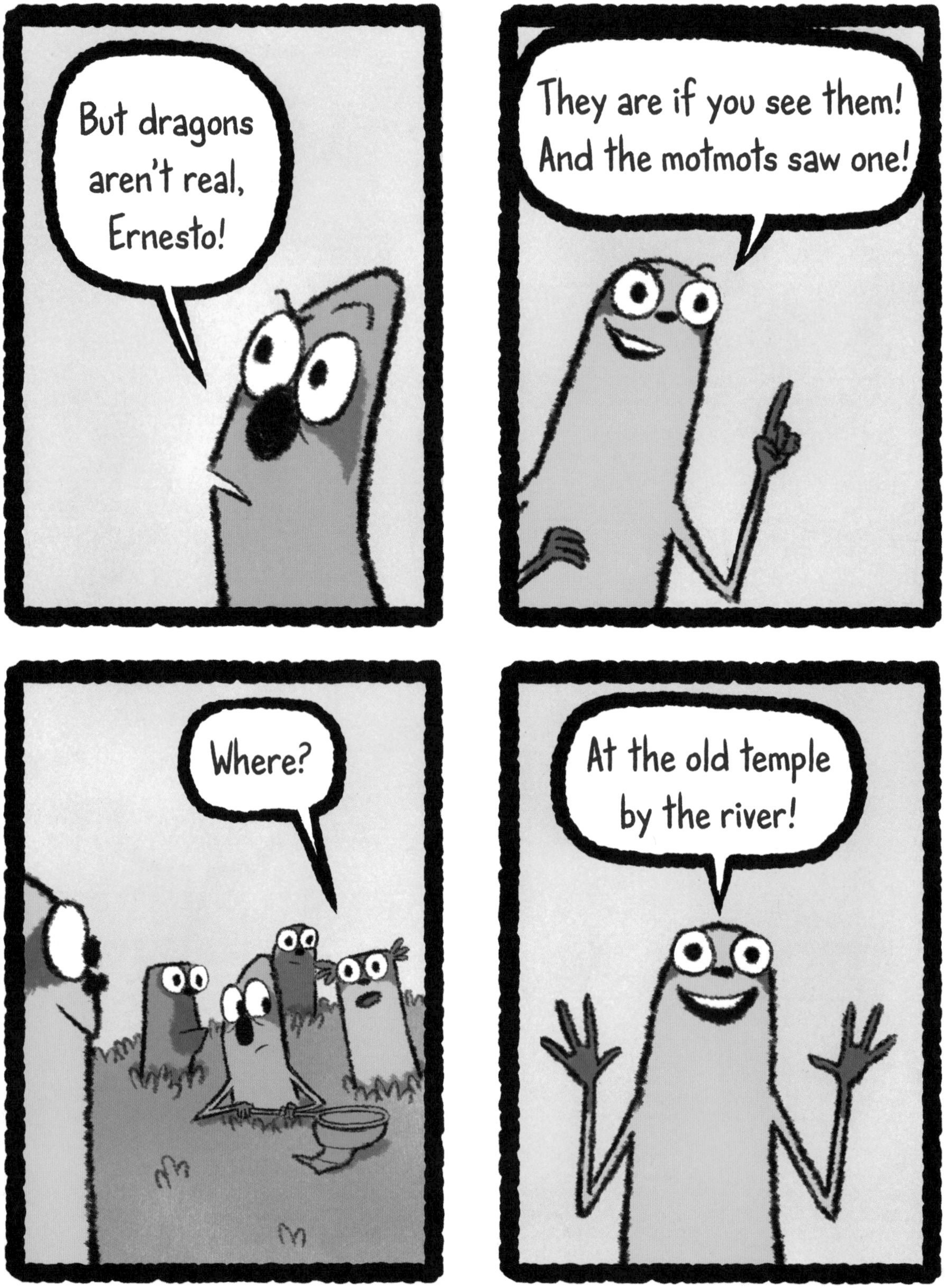
But dragons aren't real, Ernesto!
They are if you see them! And the motmots saw one!
Where?
At the old temple by the river!

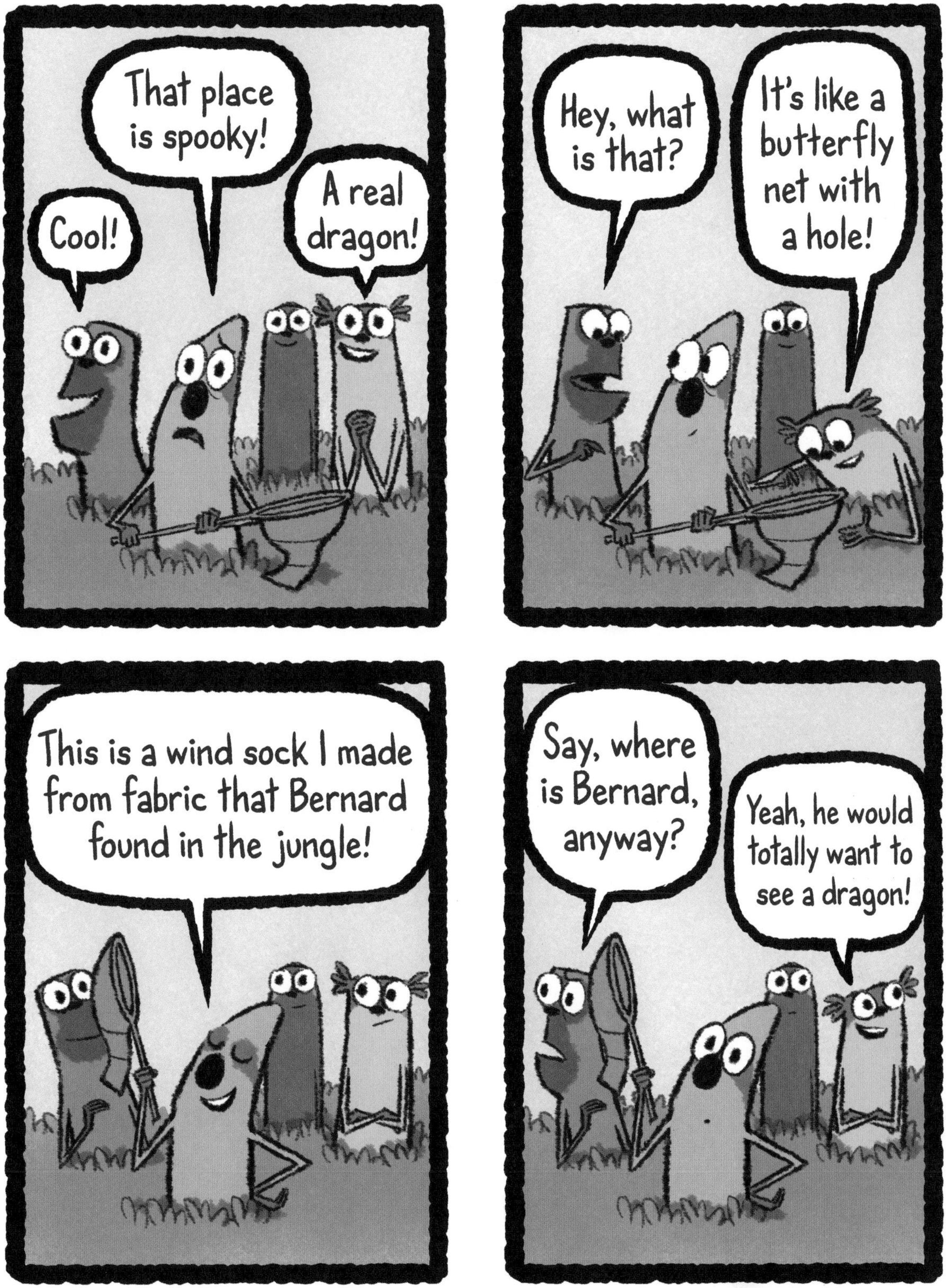
Cool!
That place is spooky!
A real dragon!
Hey, what is that?
It's like a butterfly net with a hole!
This is a wind sock I made from fabric that Bernard found in the jungle!
Say, where is Bernard, anyway?
Yeah, he would totally want to see a dragon!

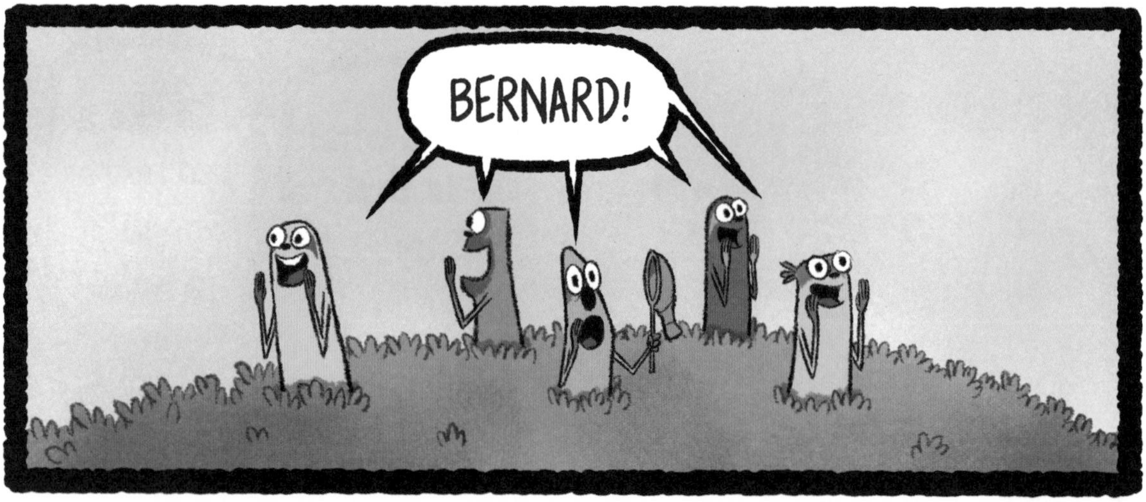
BERNARD!

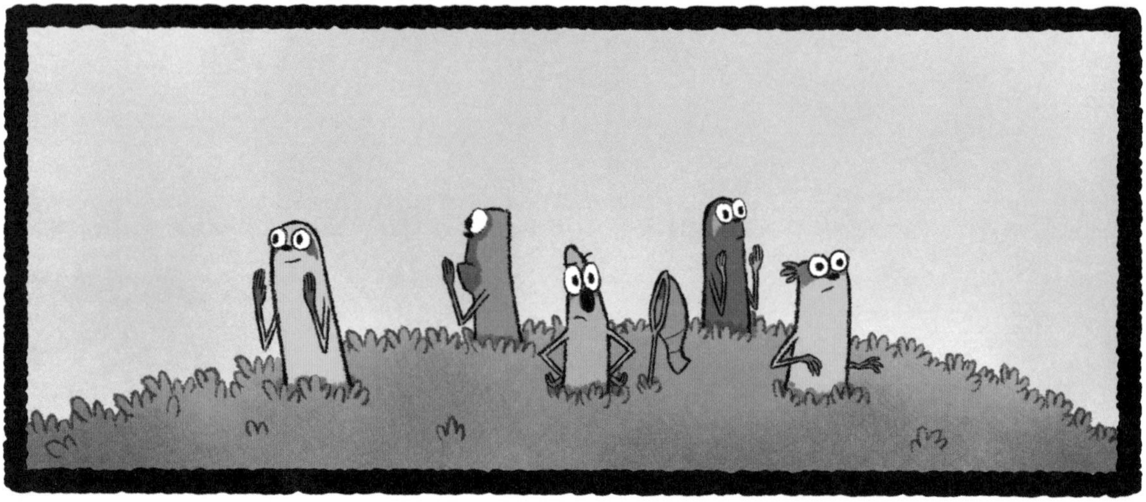

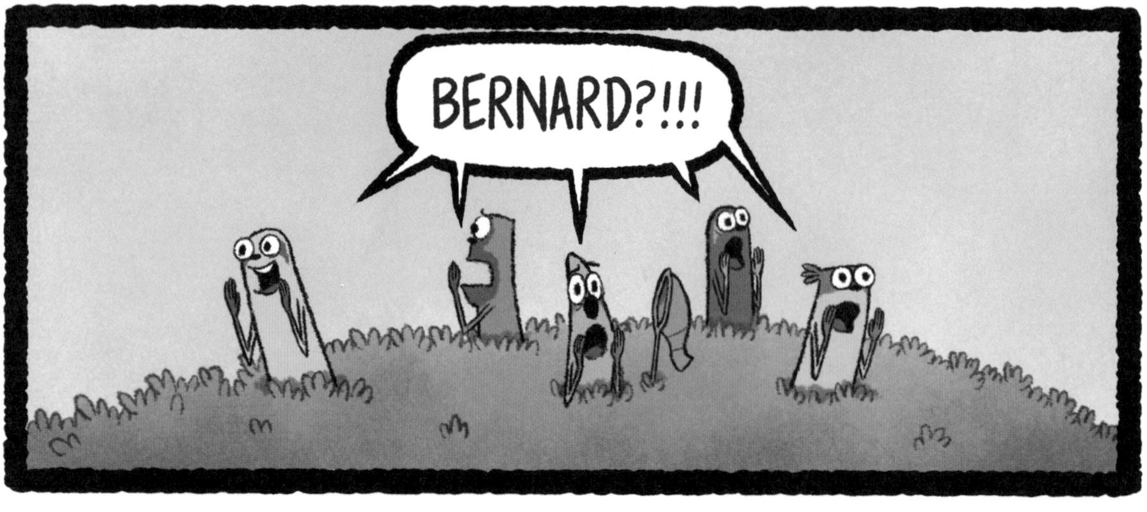
BERNARD?!!!

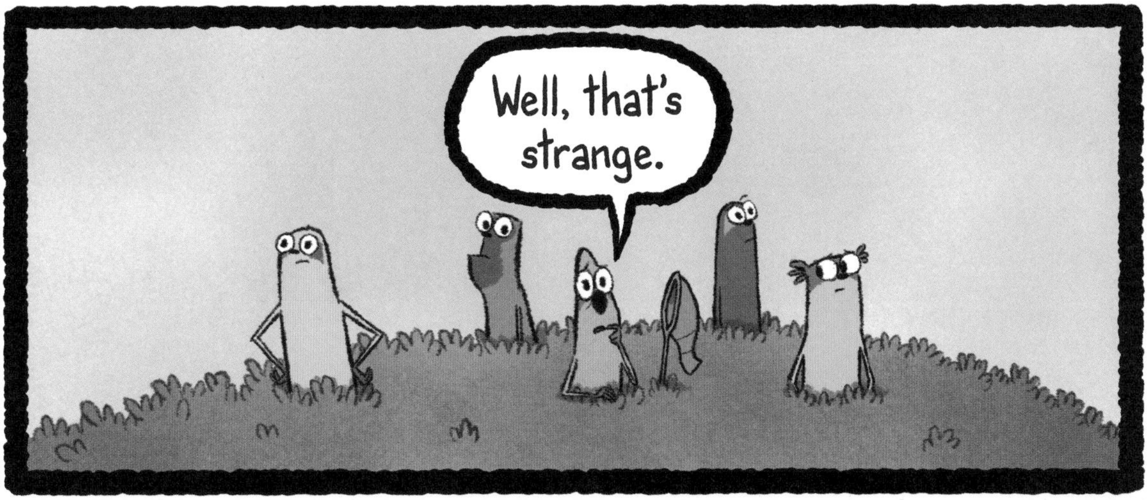
Well, that's strange.

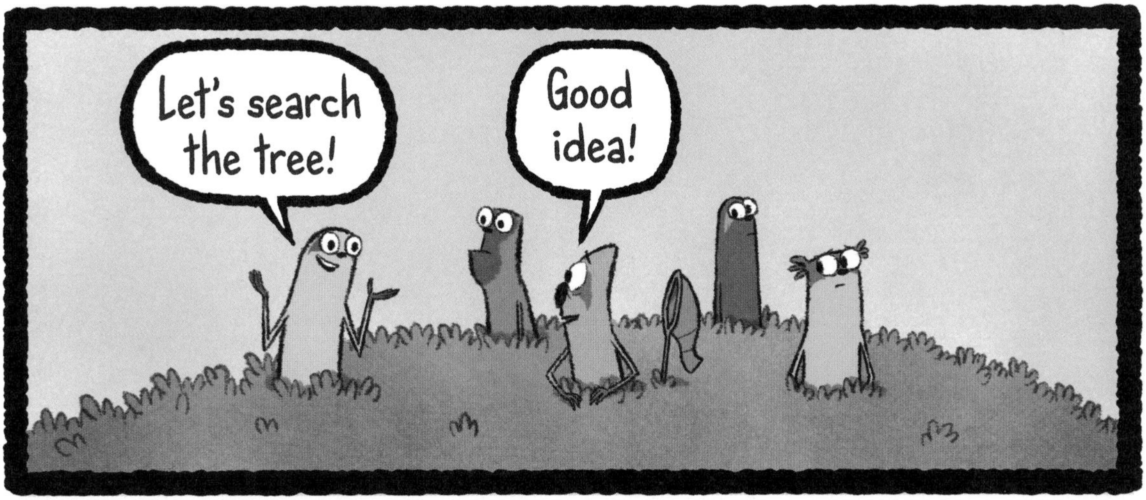
Let's search the tree!
Good idea!

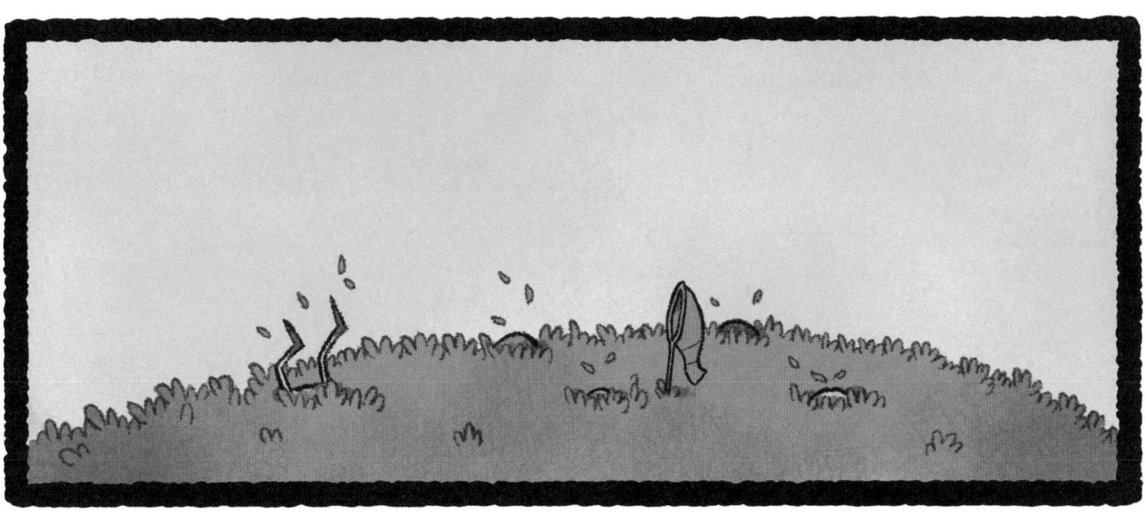

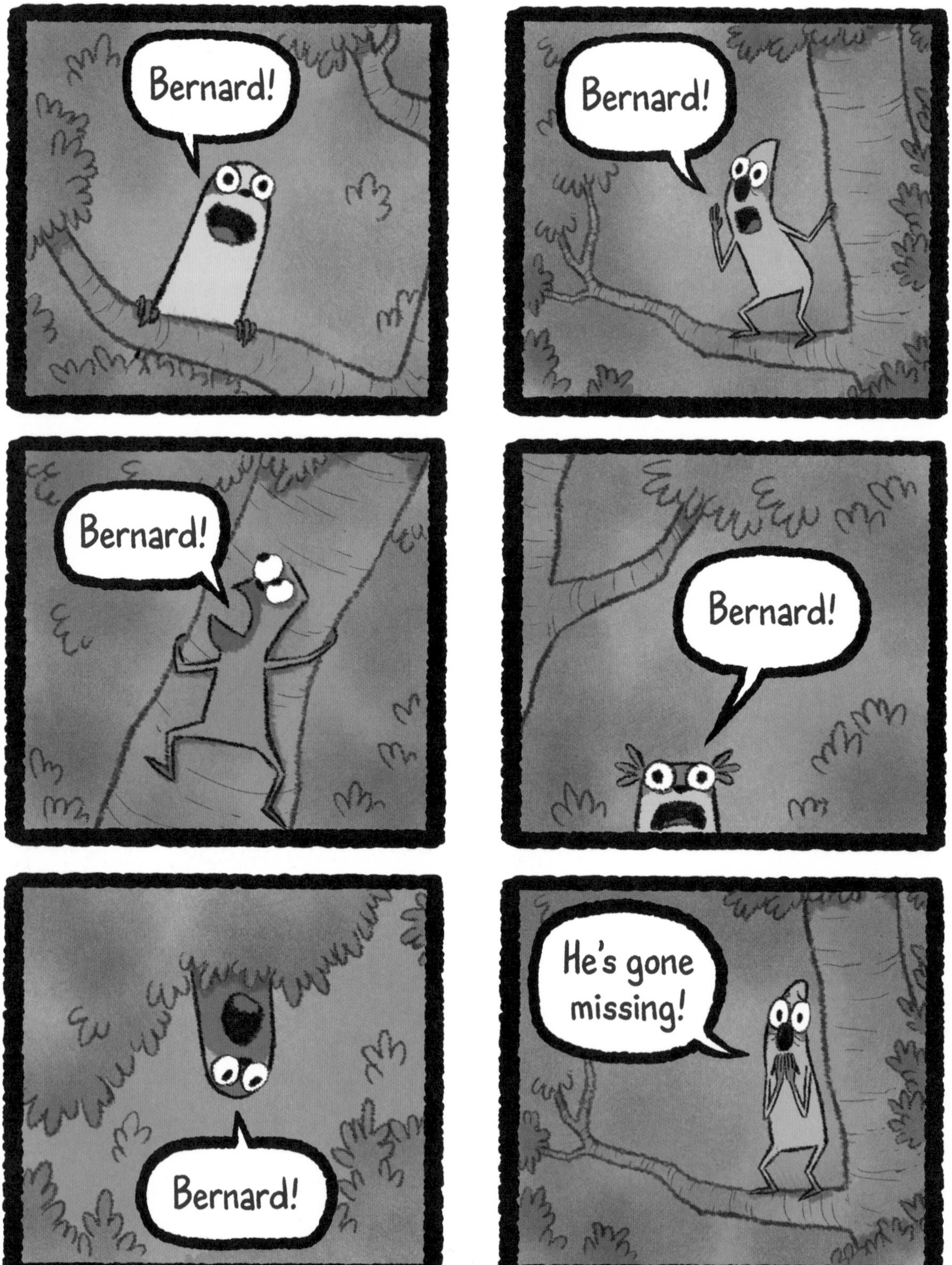
Bernard!
Bernard!
Bernard!
Bernard!
Bernard!
He's gone missing!

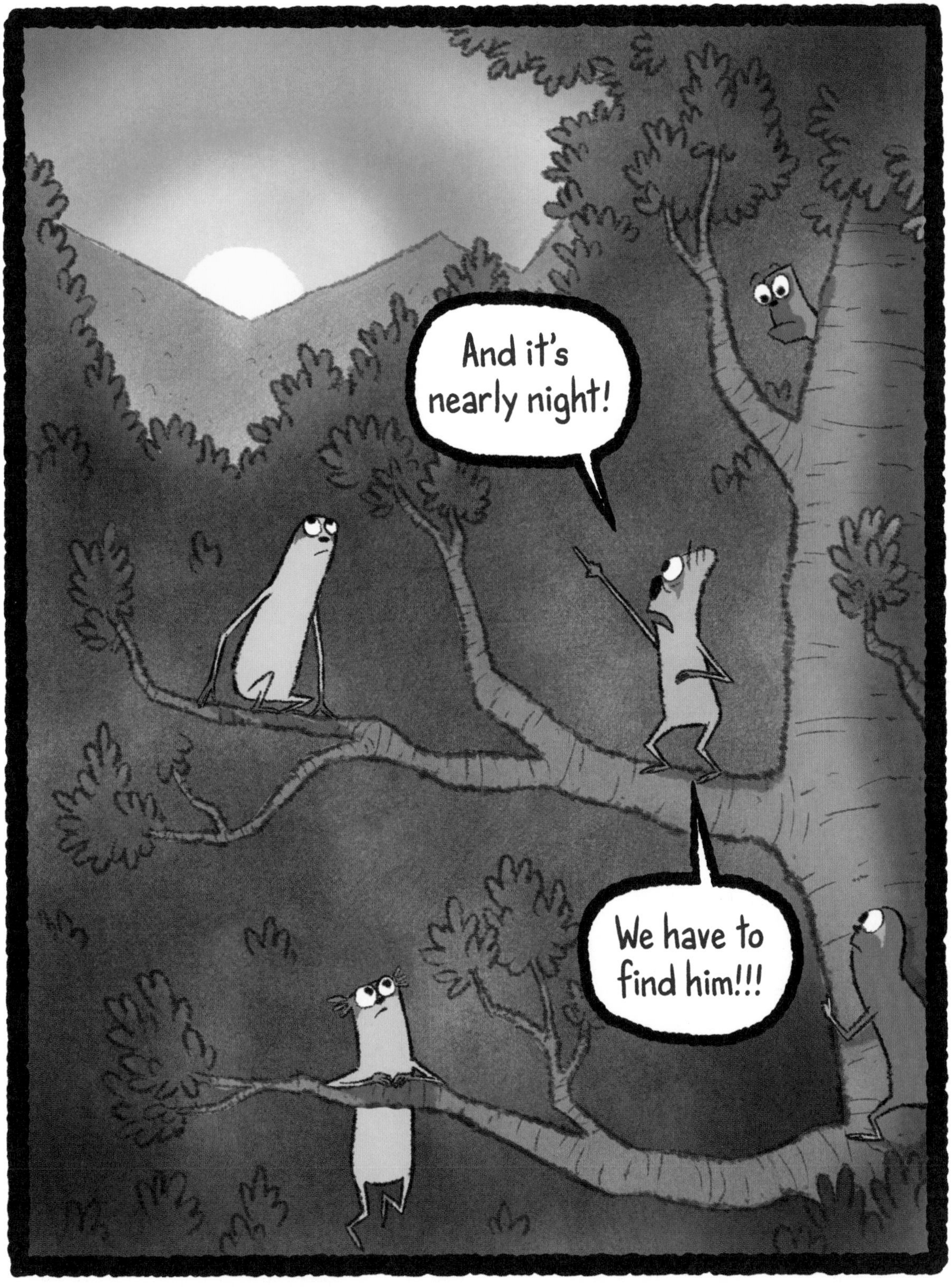
And it's nearly night!
We have to find him!!!

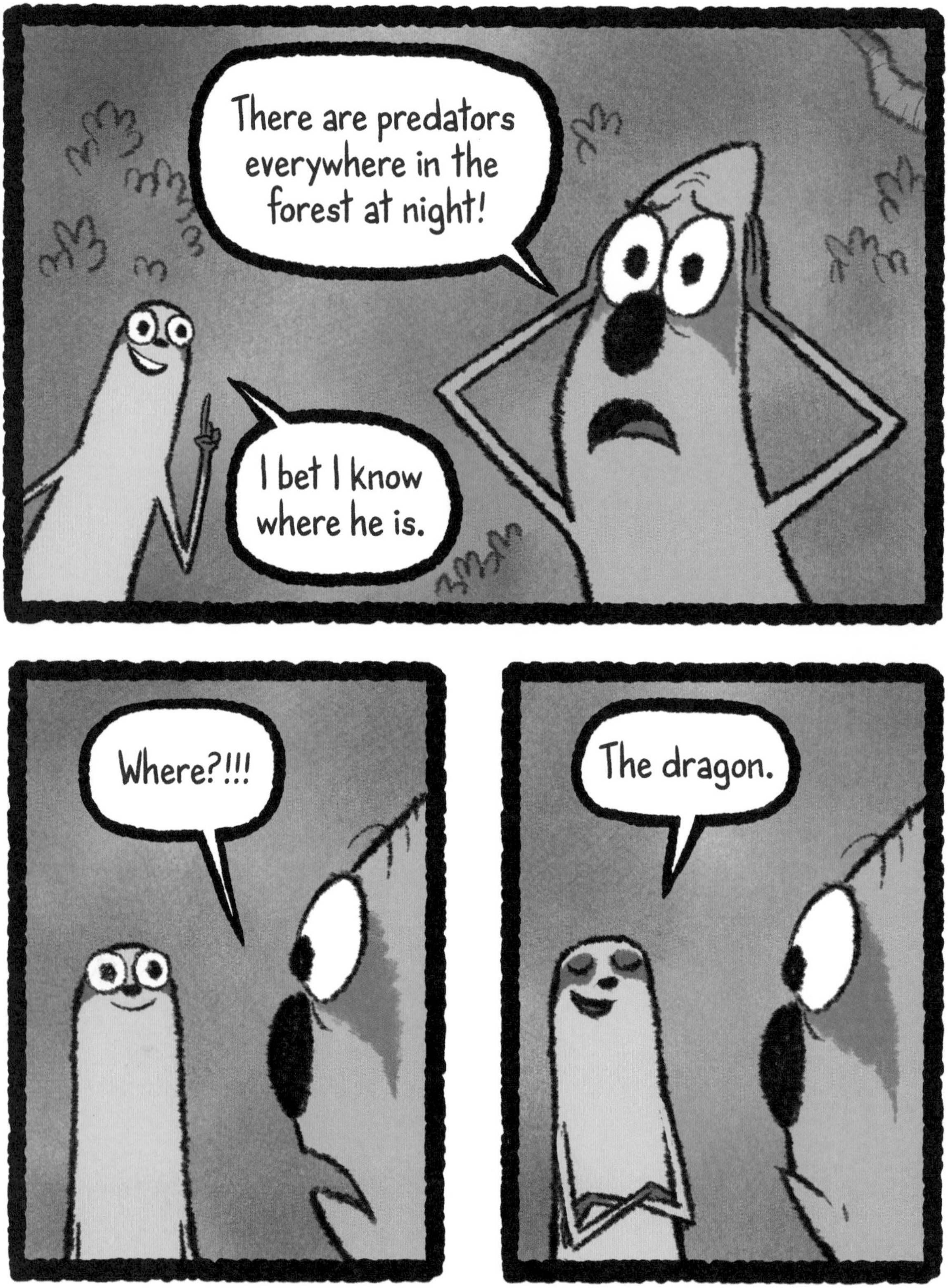
There are predators everywhere in the forest at night!
I bet I know where he is.
Where?!!!
The dragon.

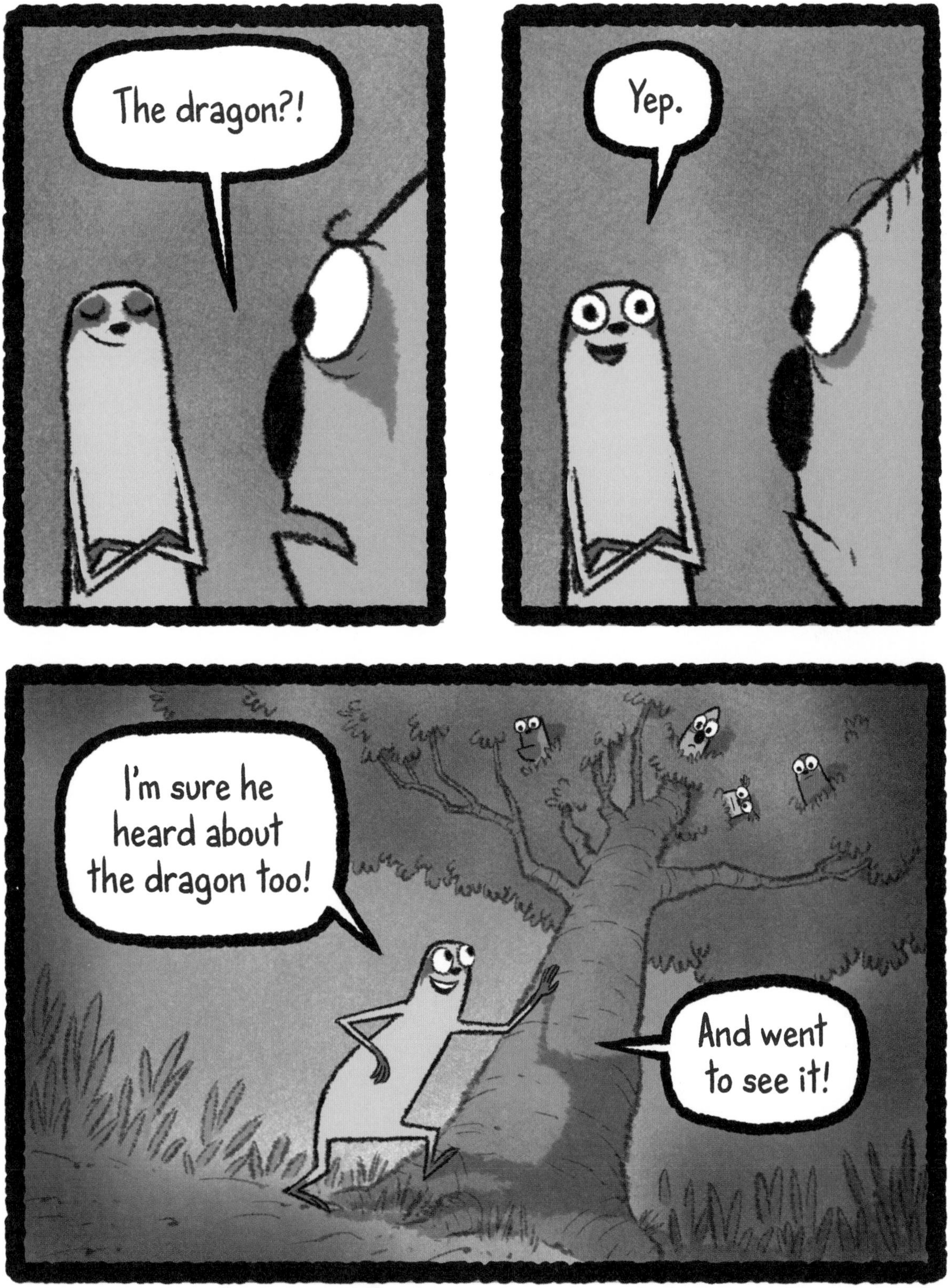
The dragon?!
Yep.
I'm sure he heard about the dragon too!
And went to see it!

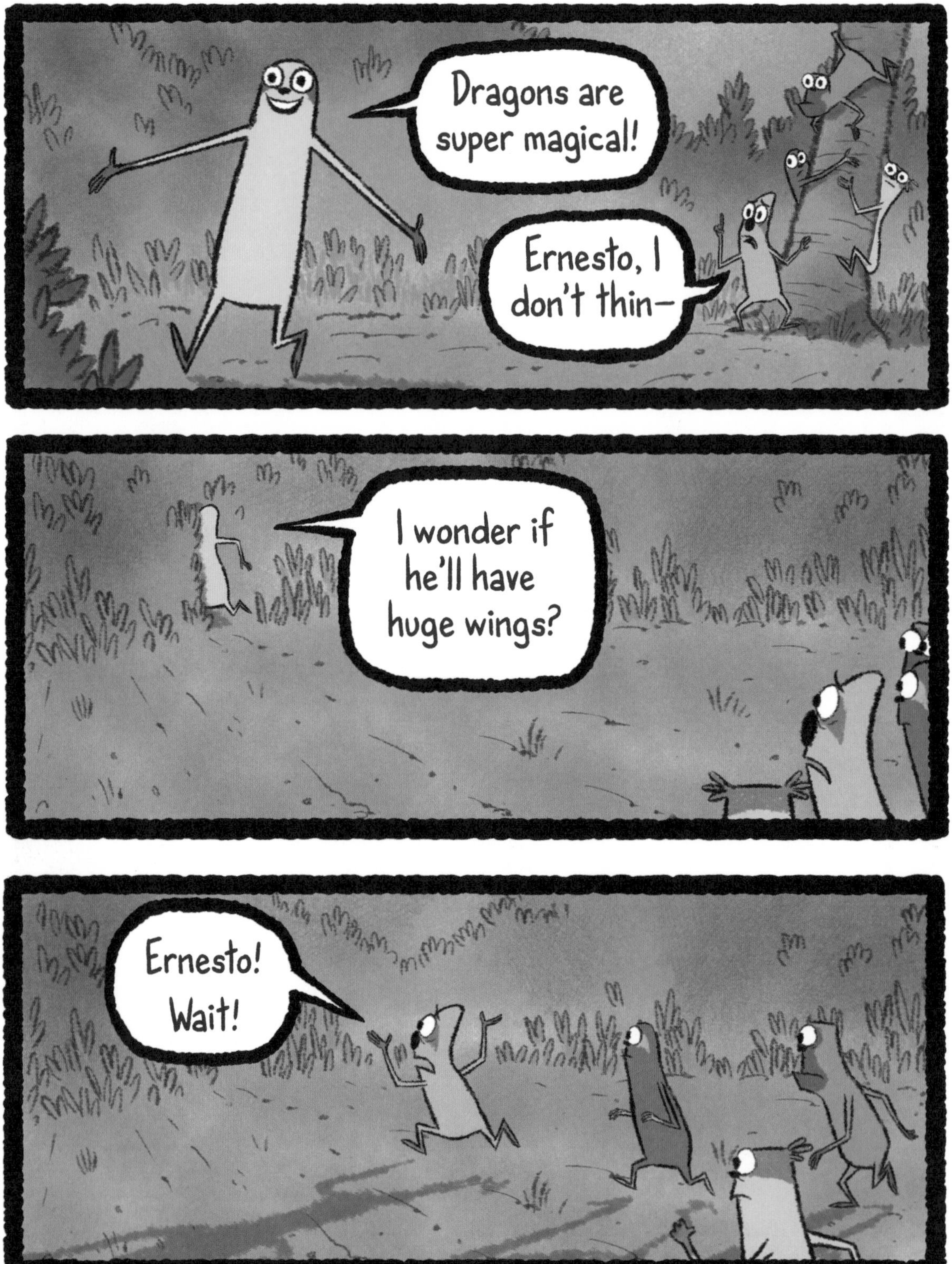
Dragons are super magical!
Ernesto, I don't thin–
I wonder if he'll have huge wings?
Ernesto! Wait!

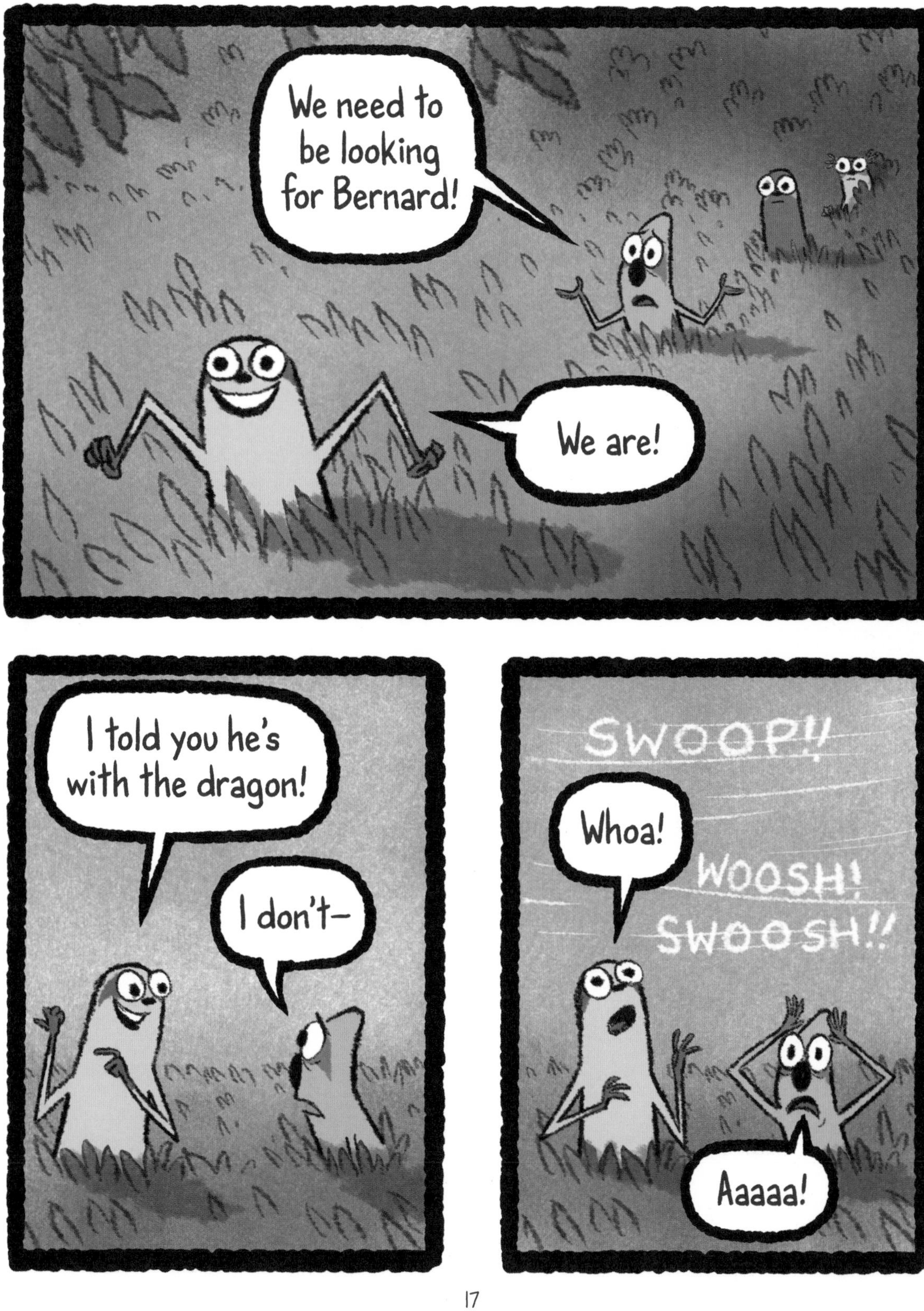
We need to be looking for Bernard!
We are!
I told you he's with the dragon!
I don't–
SWOOP!!
Whoa!
WOOSH!
SWOOSH!!
Aaaaa!

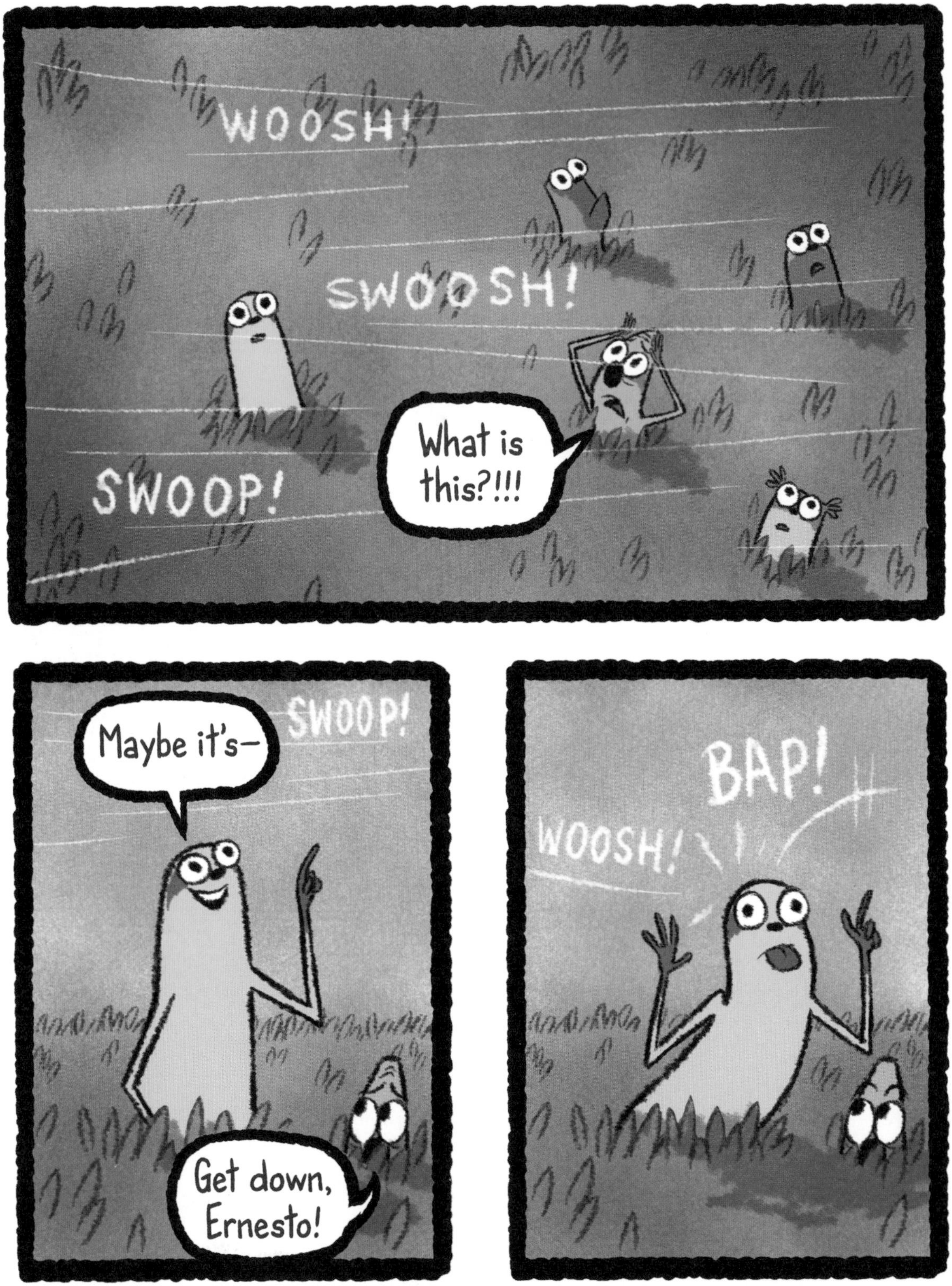
WOOSH!
SWOOSH!
SWOOP!
What is this?!!!
SWOOP!
Maybe it's—
Get down, Ernesto!
BAP!
WOOSH!

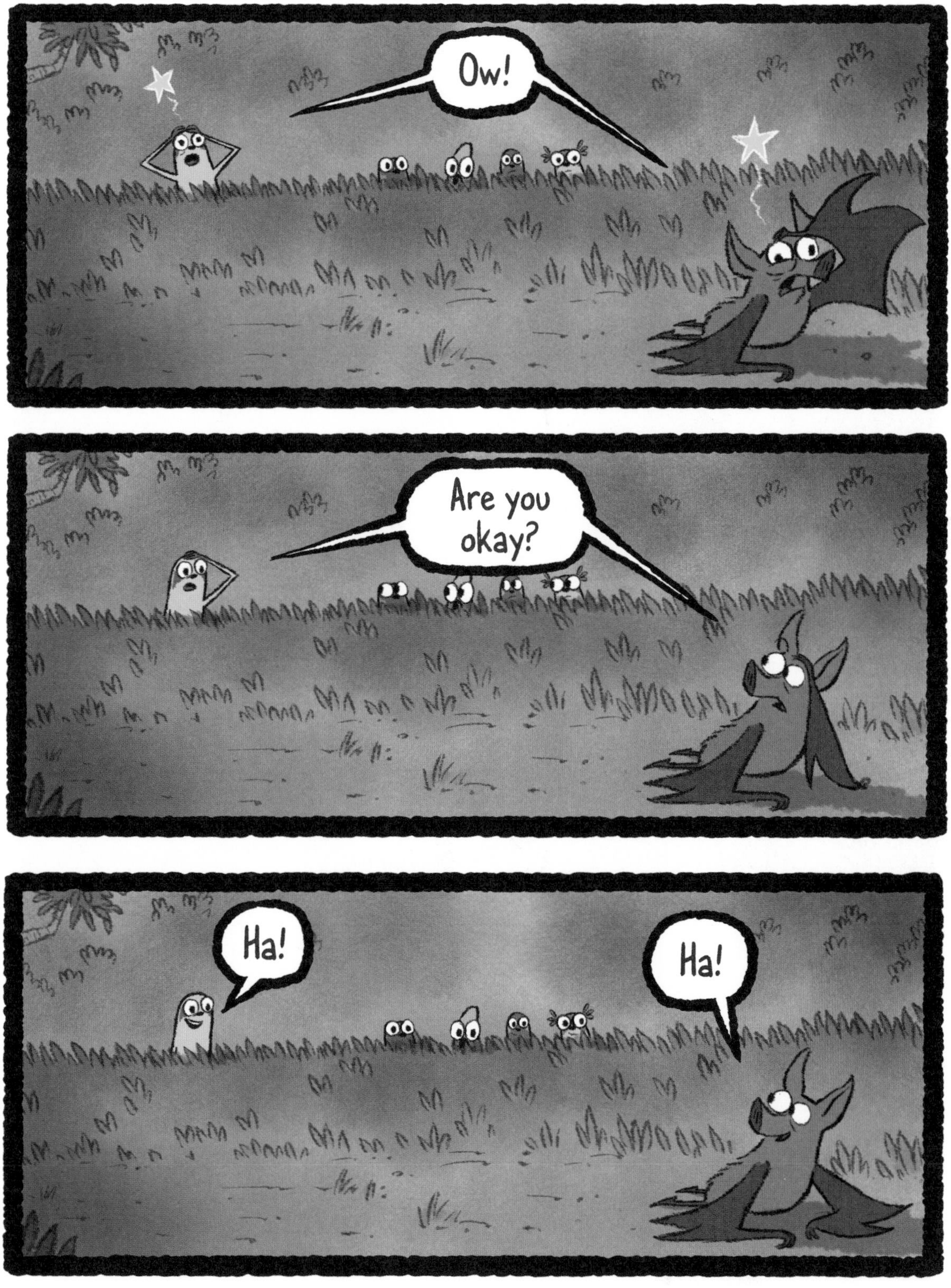
Ow!
Are you okay?
Ha!
Ha!

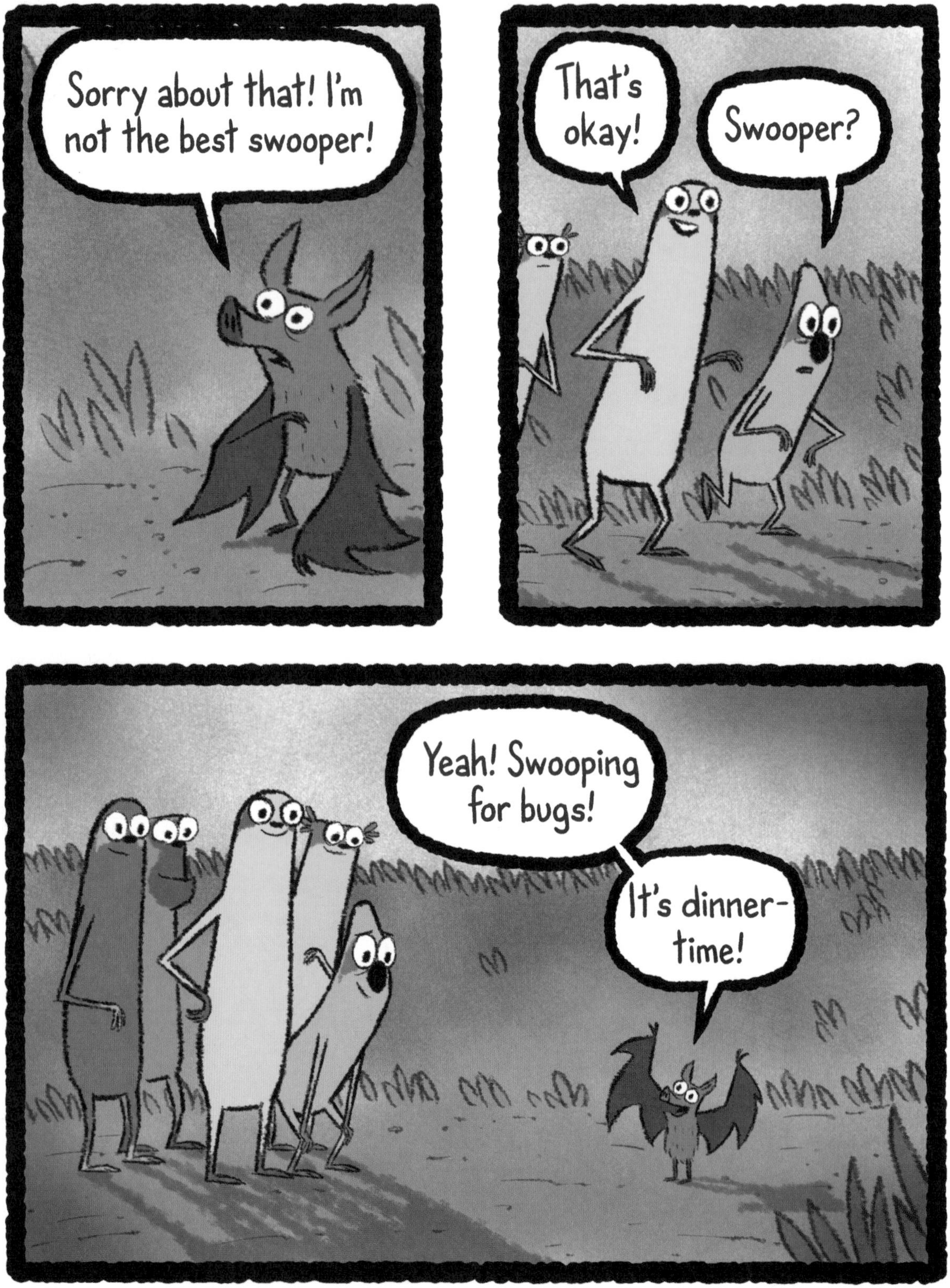
Sorry about that! I'm not the best swooper!
That's okay!
Swooper?
Yeah! Swooping for bugs!
It's dinner-time!

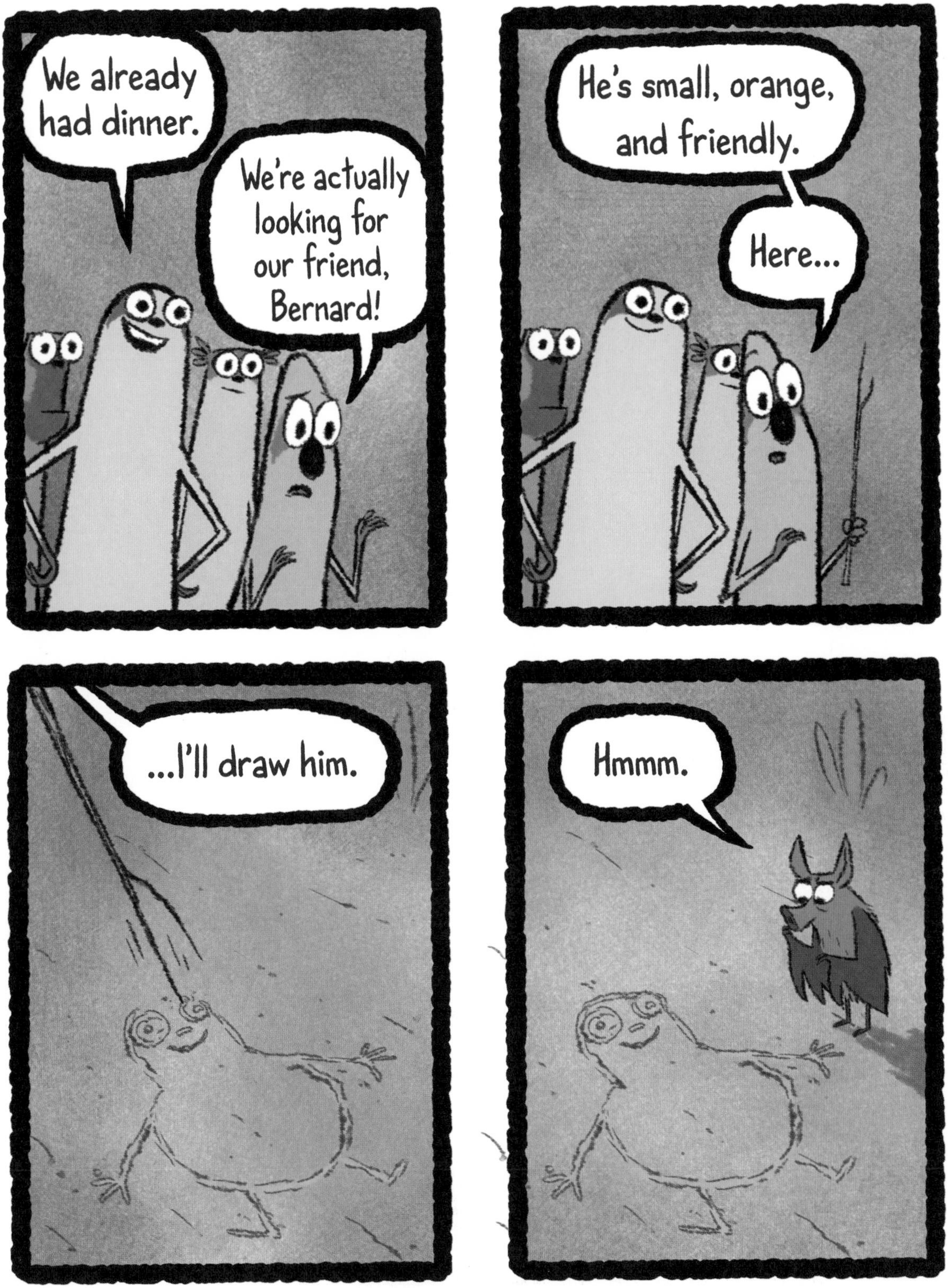
We already had dinner.
We're actually looking for our friend, Bernard!
He's small, orange, and friendly.
Here...
...I'll draw him.
Hmmm.

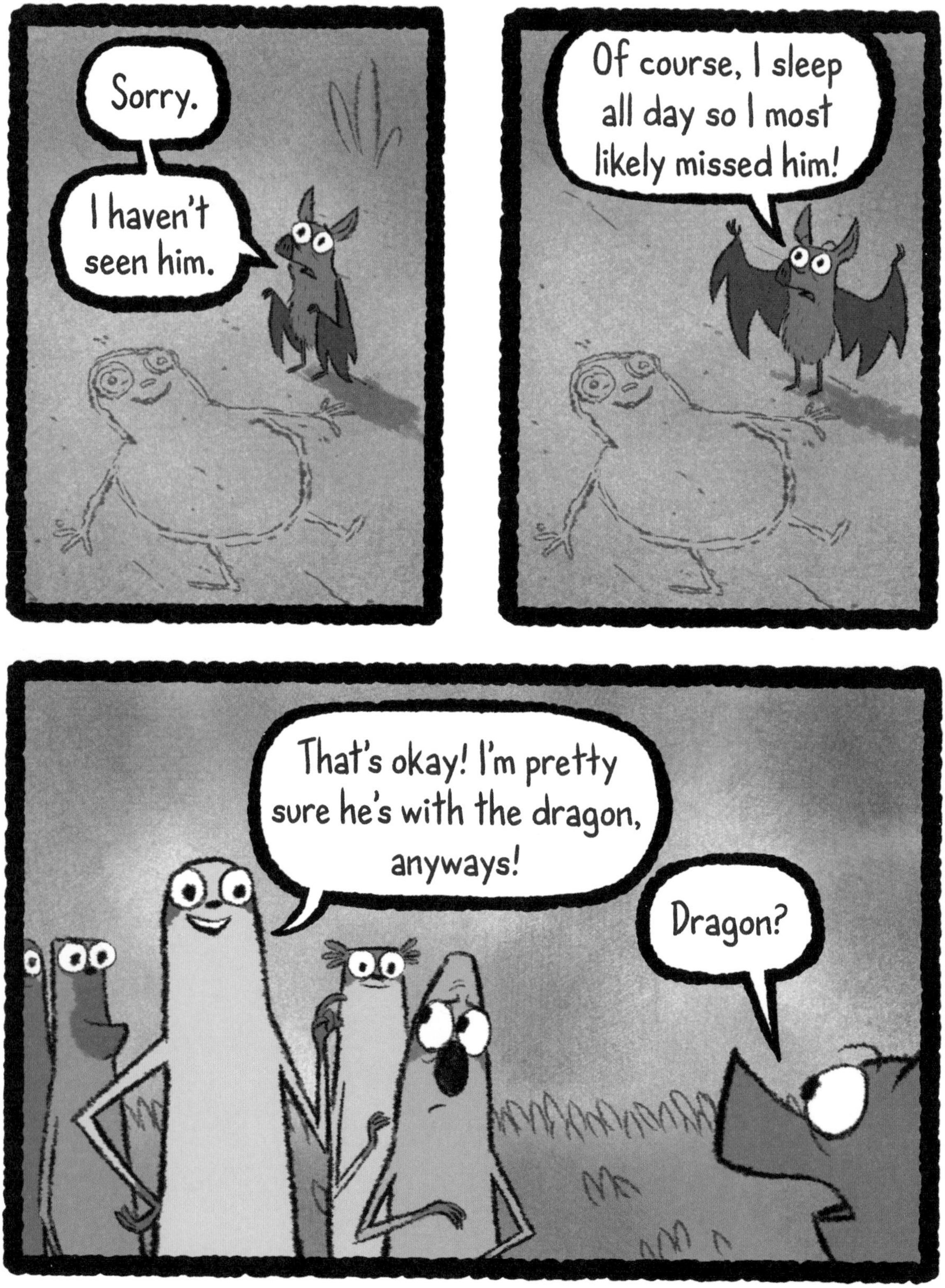
Sorry.
I haven't seen him.
Of course, I sleep all day so I most likely missed him!
That's okay! I'm pretty sure he's with the dragon, anyways!
Dragon?

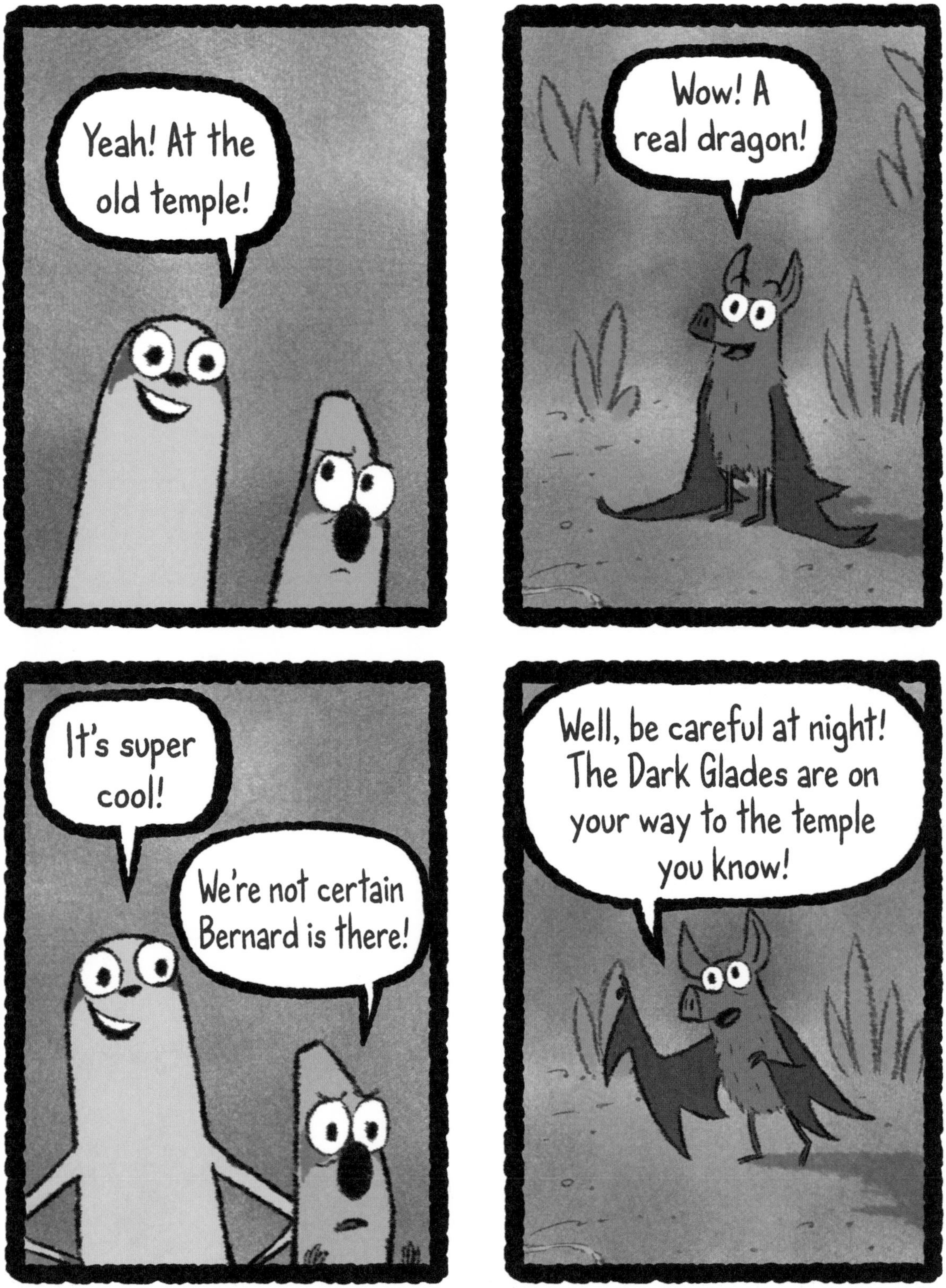
Yeah! At the old temple!
Wow! A real dragon!
It's super cool!
We're not certain Bernard is there!
Well, be careful at night! The Dark Glades are on your way to the temple you know!

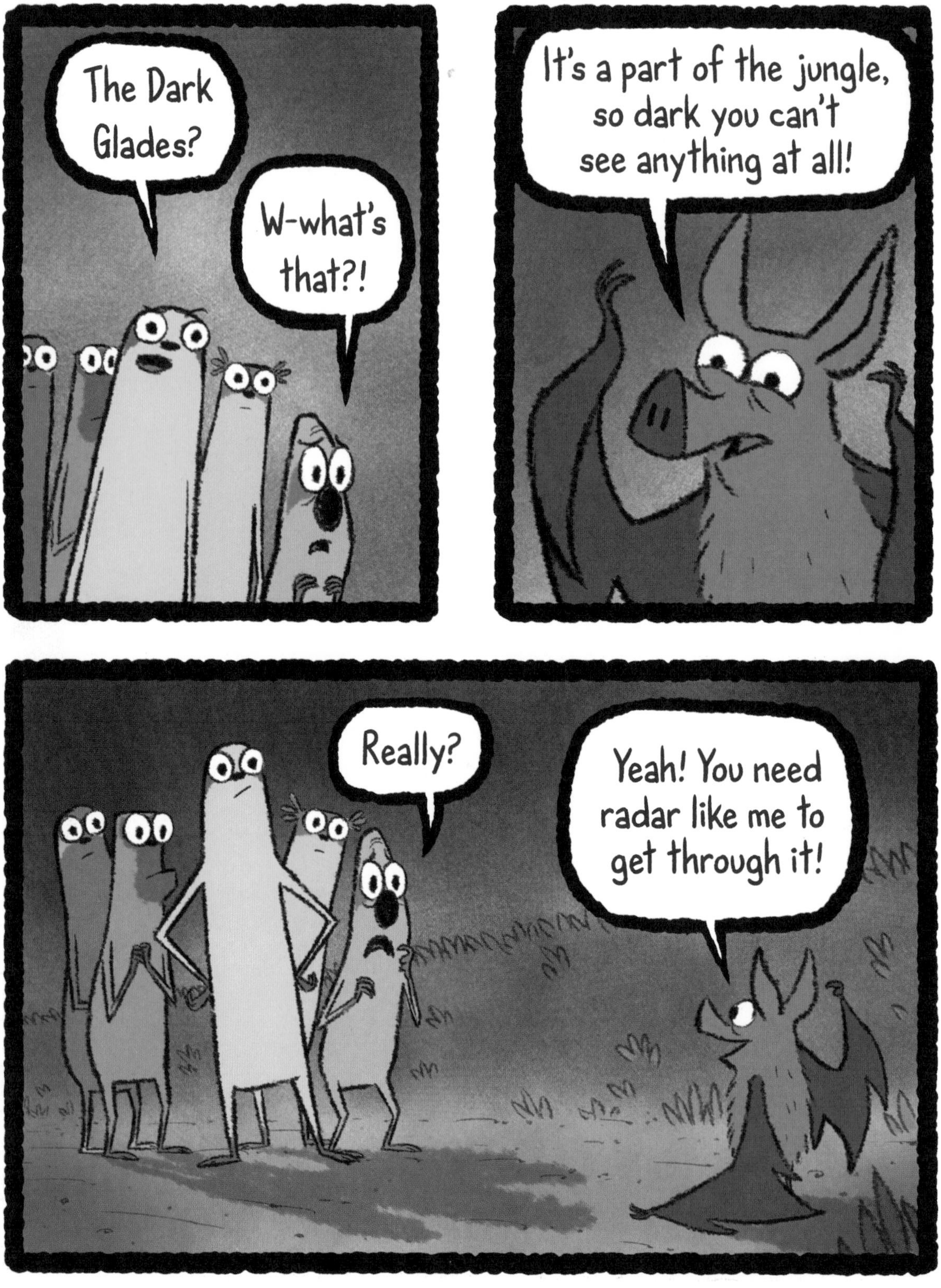
The Dark Glades?
W-what's that?!
It's a part of the jungle, so dark you can't see anything at all!
Really?
Yeah! You need radar like me to get through it!

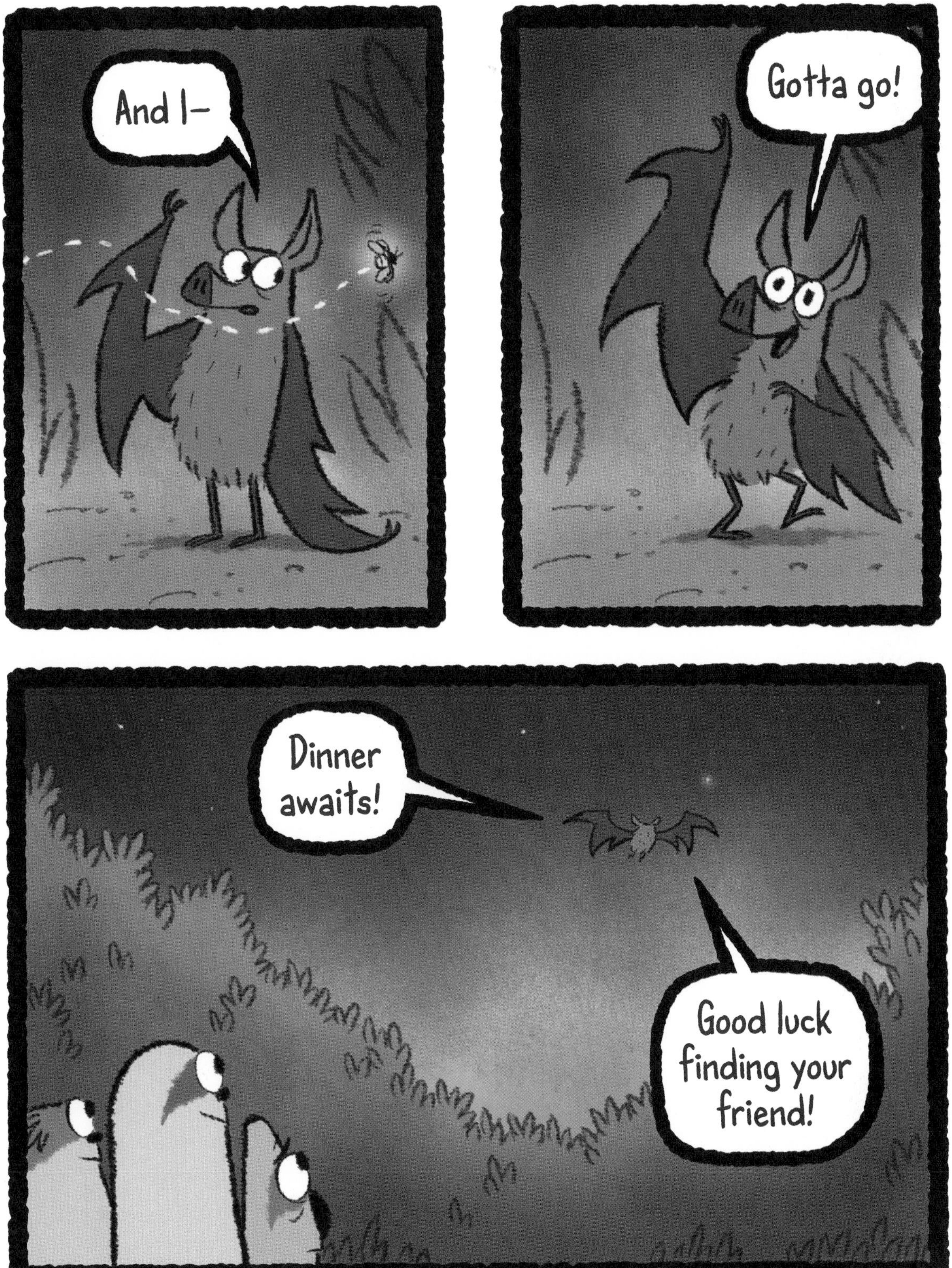
And I–
Gotta go!
Dinner awaits!
Good luck finding your friend!

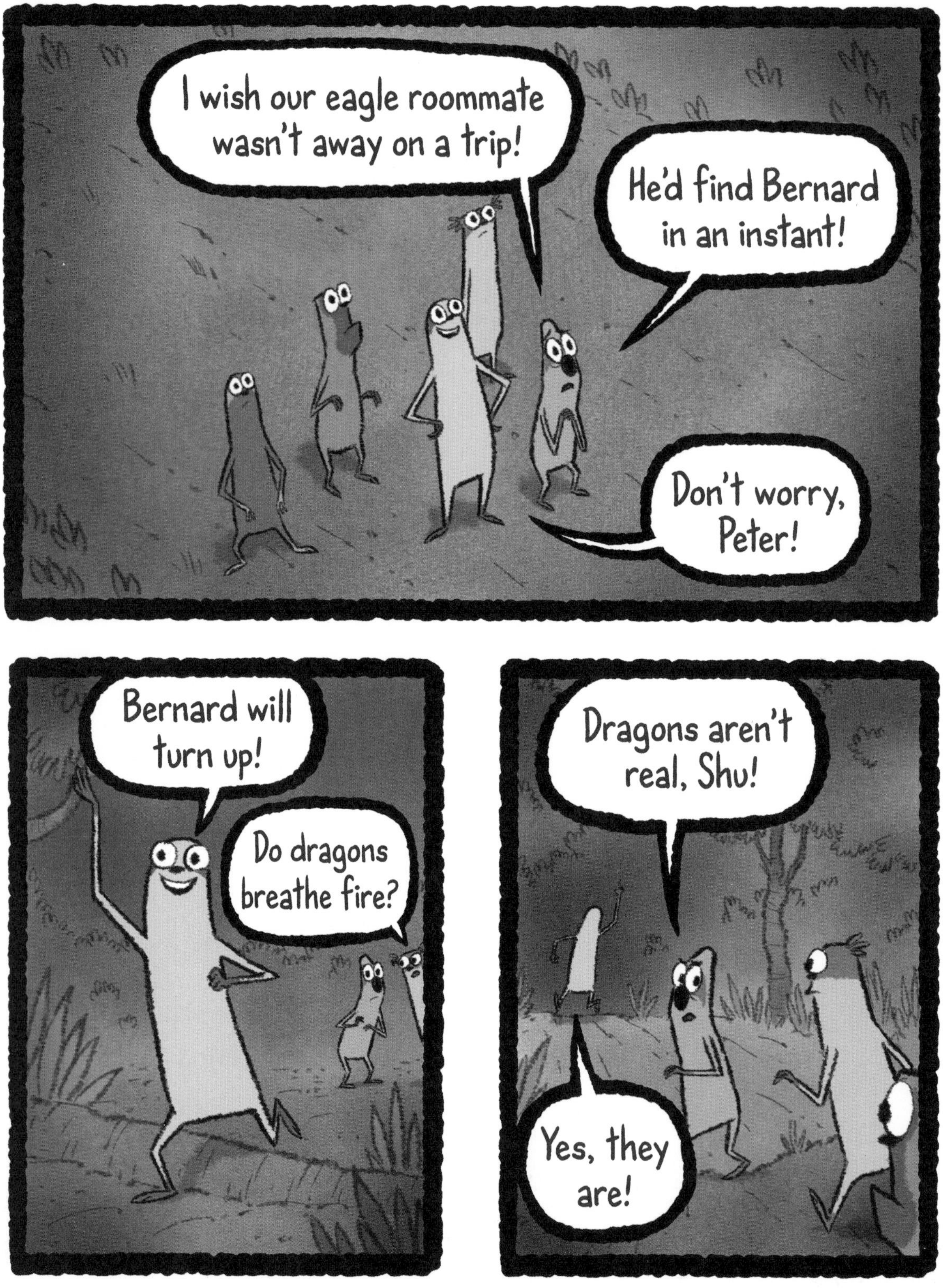
I wish our eagle roommate wasn't away on a trip!
He'd find Bernard in an instant!
Don't worry, Peter!
Bernard will turn up!
Do dragons breathe fire?
Dragons aren't real, Shu!
Yes, they are!

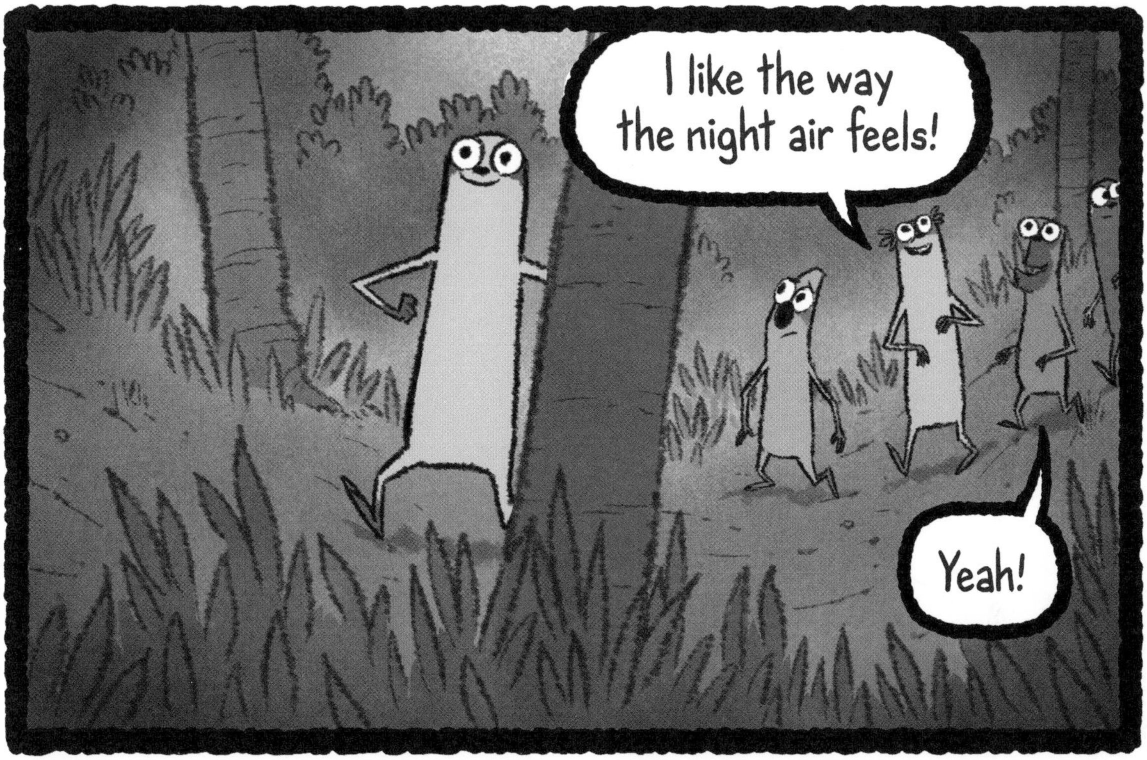
I like the way the night air feels!
Yeah!

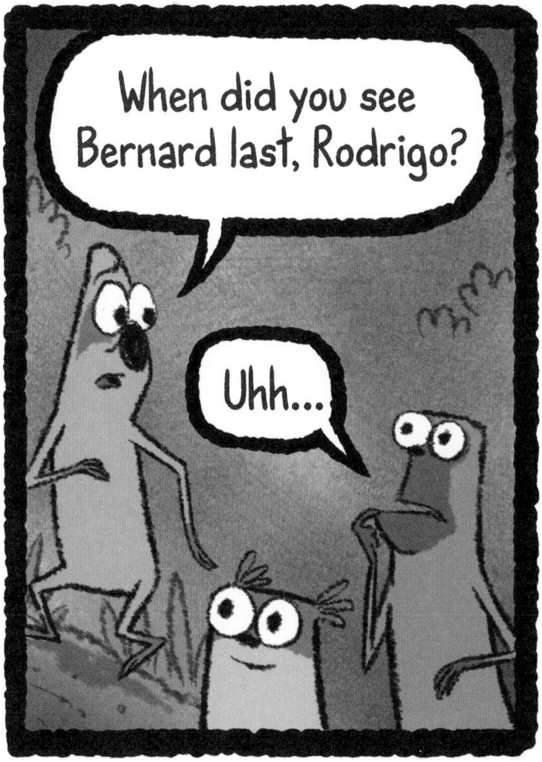
When did you see Bernard last, Rodrigo?
Uhh...

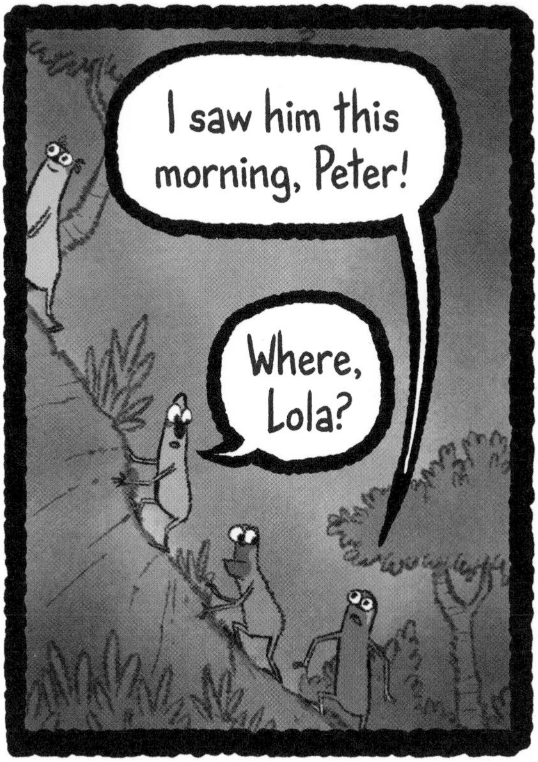
I saw him this morning, Peter!
Where, Lola?

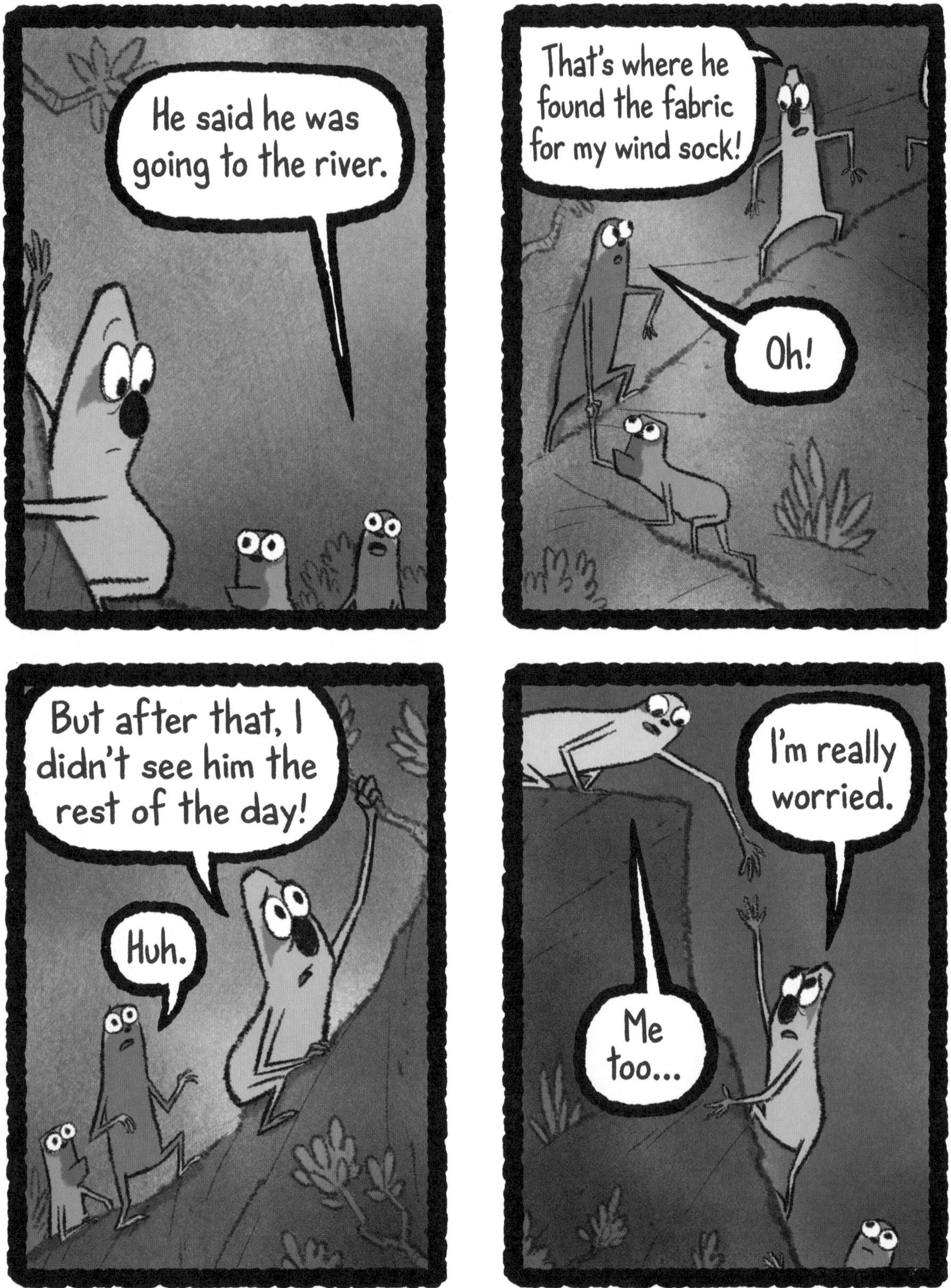
He said he was going to the river.
That's where he found the fabric for my wind sock!
Oh!
But after that, I didn't see him the rest of the day!
Huh.
I'm really worried.
Me too...

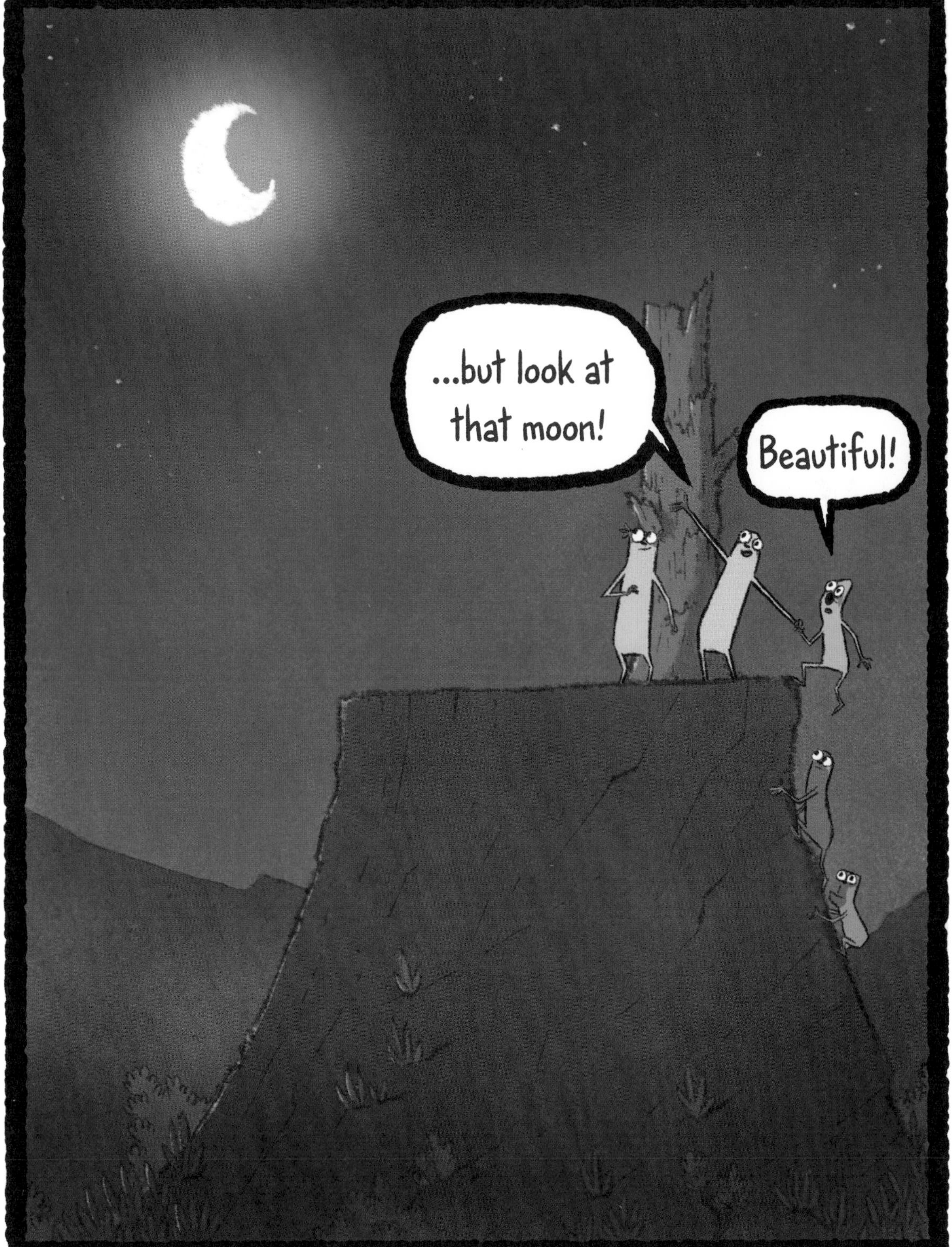
...but look at that moon!
Beautiful!

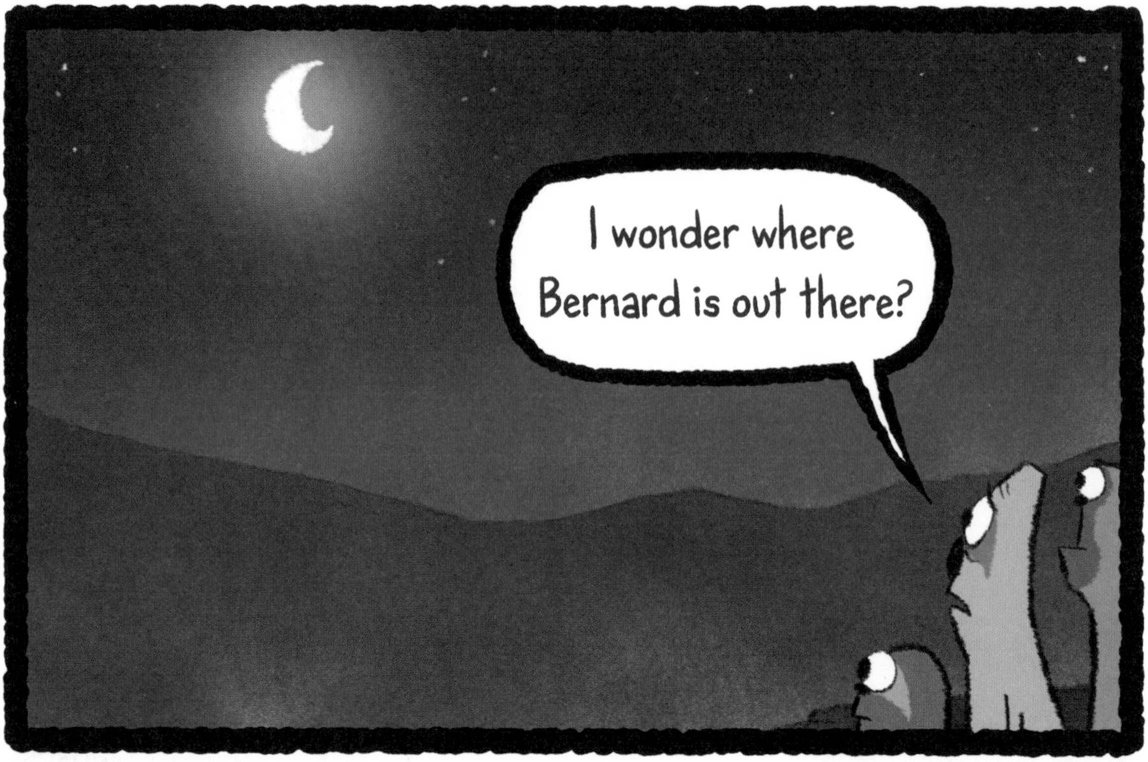
I wonder where Bernard is out there?

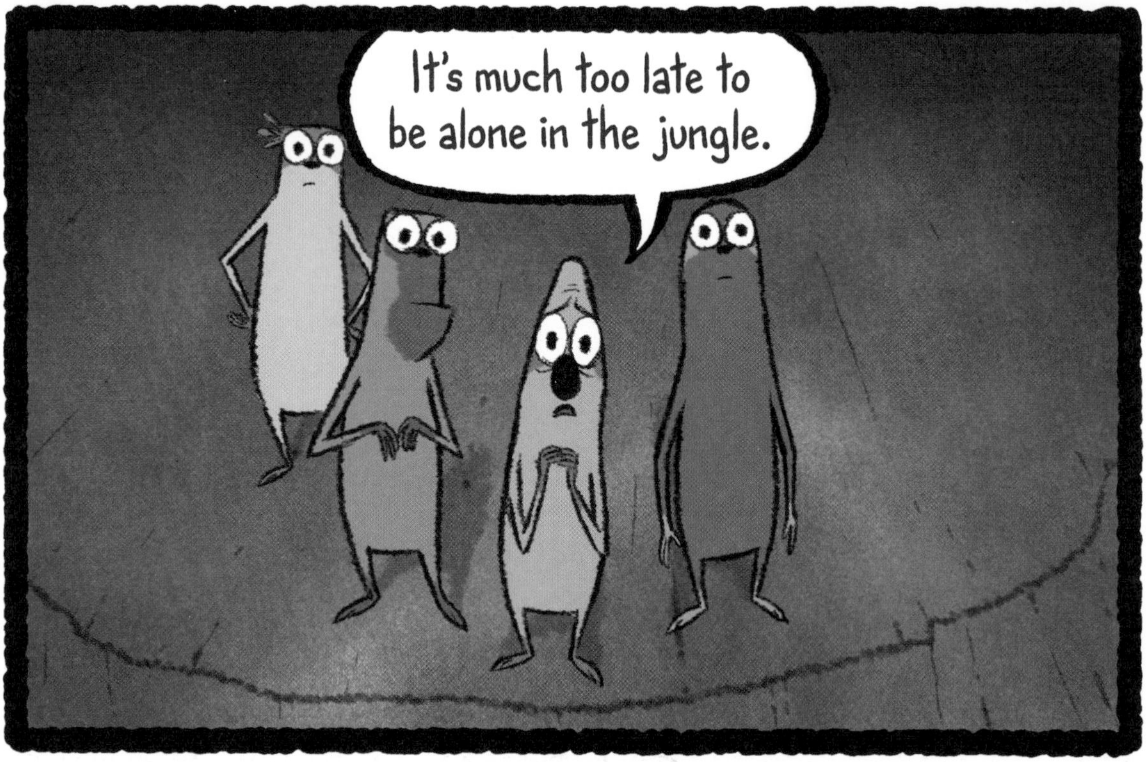
It's much too late to be alone in the jungle.

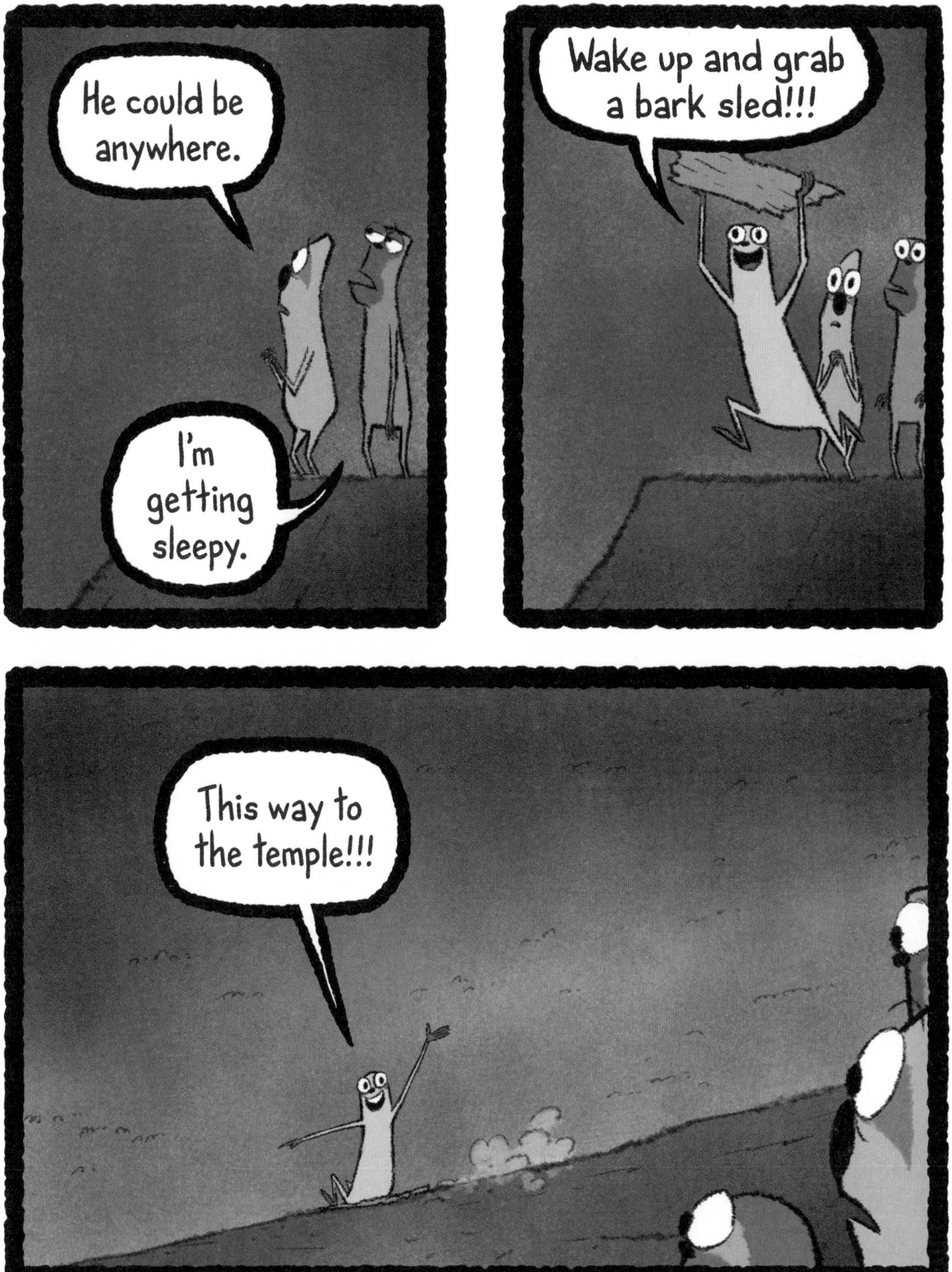
He could be anywhere.
I'm getting sleepy.
Wake up and grab a bark sled!!!
This way to the temple!!!

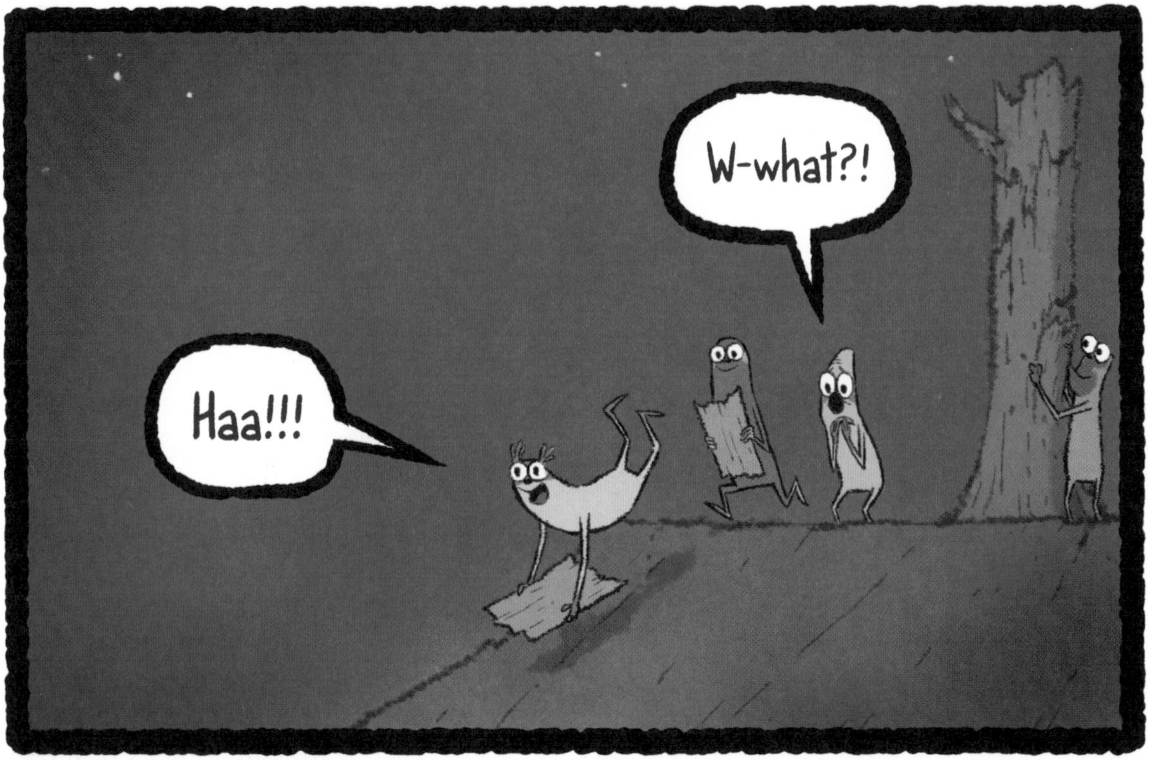
W-what?!
Haa!!!

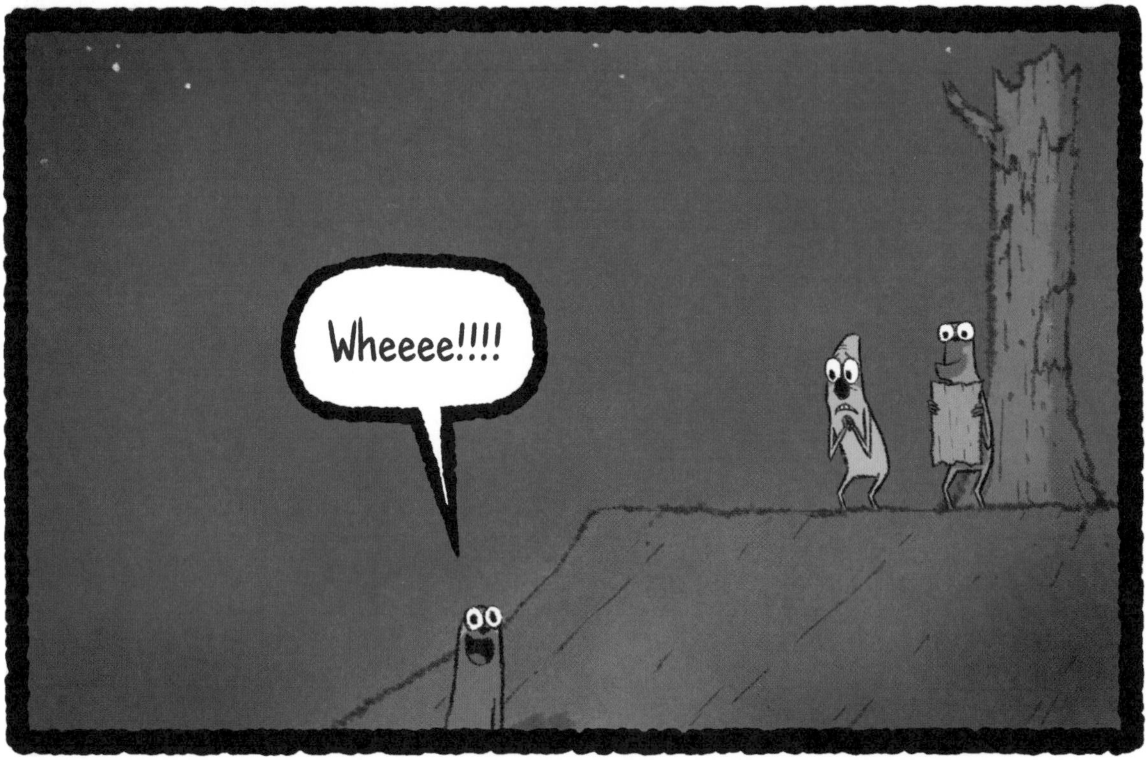
Wheeee!!!!

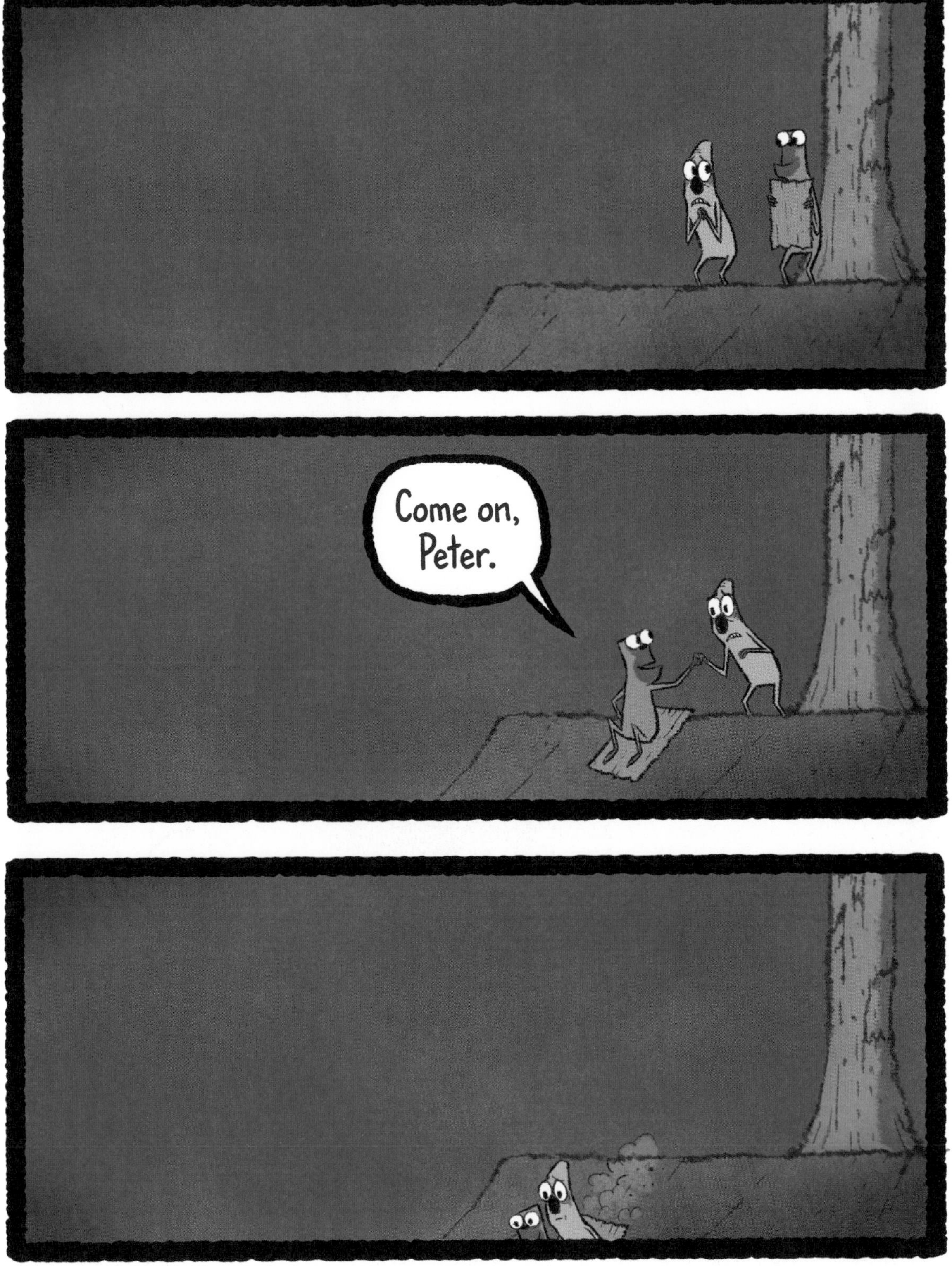
Come on, Peter.

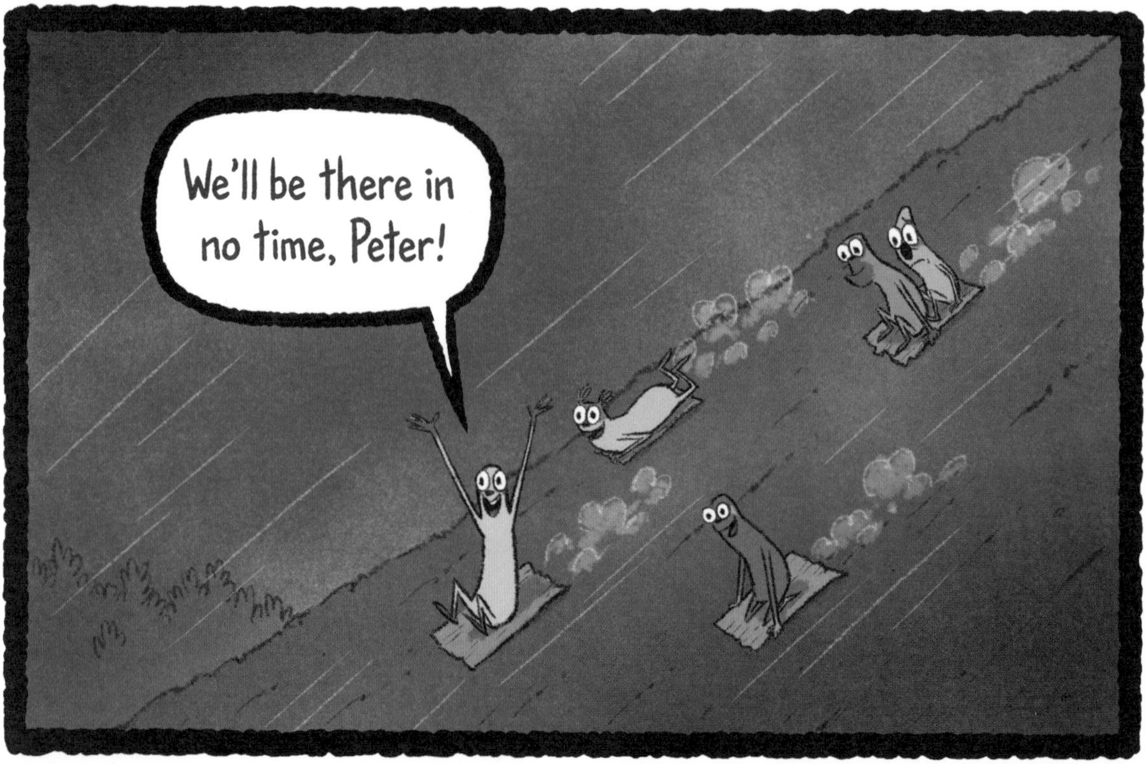
We'll be there in no time, Peter!

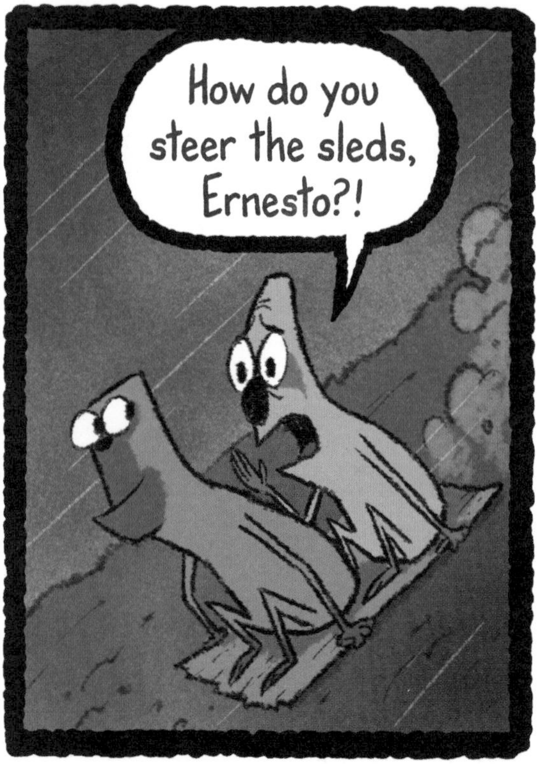
How do you steer the sleds, Ernesto?!

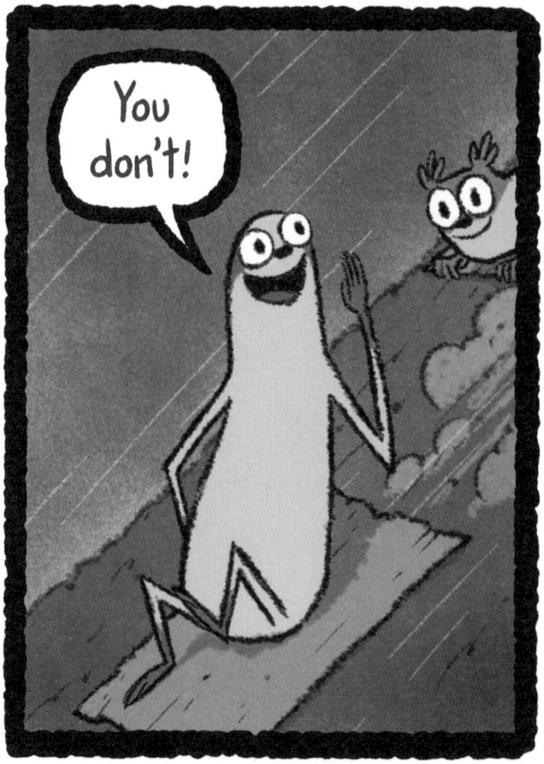
You don't!

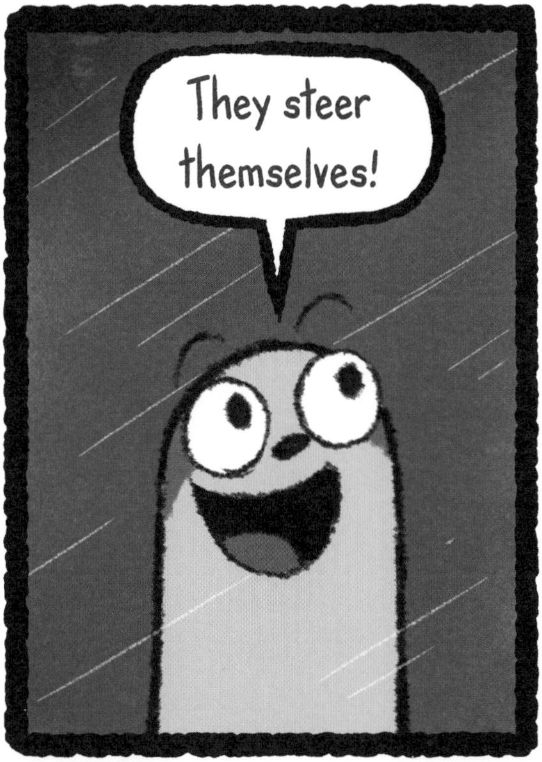
They steer themselves!

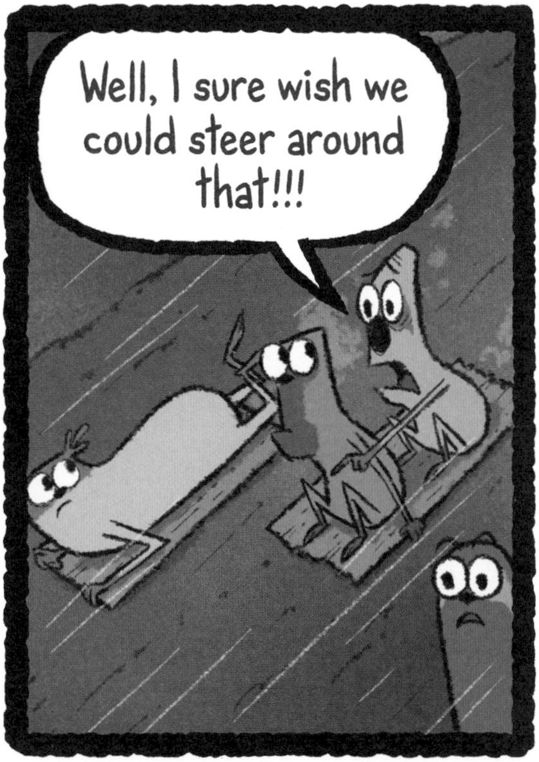
Well, I sure wish we could steer around that!!!

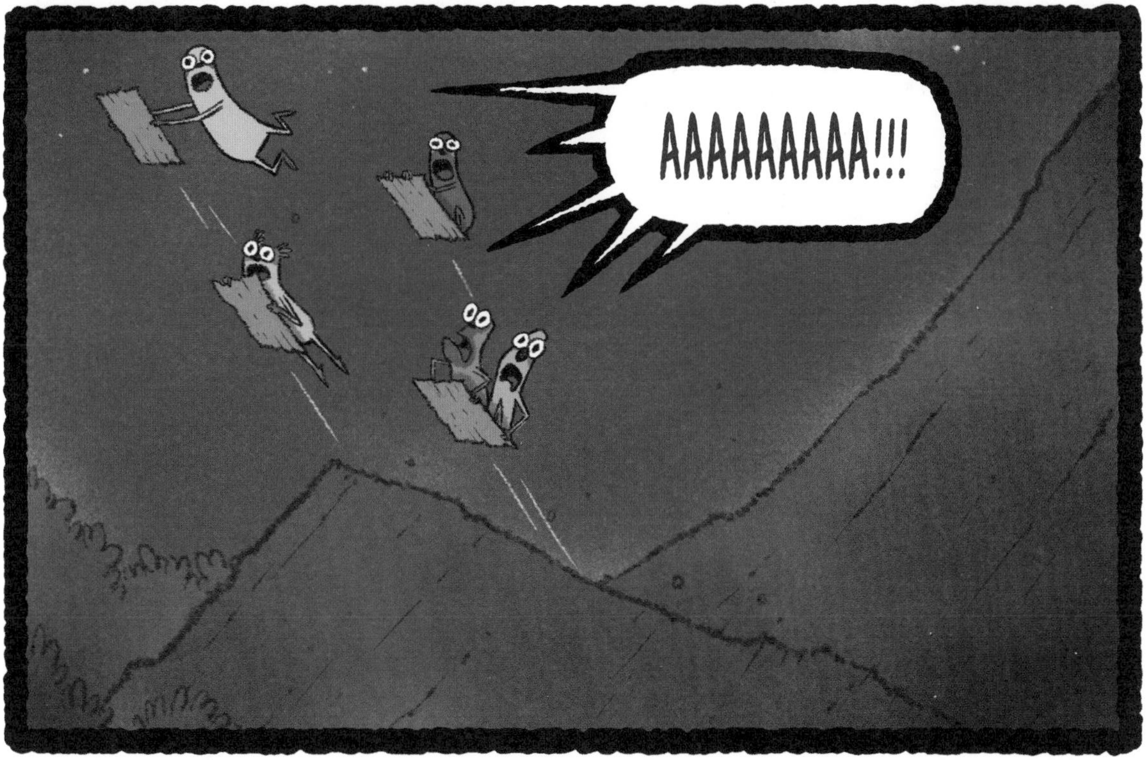
AAAAAAAAA!!!

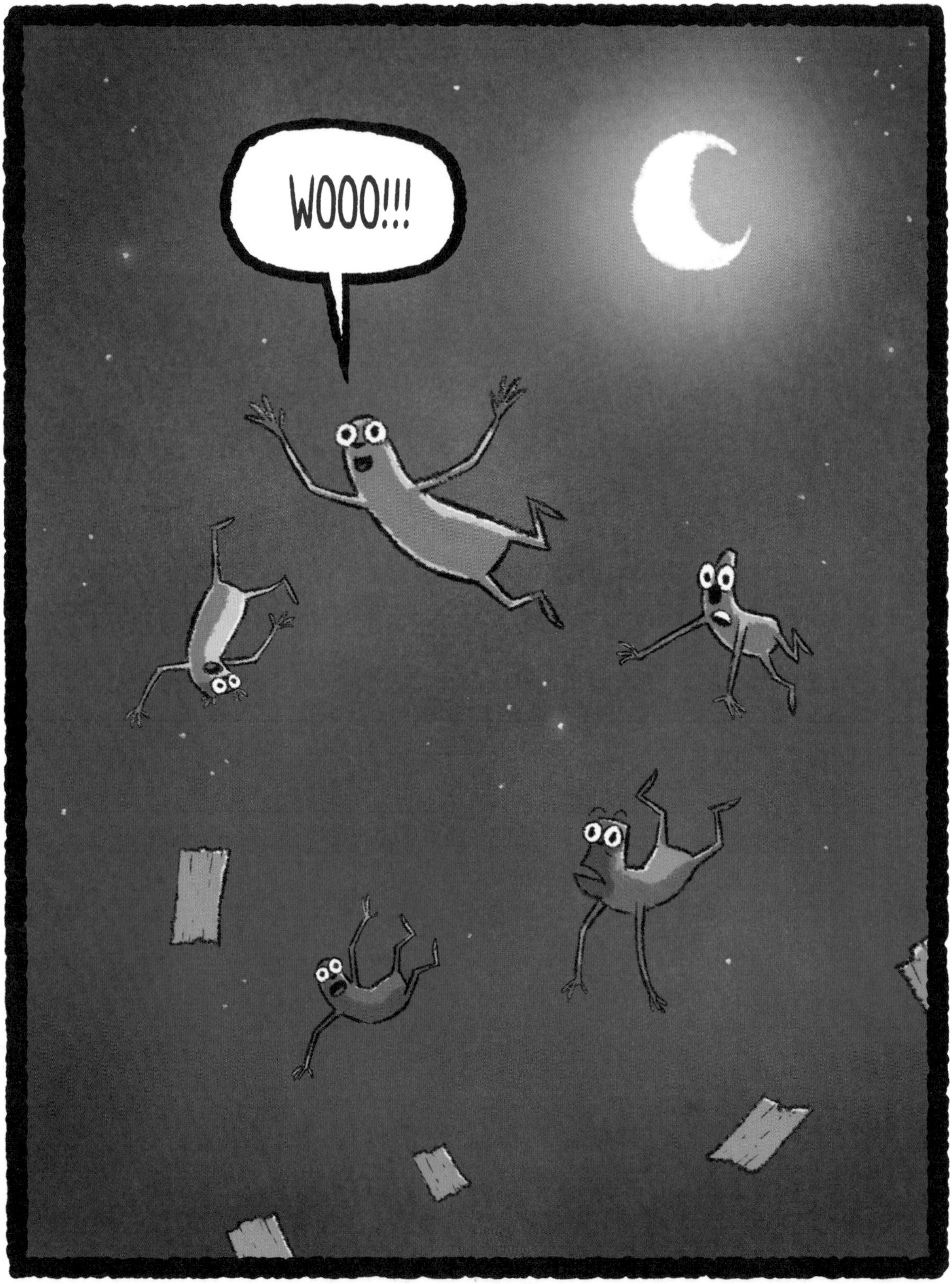
WOOO!!!

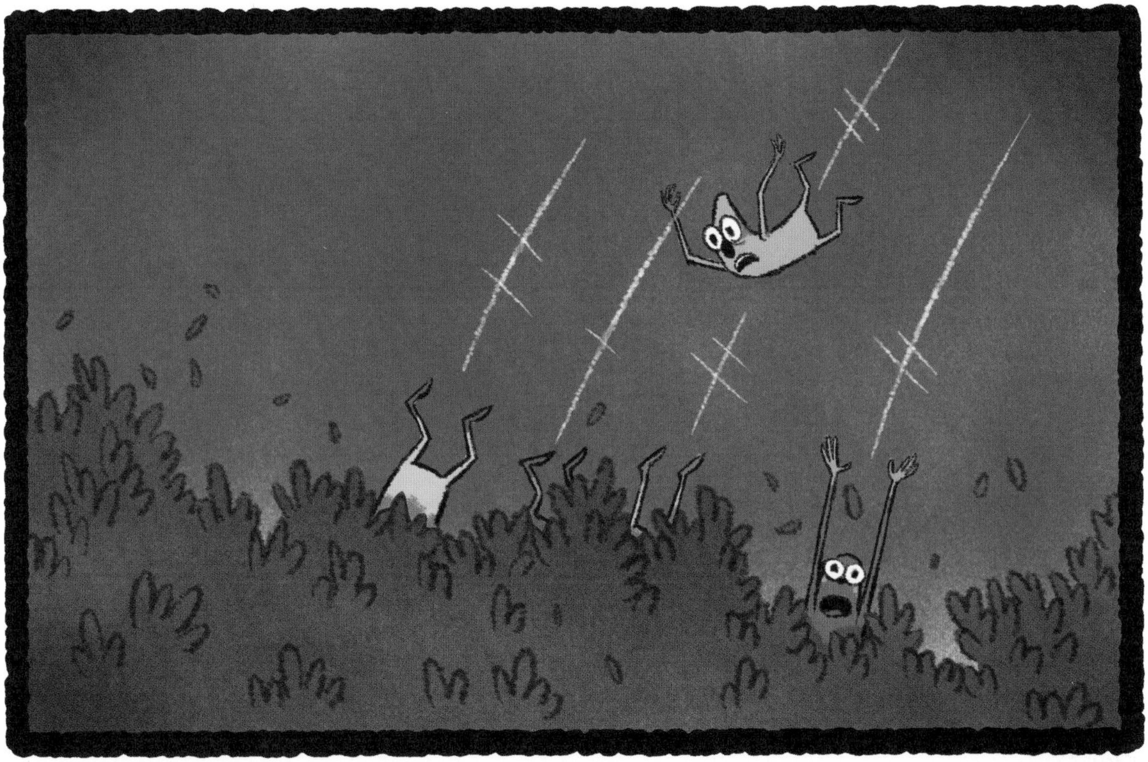

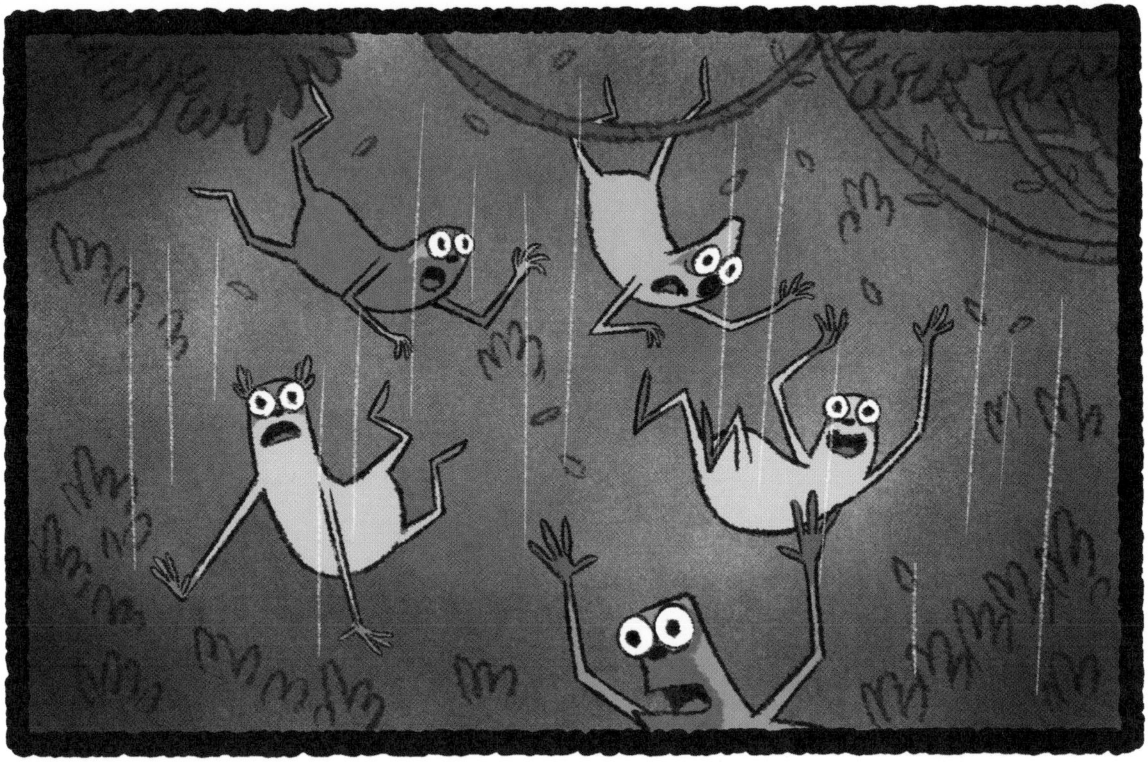

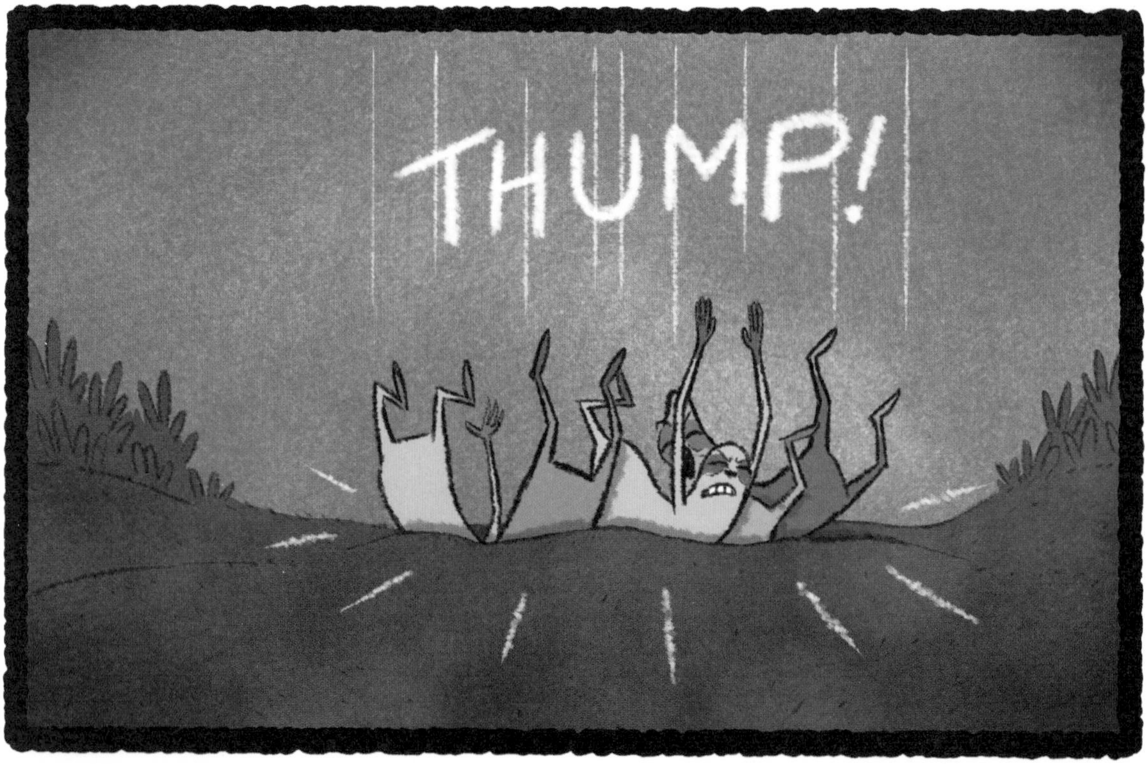
THUMP!

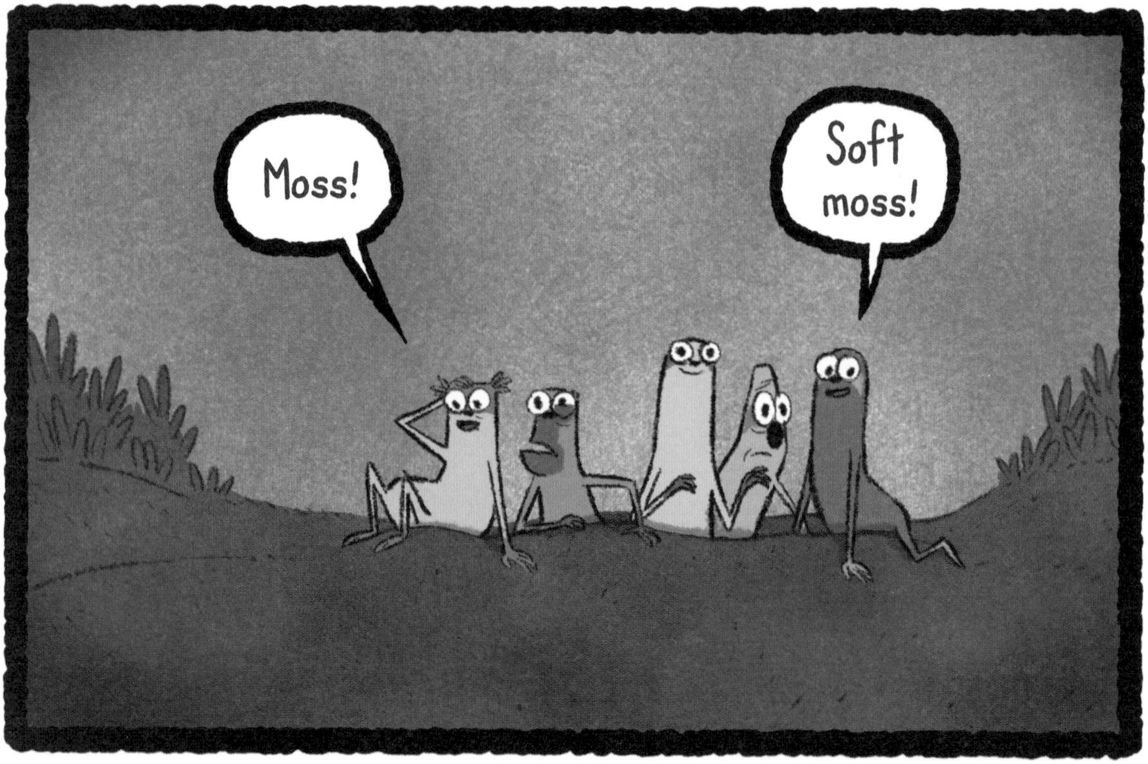
Moss!
Soft moss!

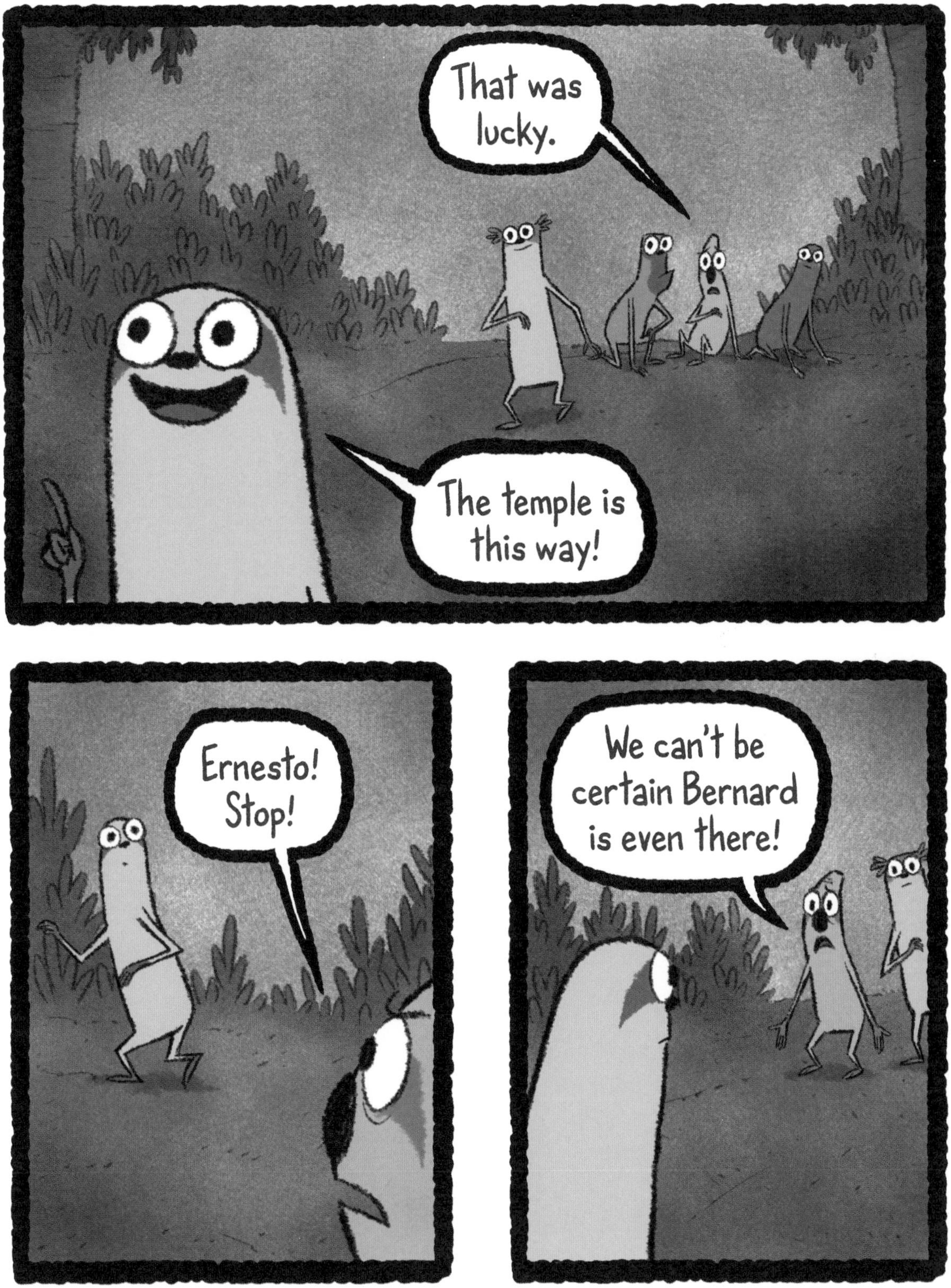
That was lucky.
The temple is this way!
Ernesto! Stop!
We can't be certain Bernard is even there!

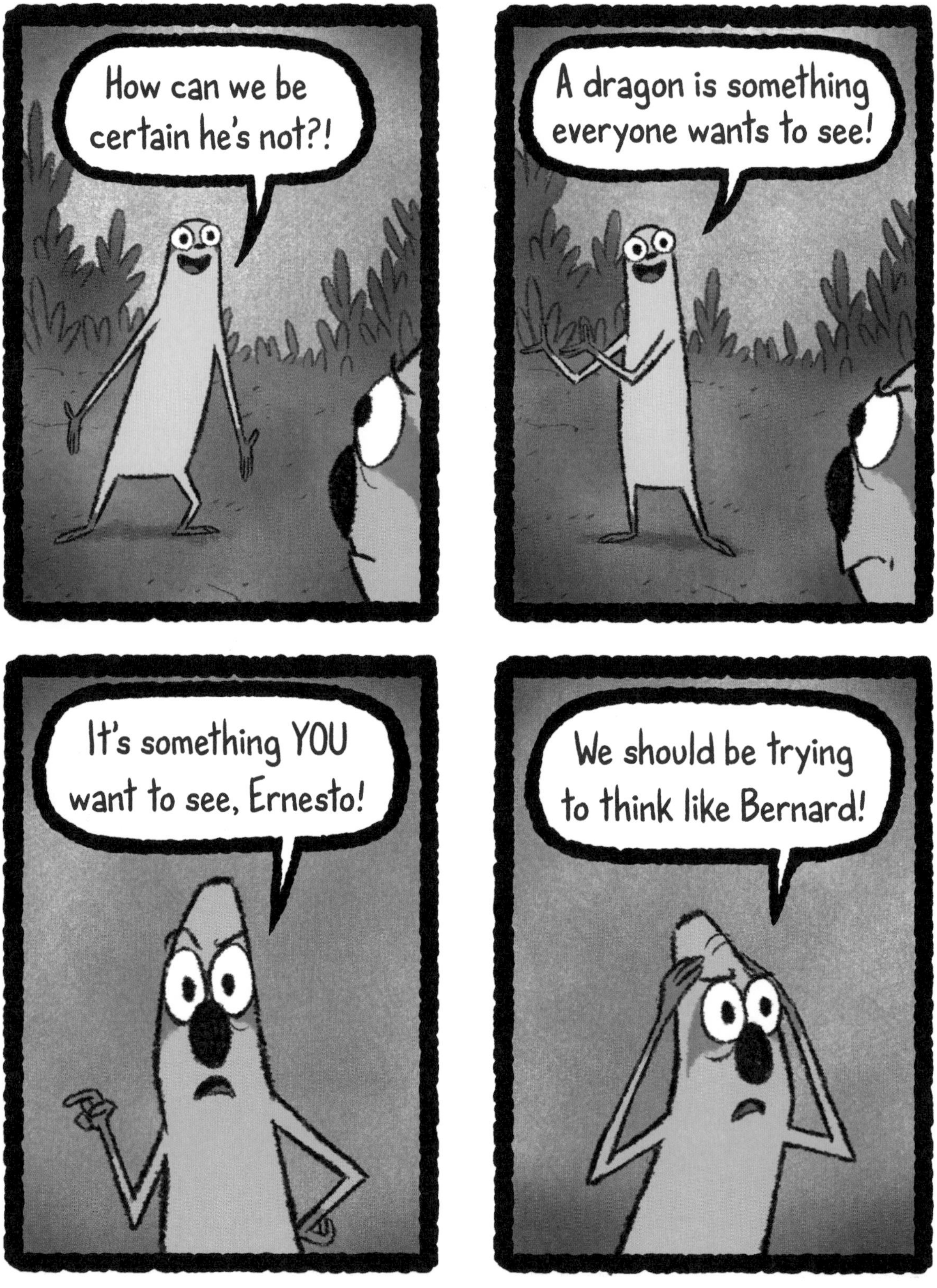
How can we be certain he's not?!
A dragon is something everyone wants to see!
It's something YOU want to see, Ernesto!
We should be trying to think like Bernard!

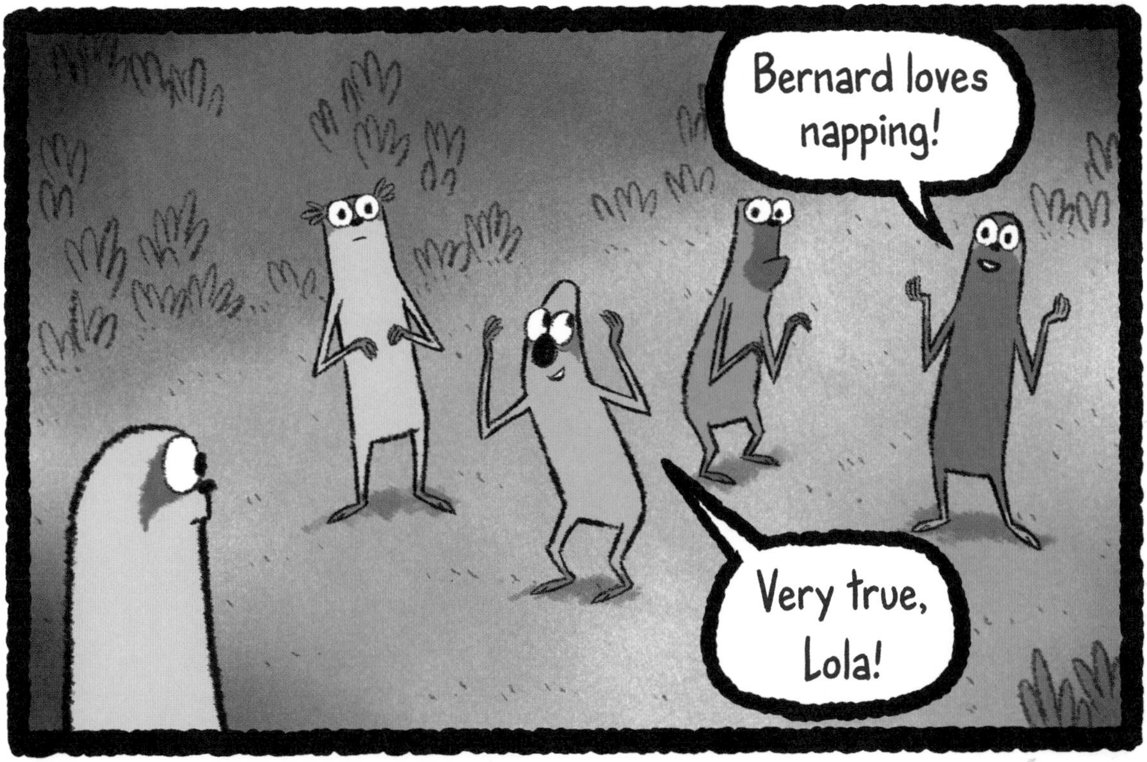
Bernard loves napping!
Very true, Lola!

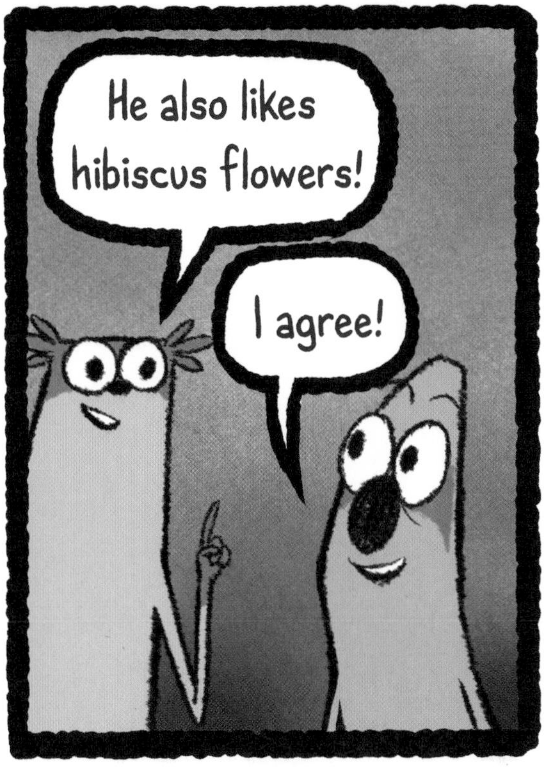
He also likes hibiscus flowers!
I agree!

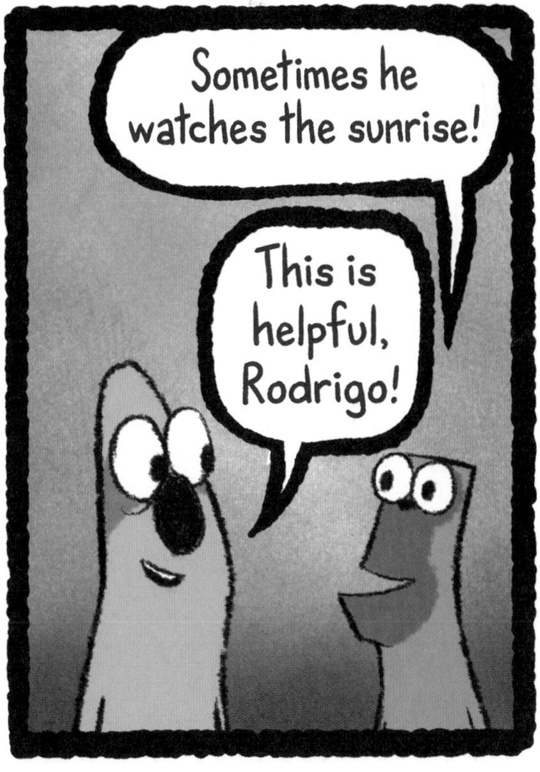
Sometimes he watches the sunrise!
This is helpful, Rodrigo!

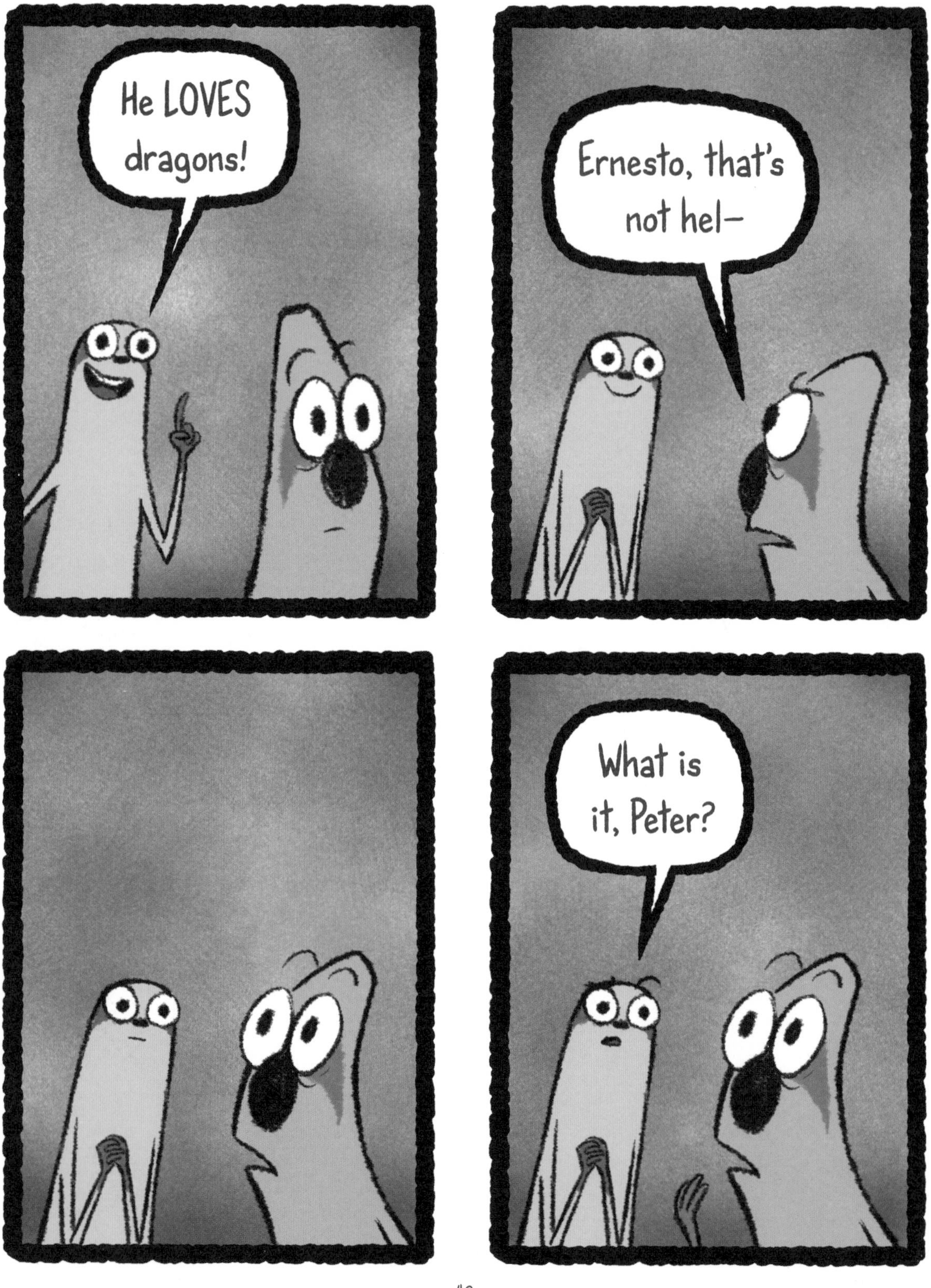
He LOVES dragons!
Ernesto, that's not hel–
What is it, Peter?

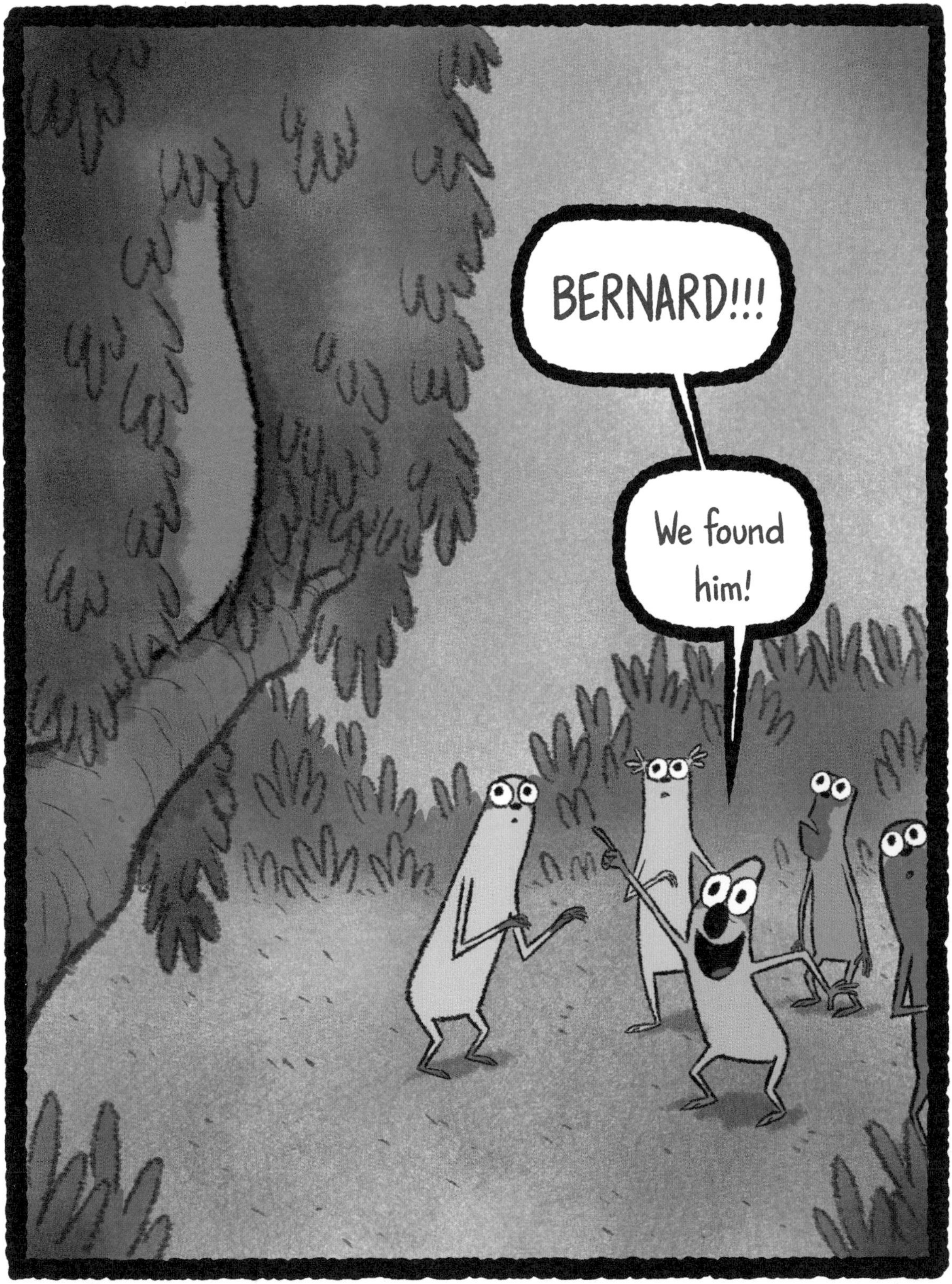

BERNARD!!!
We found him!

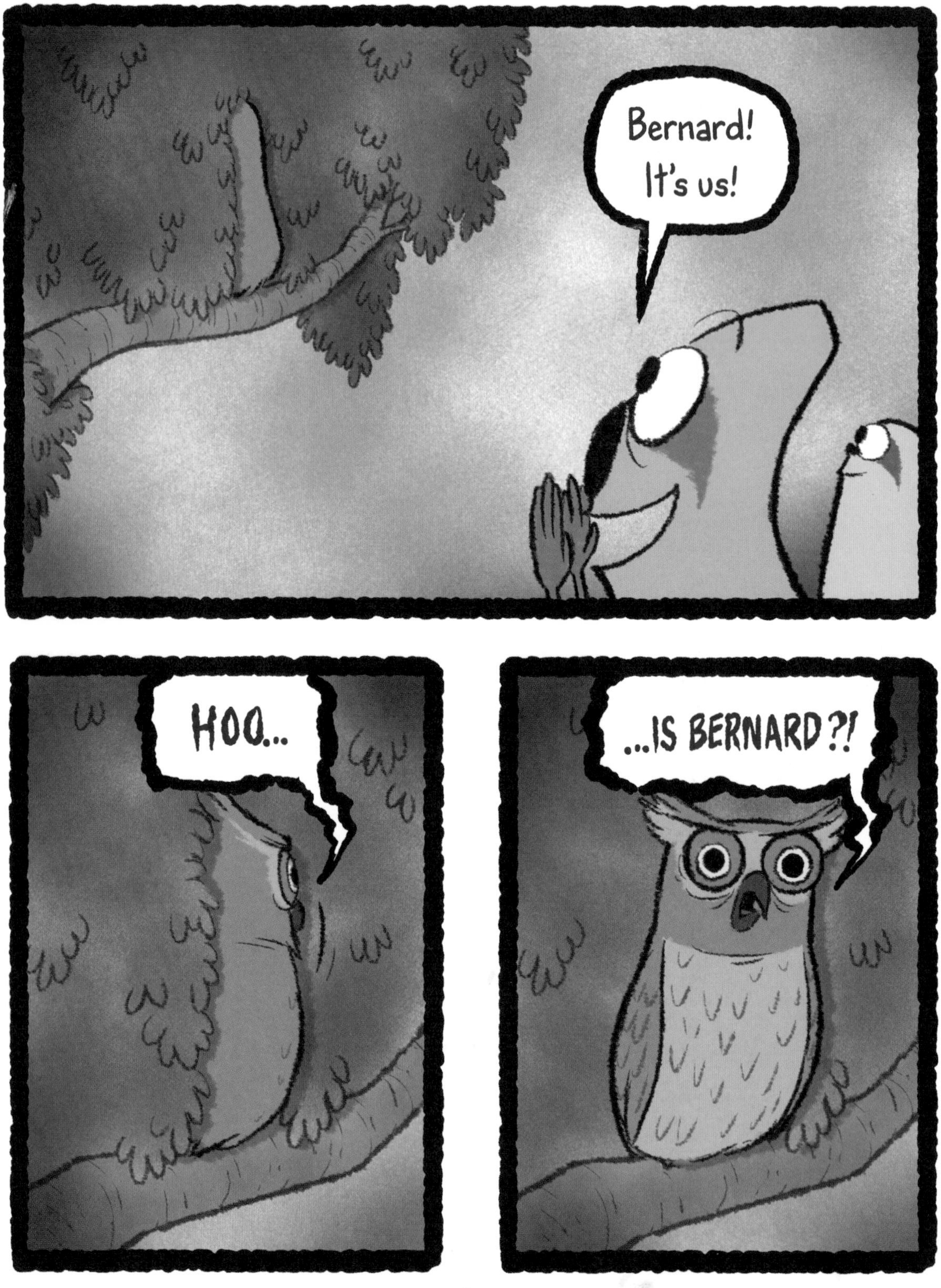
Bernard! It's us!
HOO...
...IS BERNARD?!

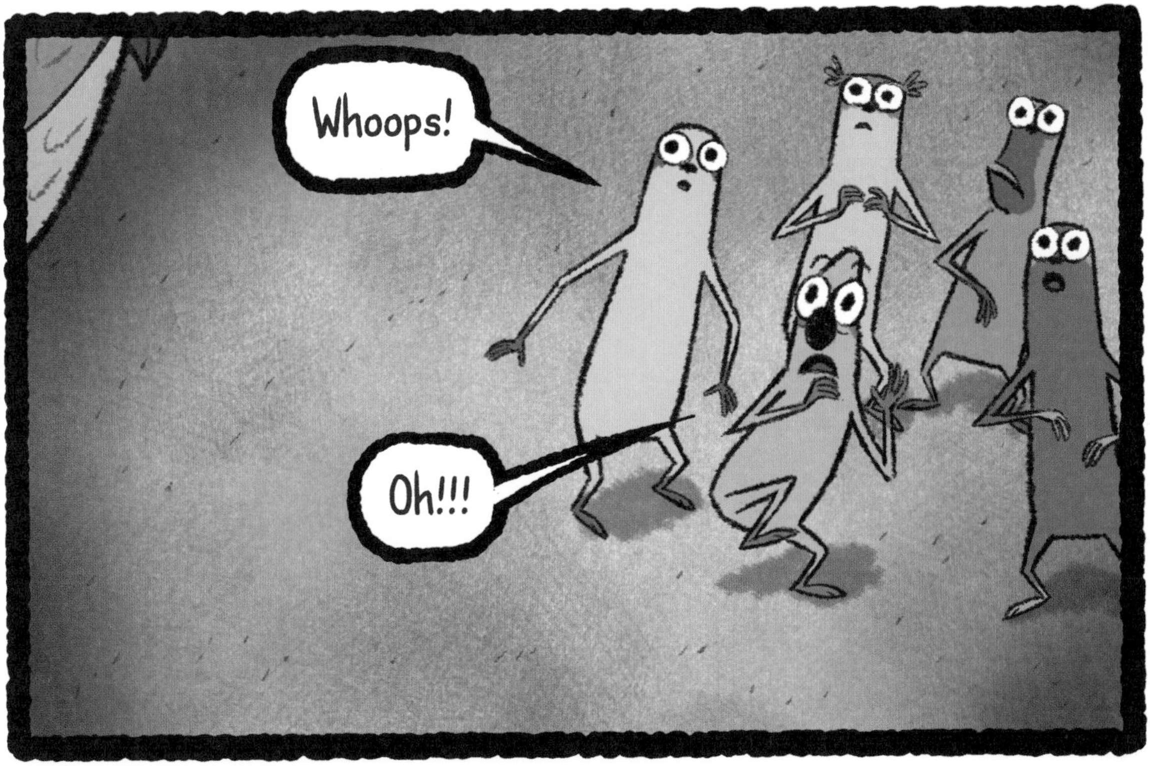
Whoops!
Oh!!!

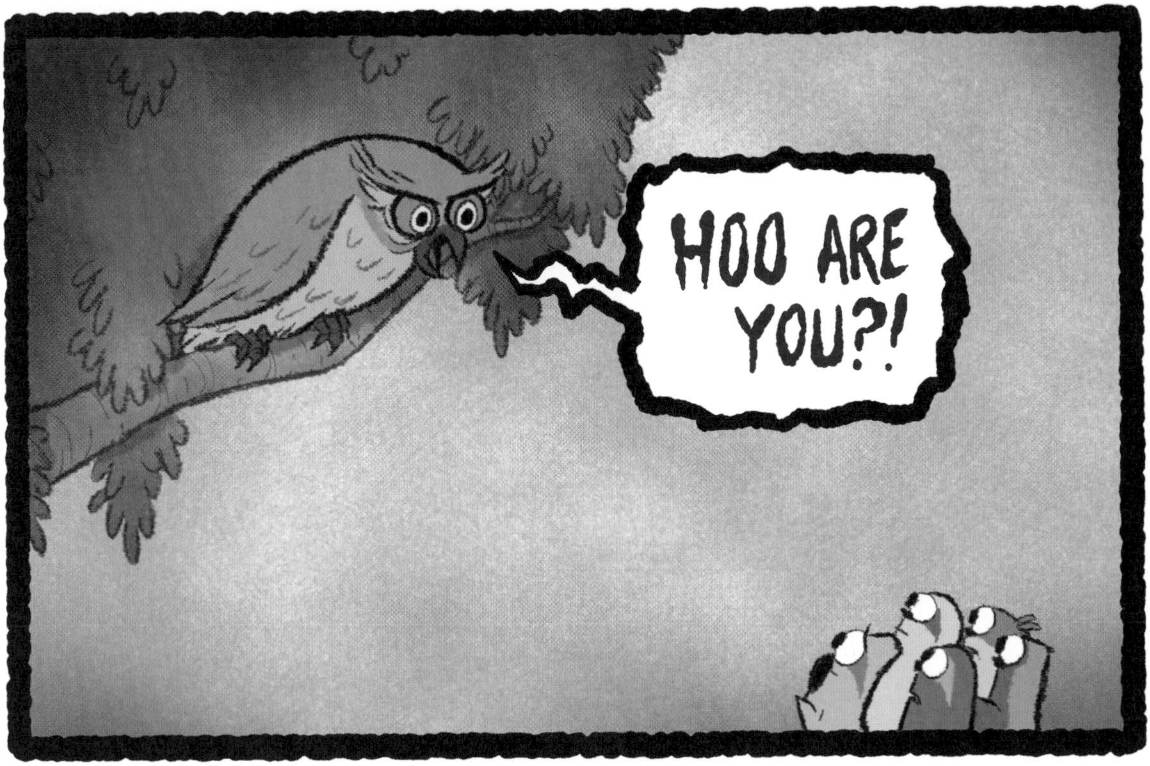
HOO ARE YOU?!

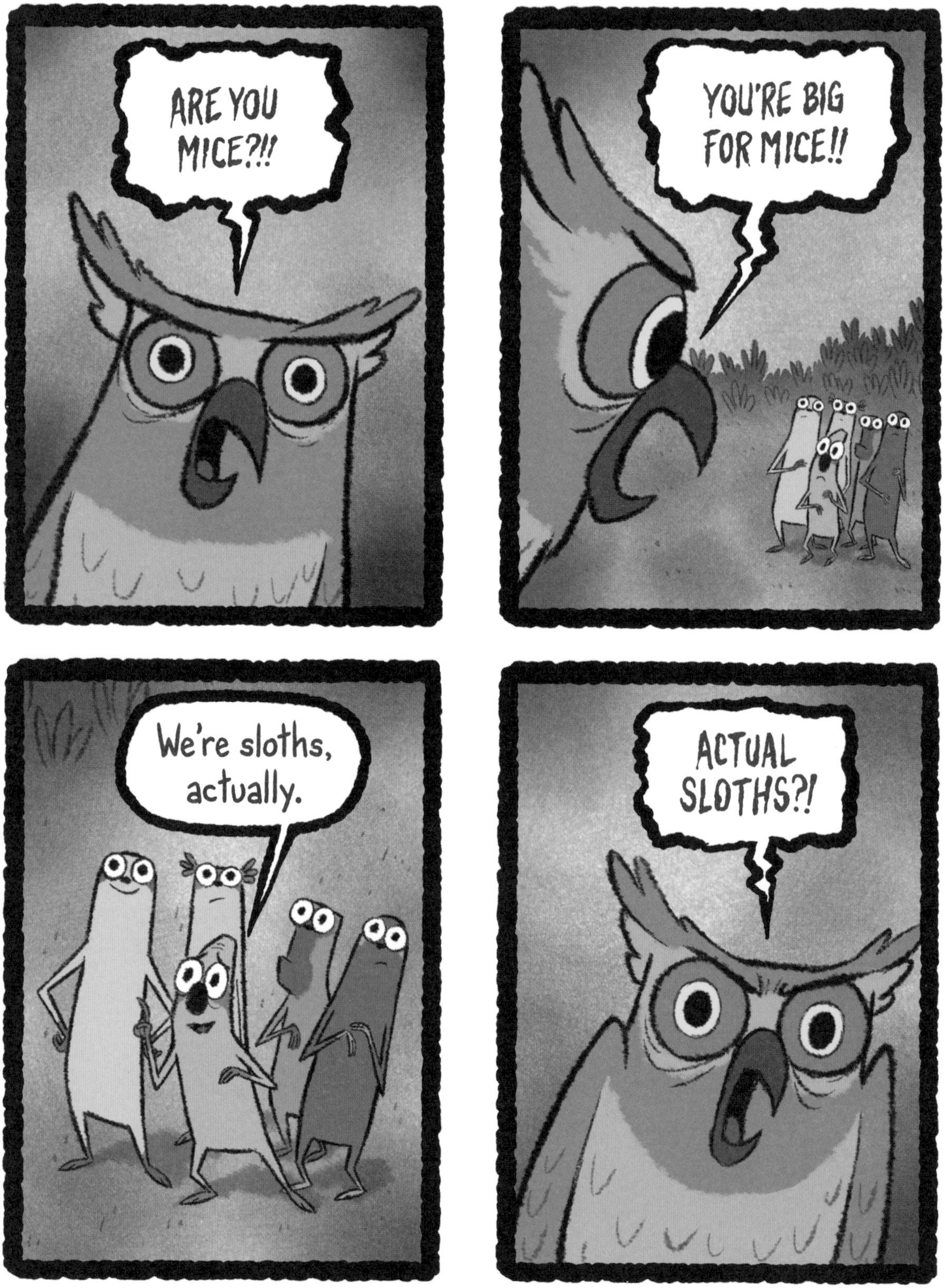
ARE YOU MICE?!!
YOU'RE BIG FOR MICE!!
We're sloths, actually.
ACTUAL SLOTHS?!

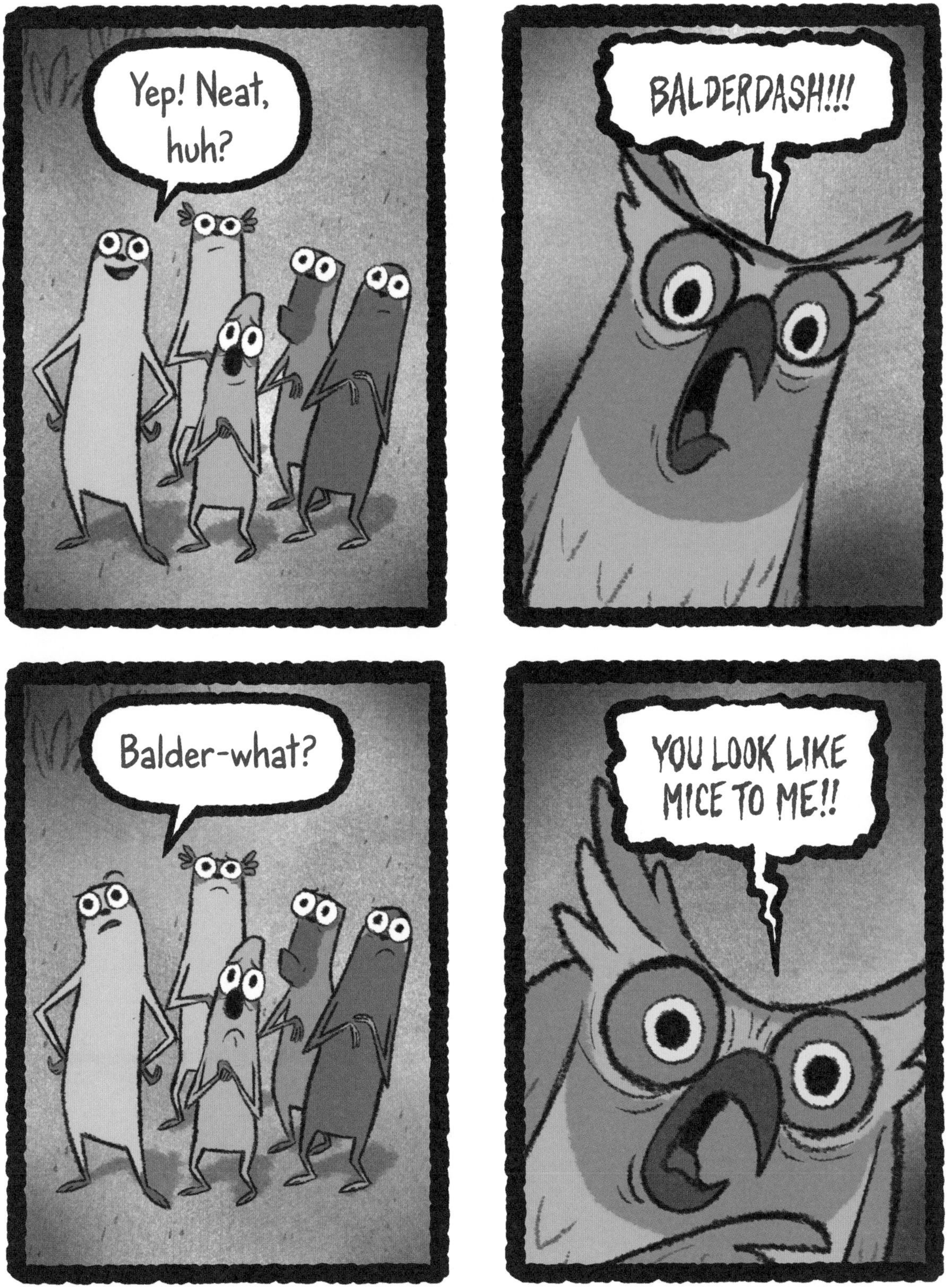
Yep! Neat, huh?
BALDERDASH!!!
Balder-what?
YOU LOOK LIKE MICE TO ME!!

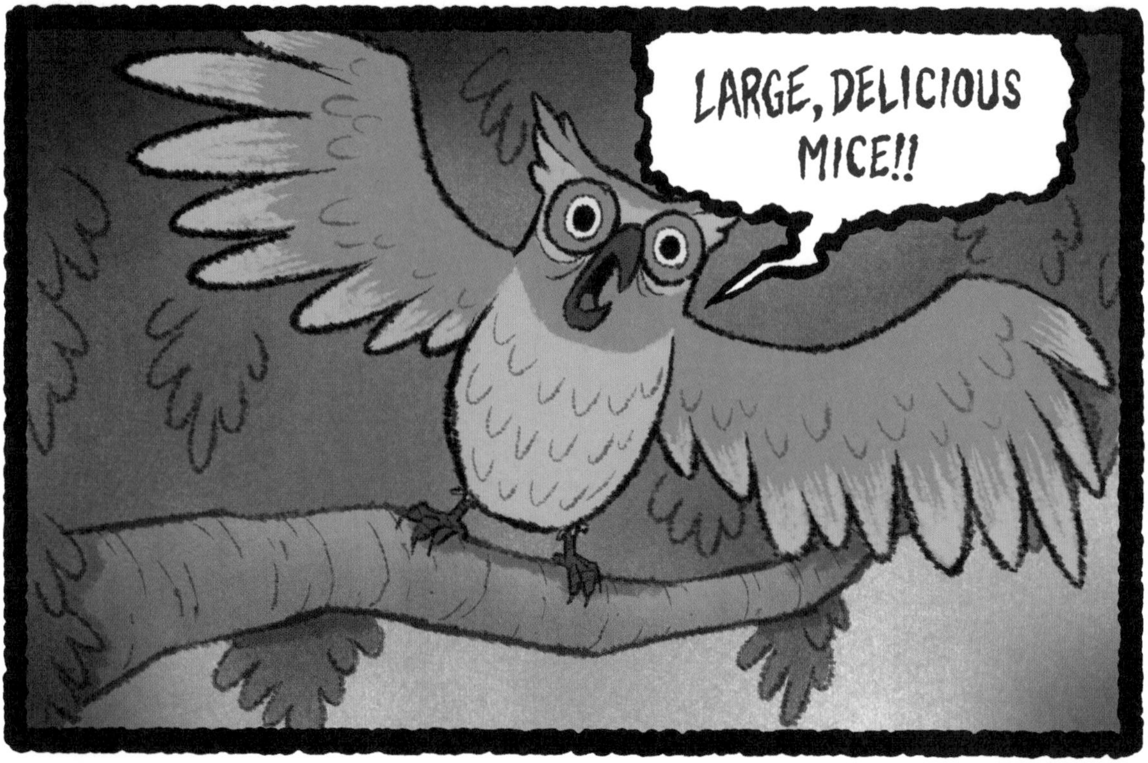
LARGE, DELICIOUS MICE!!

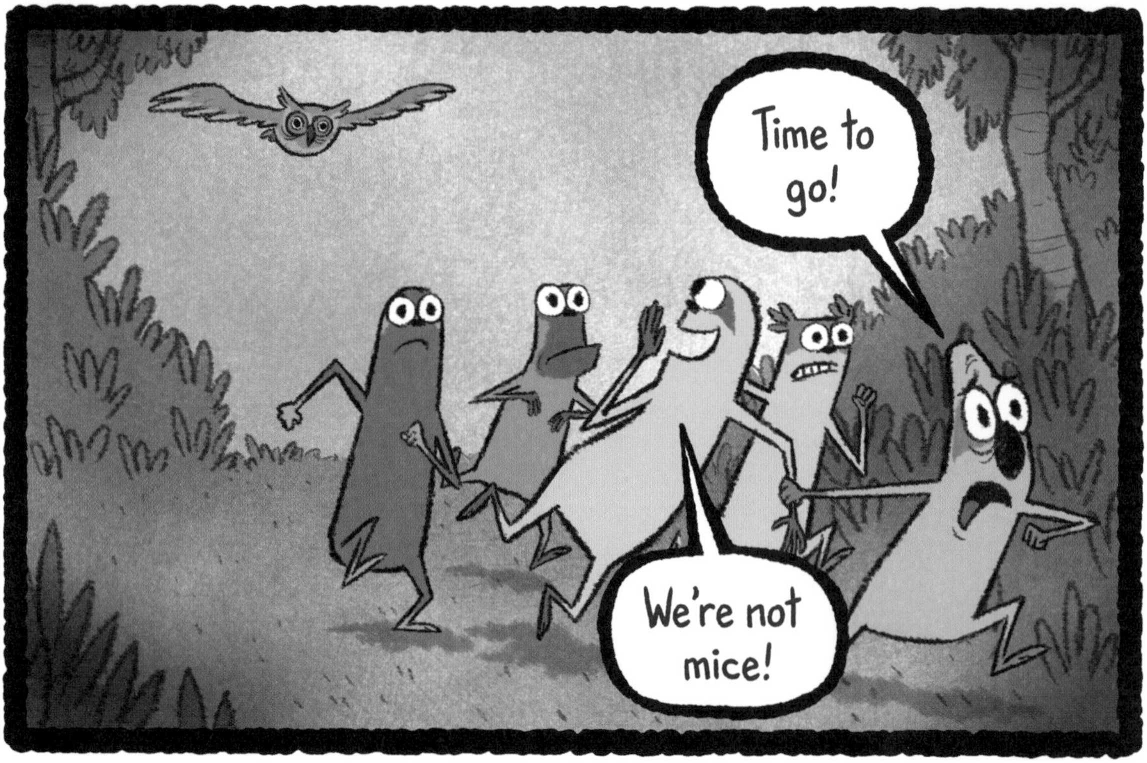
Time to go!
We're not mice!

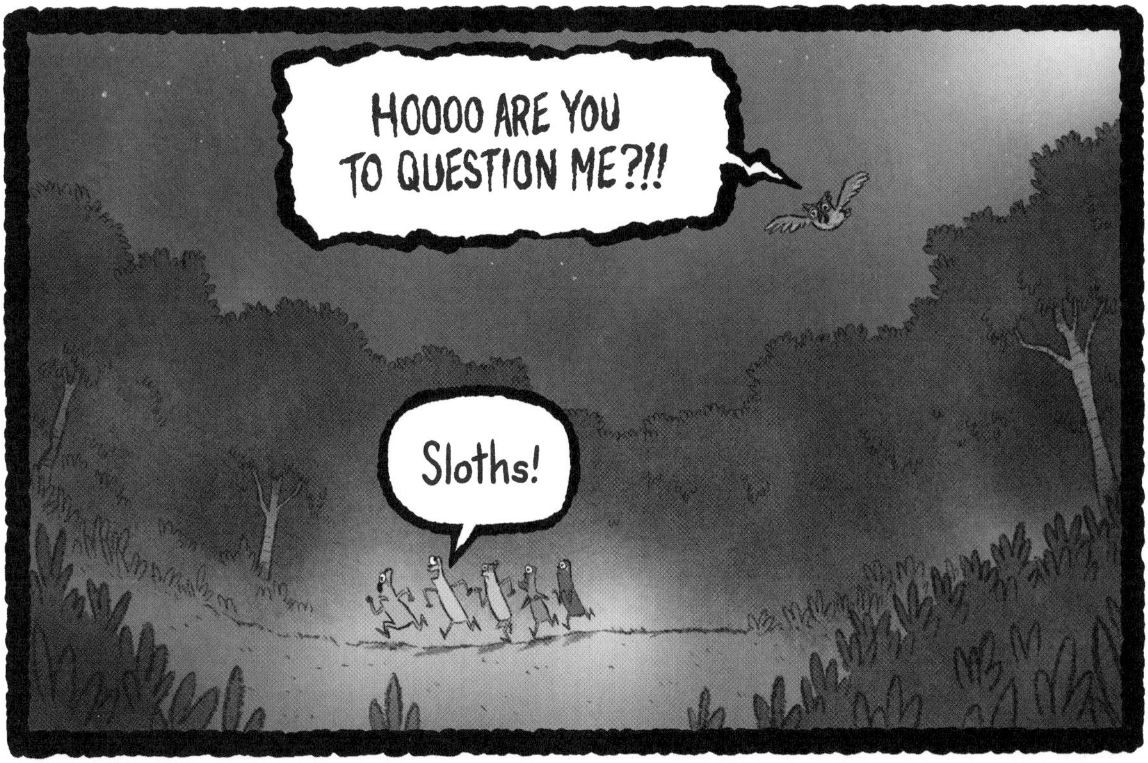
HOOOO ARE YOU TO QUESTION ME?!!
Sloths!

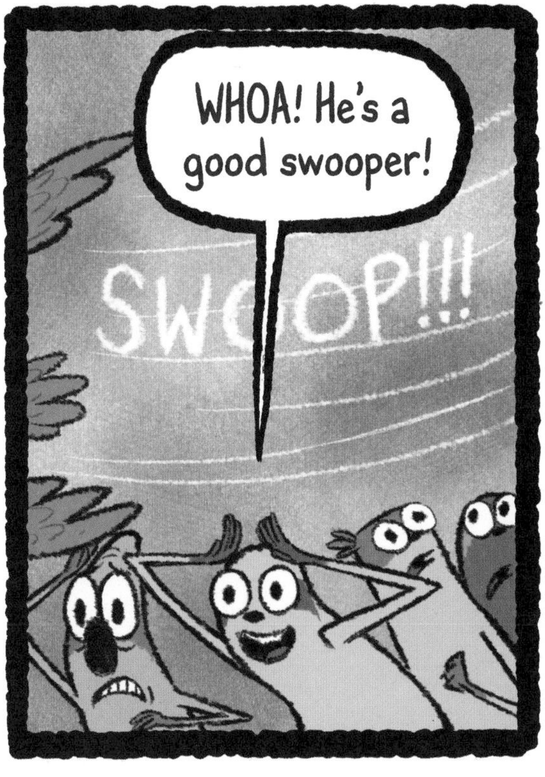
WHOA! He's a good swooper!
SWOOP!!!

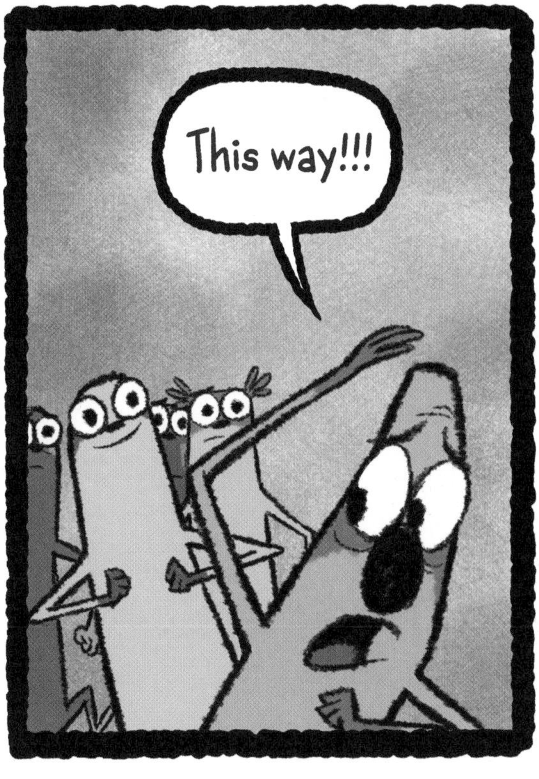
This way!!!

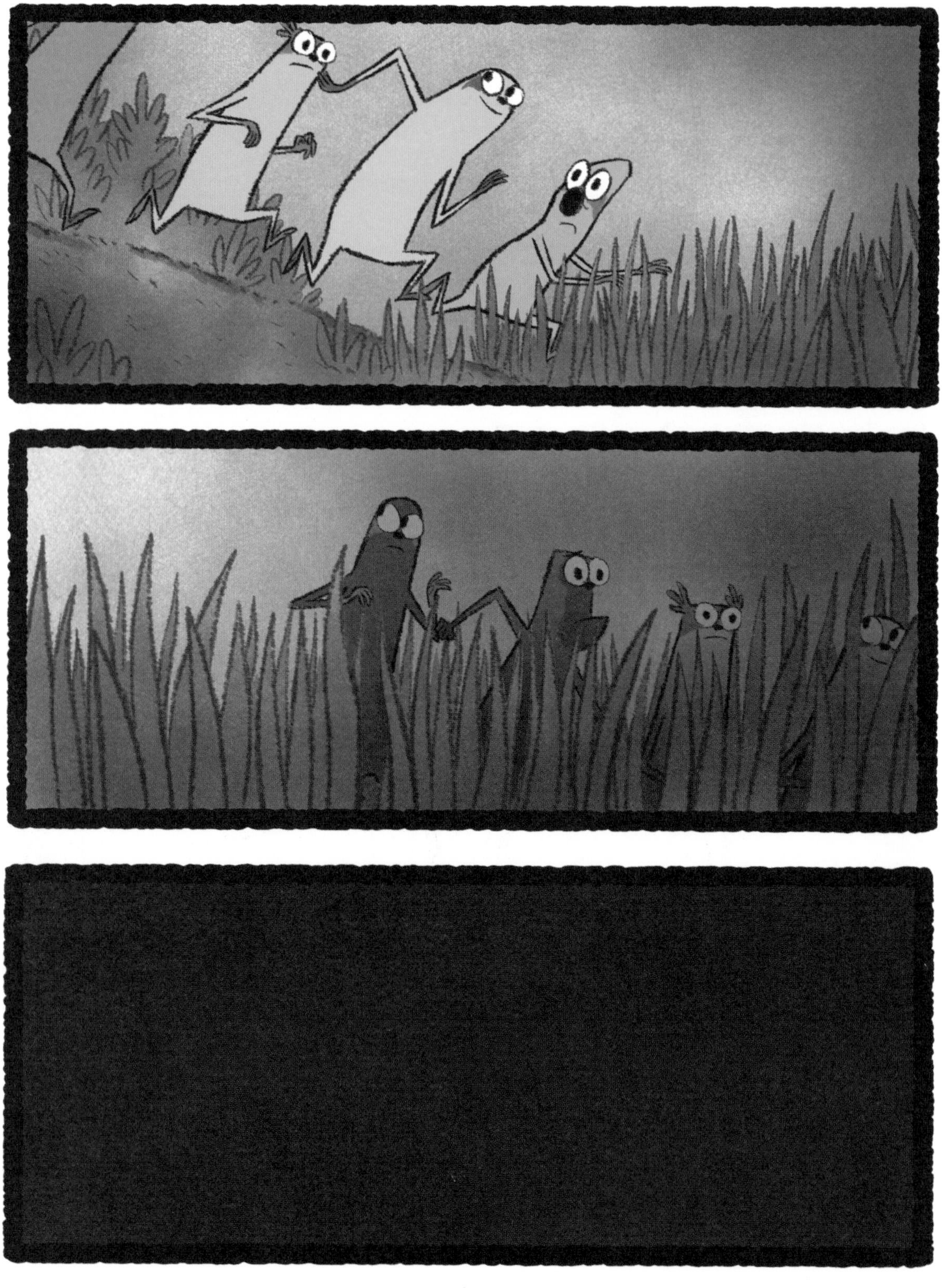

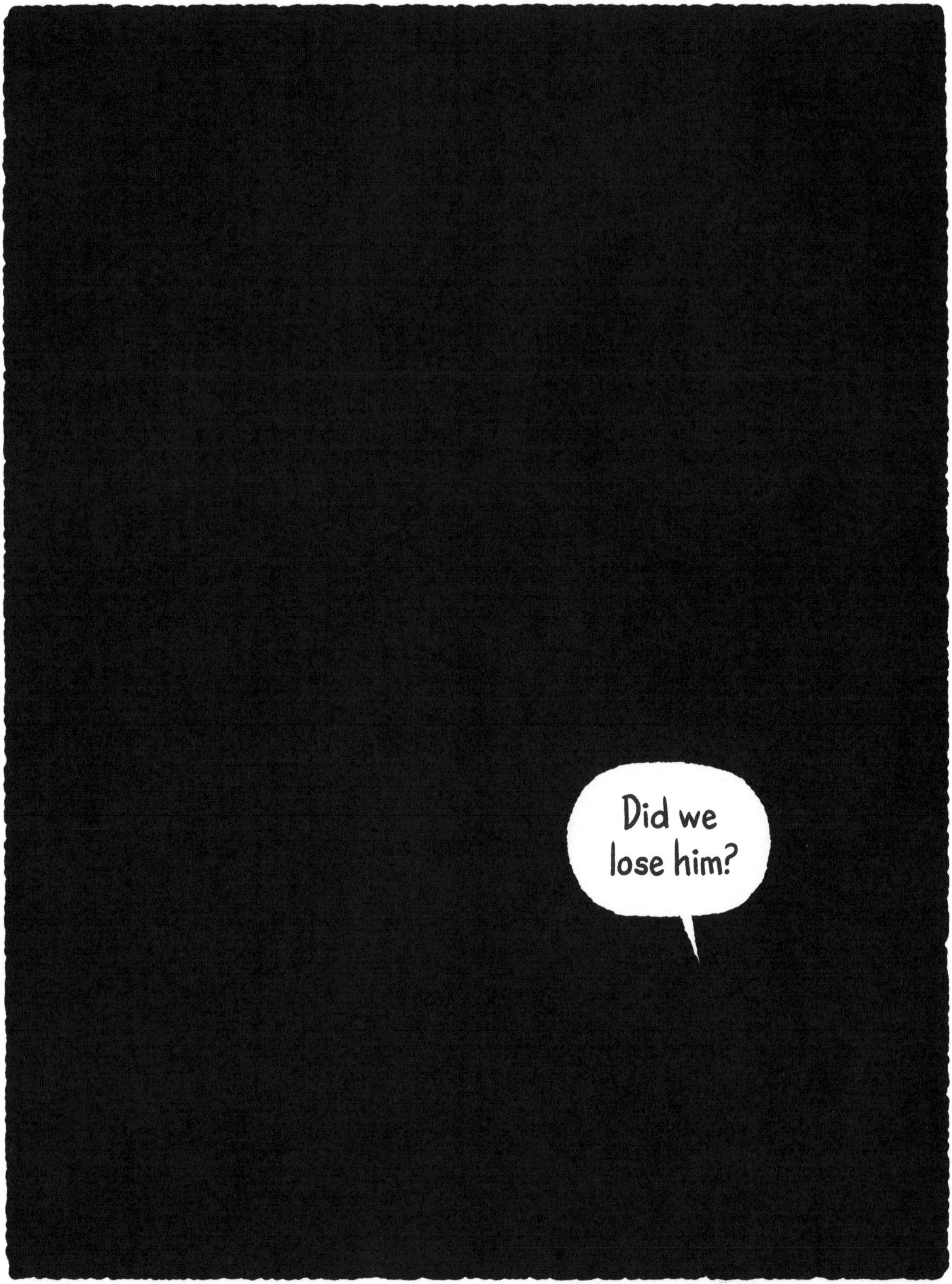
Did we lose him?

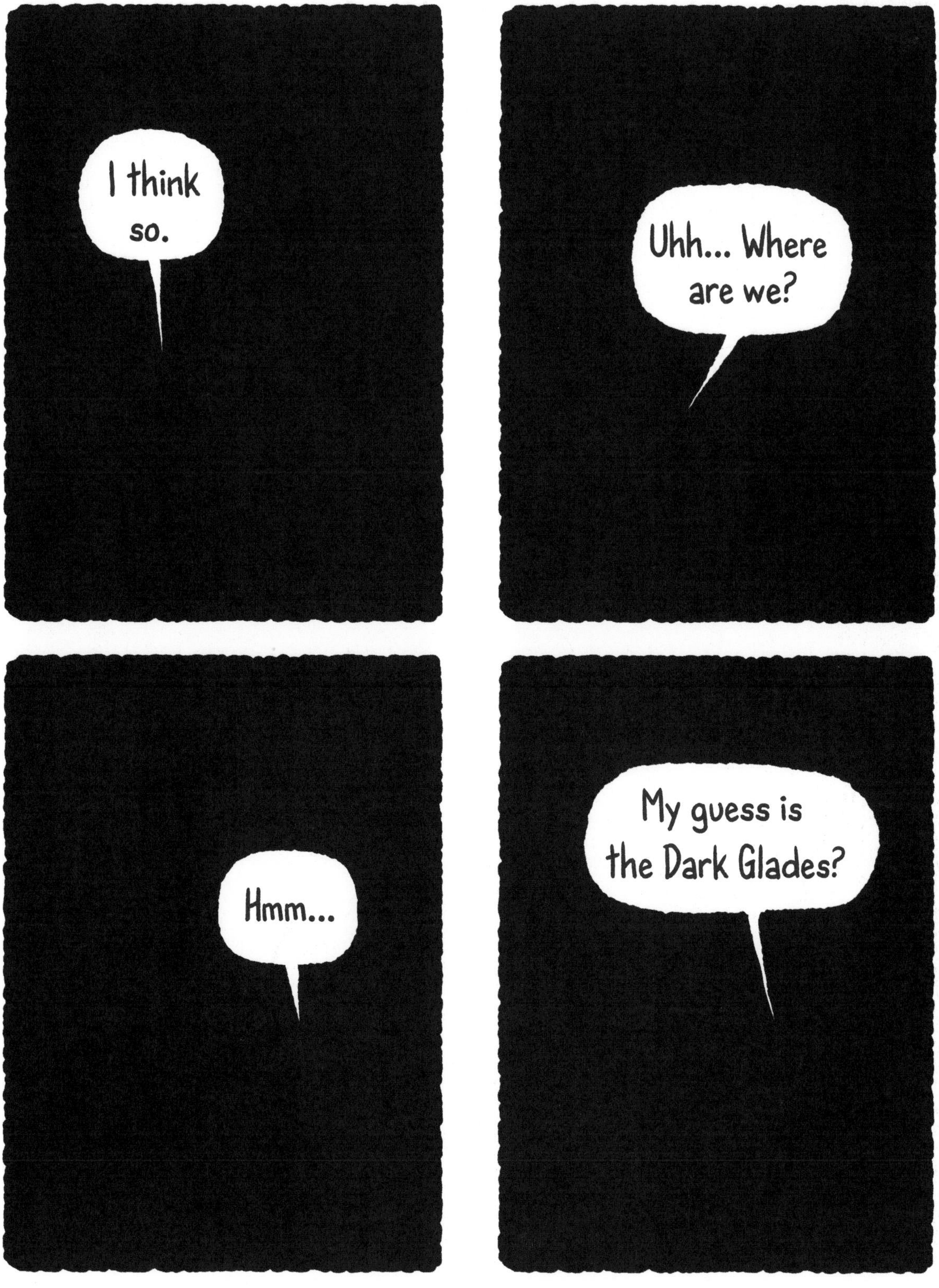
I think so.
Uhh... Where are we?
Hmm...
My guess is the Dark Glades?

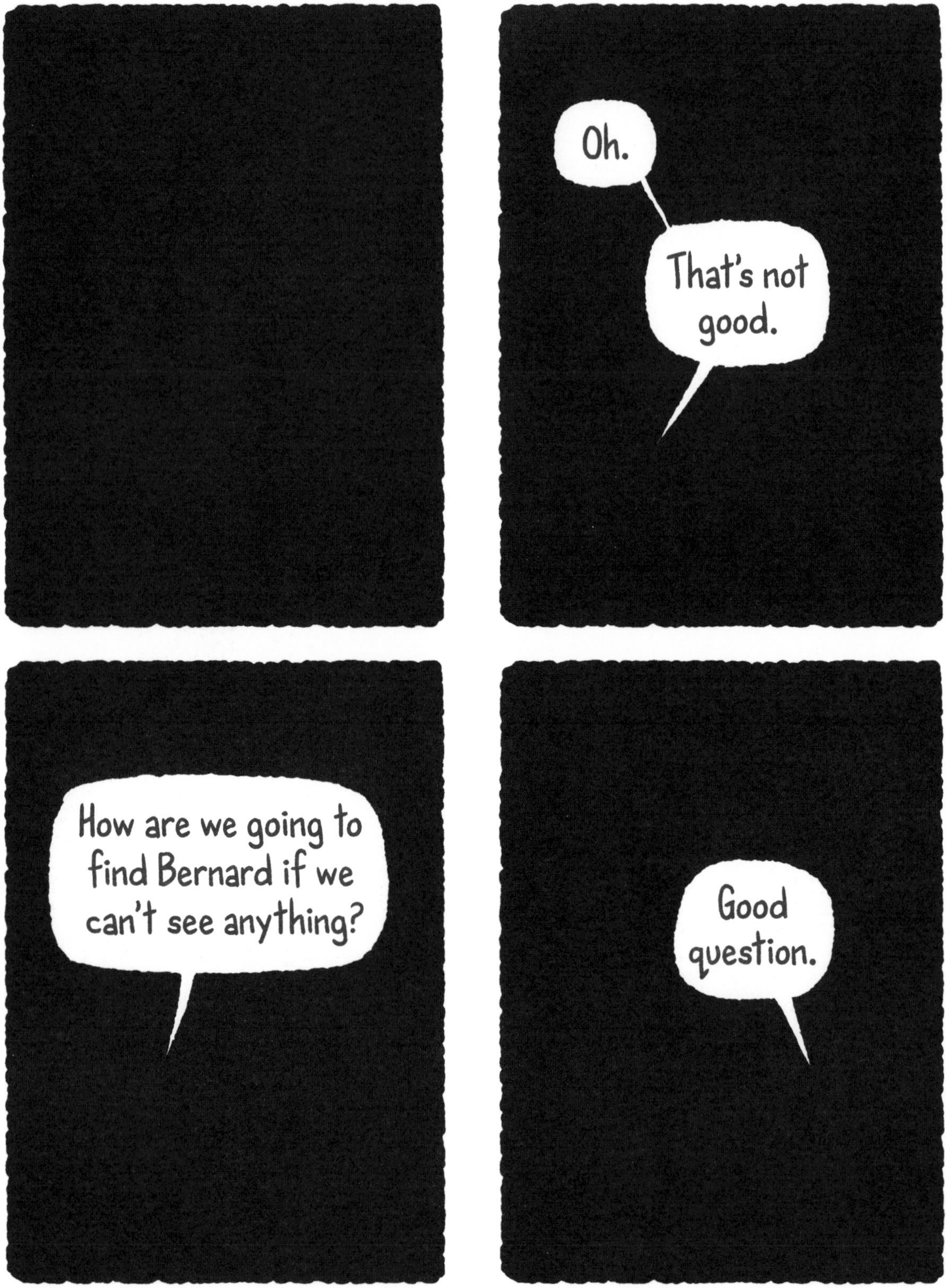
Oh.
That's not good.
How are we going to find Bernard if we can't see anything?
Good question.

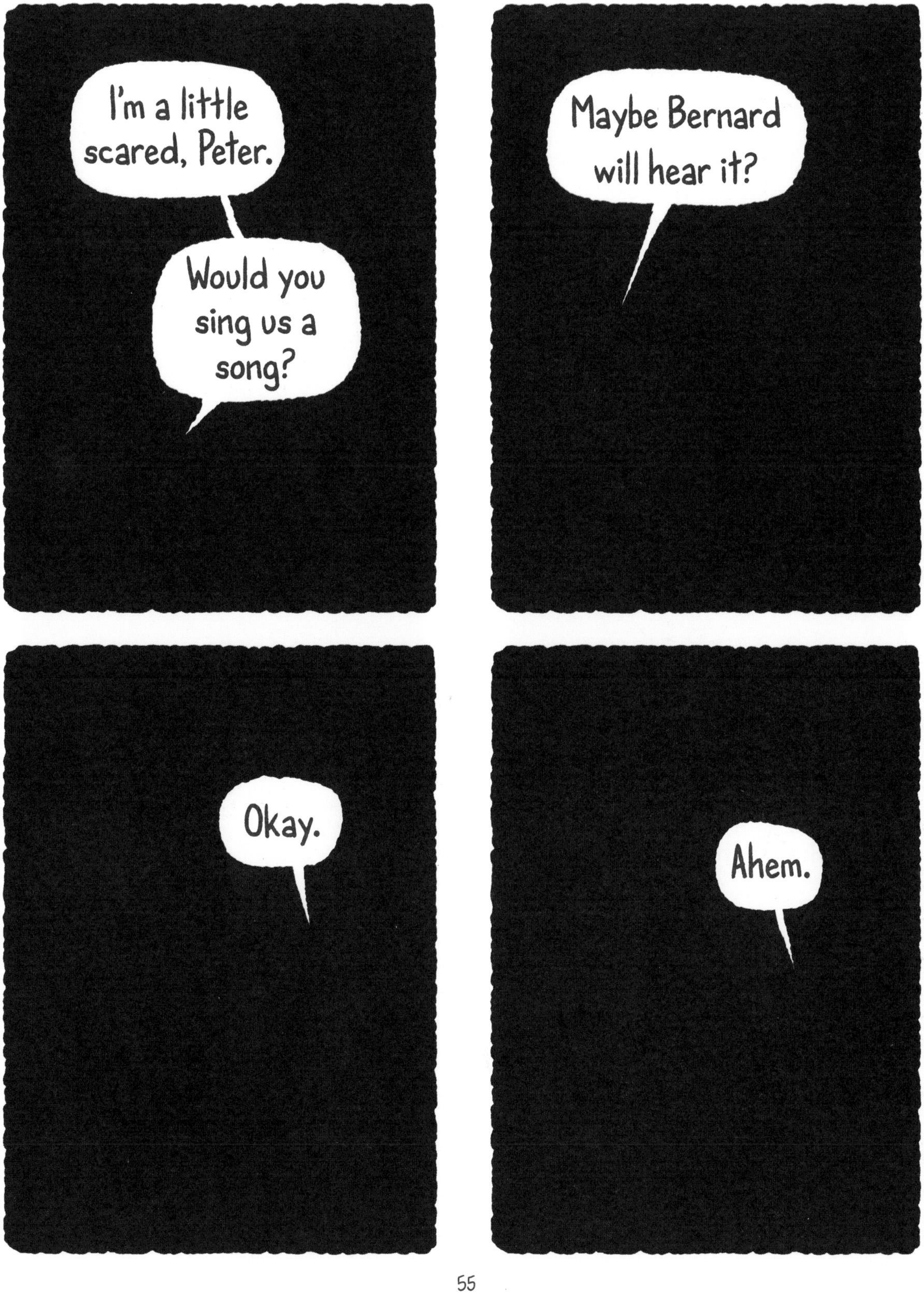
I'm a little scared, Peter.
Would you sing us a song?
Maybe Bernard will hear it?
Okay.
Ahem.

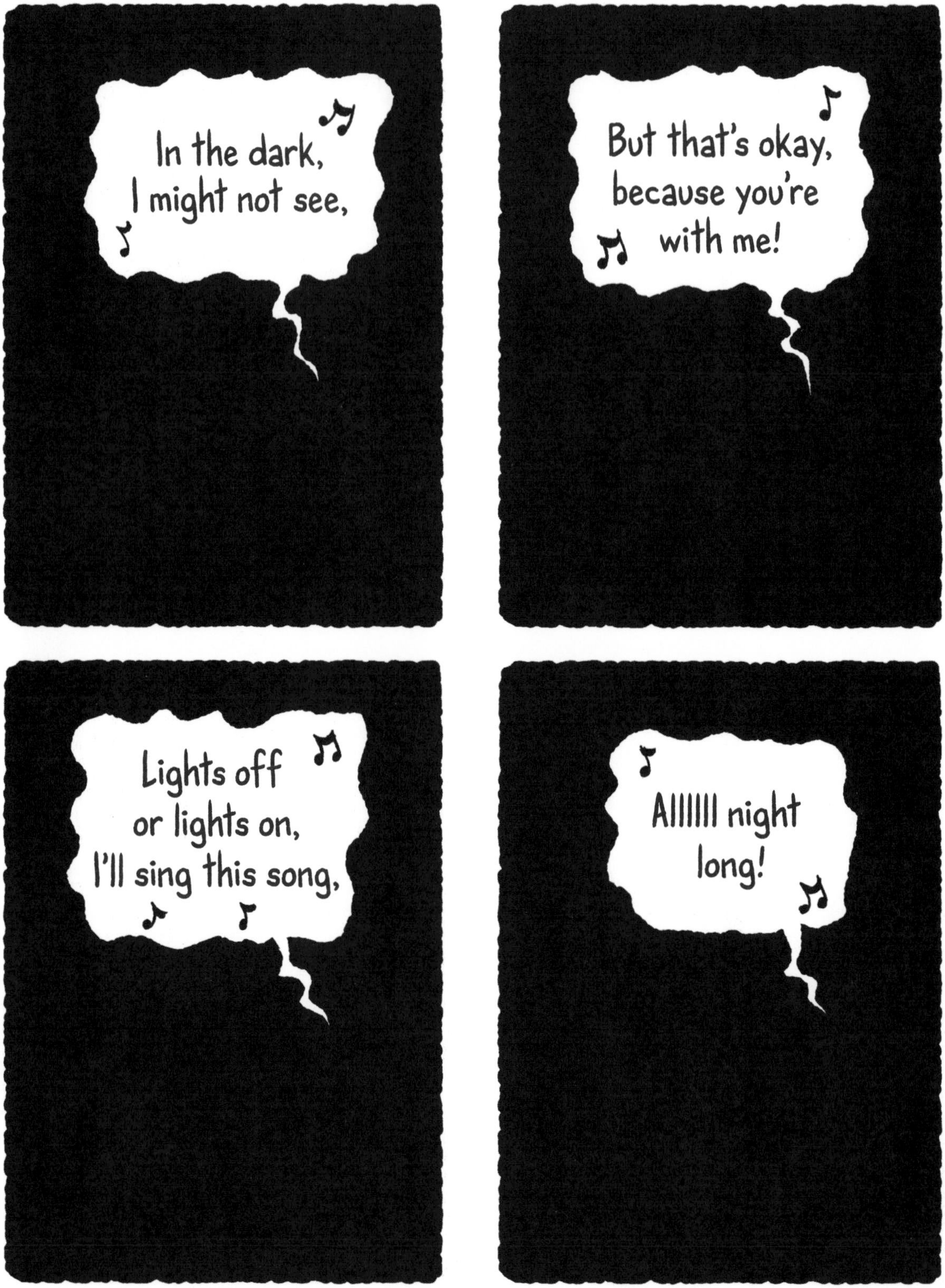
In the dark, I might not see,
But that's okay, because you're with me!
Lights off or lights on, I'll sing this song,
Alllllll night long!

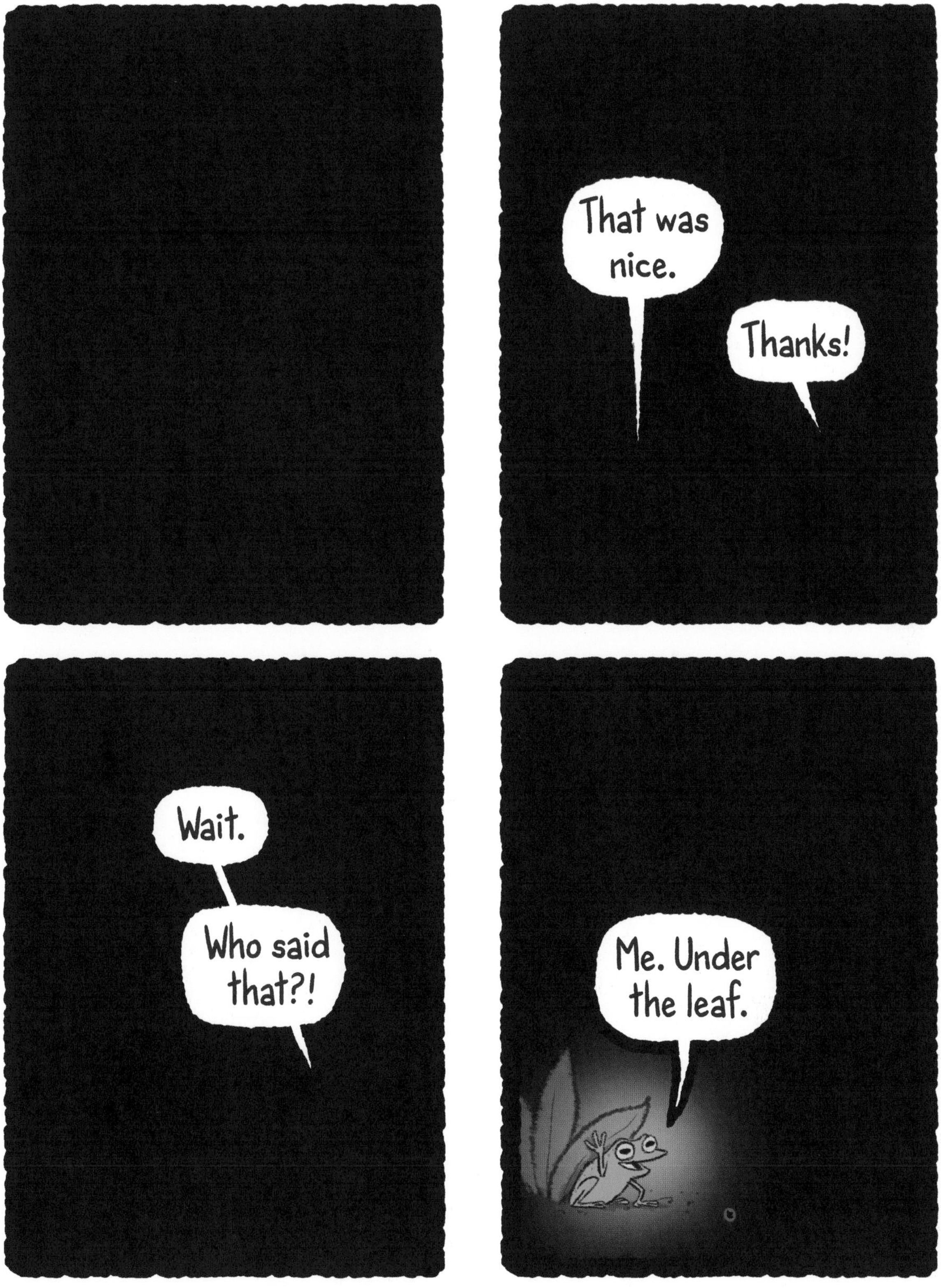
That was nice.
Thanks!
Wait.
Who said that?!
Me. Under the leaf.

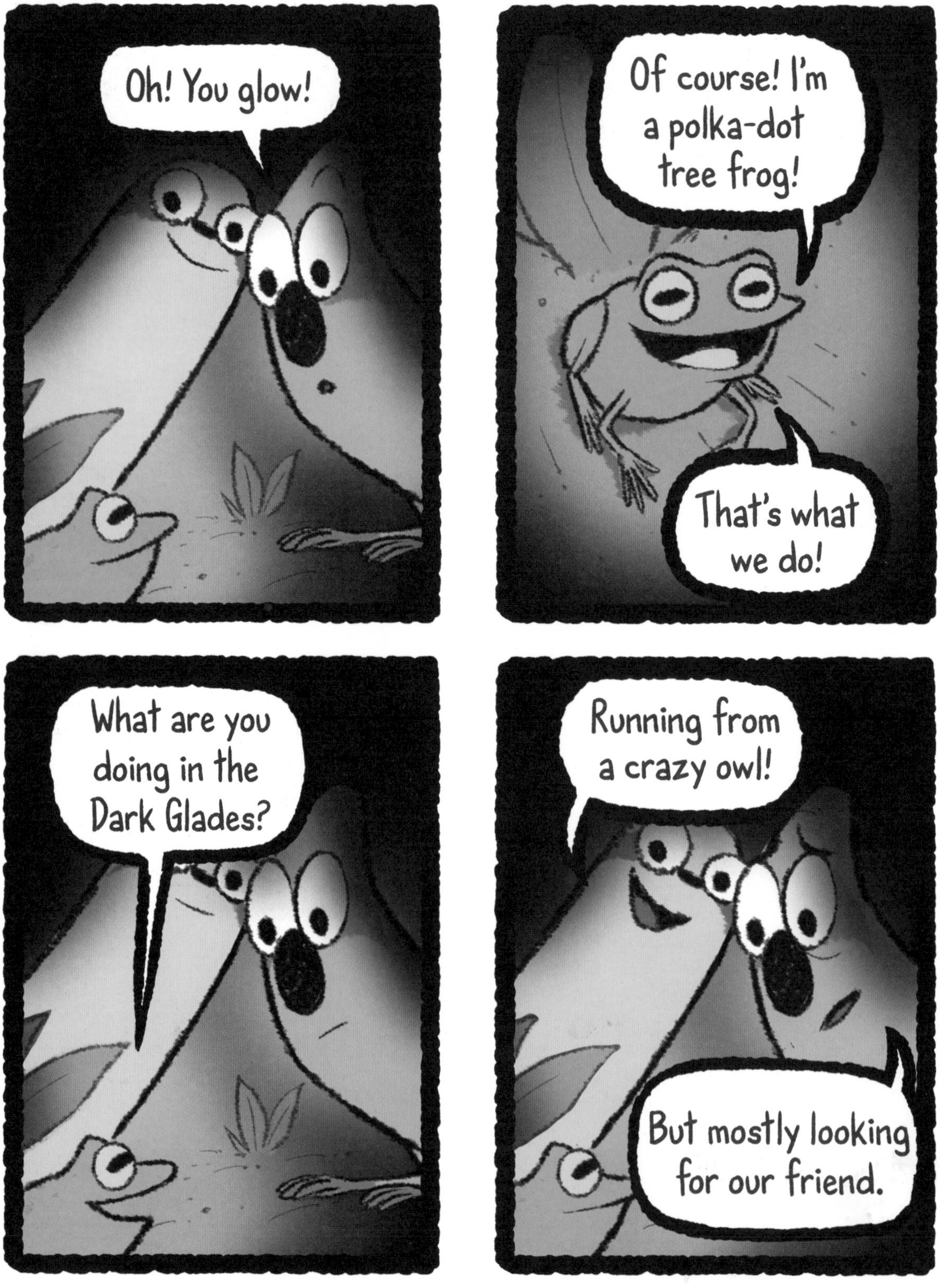
Oh! You glow!
Of course! I'm a polka-dot tree frog!
That's what we do!
What are you doing in the Dark Glades?
Running from a crazy owl!
But mostly looking for our friend.

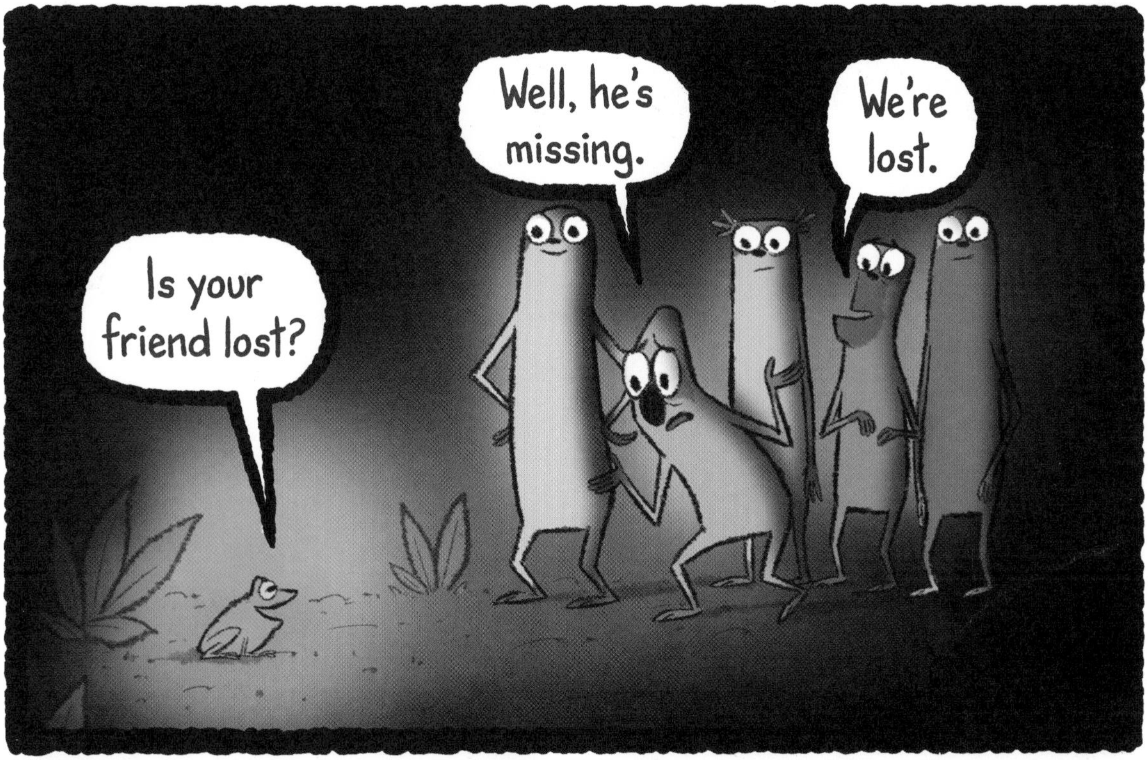
Is your friend lost?
Well, he's missing.
We're lost.

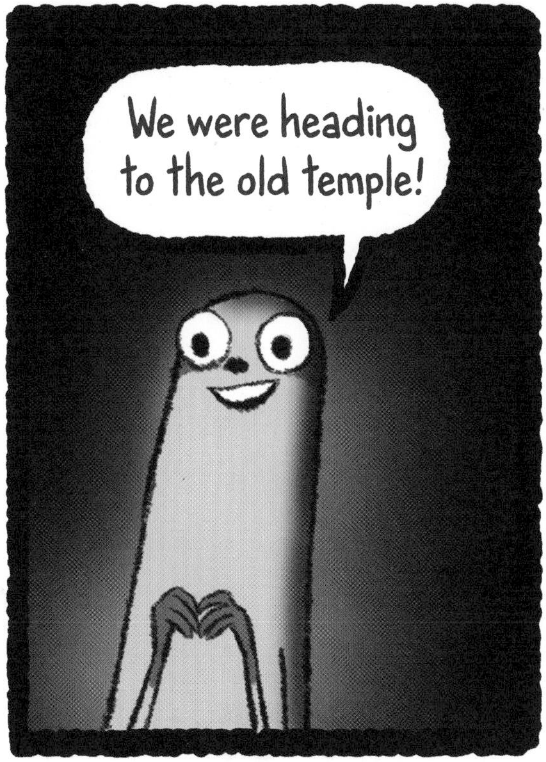
We were heading to the old temple!

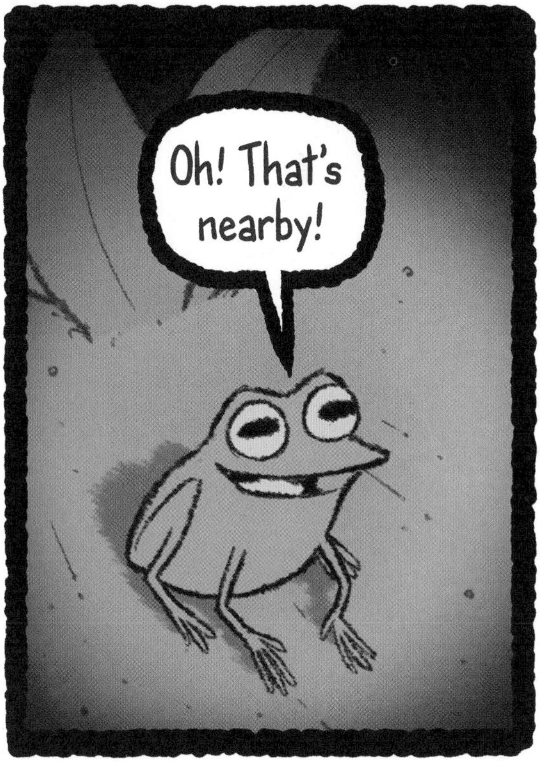
Oh! That's nearby!

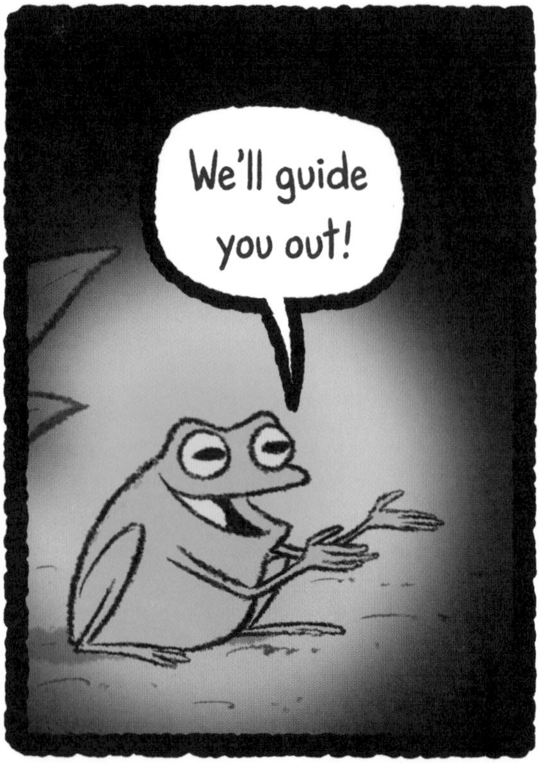
We'll guide you out!

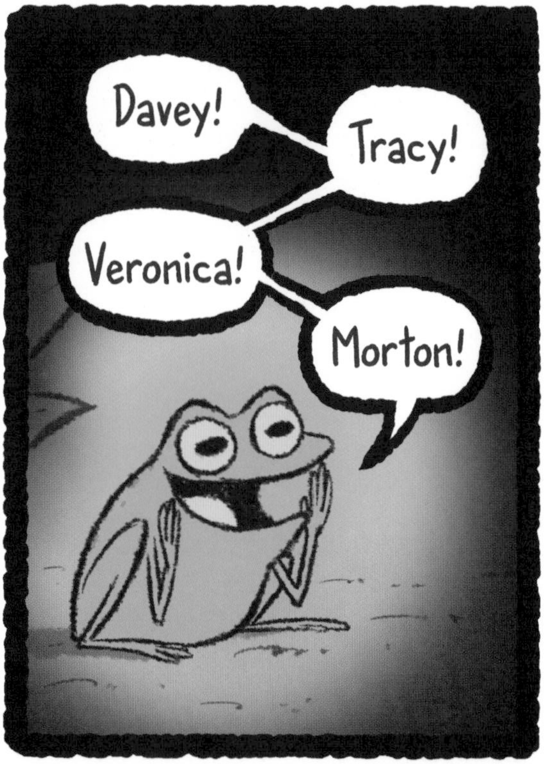
Davey!
Tracy!
Veronica!
Morton!

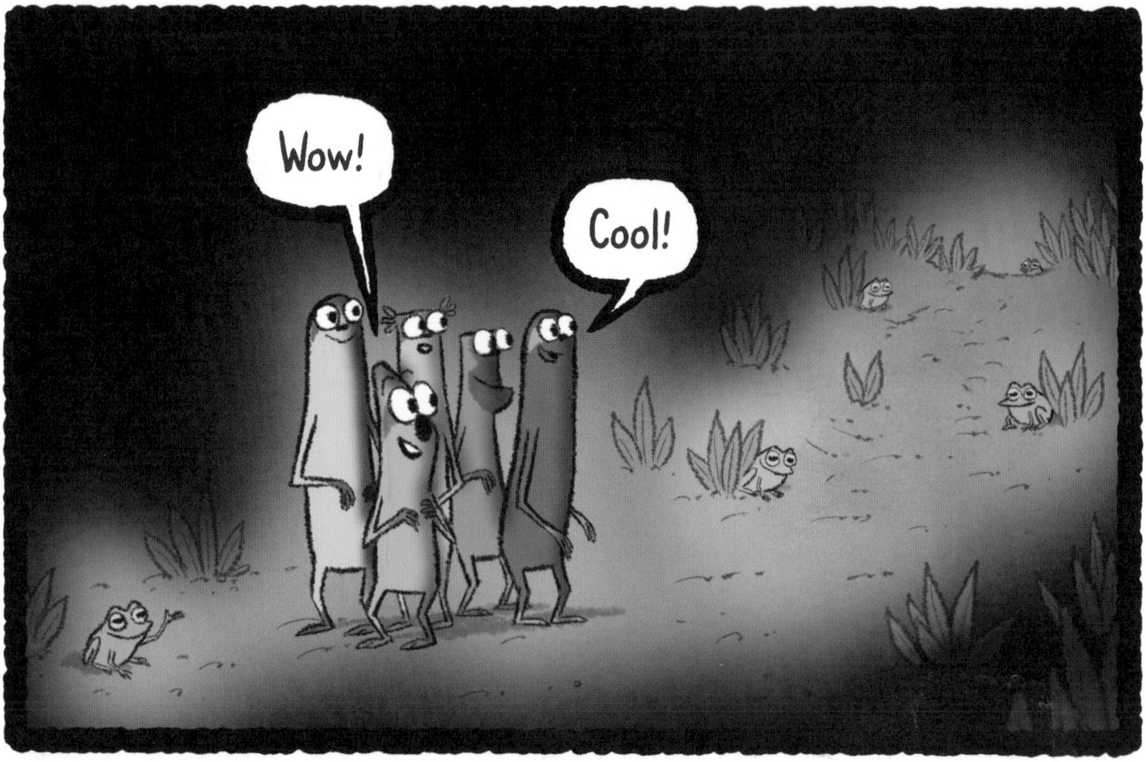
Wow!
Cool!

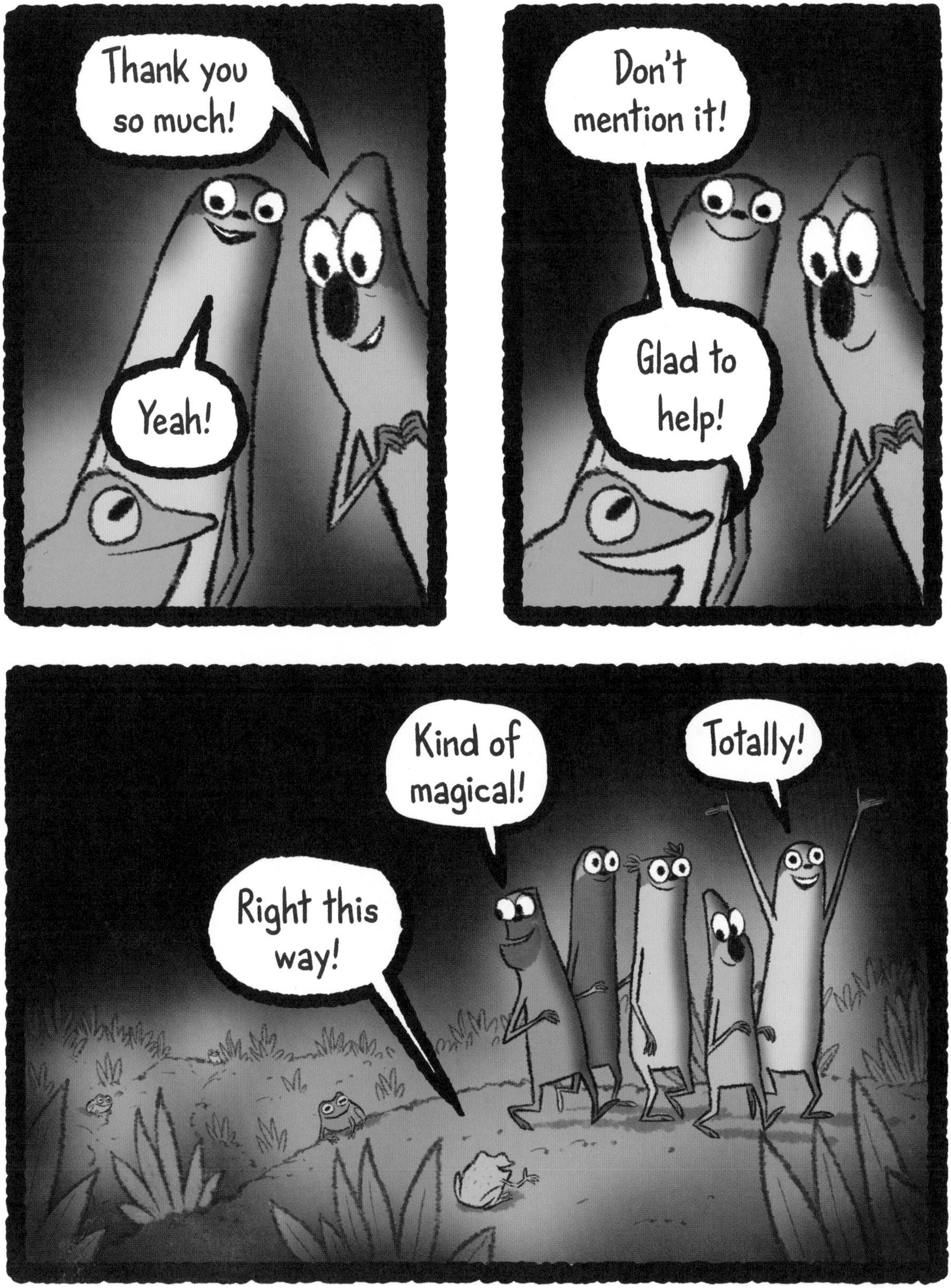
Thank you so much!
Yeah!
Don't mention it!
Glad to help!
Right this way!
Kind of magical!
Totally!

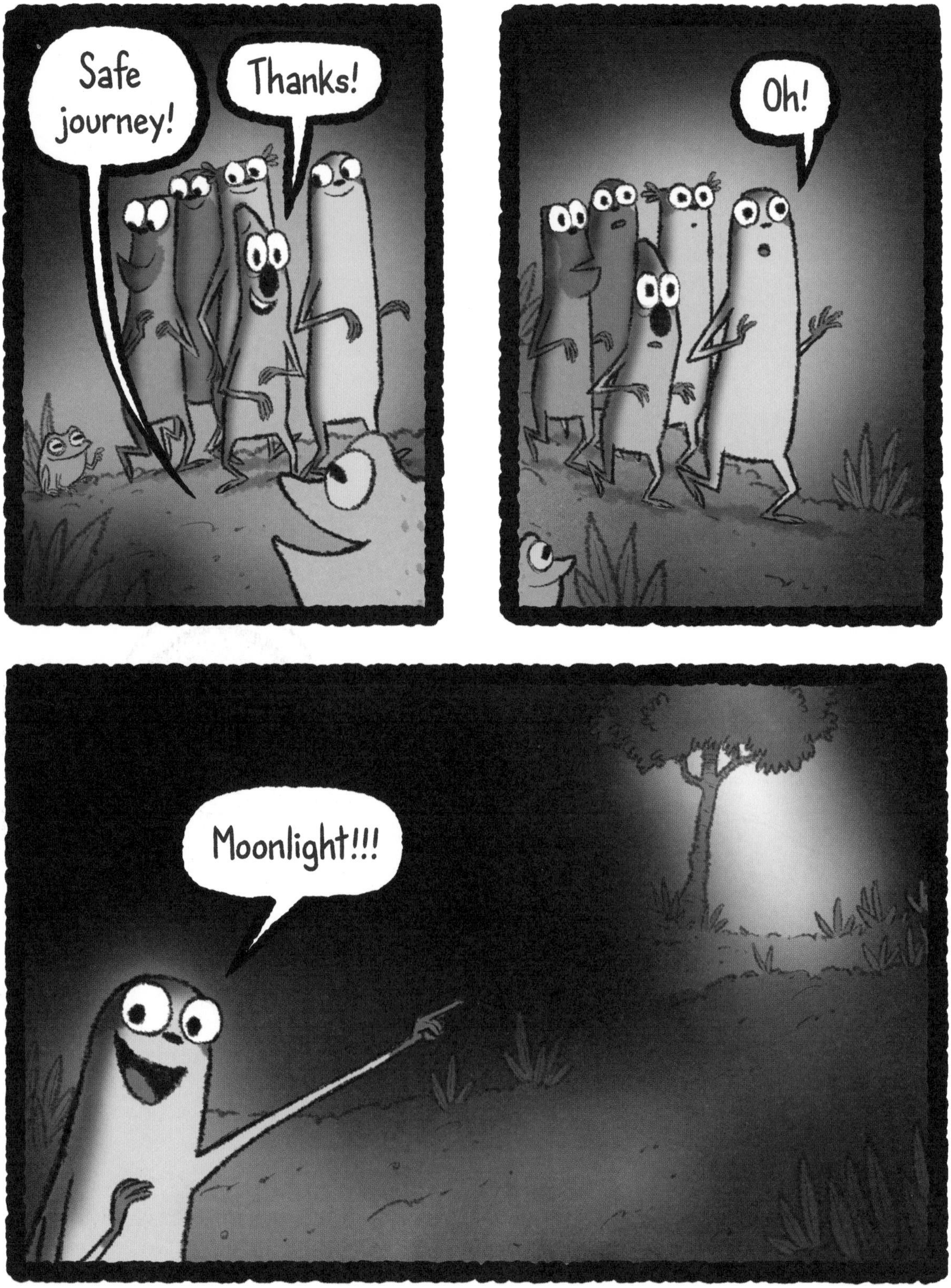
Safe journey!
Thanks!
Oh!
Moonlight!!!

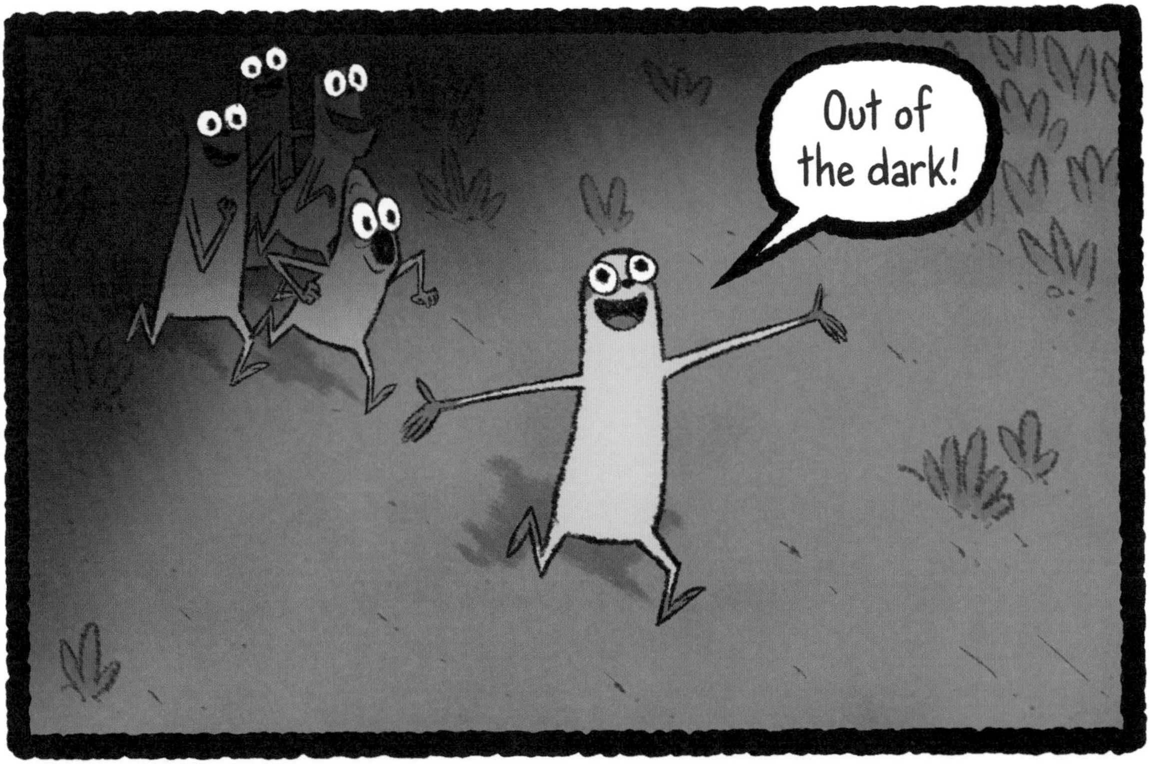
Out of the dark!

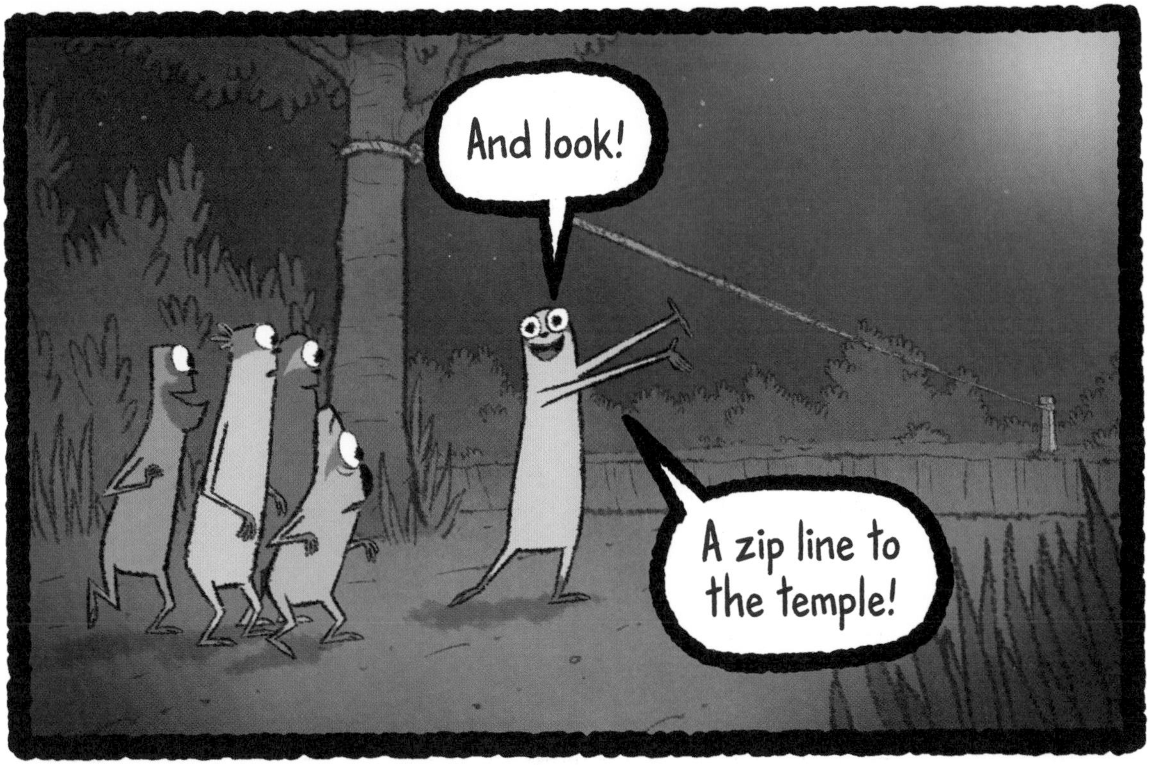
And look!
A zip line to the temple!

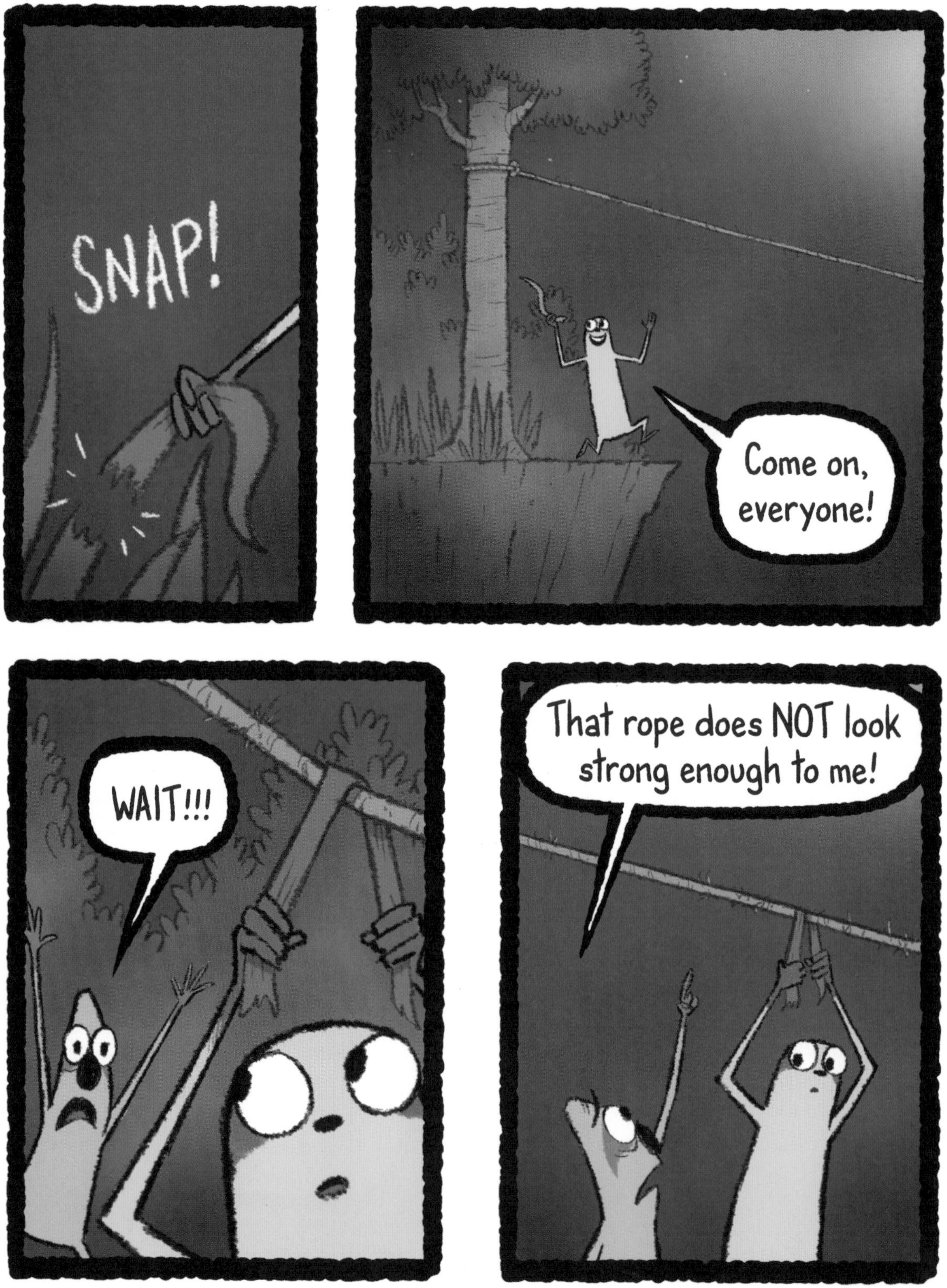
SNAP!
Come on, everyone!
WAIT!!!
That rope does NOT look strong enough to me!

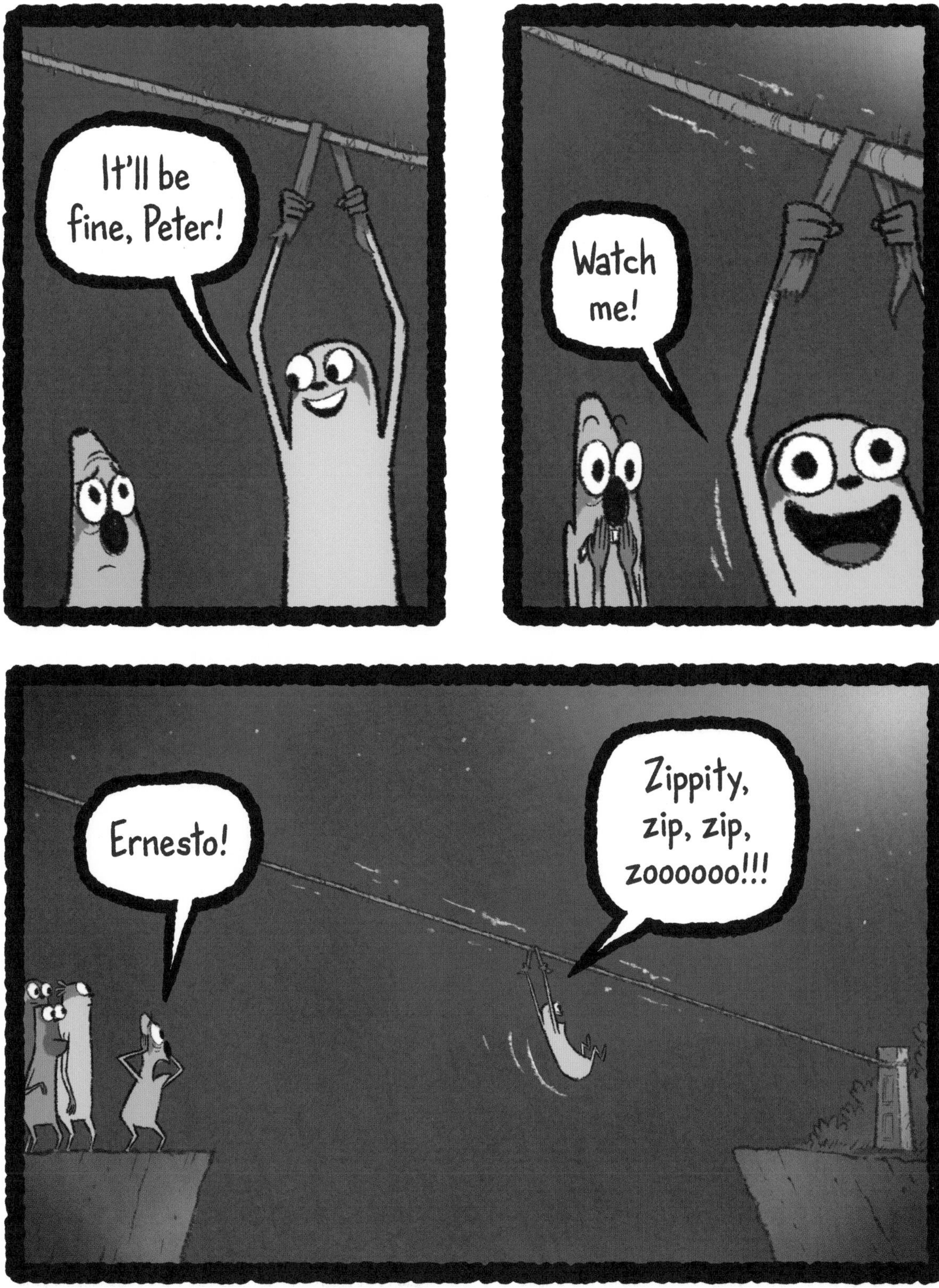
It'll be fine, Peter!
Watch me!
Ernesto!
Zippity, zip, zip, zoooooo!!!

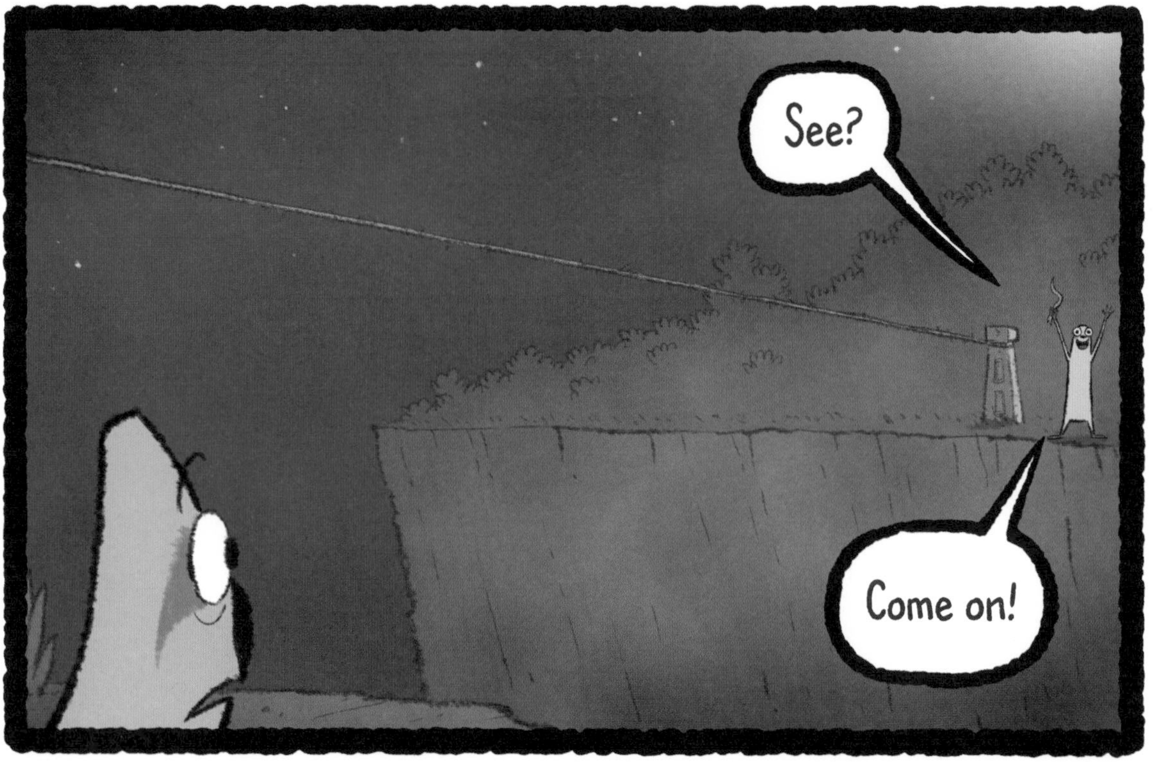
See?
Come on!

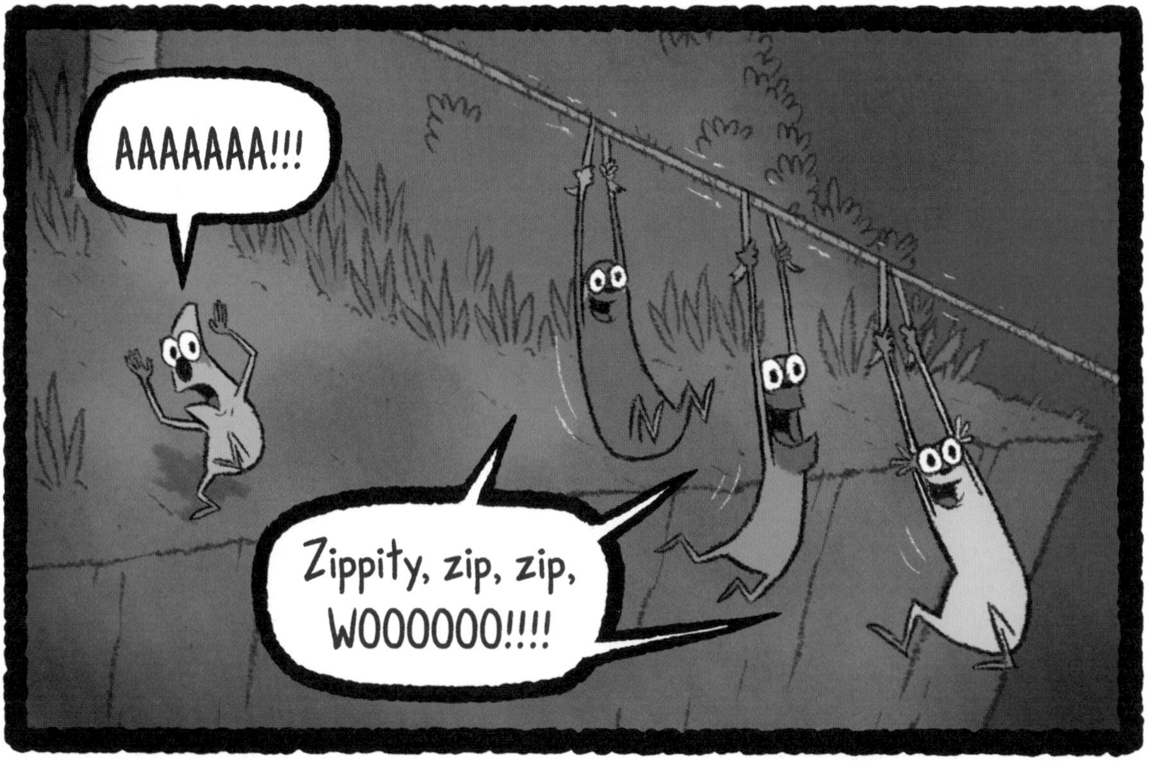
AAAAAAA!!!
Zippity, zip, zip, WOOOOOO!!!!

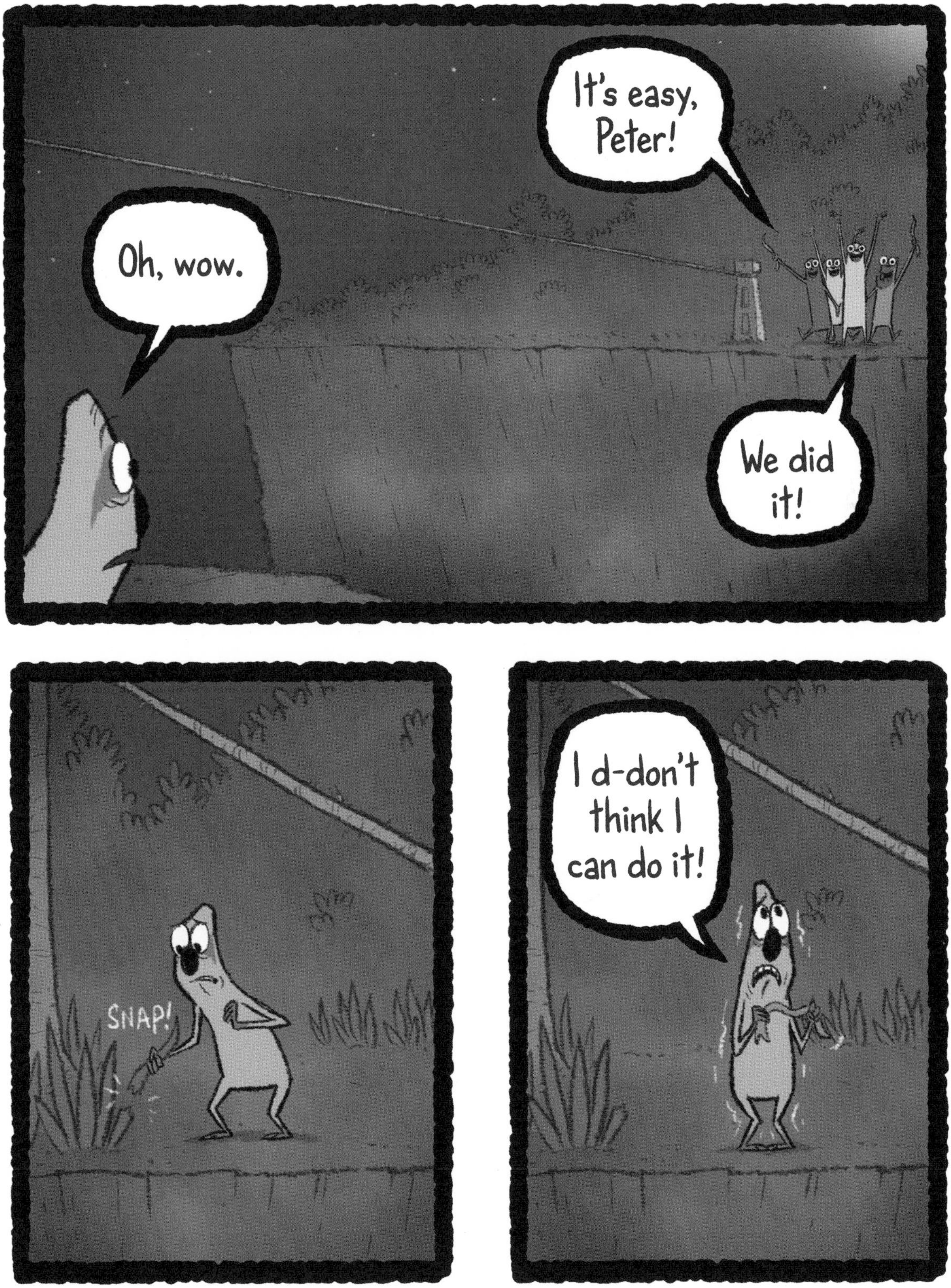
Oh, wow.
It's easy, Peter!
We did it!
SNAP!
I d-don't think I can do it!

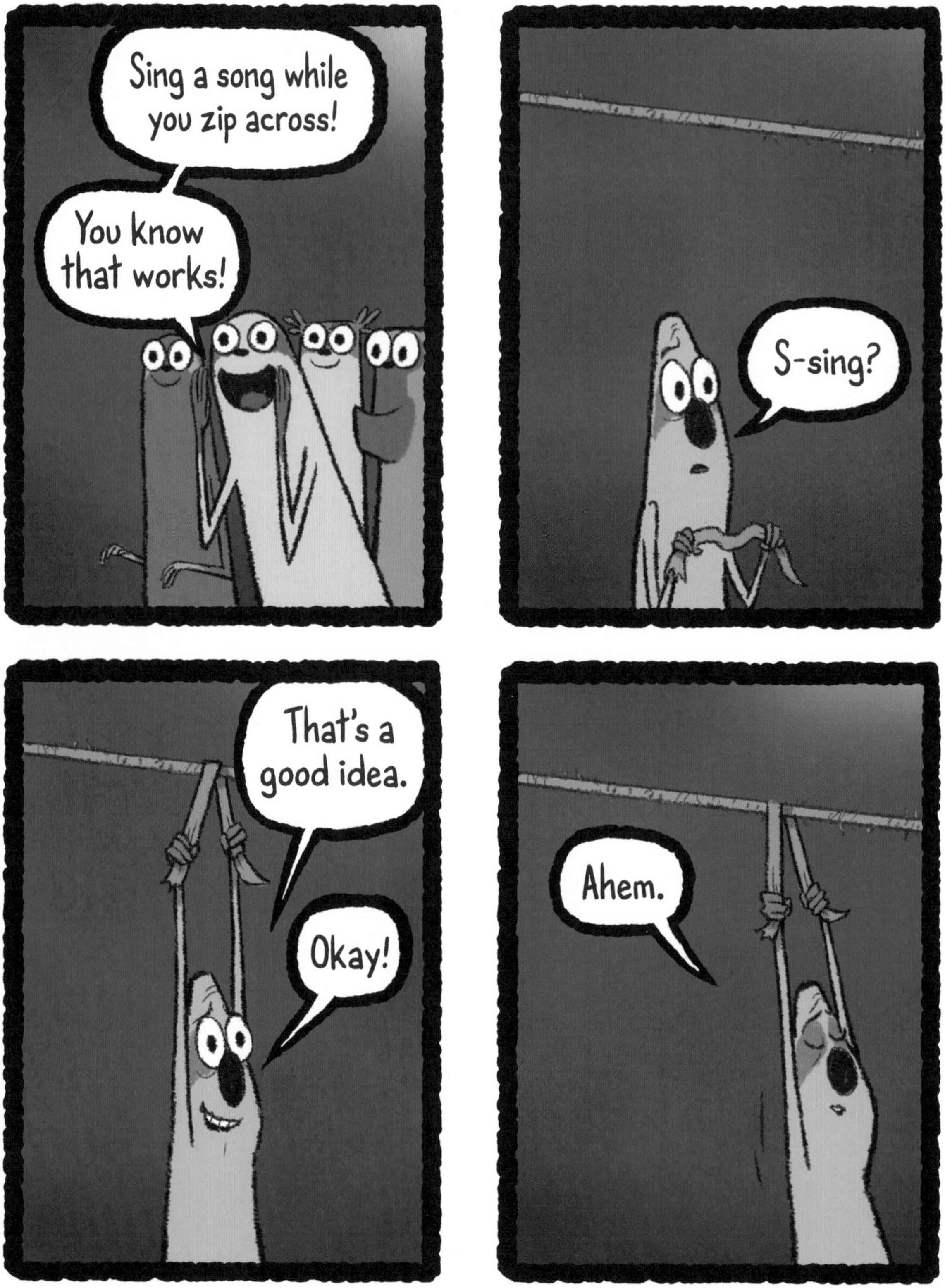
Sing a song while you zip across!
You know that works!
S-sing?
That's a good idea.
Okay!
Ahem.

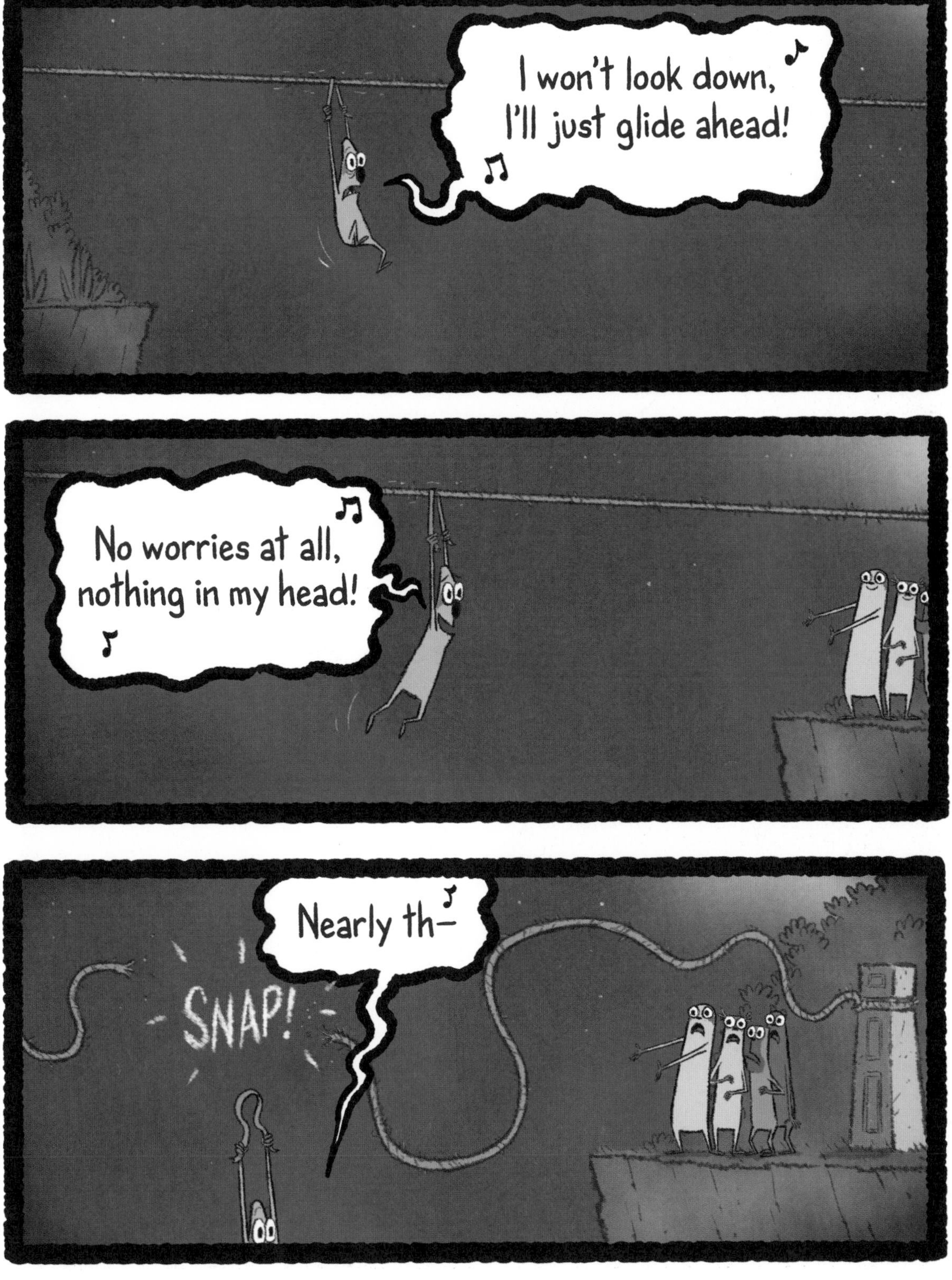
I won't look down, I'll just glide ahead!
No worries at all, nothing in my head!
Nearly th—
SNAP!

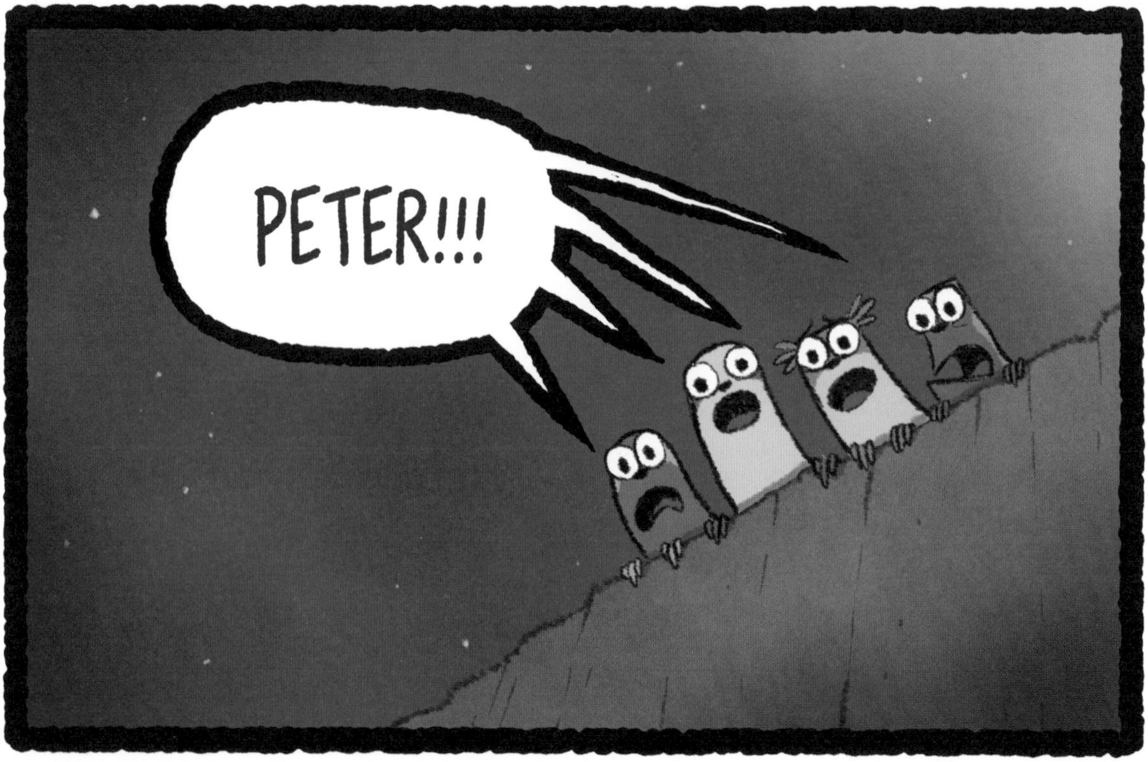
PETER!!!

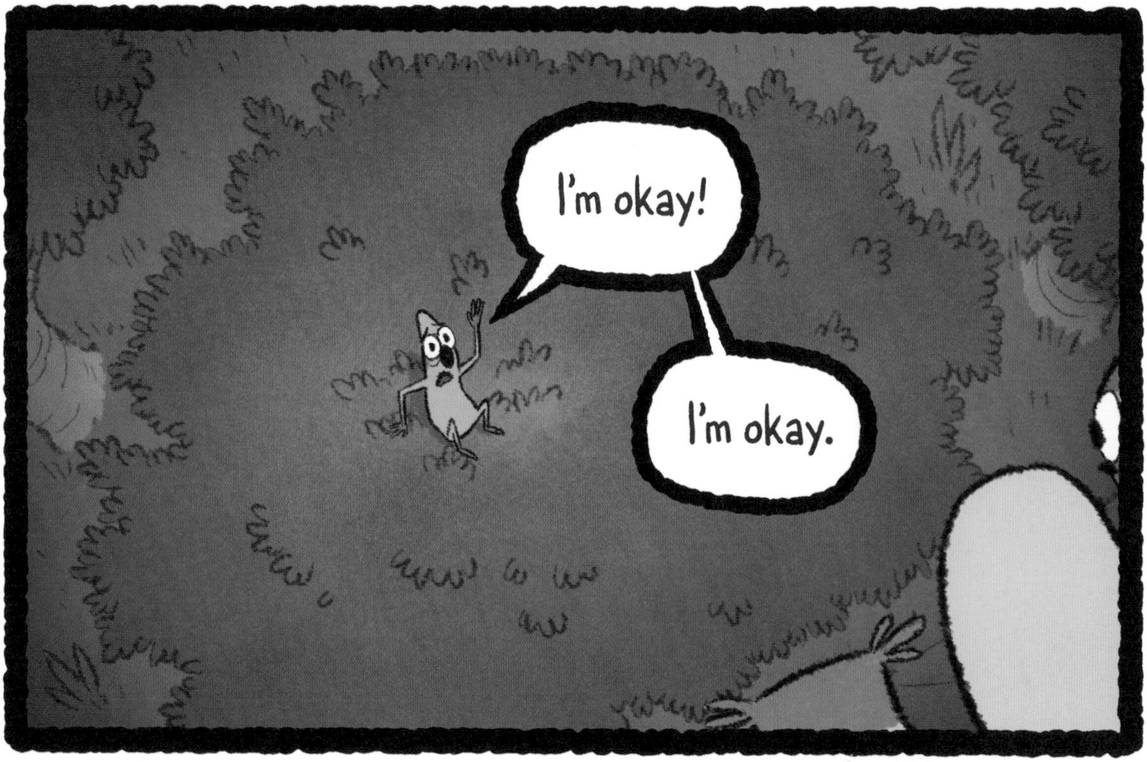
I'm okay!
I'm okay.

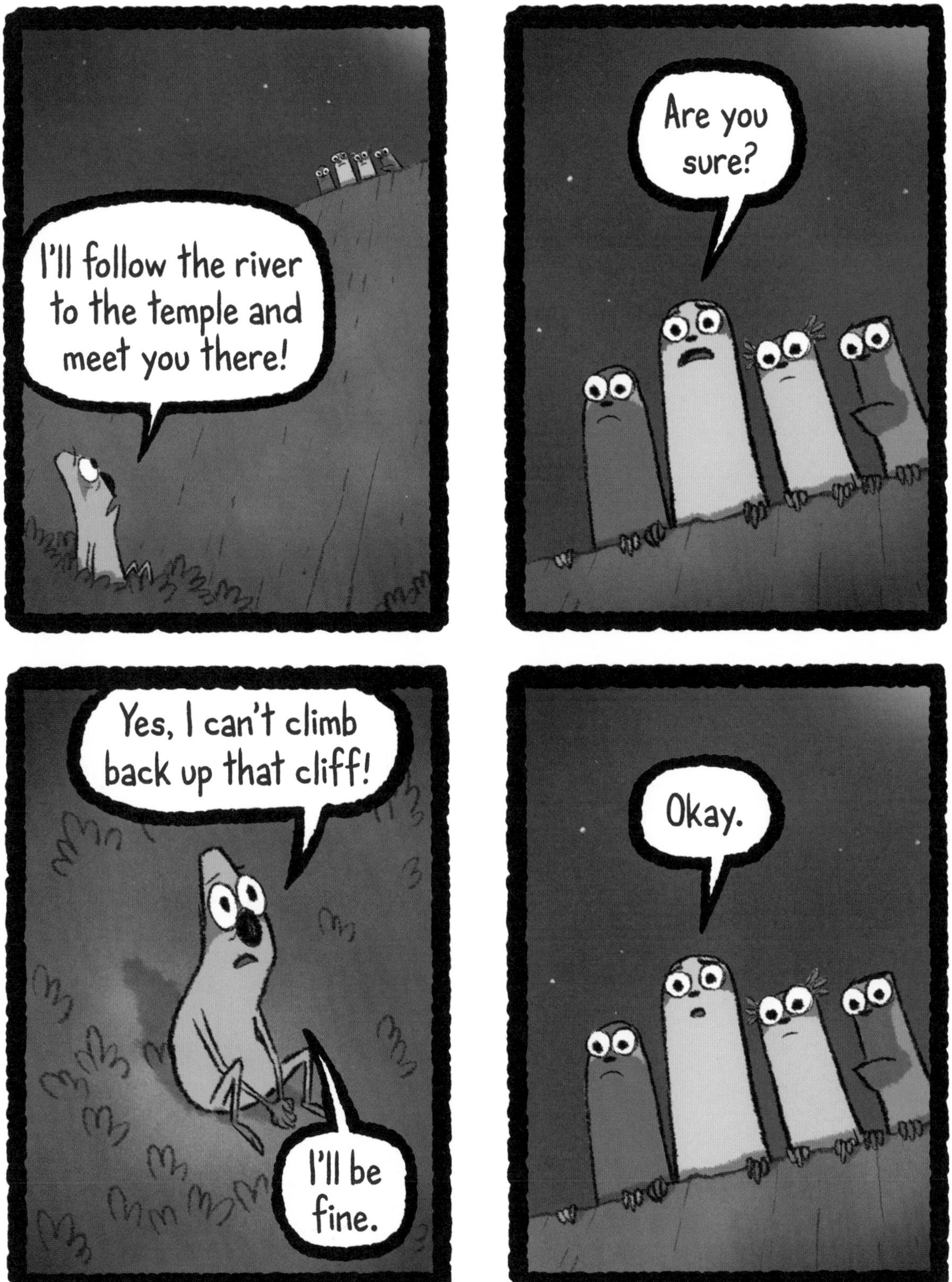
I'll follow the river to the temple and meet you there!
Are you sure?
Yes, I can't climb back up that cliff!
I'll be fine.
Okay.

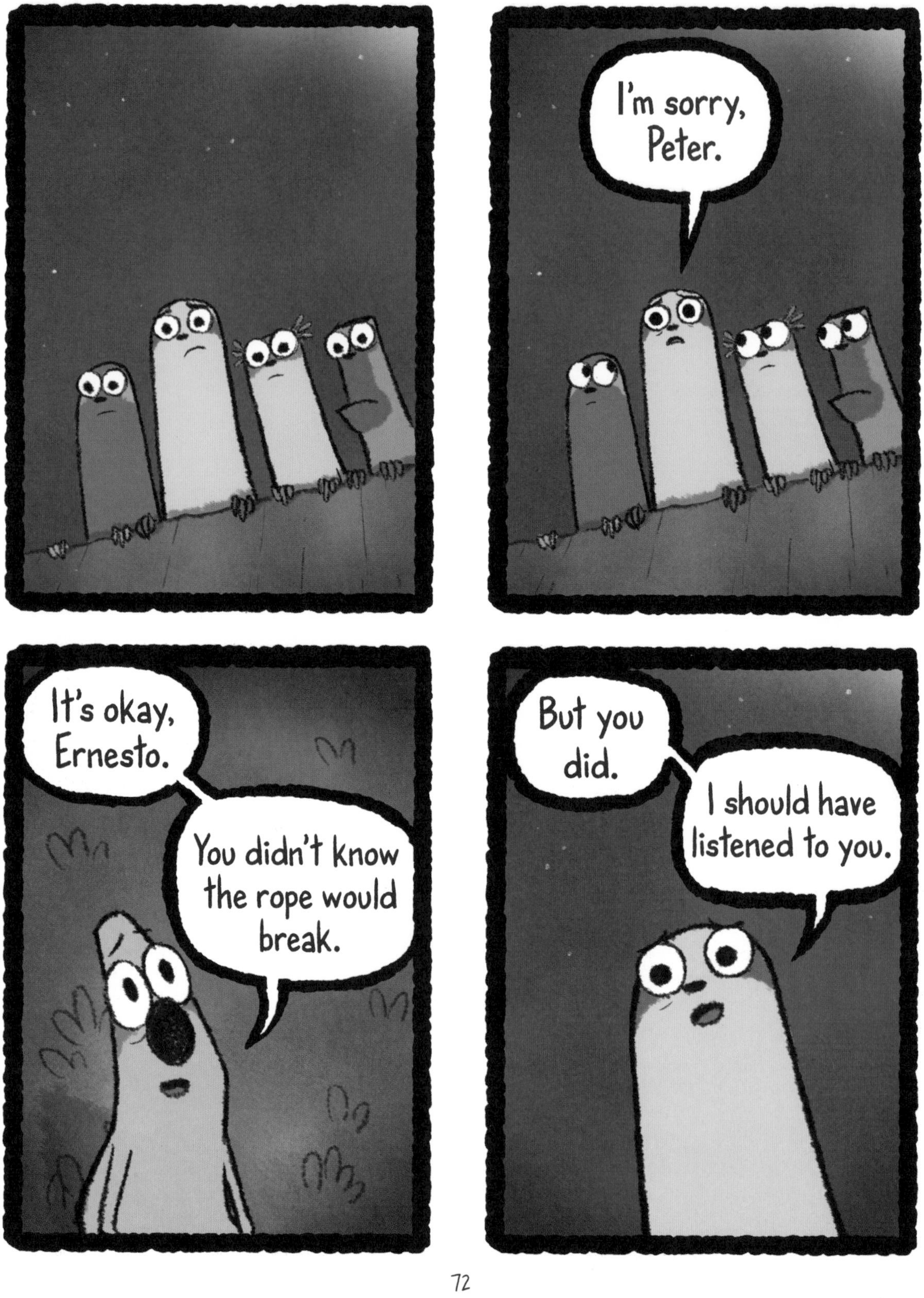
I'm sorry, Peter.
It's okay, Ernesto.
You didn't know the rope would break.
But you did.
I should have listened to you.

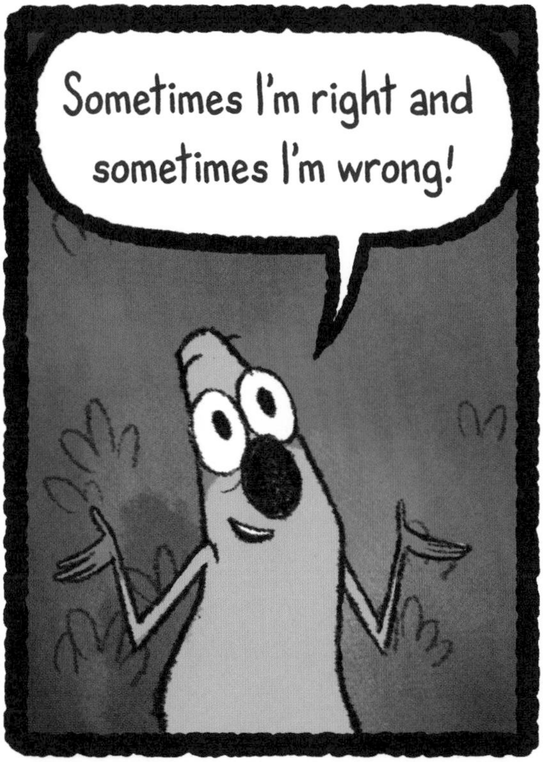
Sometimes I'm right and sometimes I'm wrong!

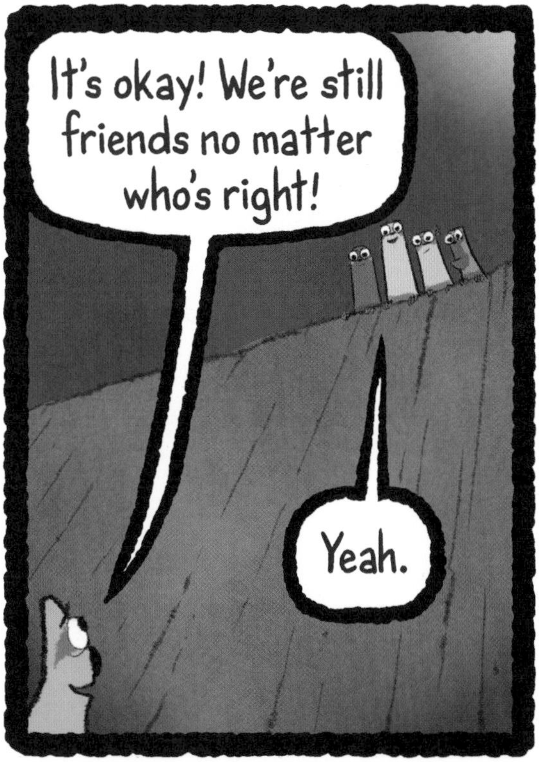
It's okay! We're still friends no matter who's right!
Yeah.

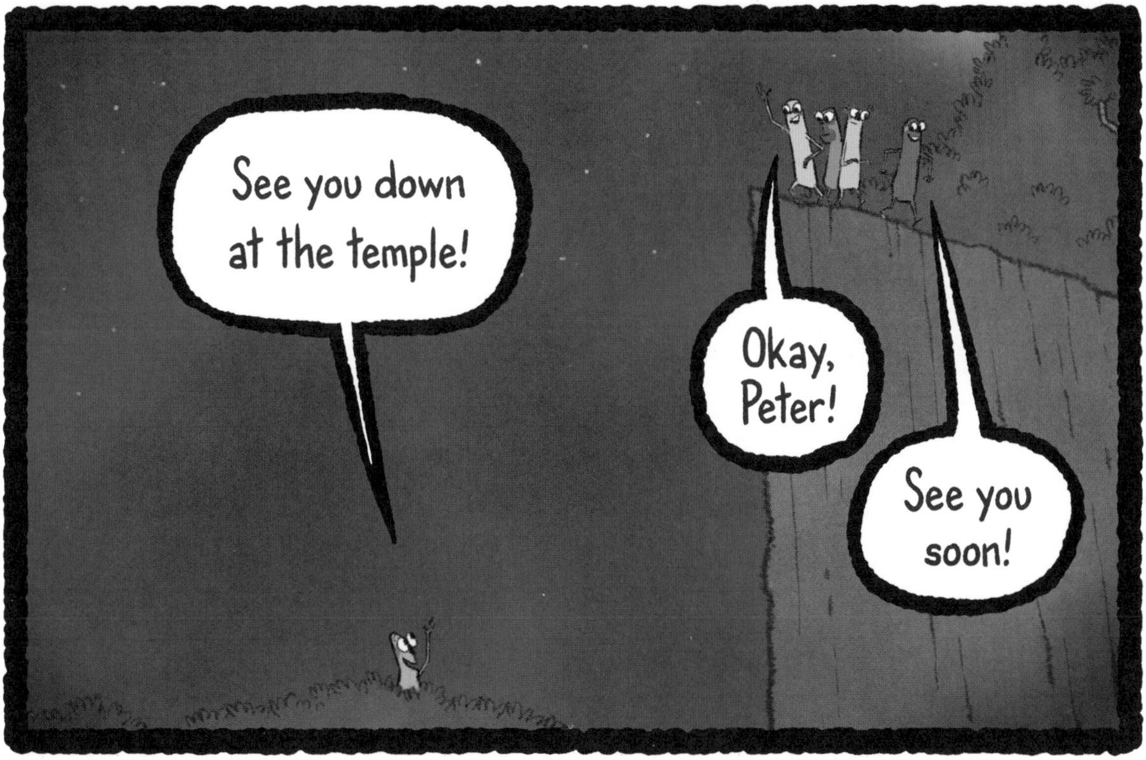
See you down at the temple!
Okay, Peter!
See you soon!

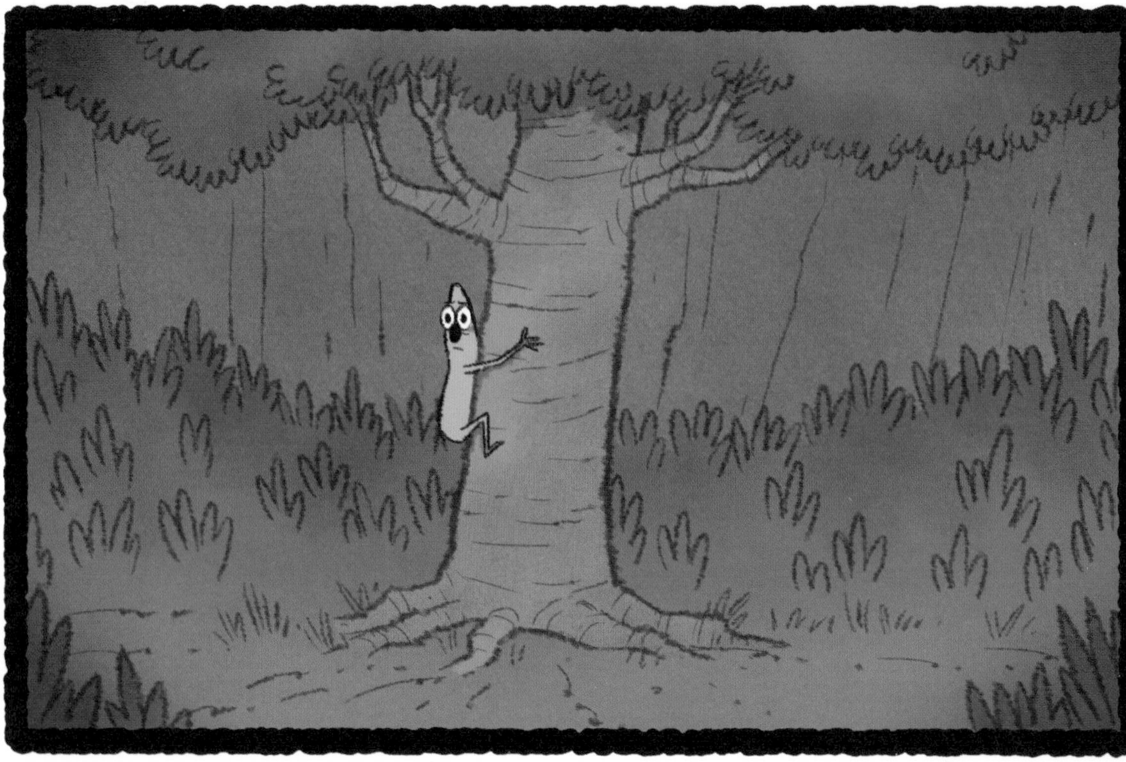

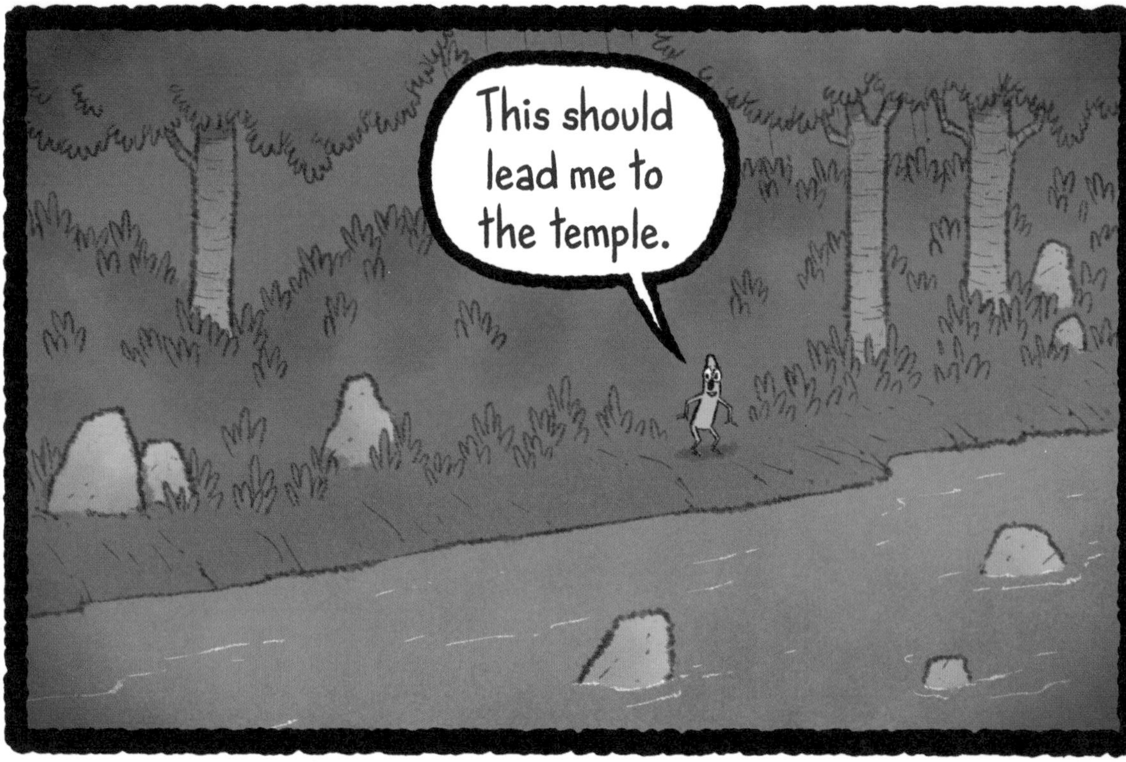
This should lead me to the temple.

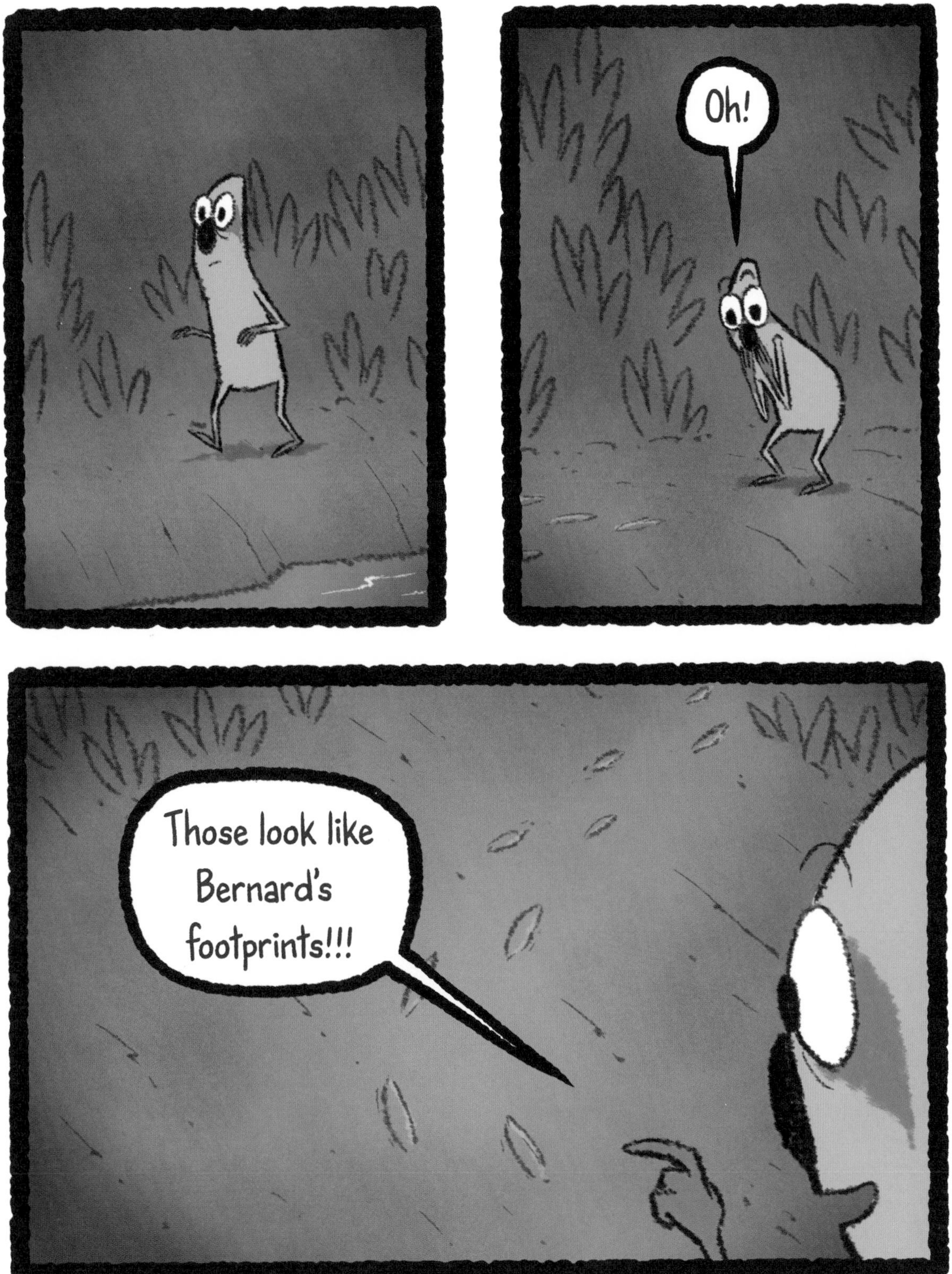
Oh!
Those look like Bernard's footprints!!!

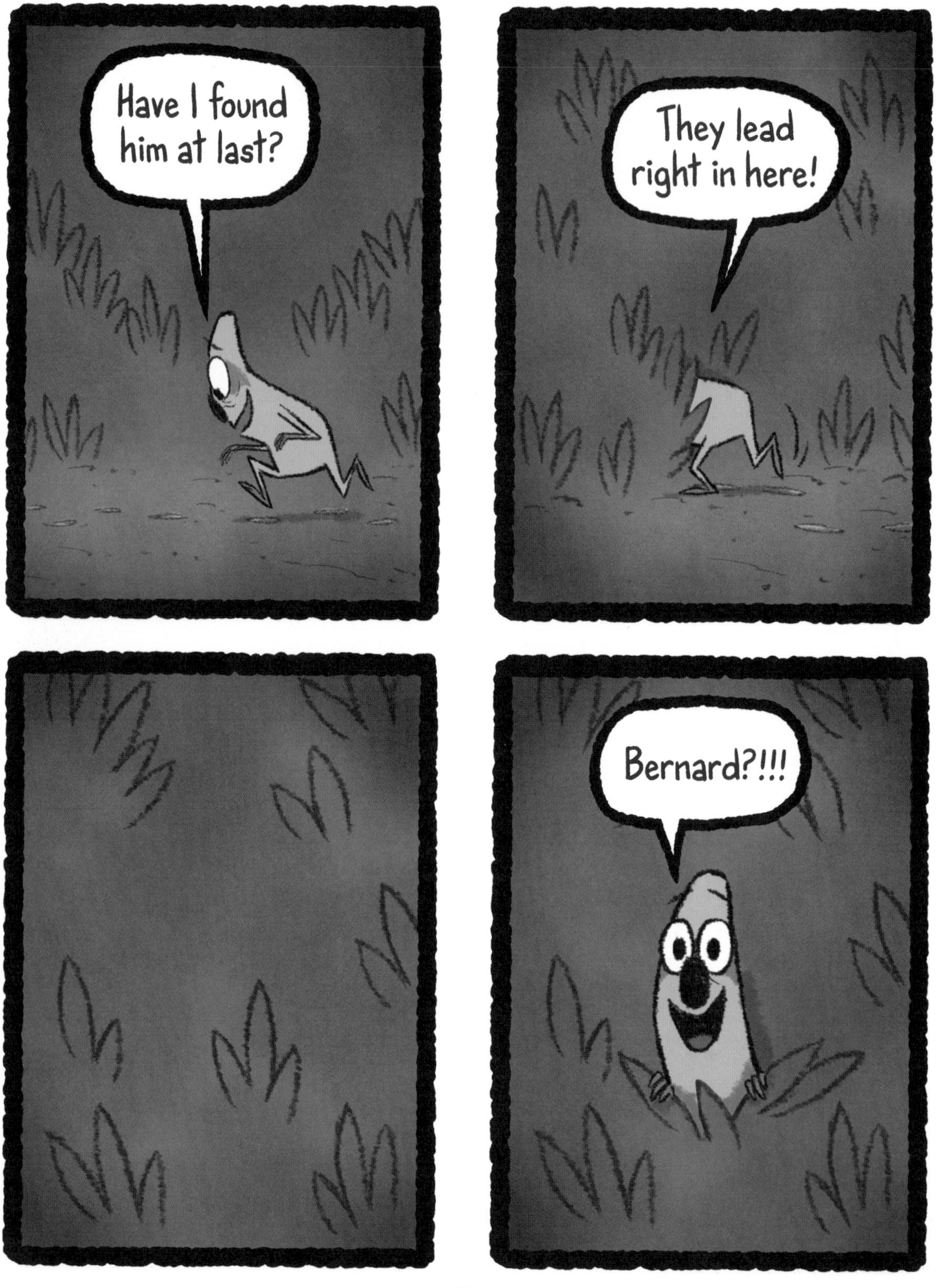
Have I found him at last?
They lead right in here!
Bernard?!!!

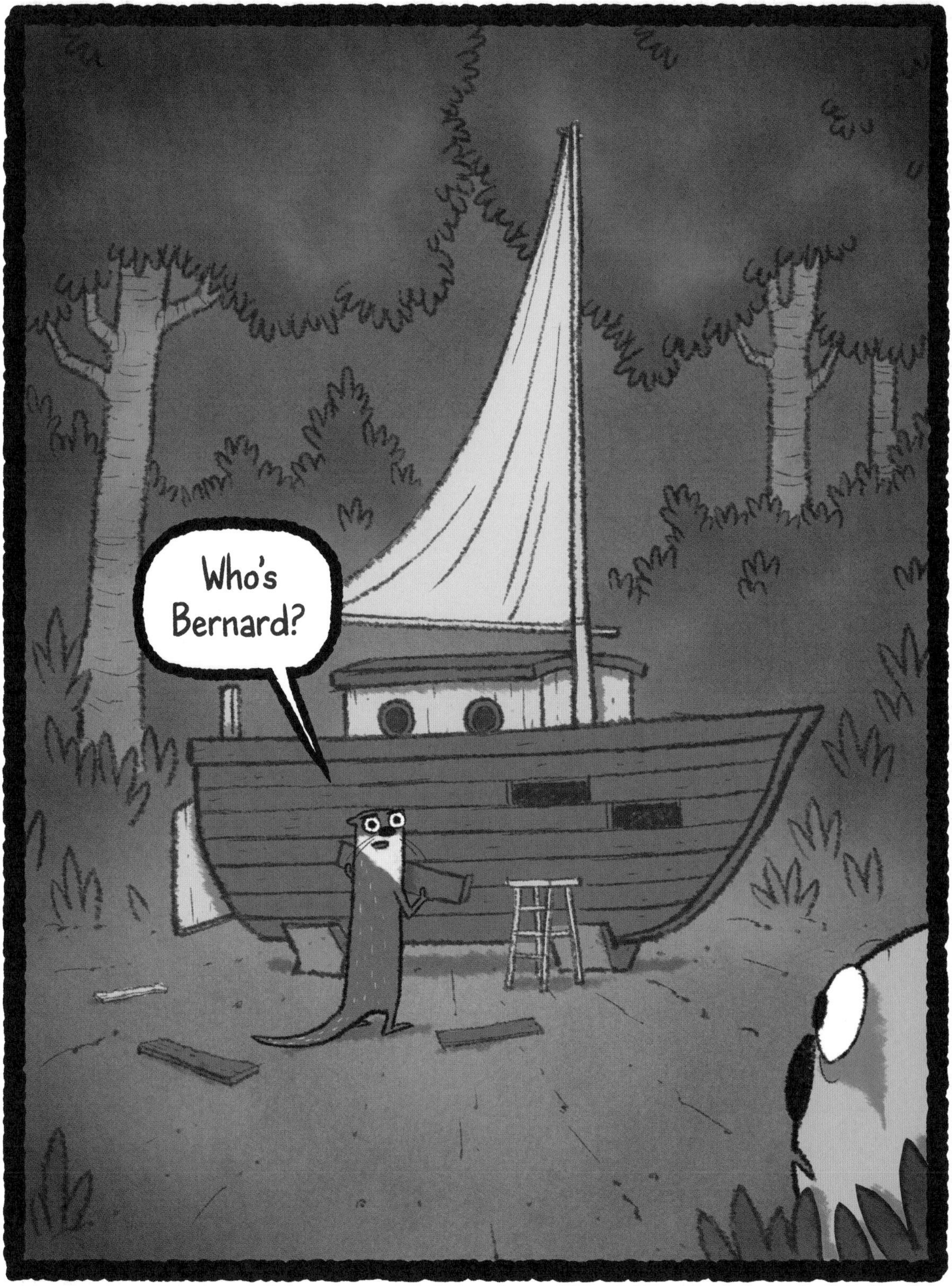
Who's Bernard?

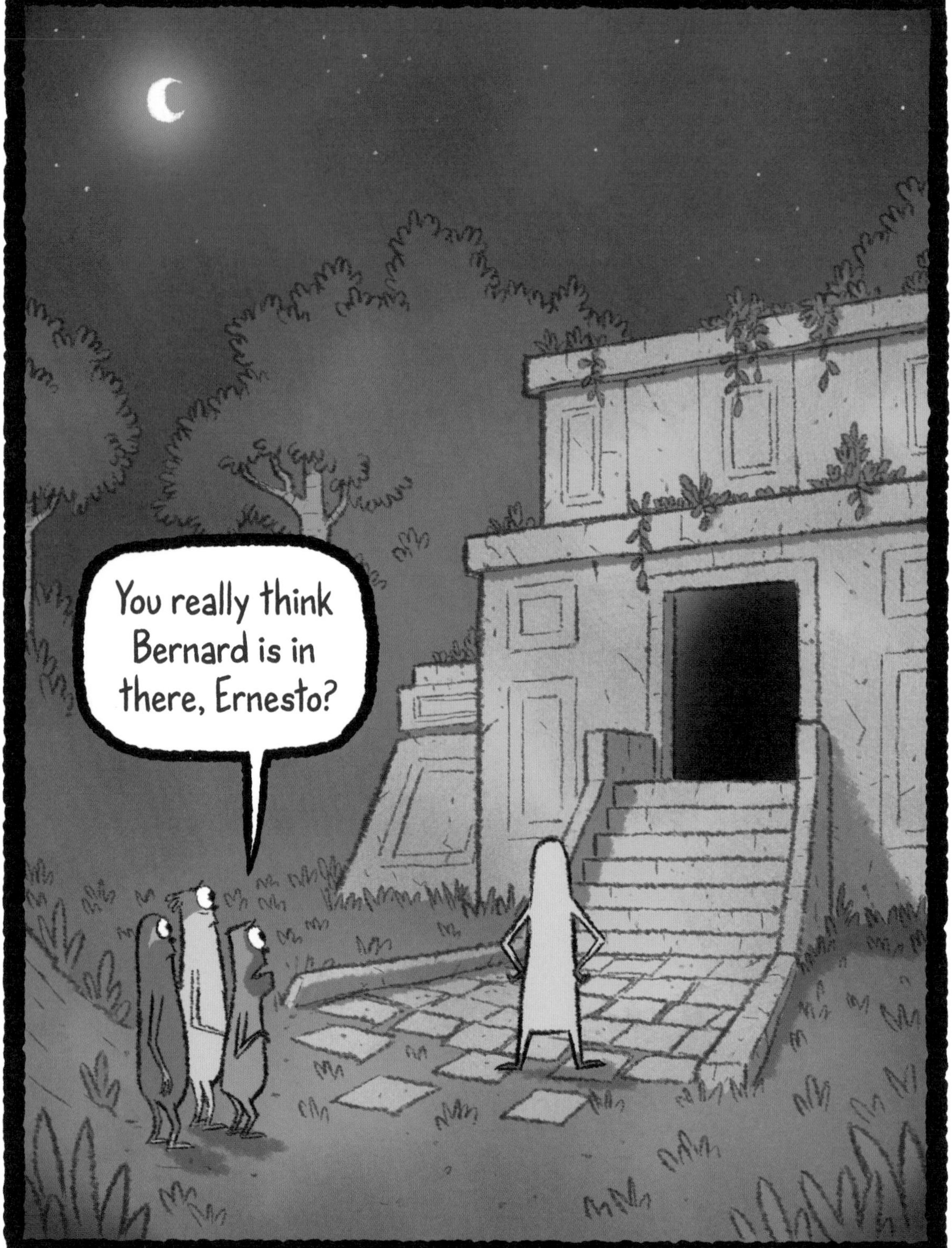
You really think Bernard is in there, Ernesto?

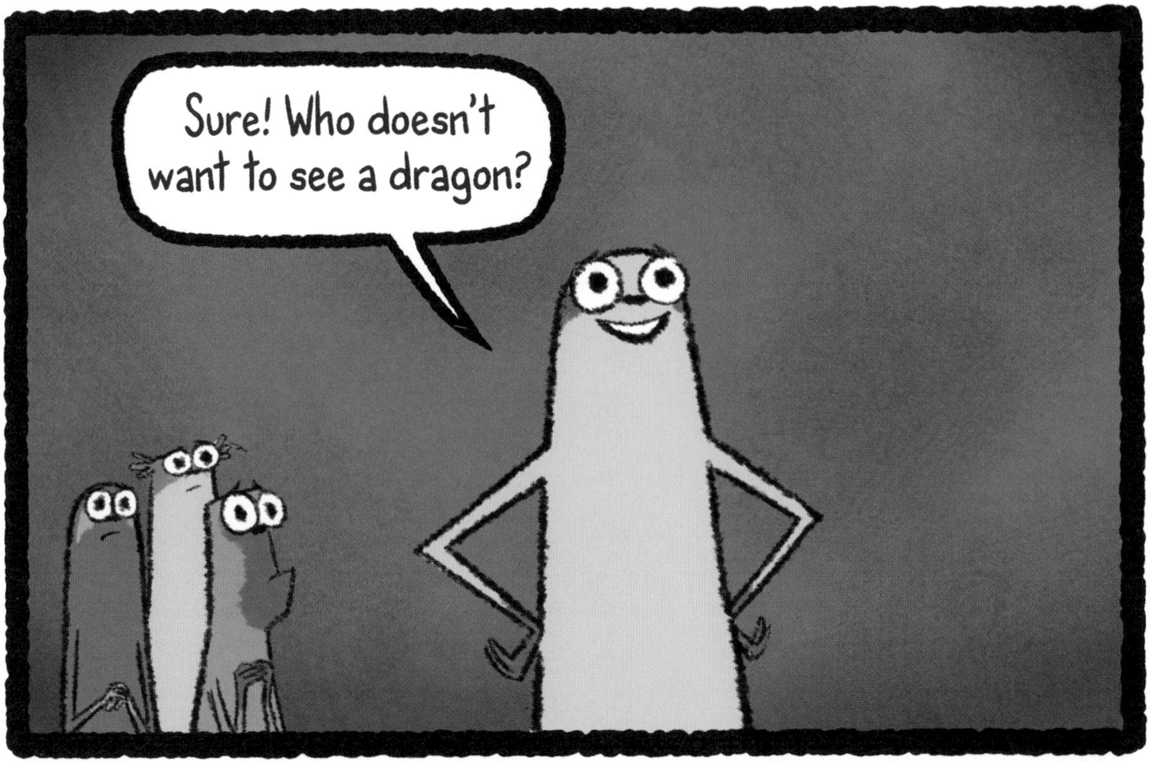
Sure! Who doesn't want to see a dragon?

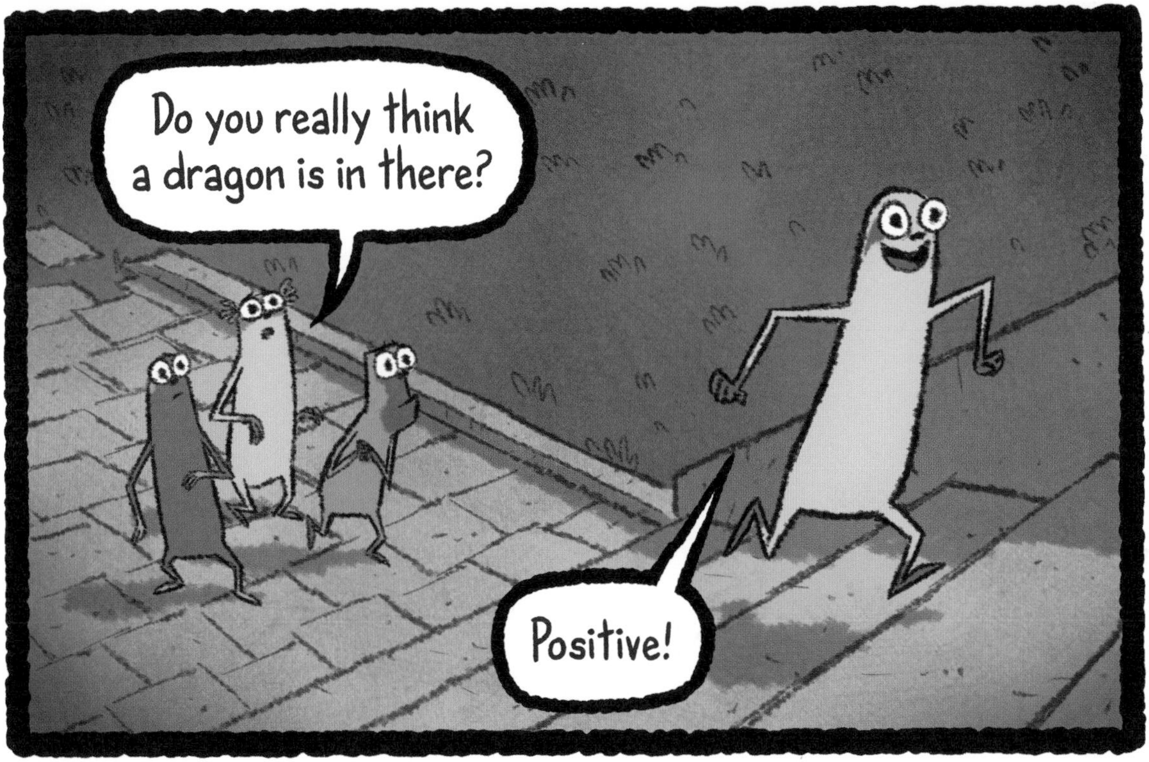
Do you really think a dragon is in there?
Positive!

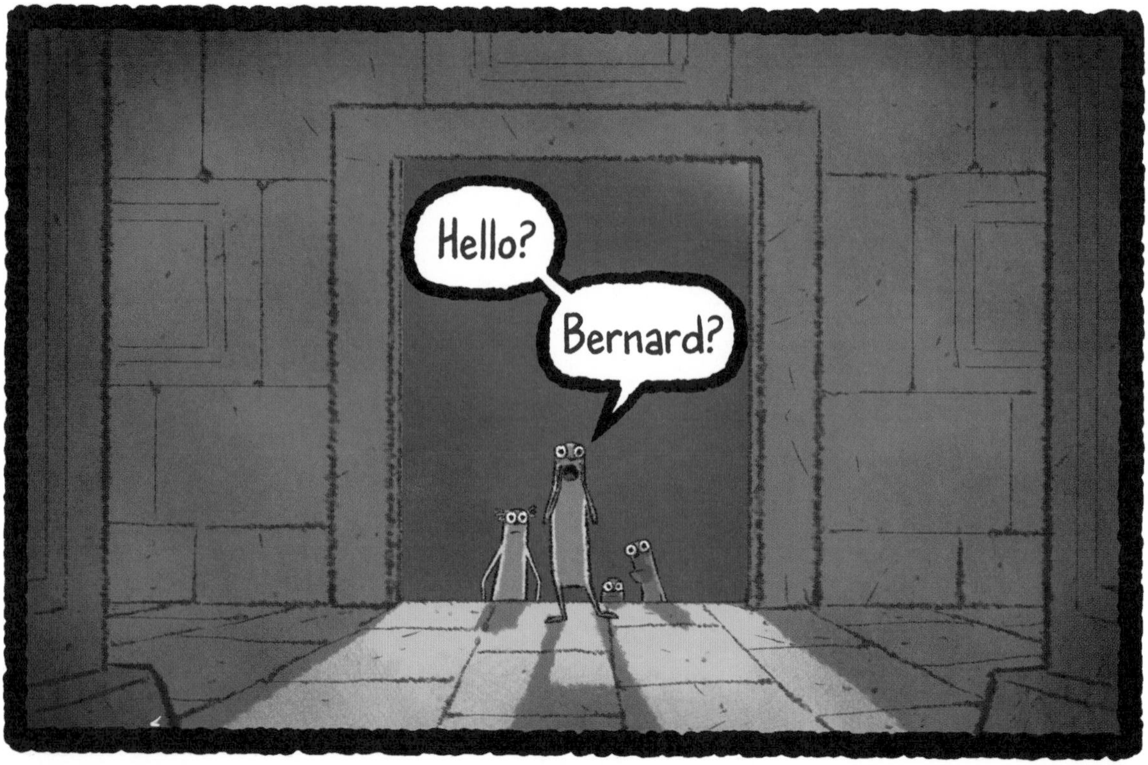
Hello?
Bernard?

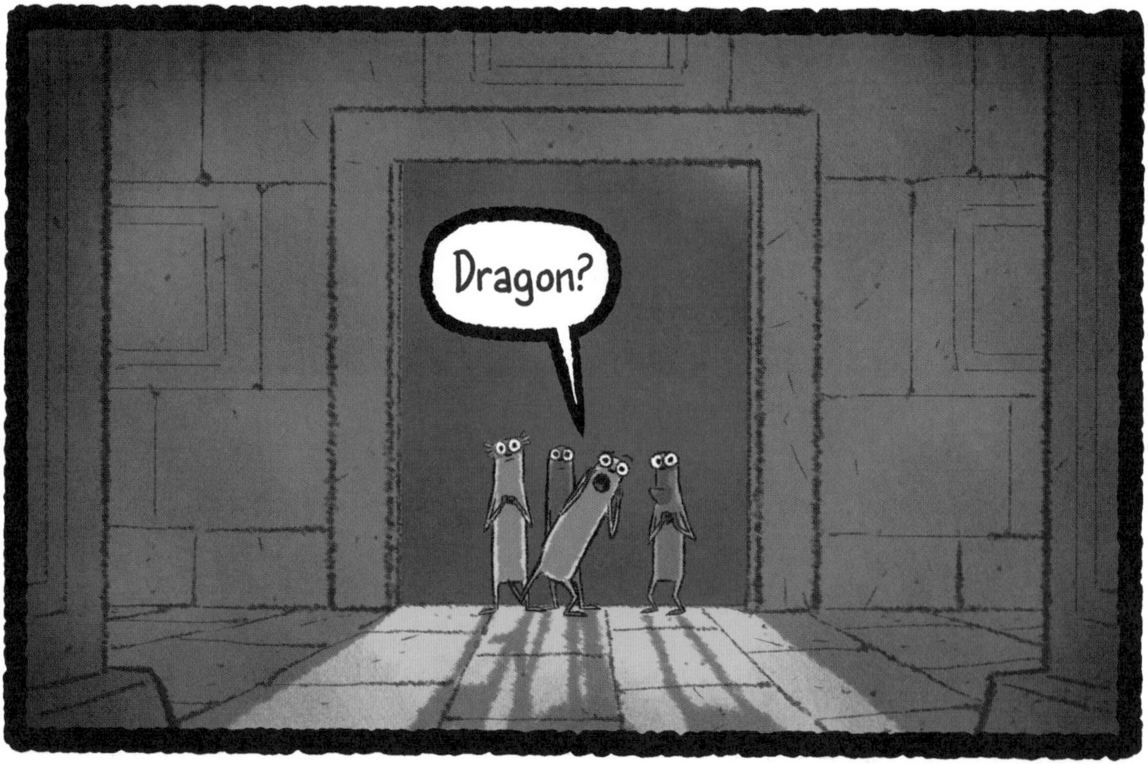
Dragon?

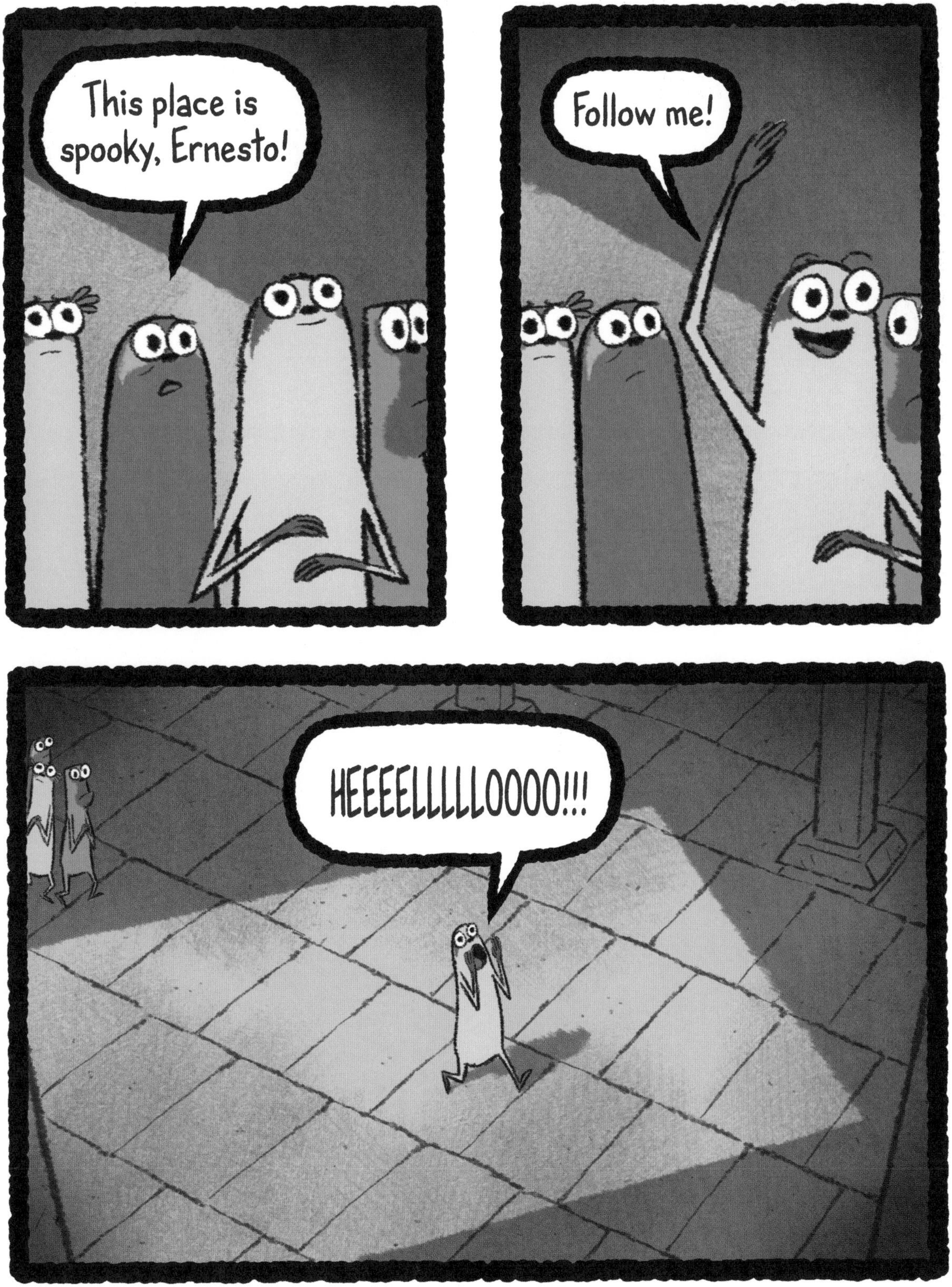
This place is spooky, Ernesto!
Follow me!
HEEEELLLLLOOOO!!!

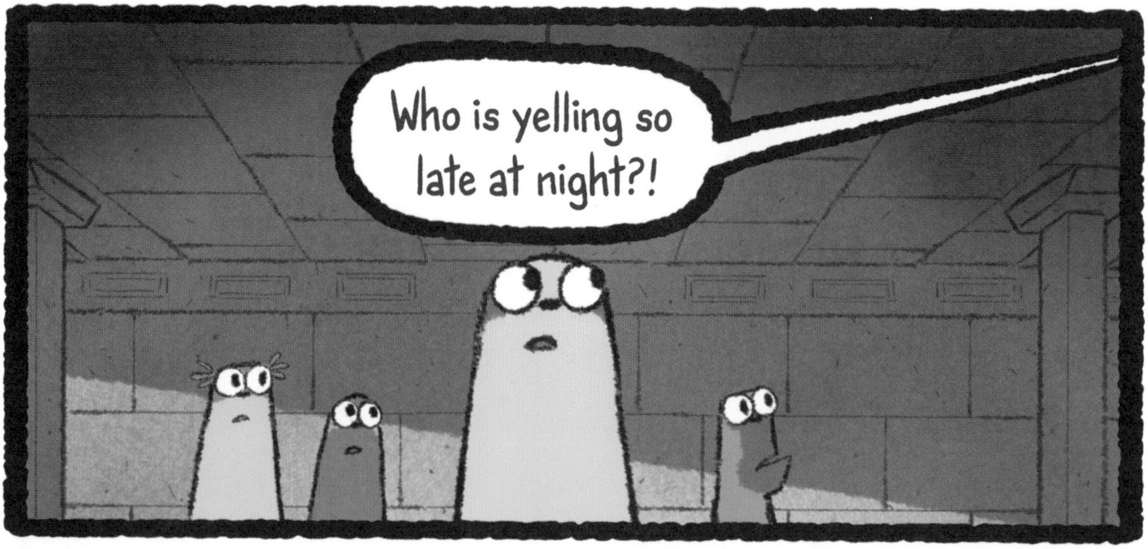
Who is yelling so late at night?!

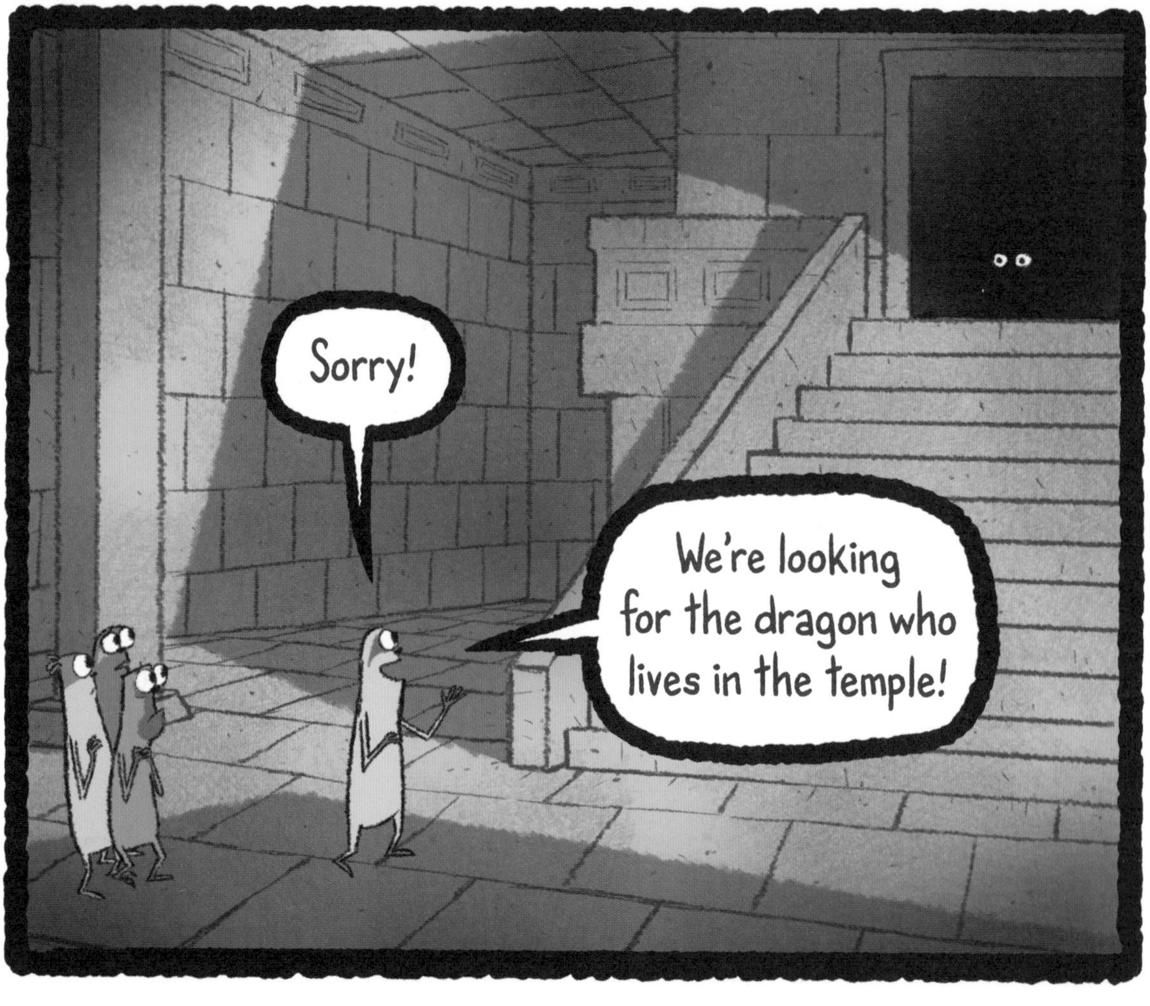
Sorry!
We're looking for the dragon who lives in the temple!

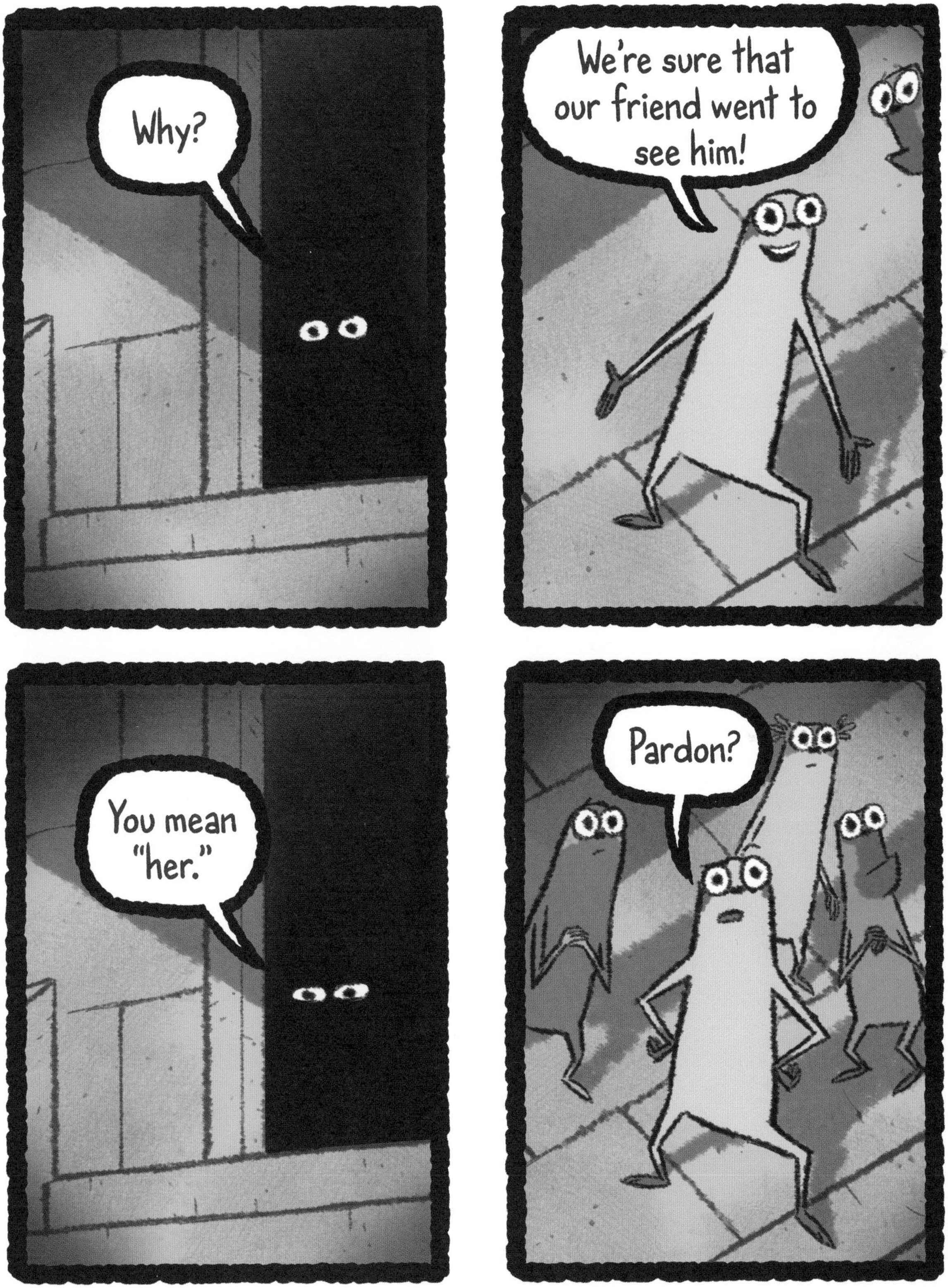
Why?
We're sure that our friend went to see him!
You mean "her."
Pardon?

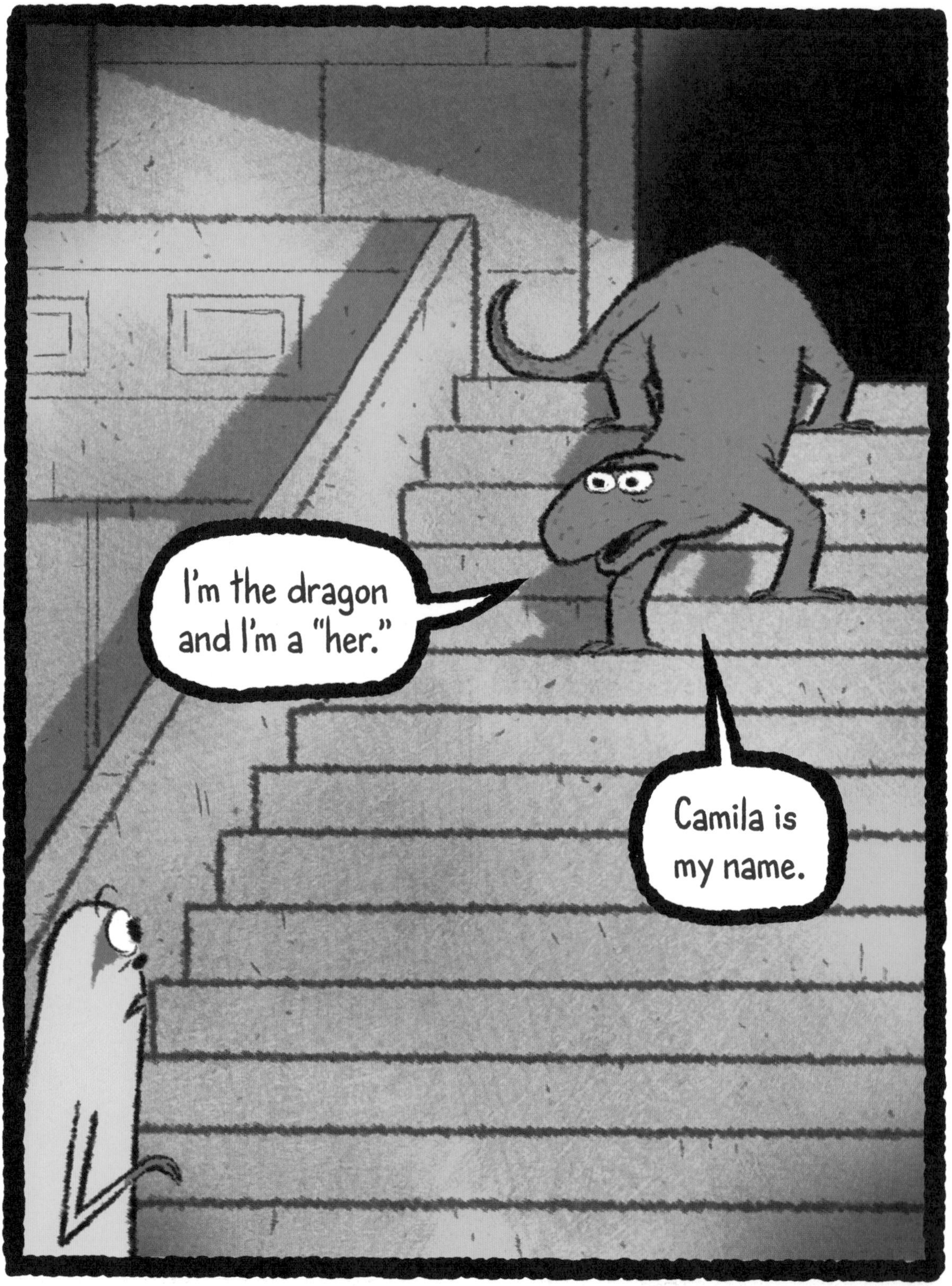
I'm the dragon and I'm a "her."
Camila is my name.

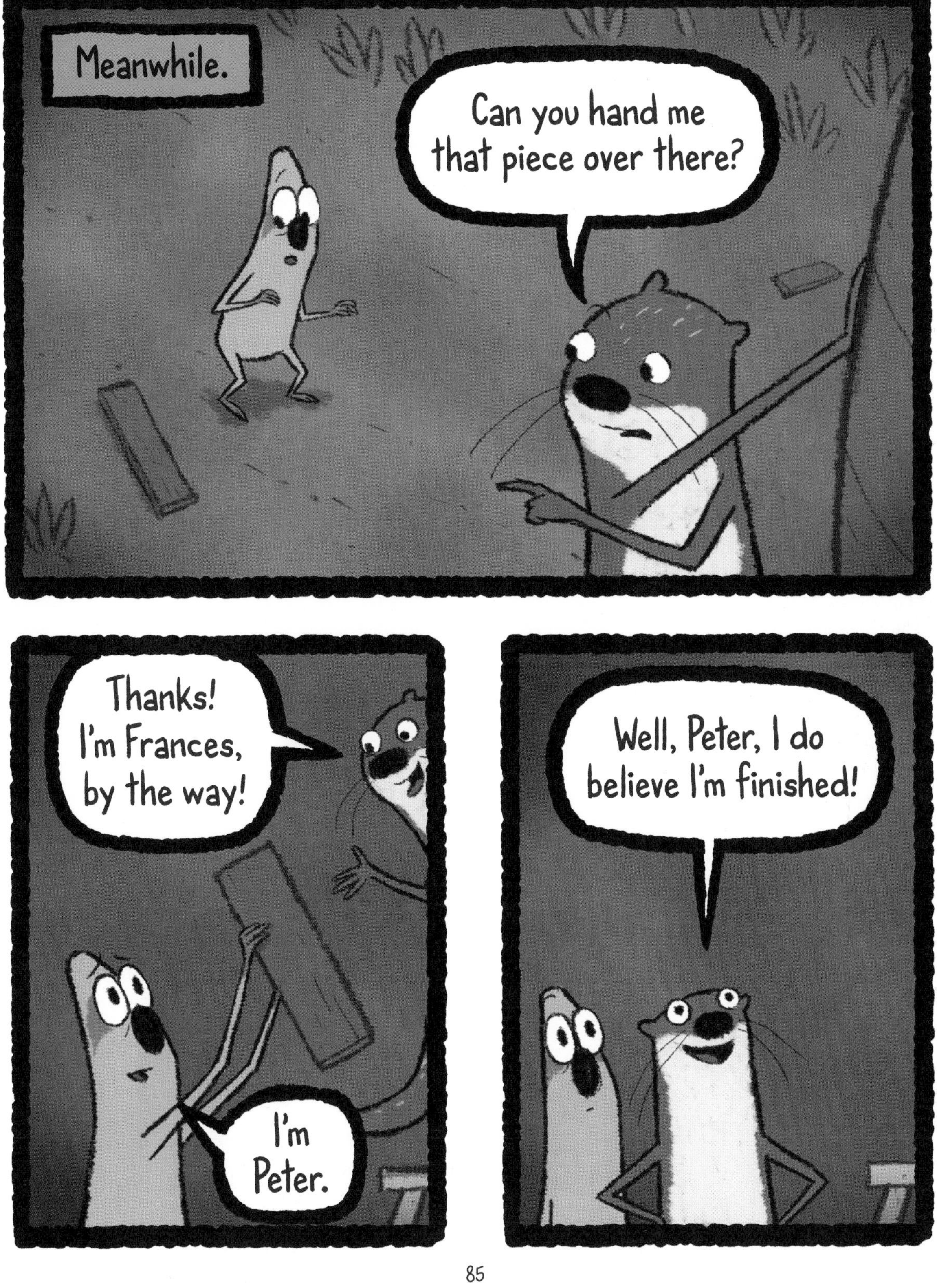
Meanwhile.
Can you hand me that piece over there?
Thanks! I'm Frances, by the way!
I'm Peter.
Well, Peter, I do believe I'm finished!

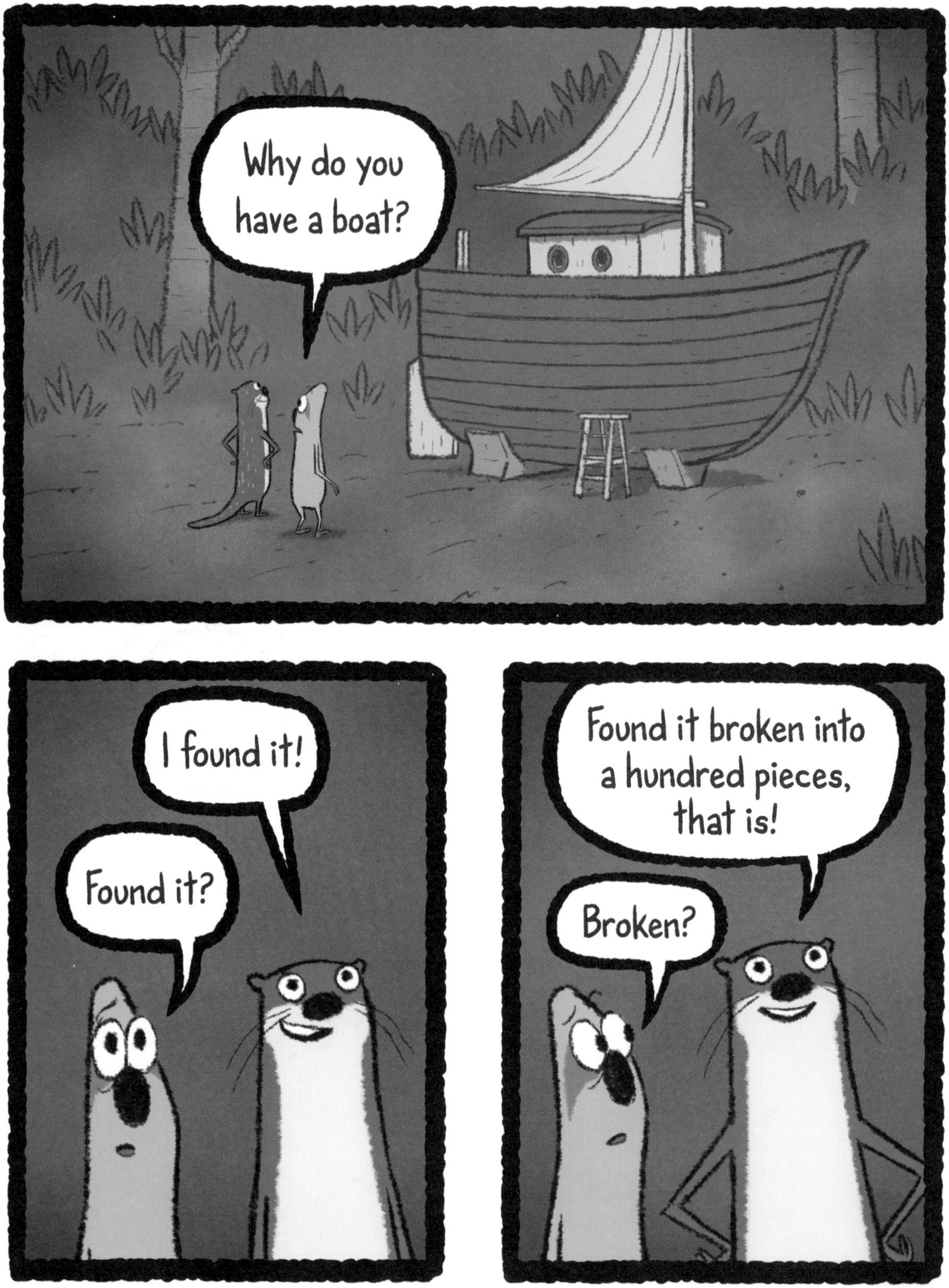
Why do you have a boat?
I found it!
Found it?
Found it broken into a hundred pieces, that is!
Broken?

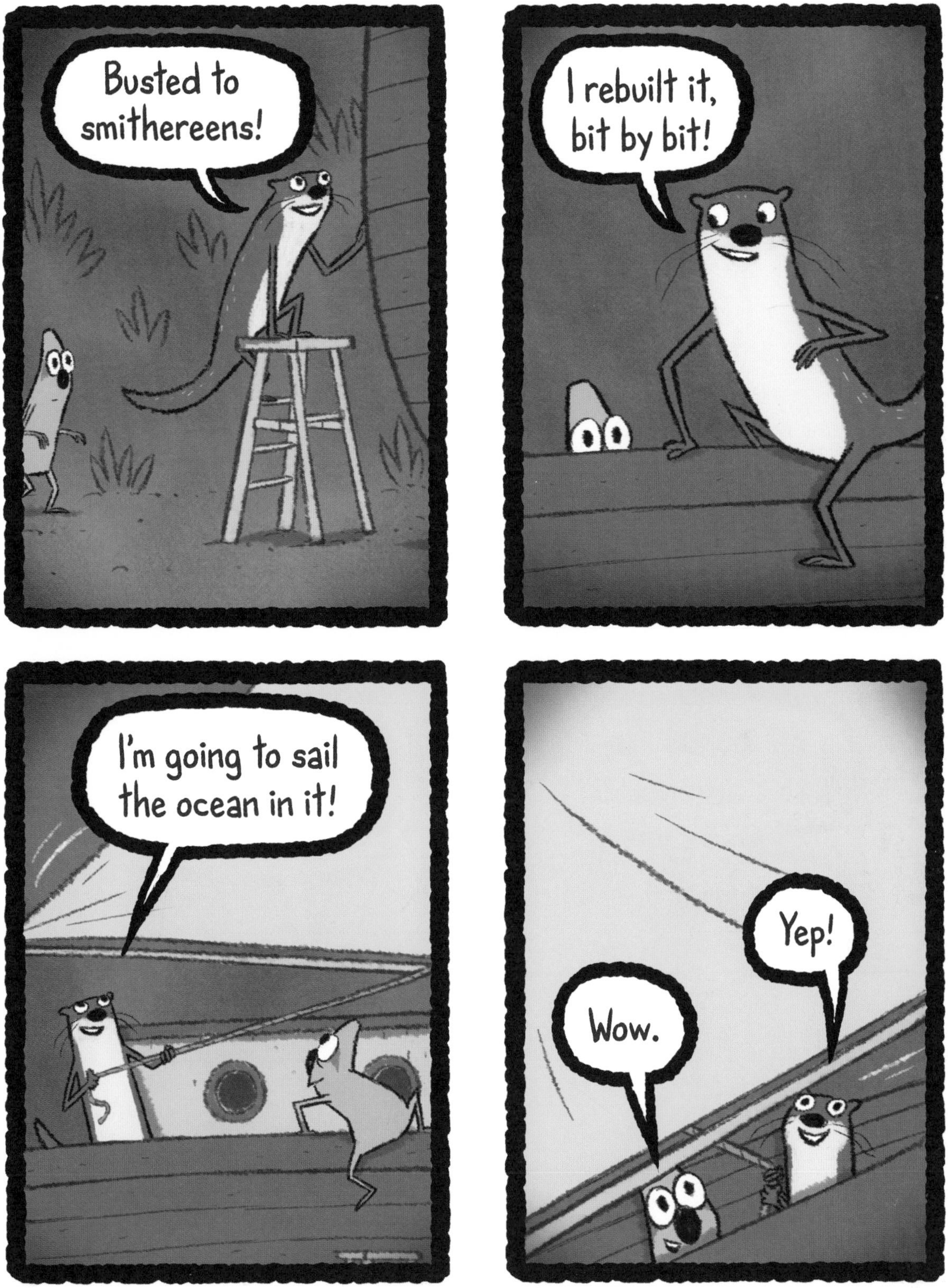
Busted to smithereens!
I rebuilt it, bit by bit!
I'm going to sail the ocean in it!
Yep!
Wow.

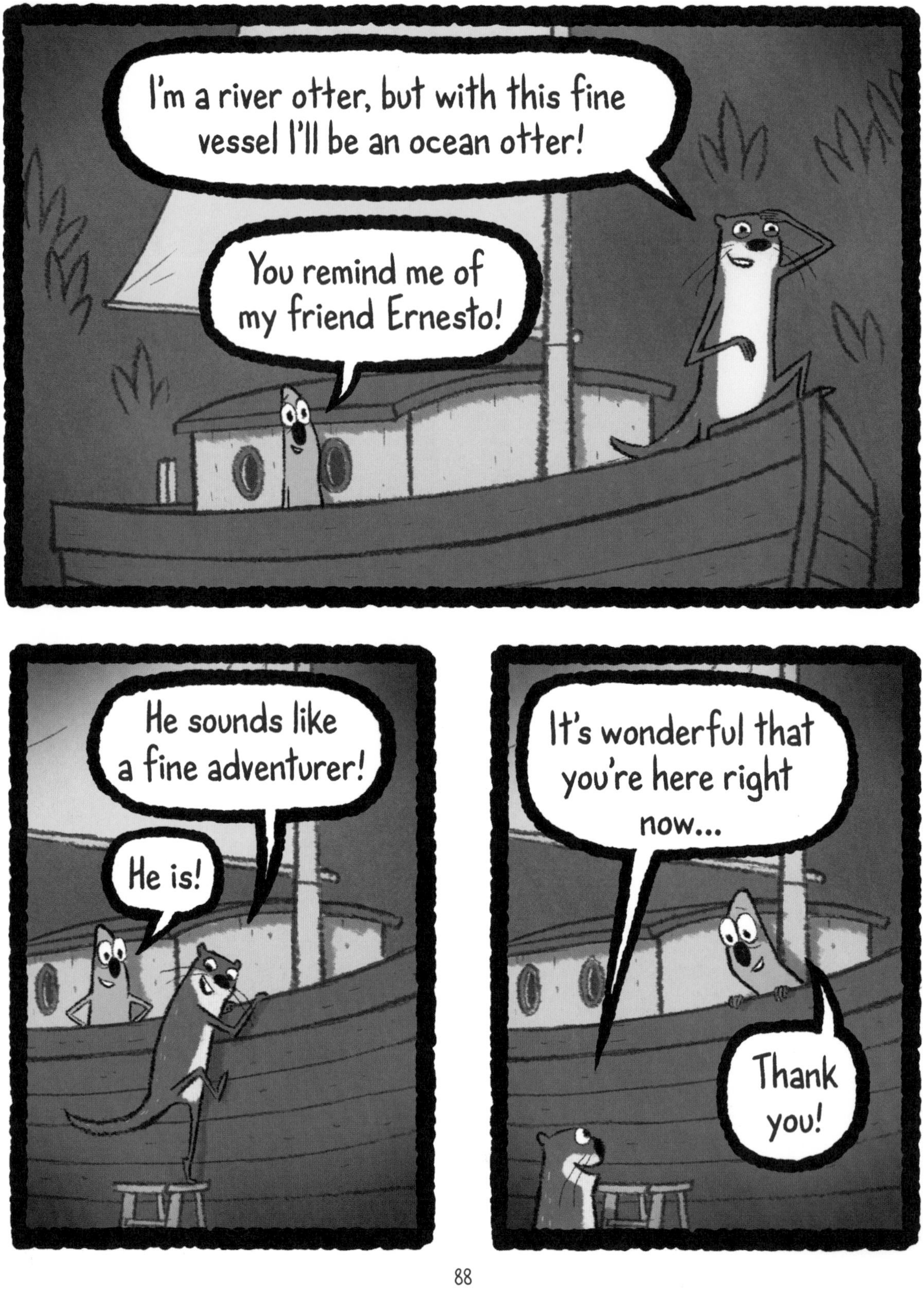
I'm a river otter, but with this fine vessel I'll be an ocean otter!
You remind me of my friend Ernesto!
He sounds like a fine adventurer!
He is!
It's wonderful that you're here right now...
Thank you!

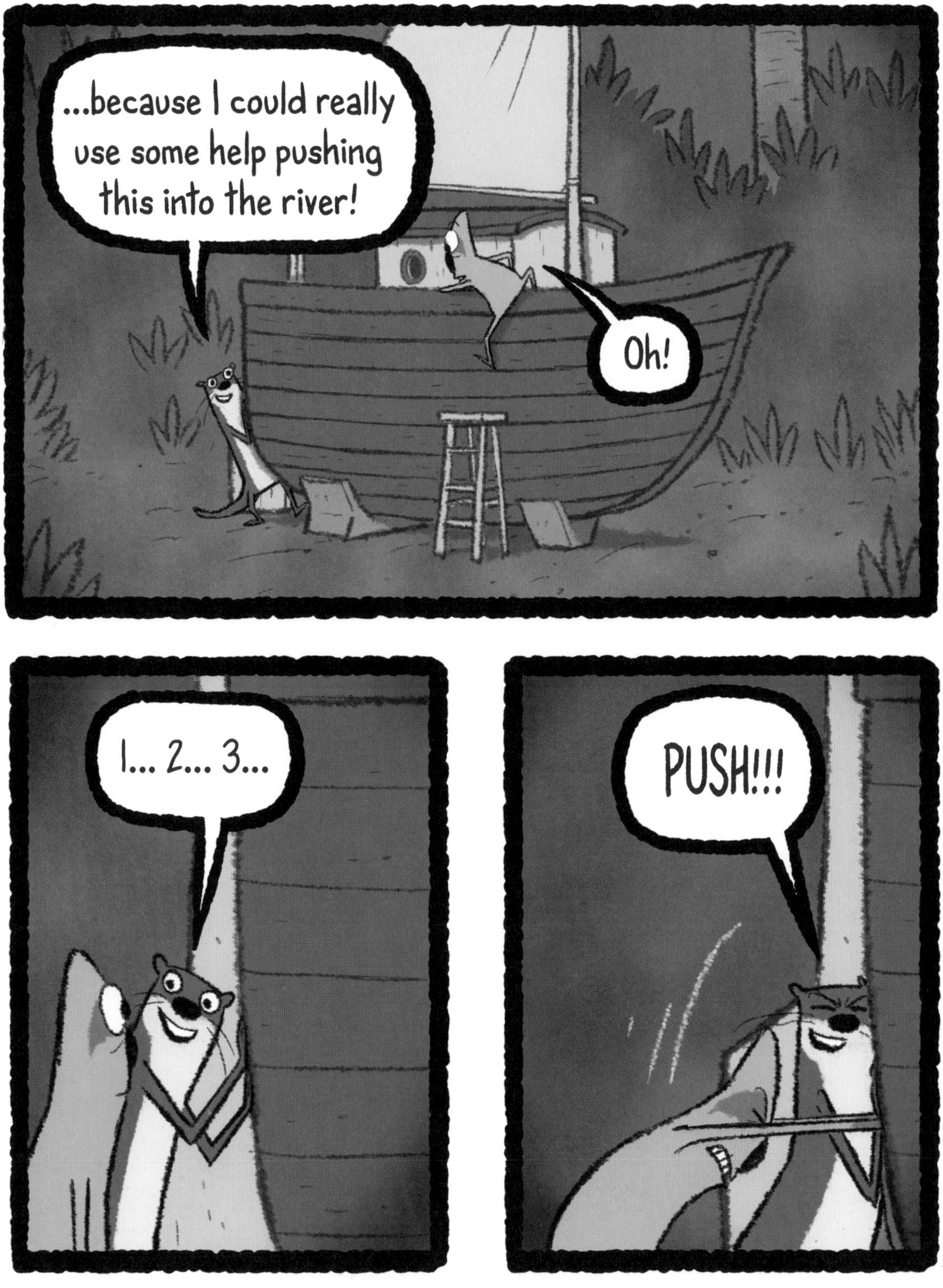
...because I could really use some help pushing this into the river!
Oh!
1... 2... 3...
PUSH!!!

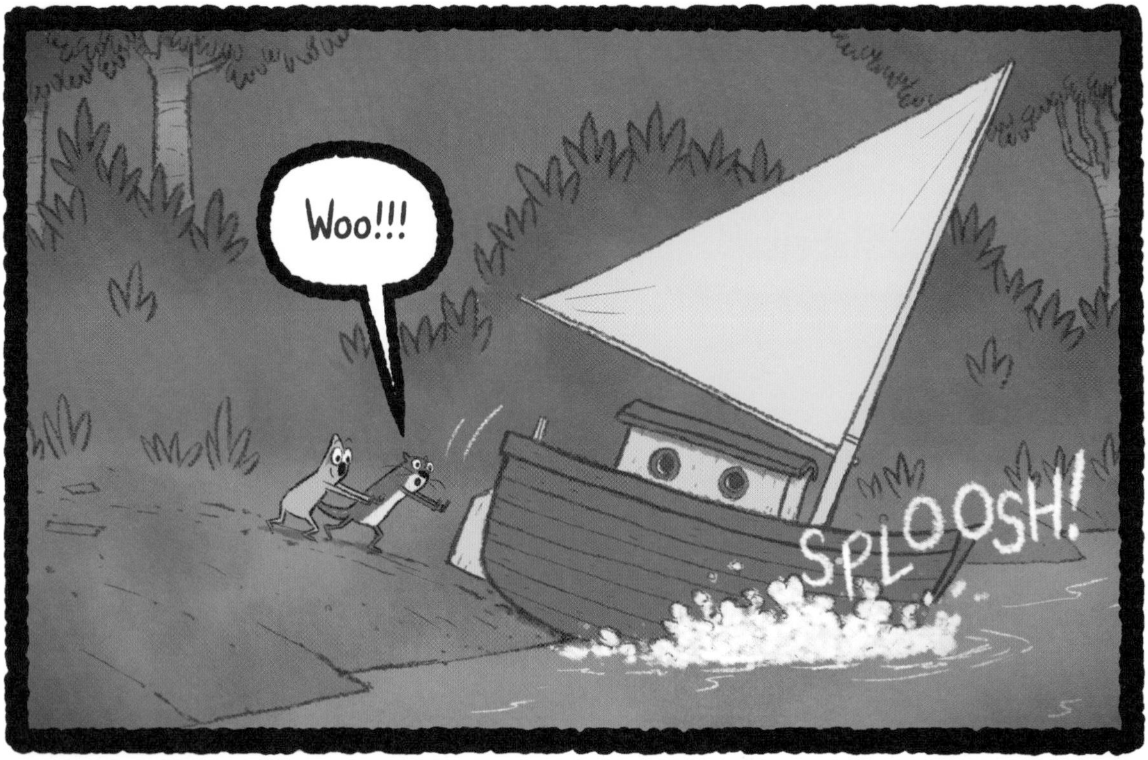
Woo!!!
SPLOOSH!

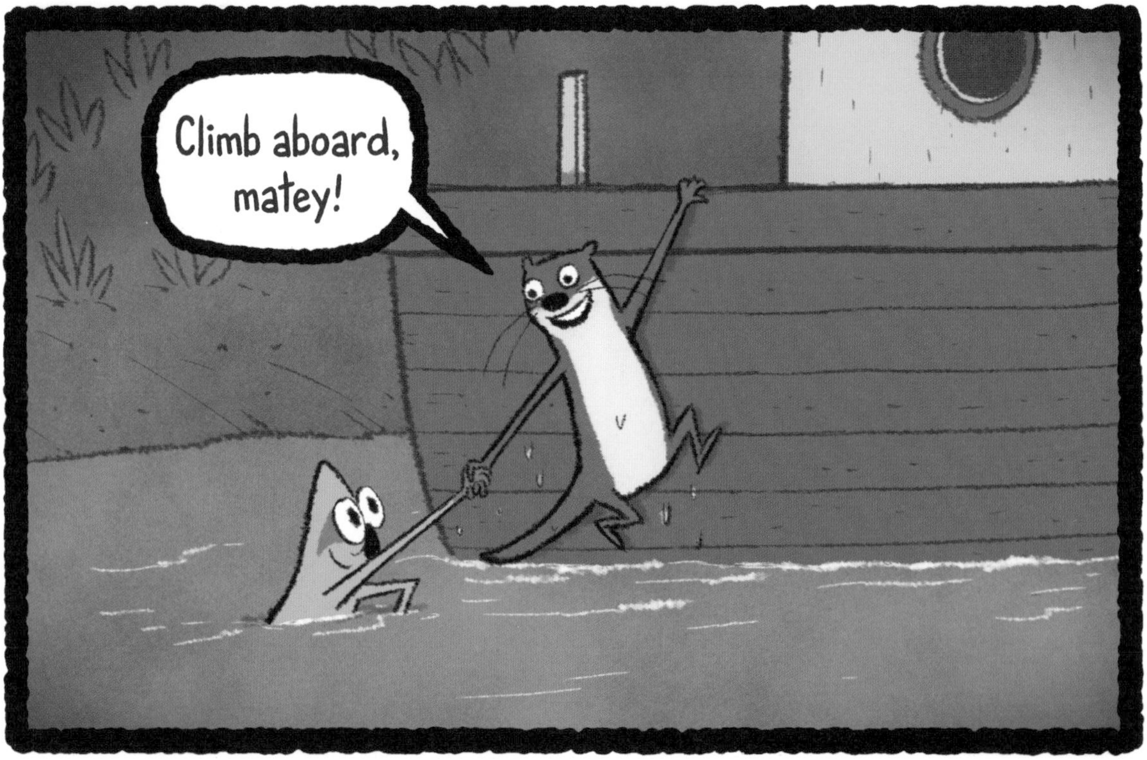
Climb aboard, matey!

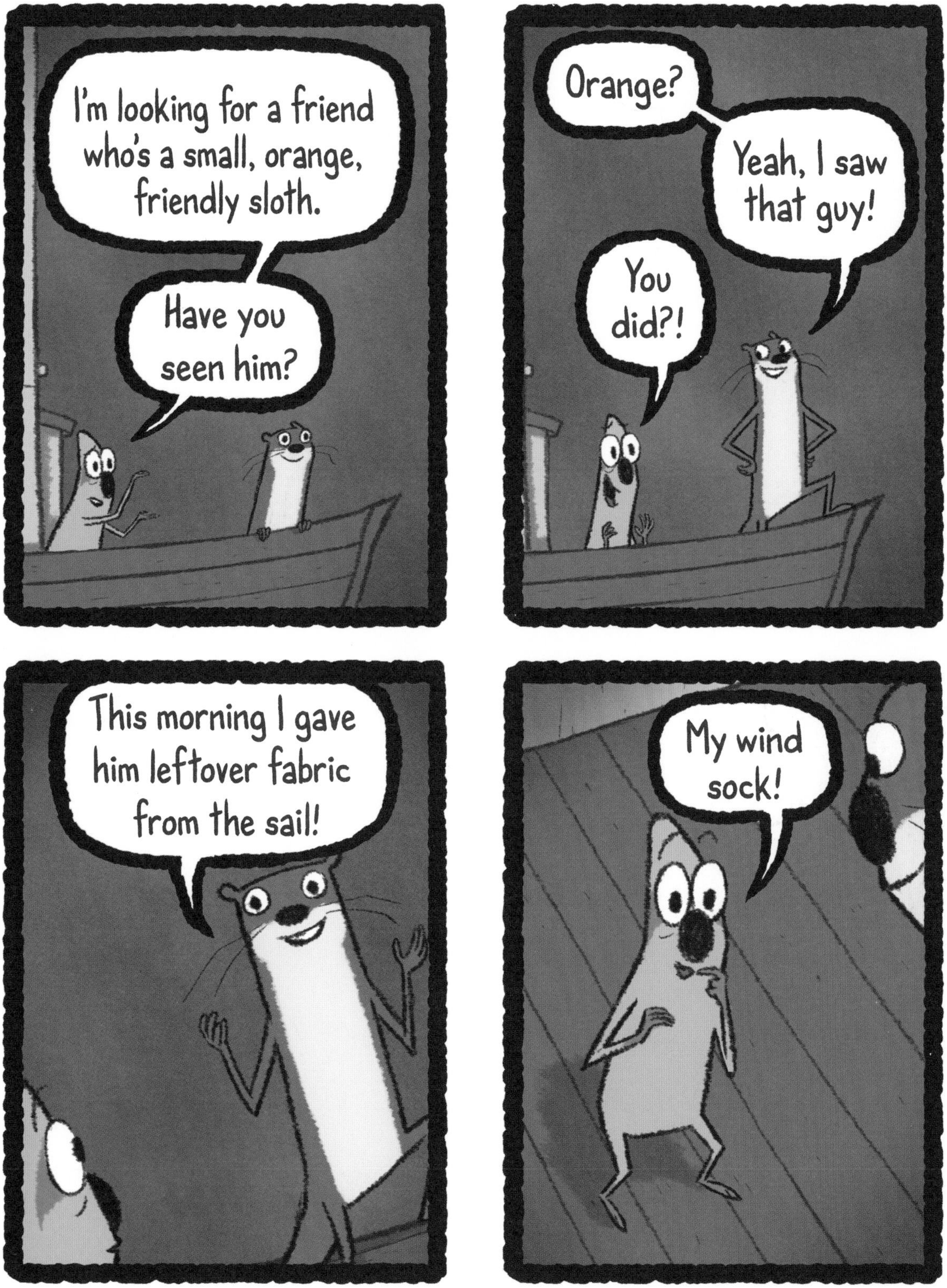
I'm looking for a friend who's a small, orange, friendly sloth.
Have you seen him?
Orange?
Yeah, I saw that guy!
You did?!
This morning I gave him leftover fabric from the sail!
My wind sock!

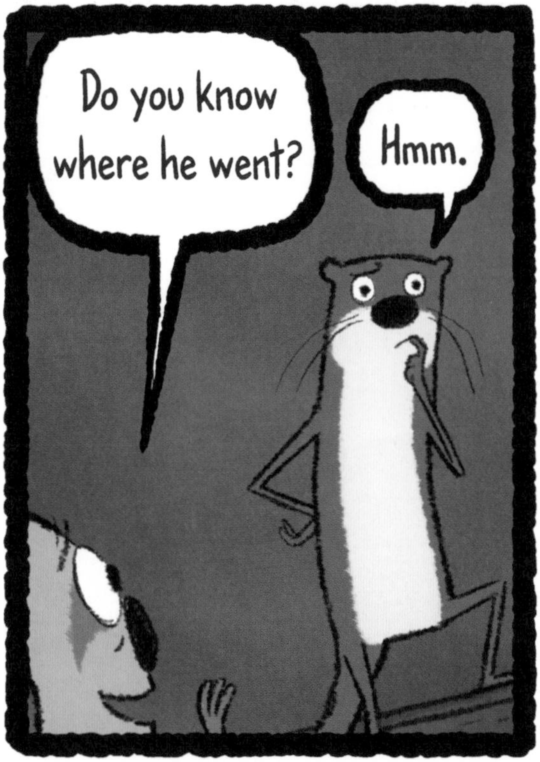
Do you know where he went?
Hmm.

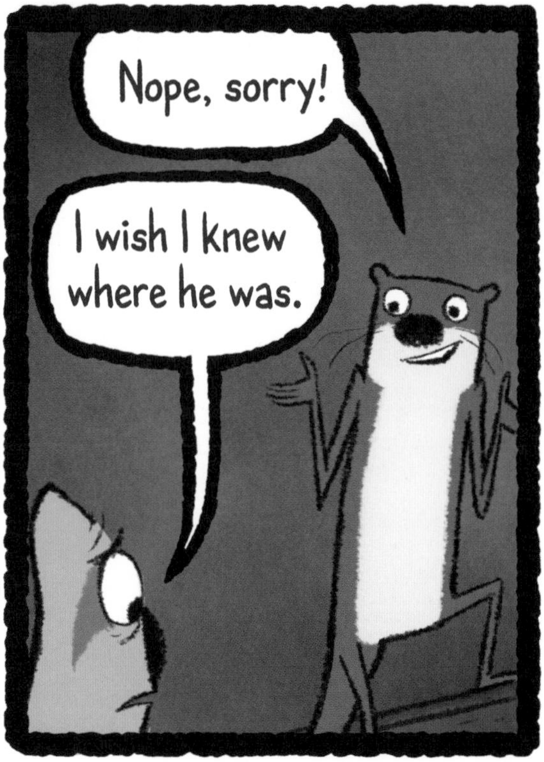
Nope, sorry!
I wish I knew where he was.

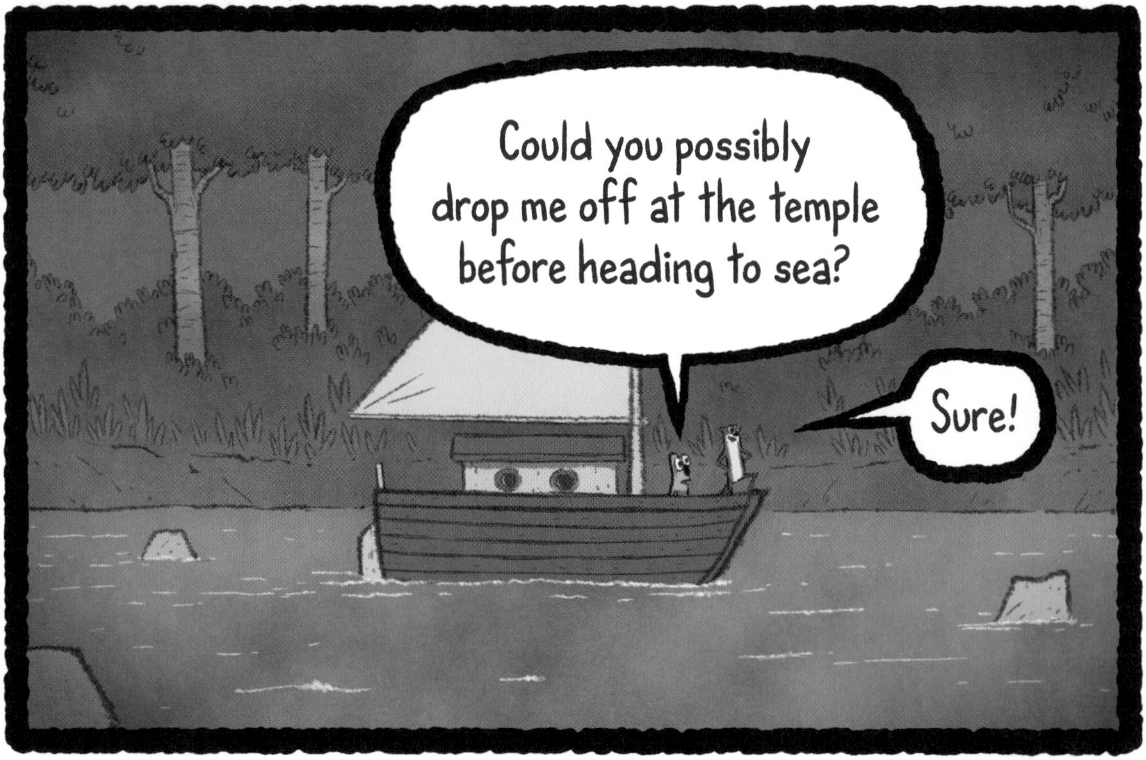
Could you possibly drop me off at the temple before heading to sea?
Sure!

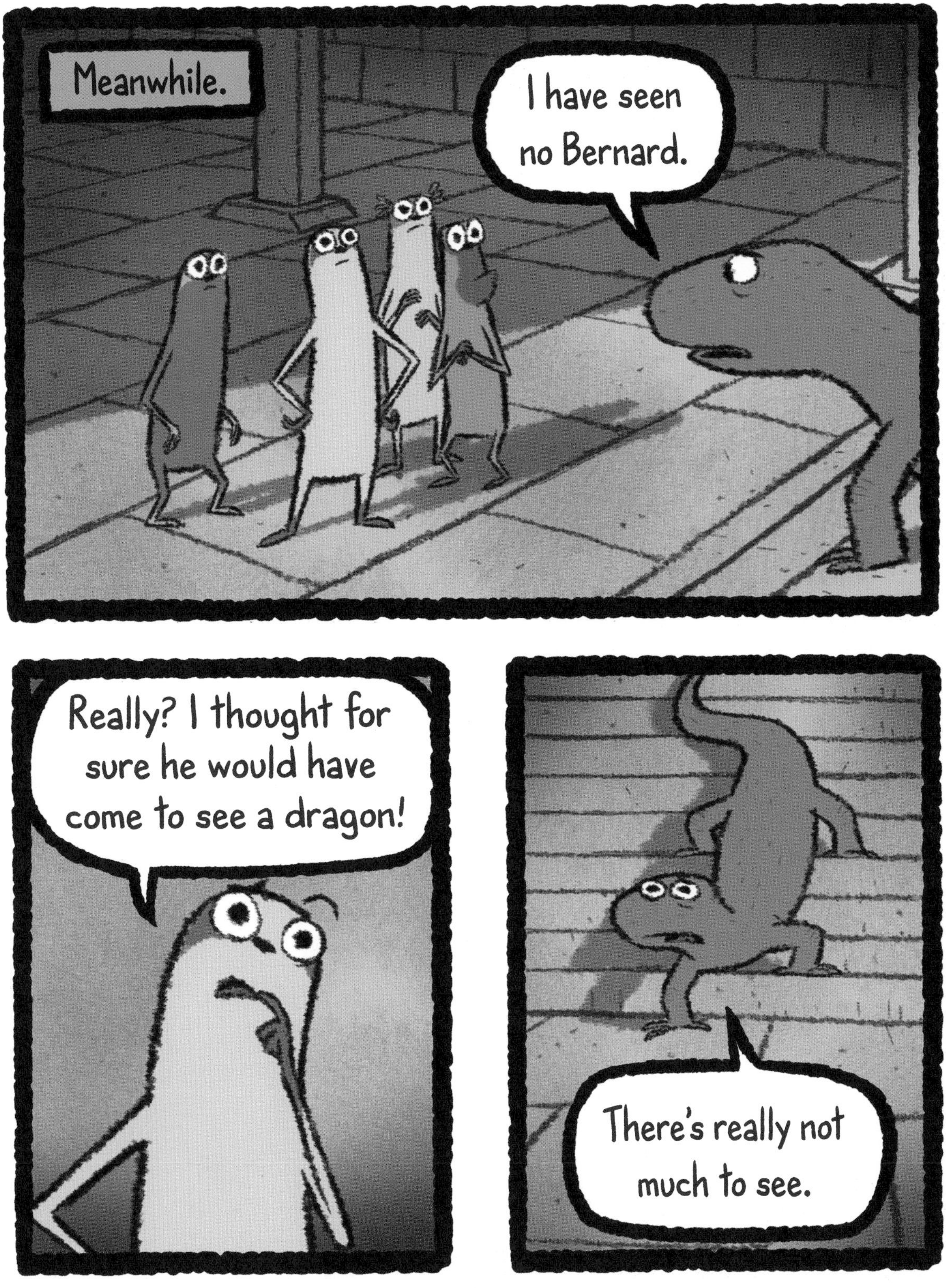
Meanwhile.
I have seen no Bernard.
Really? I thought for sure he would have come to see a dragon!
There's really not much to see.

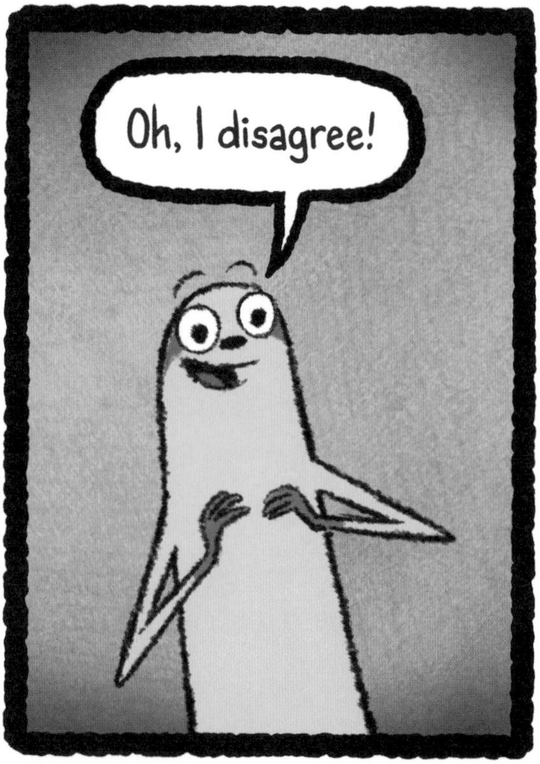
Oh, I disagree!

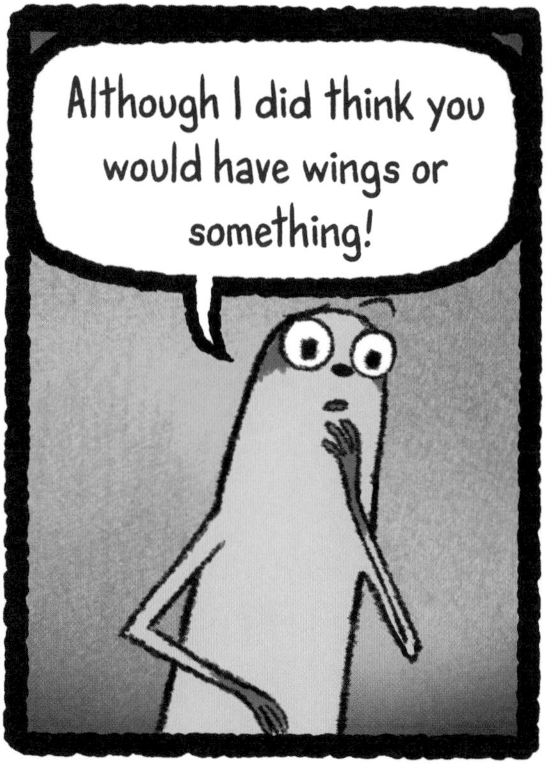
Although I did think you would have wings or something!

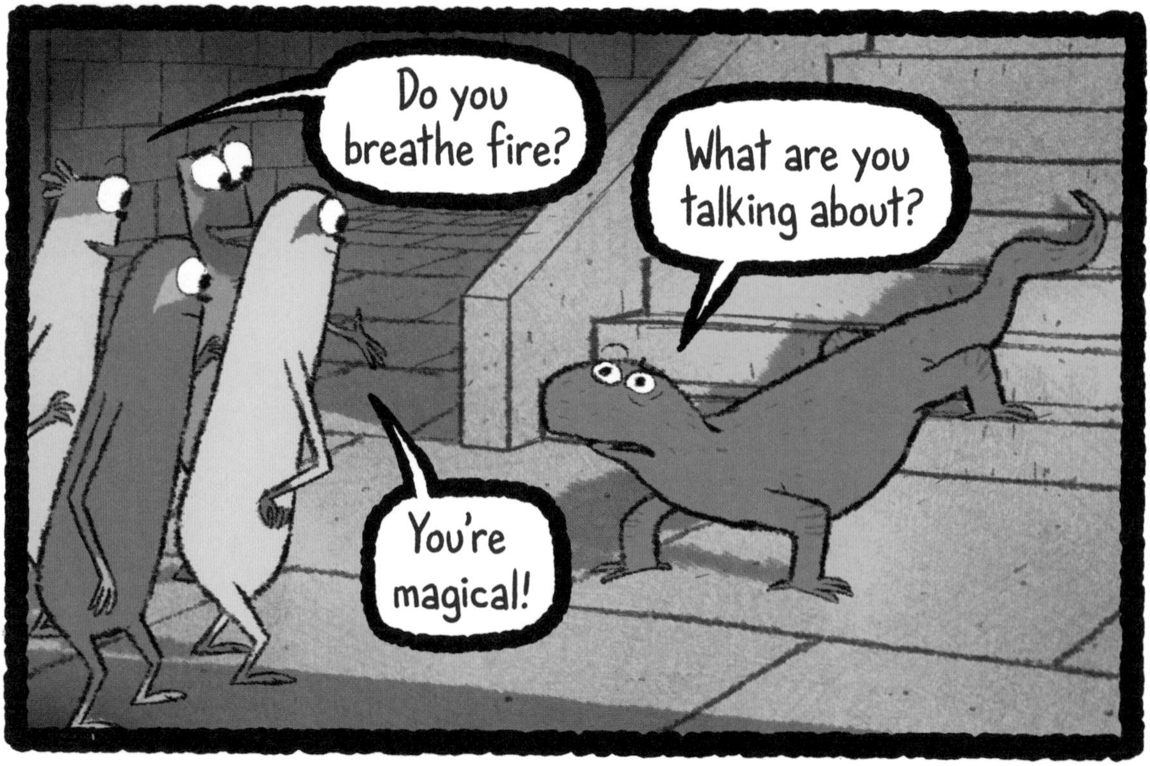
Do you breathe fire?
You're magical!
What are you talking about?

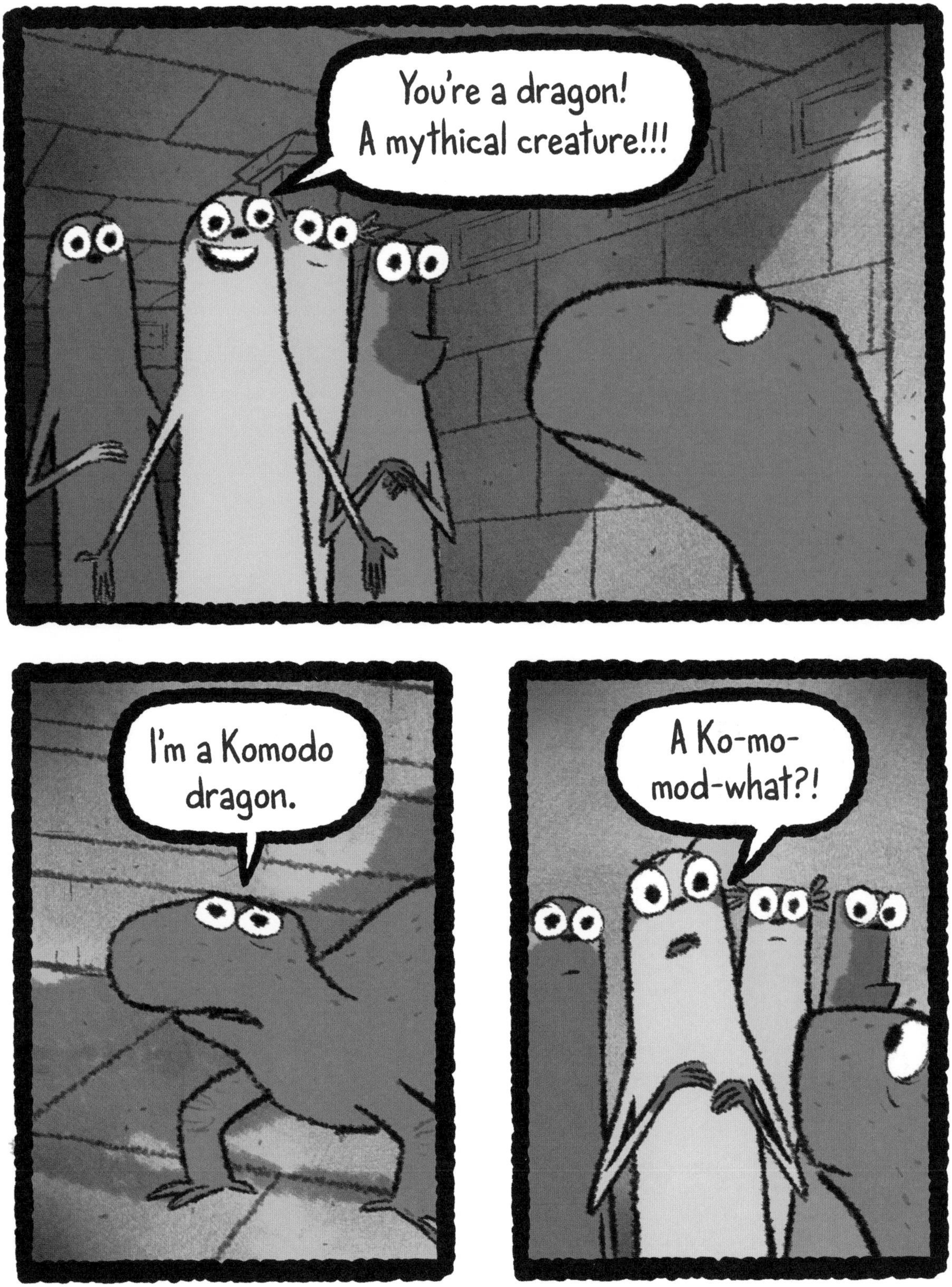
You're a dragon! A mythical creature!!!
I'm a Komodo dragon.
A Ko-mo-mod-what?!

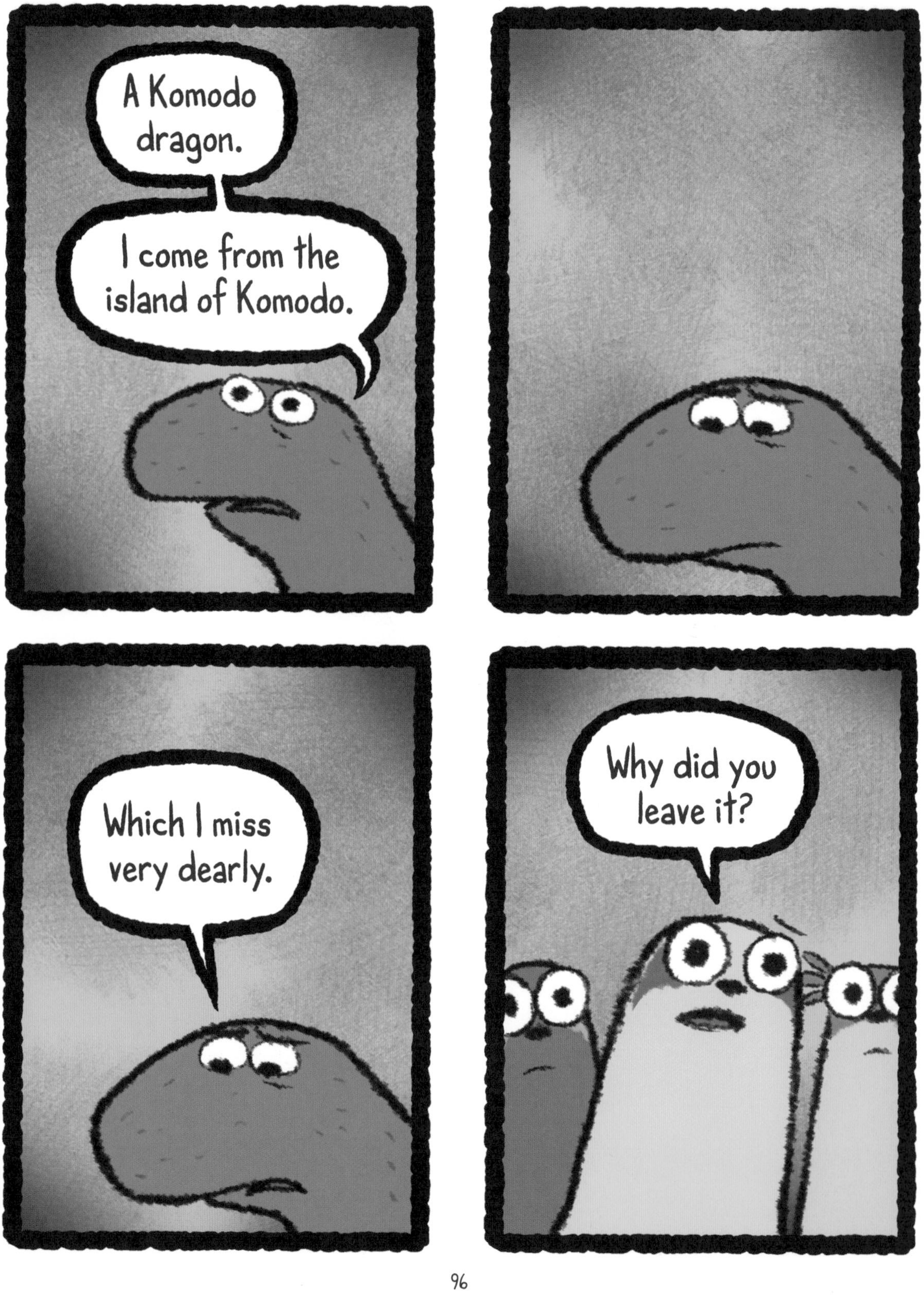
A Komodo dragon.
I come from the island of Komodo.
Which I miss very dearly.
Why did you leave it?

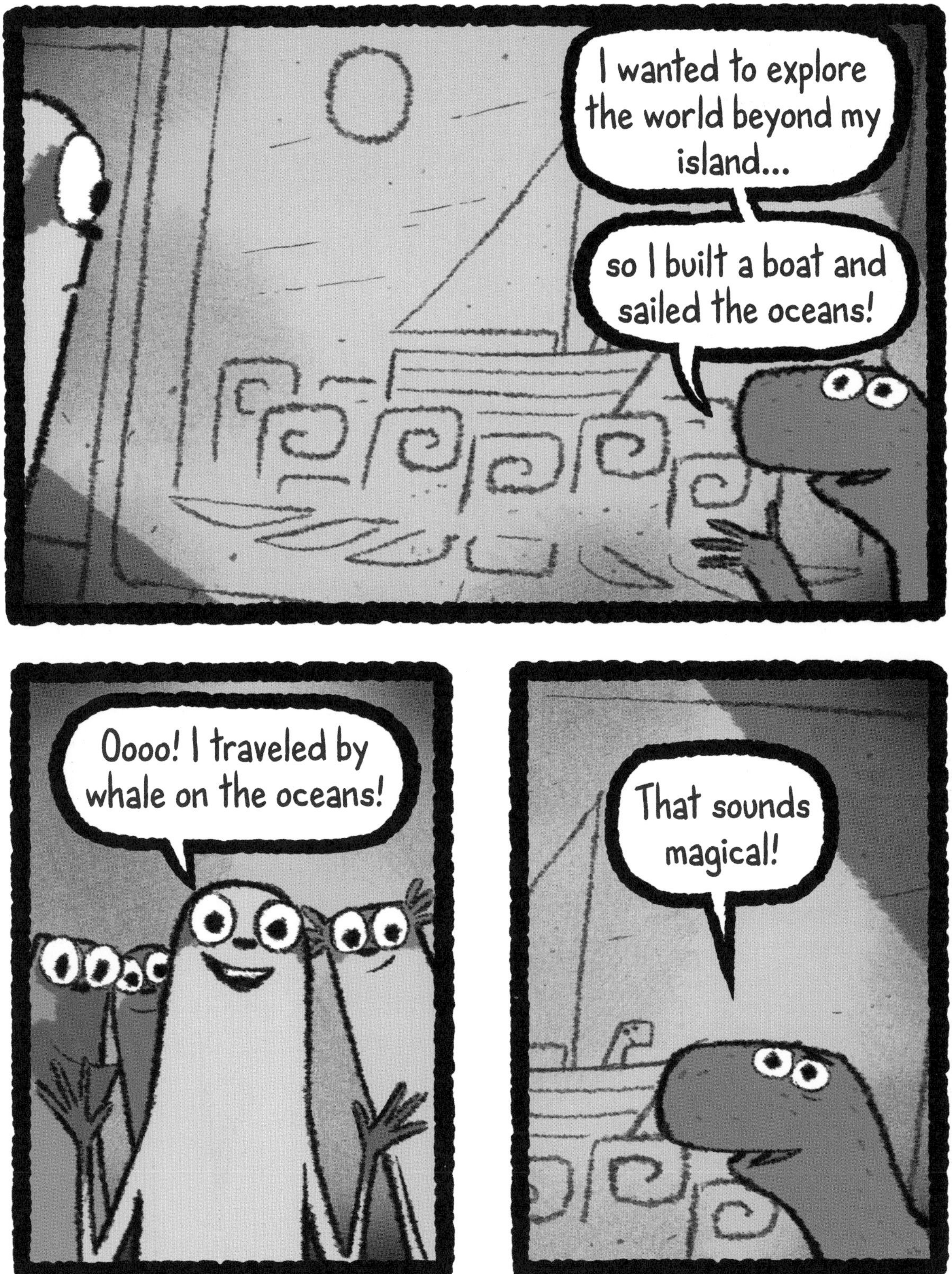
I wanted to explore the world beyond my island...
so I built a boat and sailed the oceans!
Oooo! I traveled by whale on the oceans!
That sounds magical!

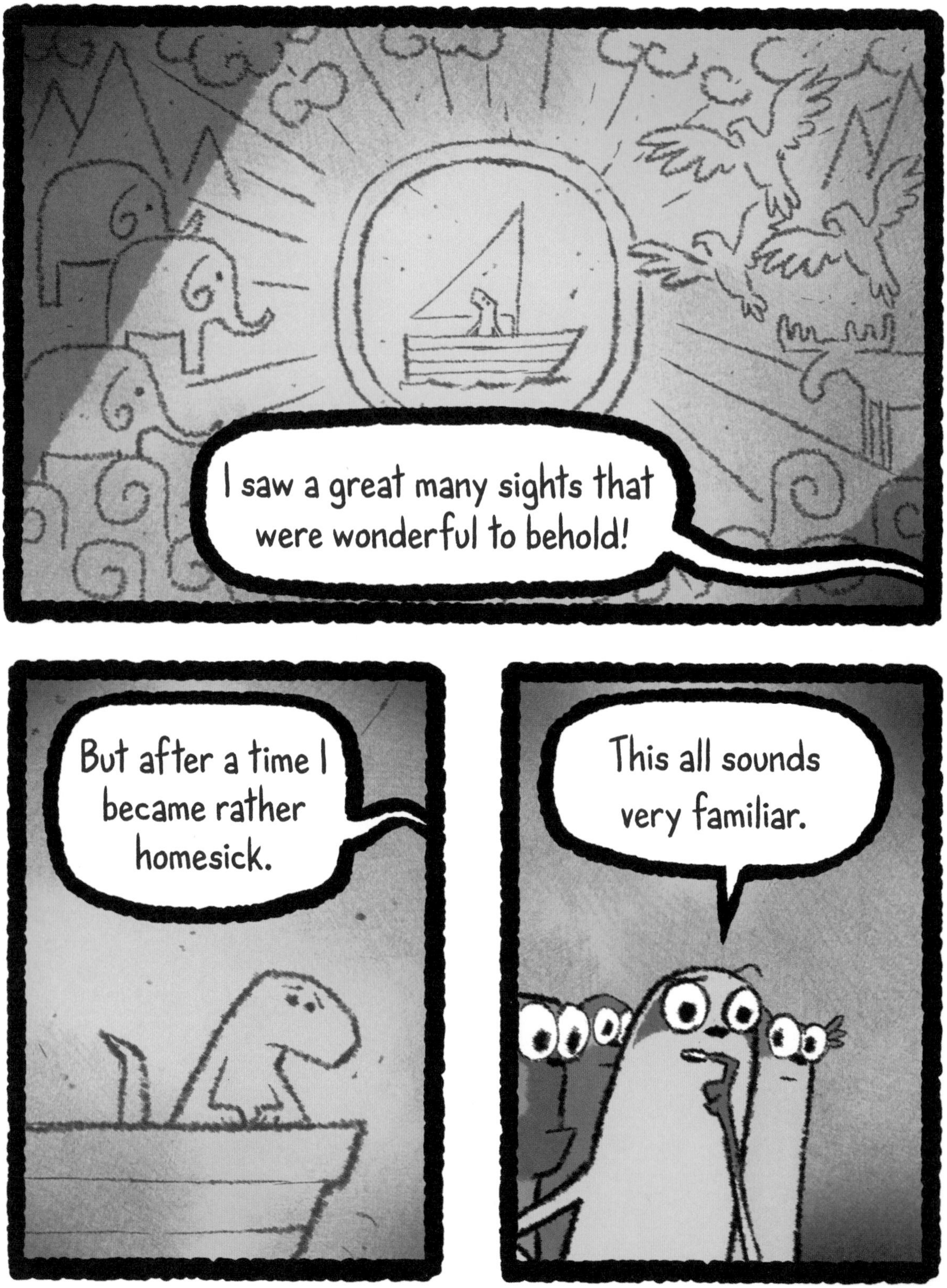
I saw a great many sights that were wonderful to behold!
But after a time I became rather homesick.
This all sounds very familiar.

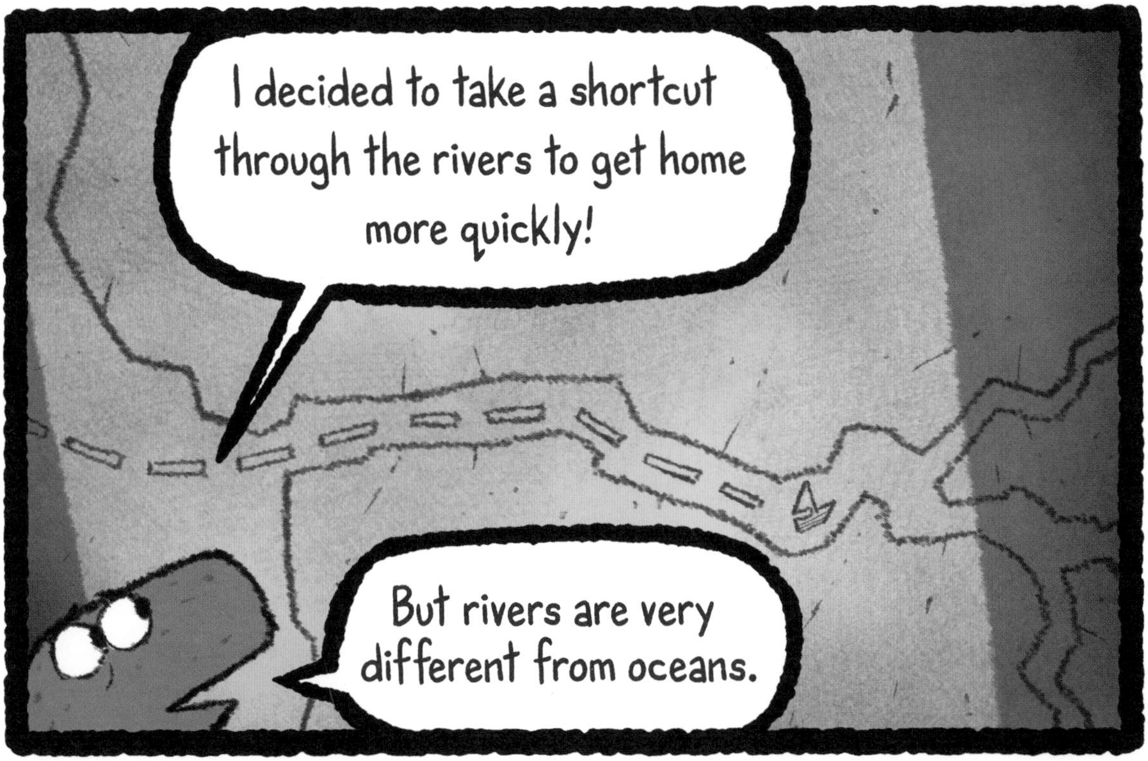
I decided to take a shortcut through the rivers to get home more quickly!
But rivers are very different from oceans.

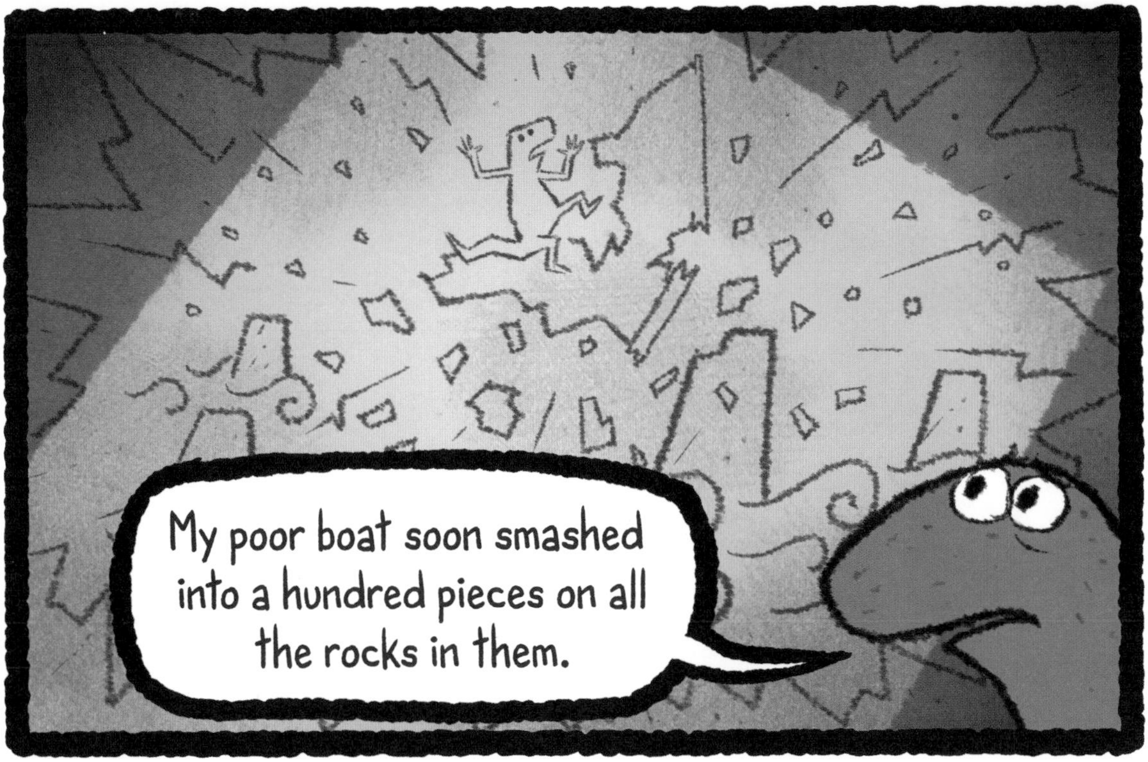
My poor boat soon smashed into a hundred pieces on all the rocks in them.

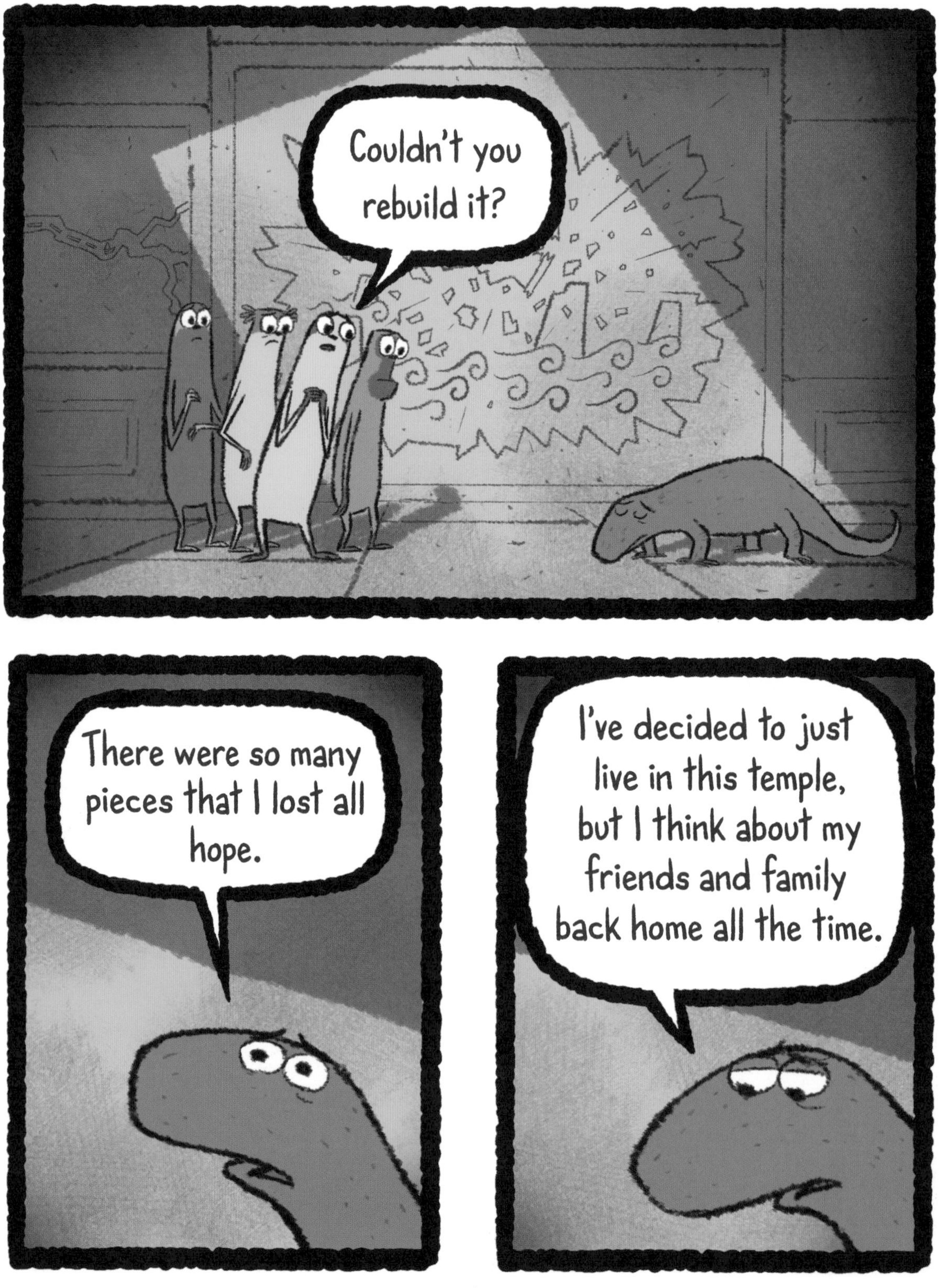

Couldn't you rebuild it?
There were so many pieces that I lost all hope.
I've decided to just live in this temple, but I think about my friends and family back home all the time.

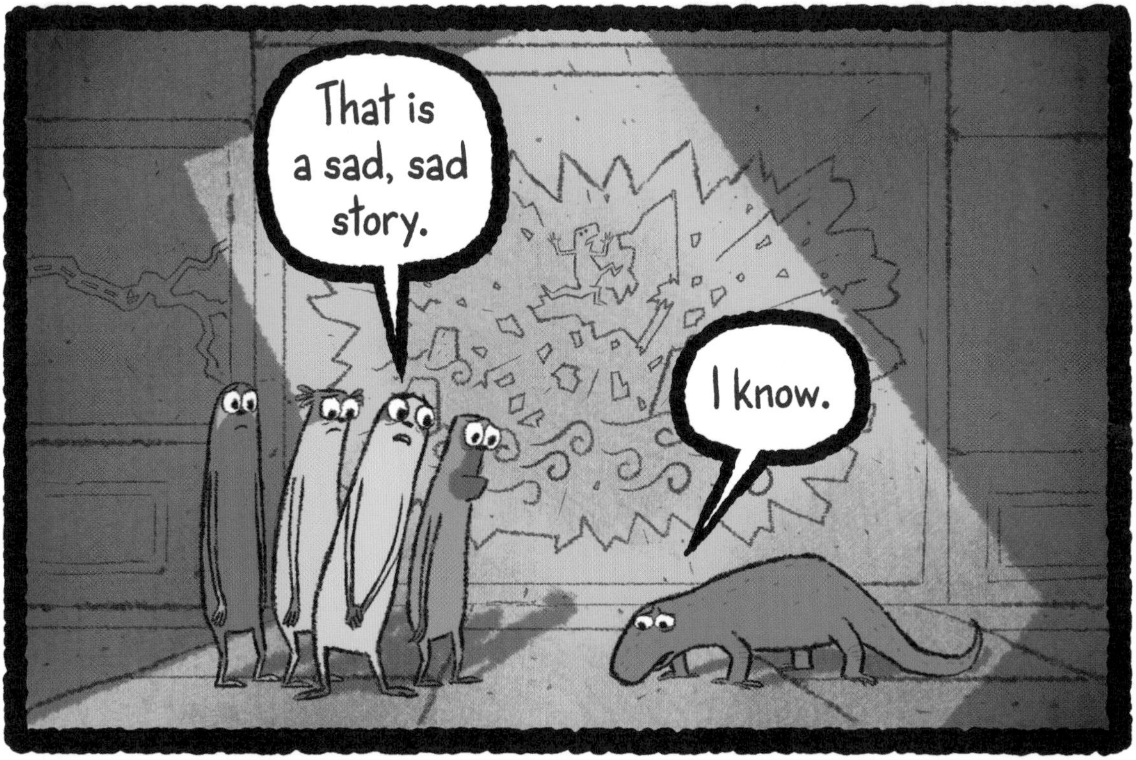
That is a sad, sad story.
I know.

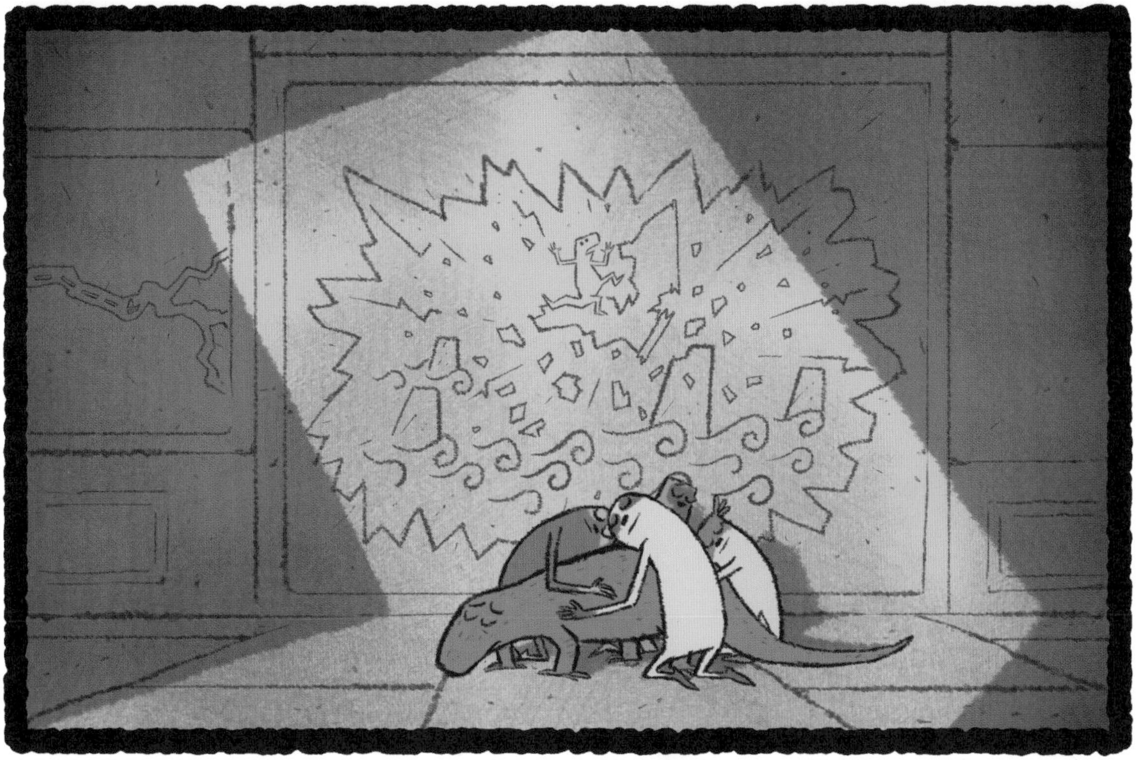

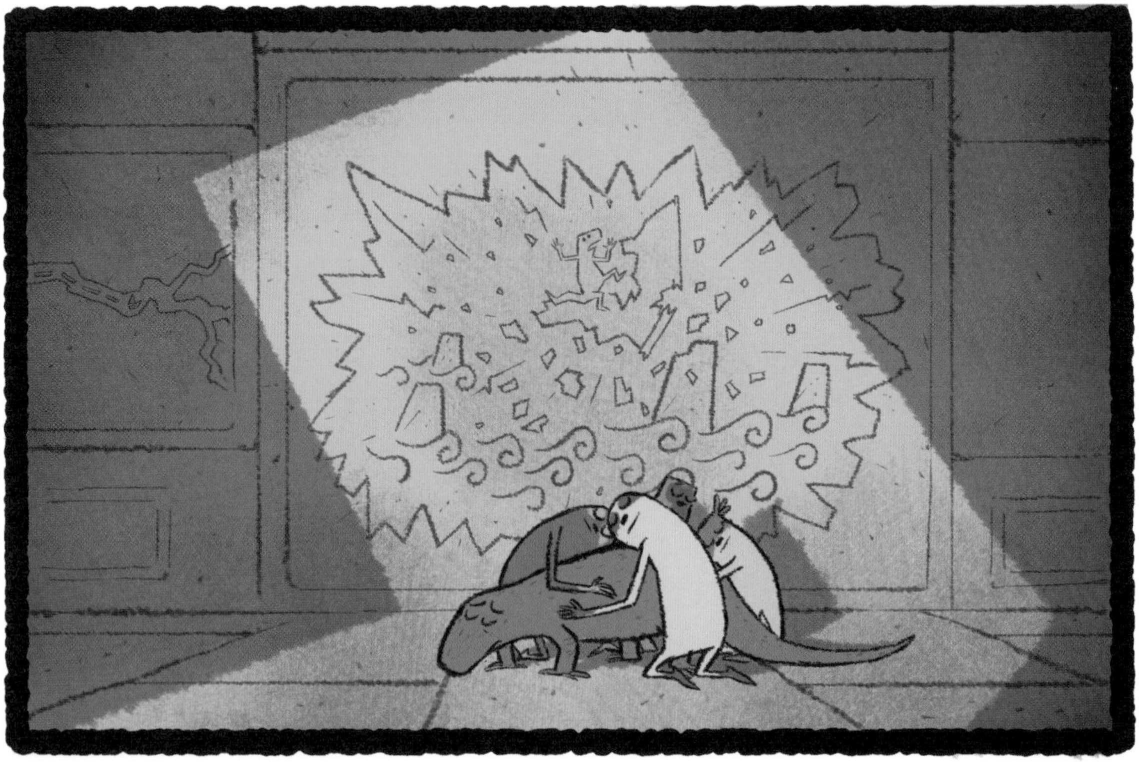

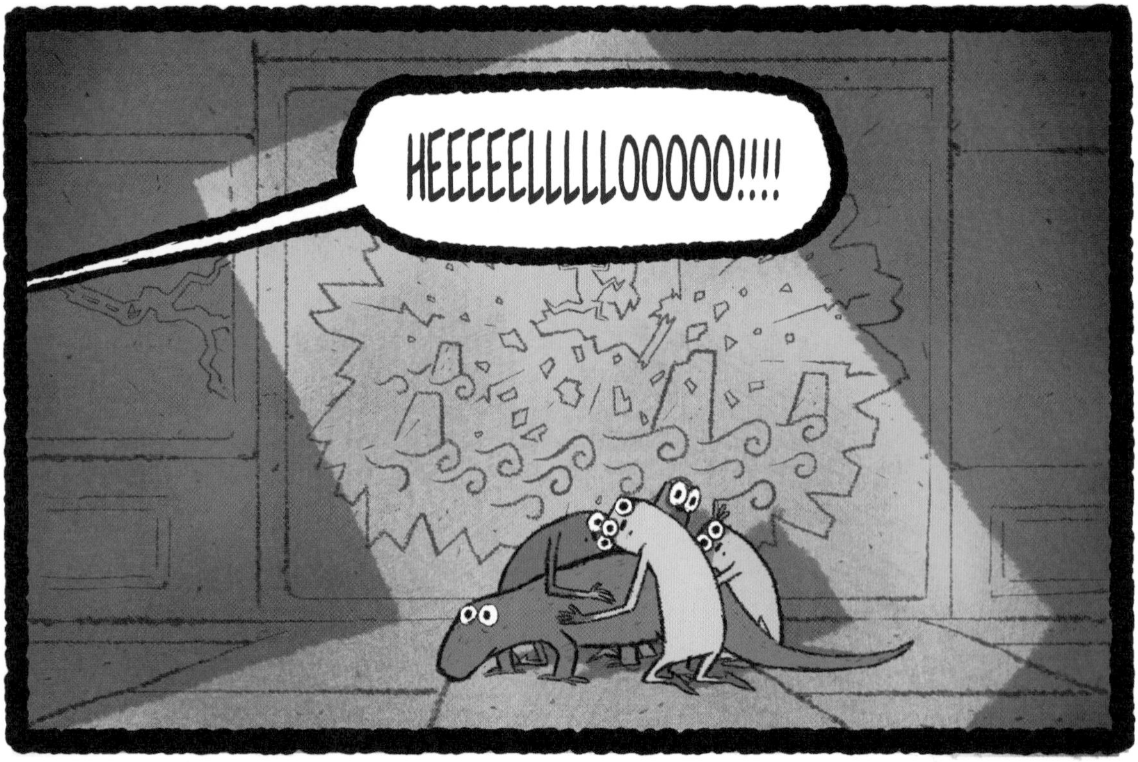
HEEEEELLLLLOOOOO!!!!

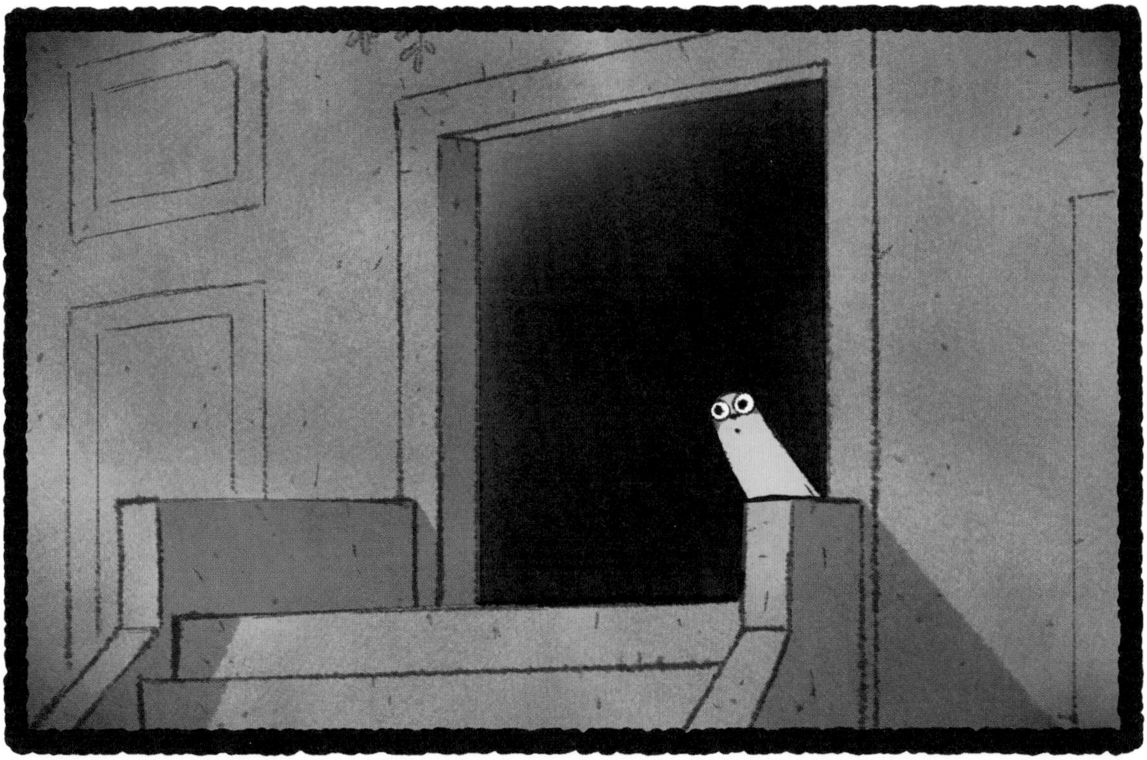

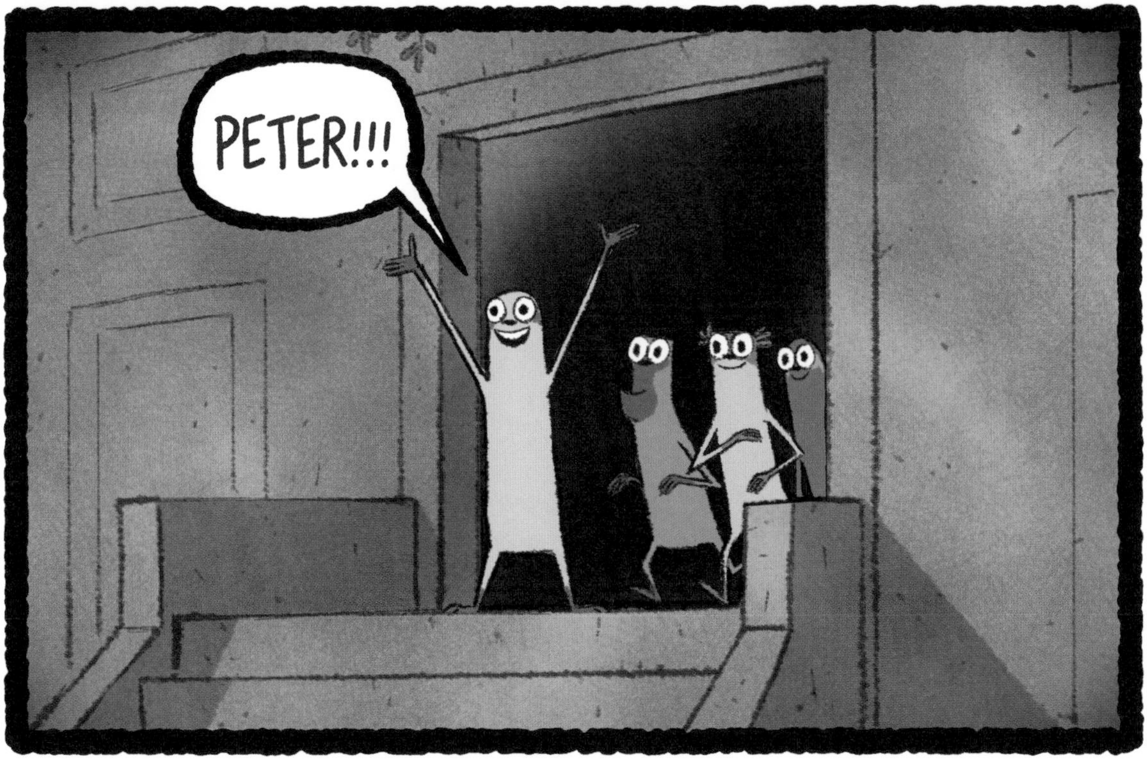
PETER!!!

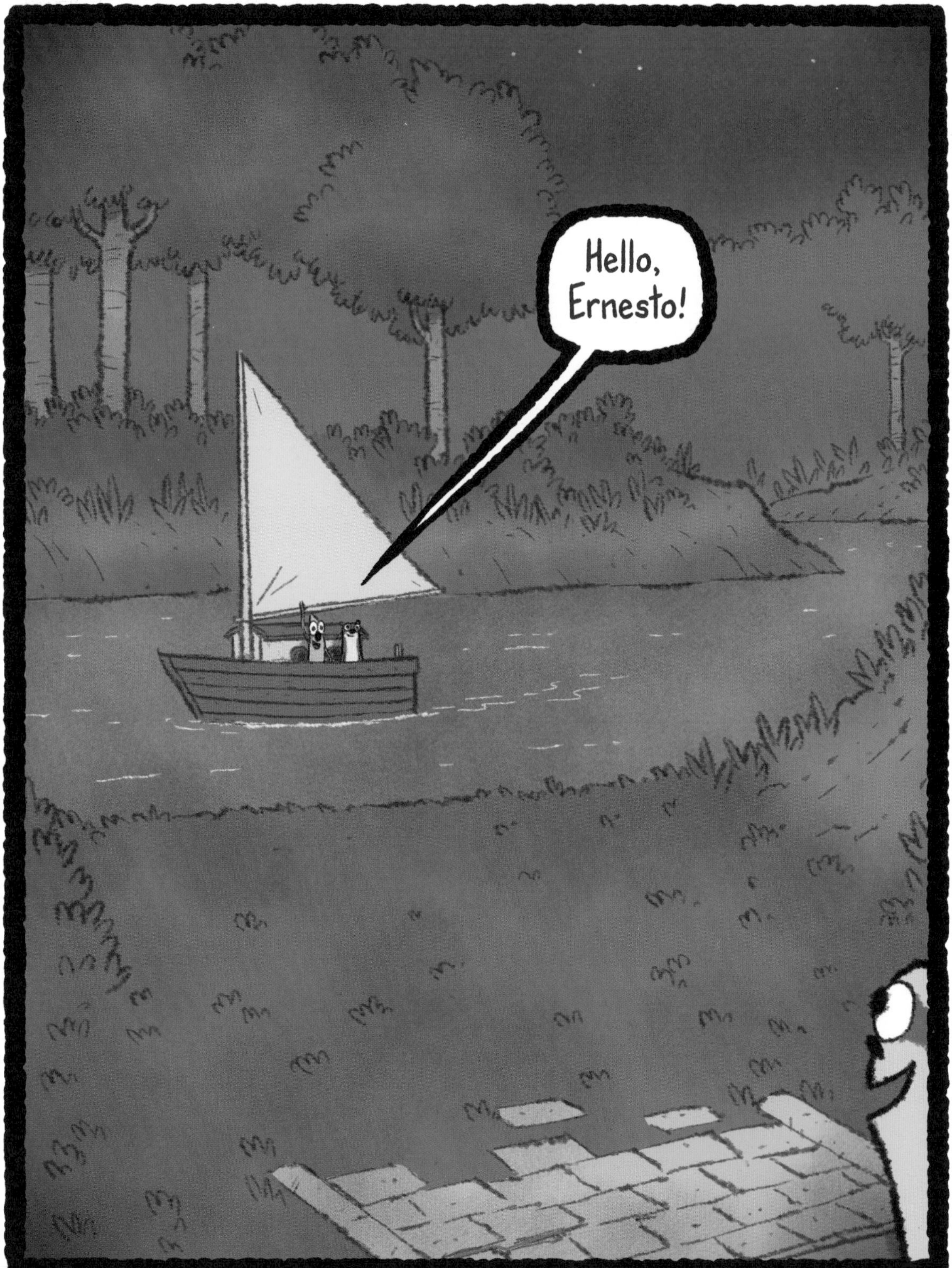
Hello, Ernesto!

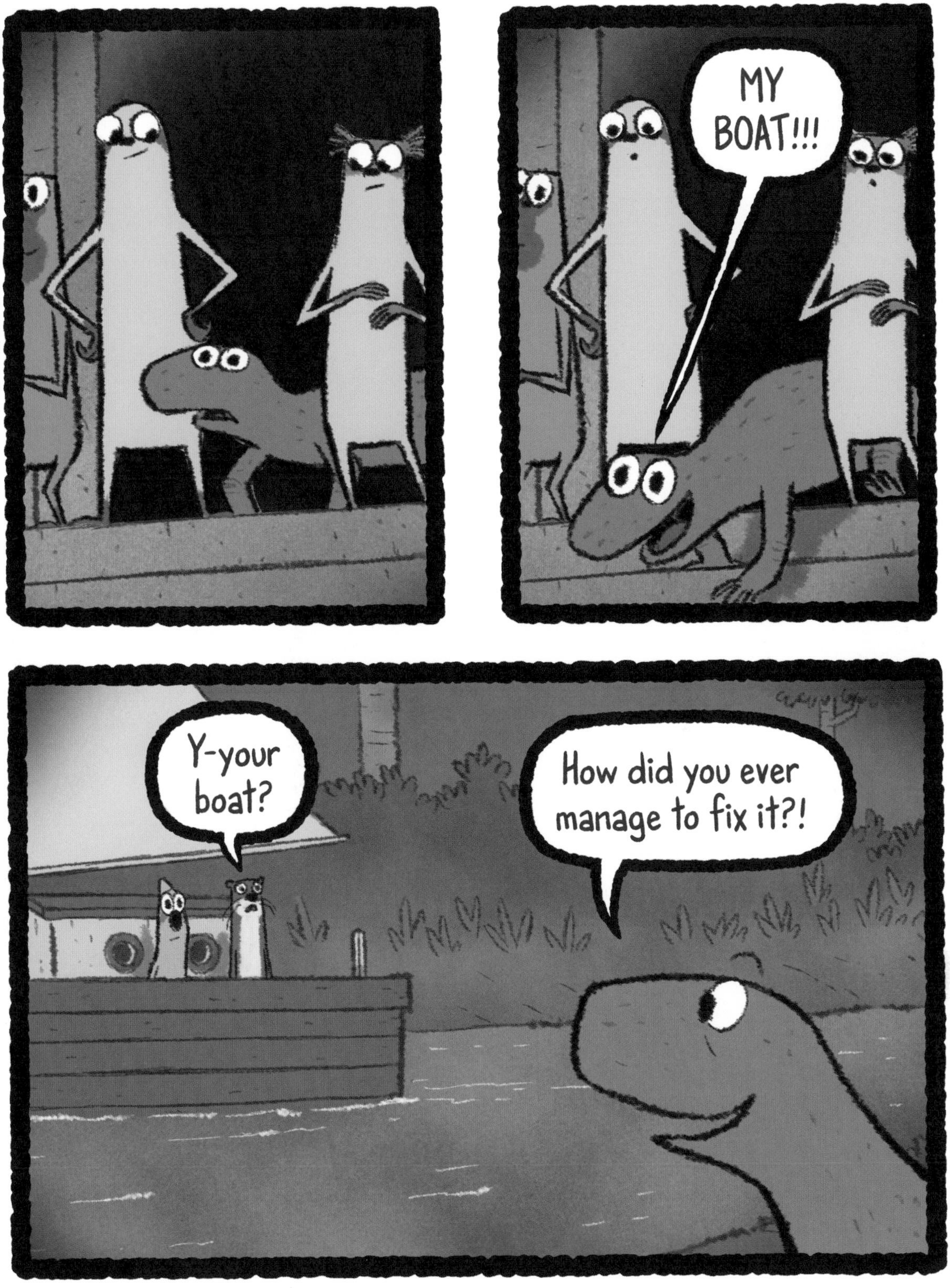
MY BOAT!!!
Y-your boat?
How did you ever manage to fix it?!

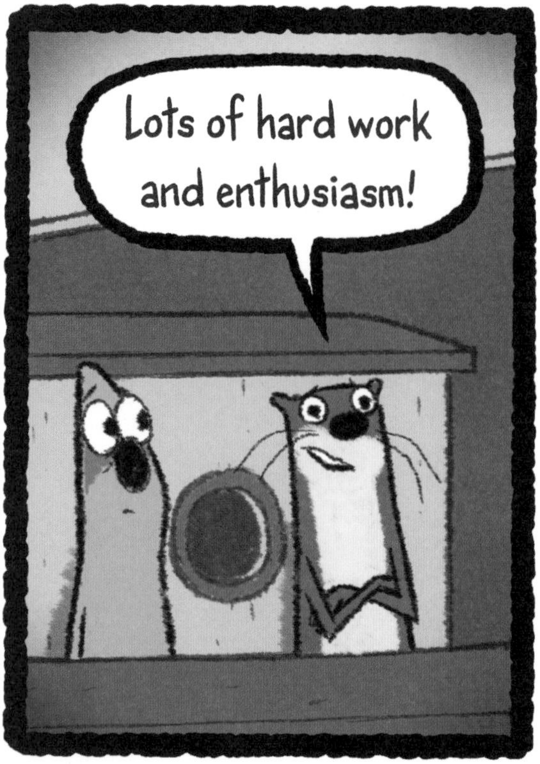
Lots of hard work and enthusiasm!

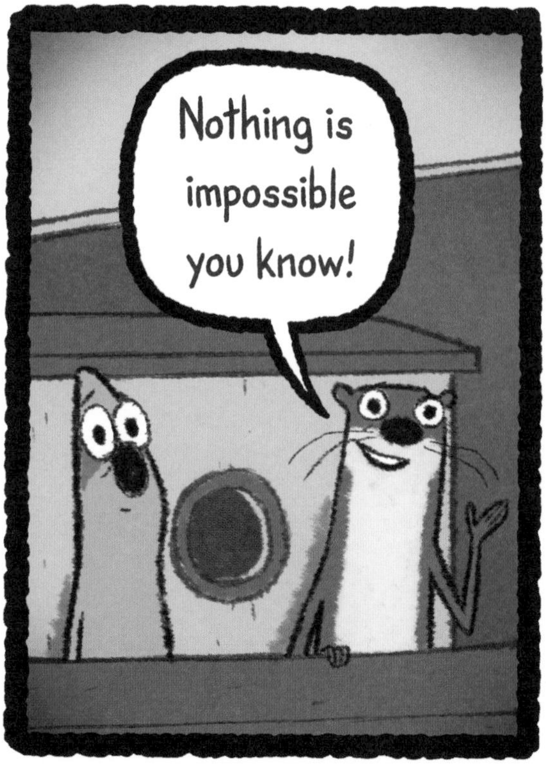
Nothing is impossible you know!

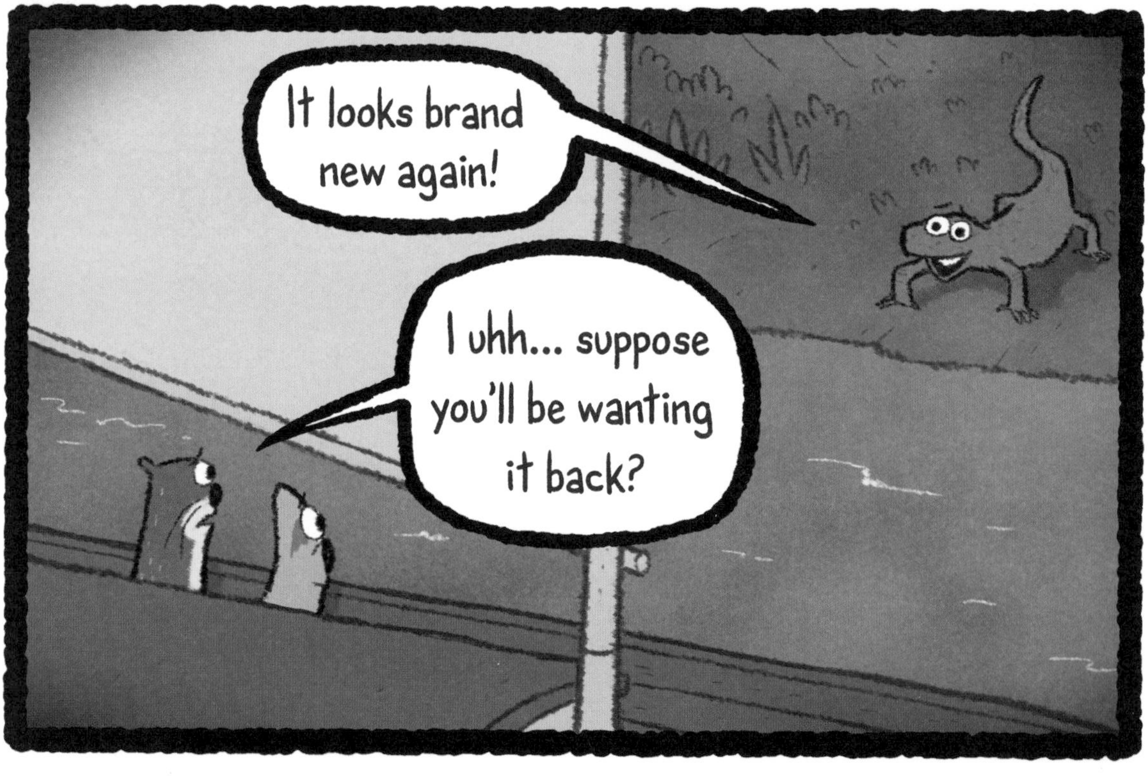
It looks brand new again!
I uhh... suppose you'll be wanting it back?

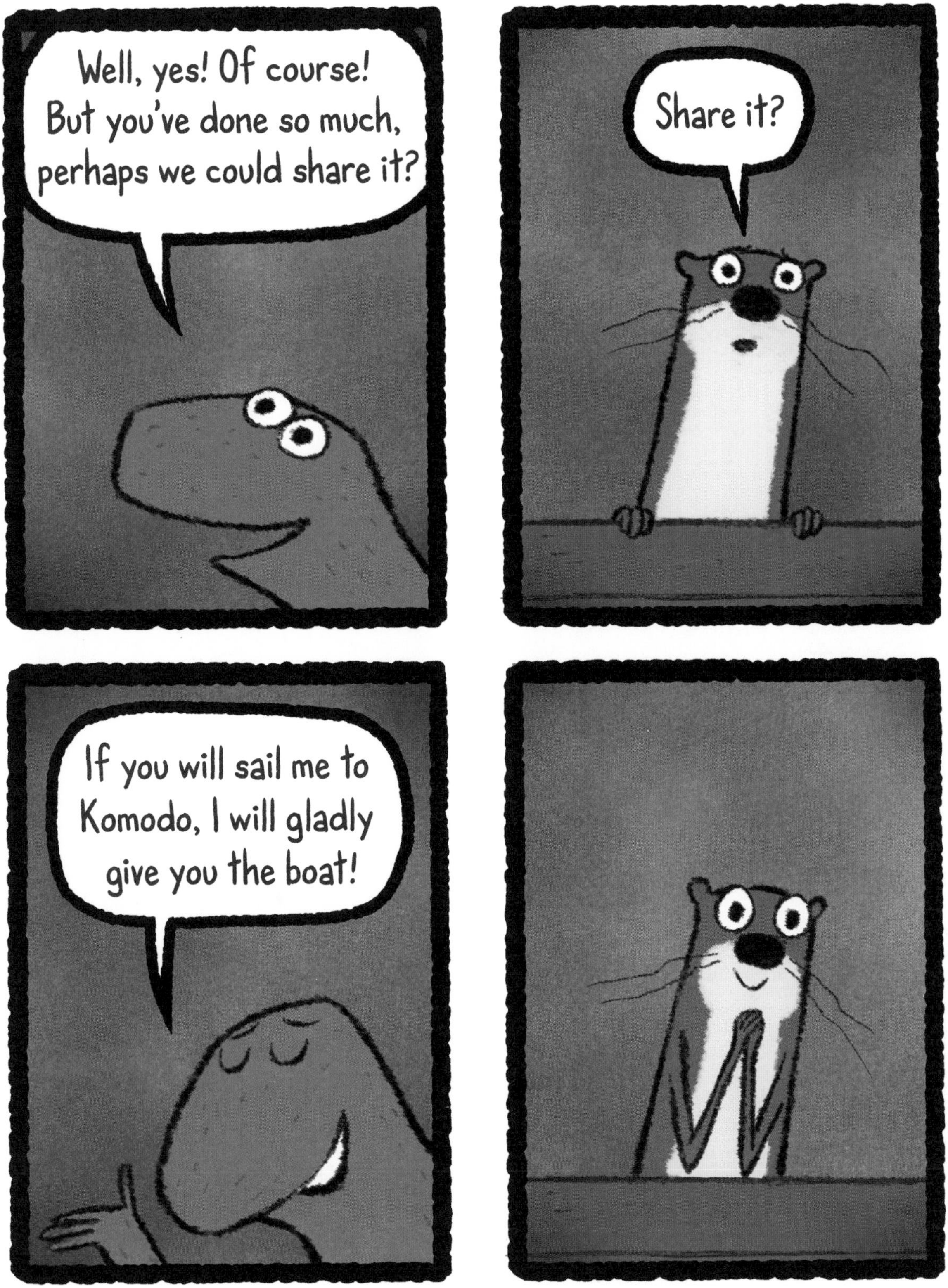
Well, yes! Of course! But you've done so much, perhaps we could share it?
Share it?
If you will sail me to Komodo, I will gladly give you the boat!

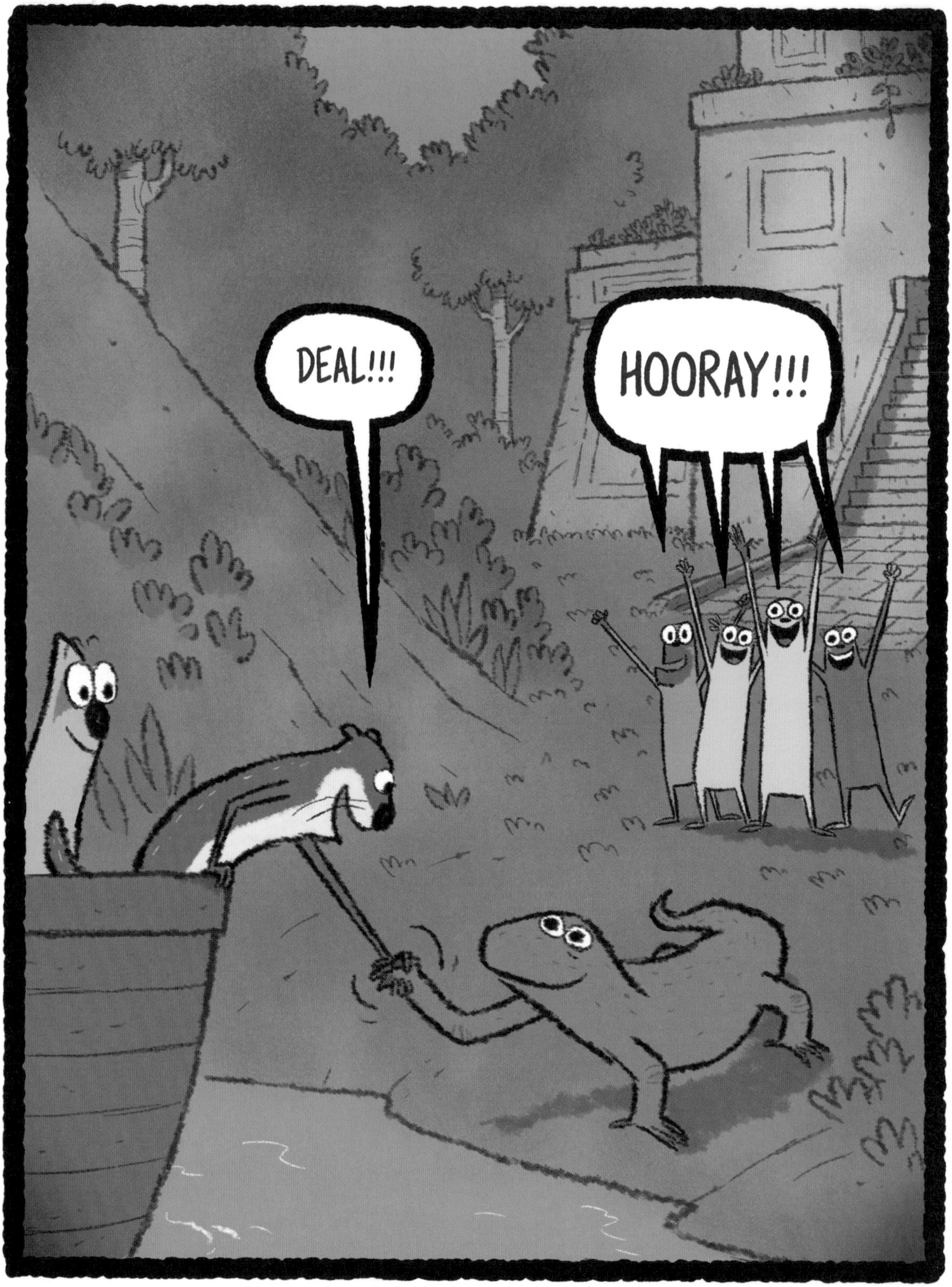
DEAL!!!
HOORAY!!!

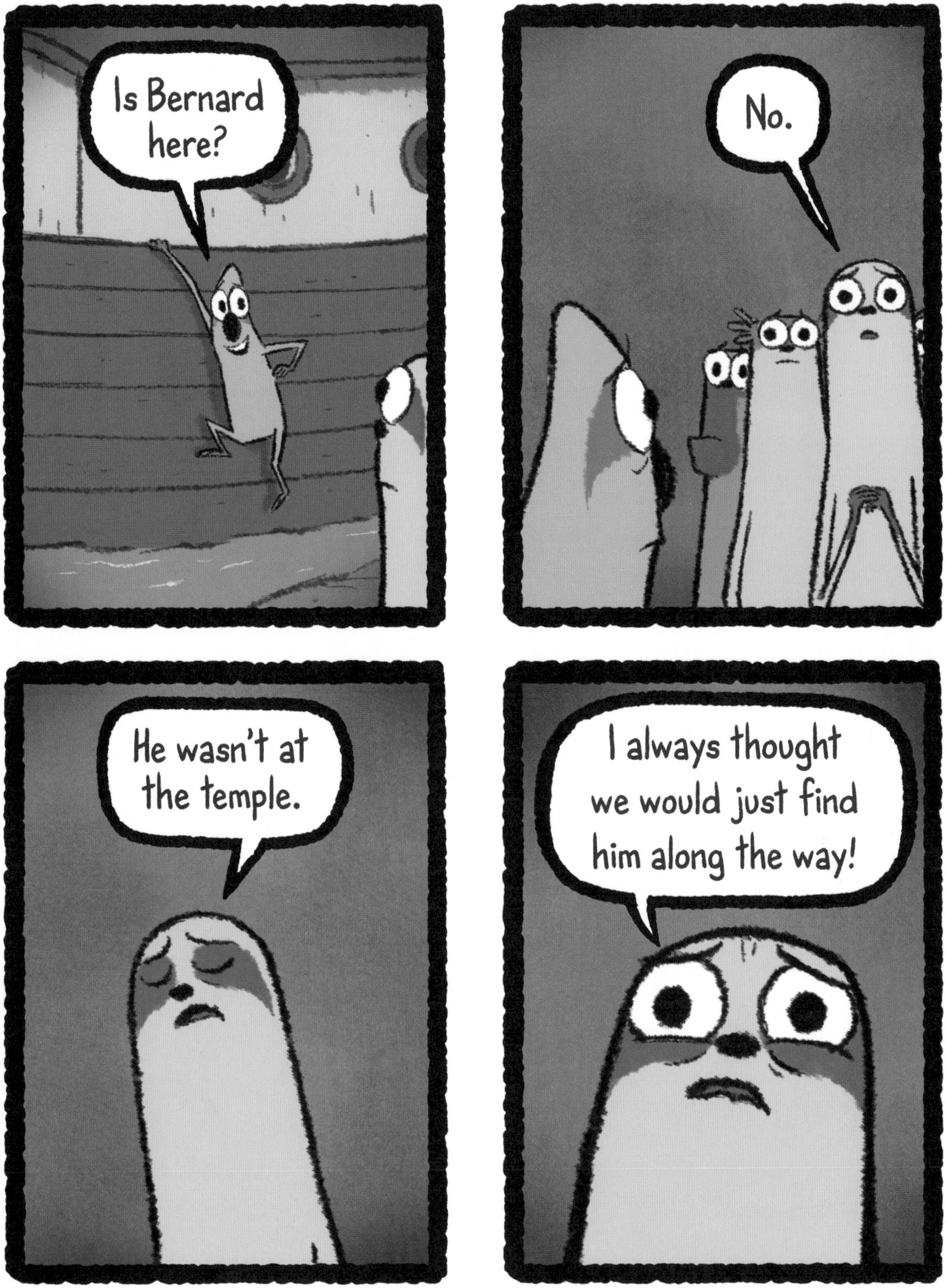

Is Bernard here?
No.
He wasn't at the temple.
I always thought we would just find him along the way!

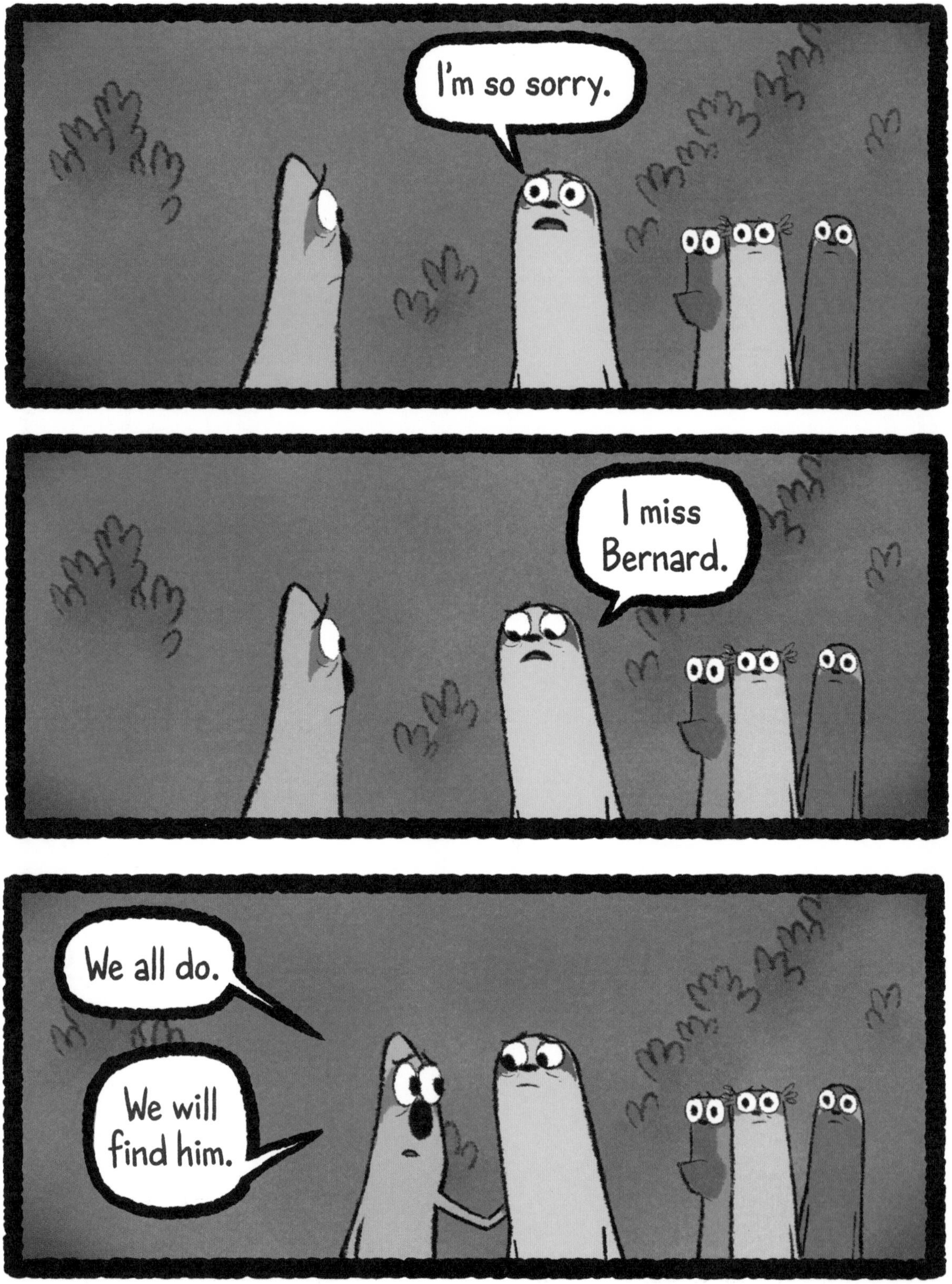
I'm so sorry.
I miss Bernard.
We all do.
We will find him.

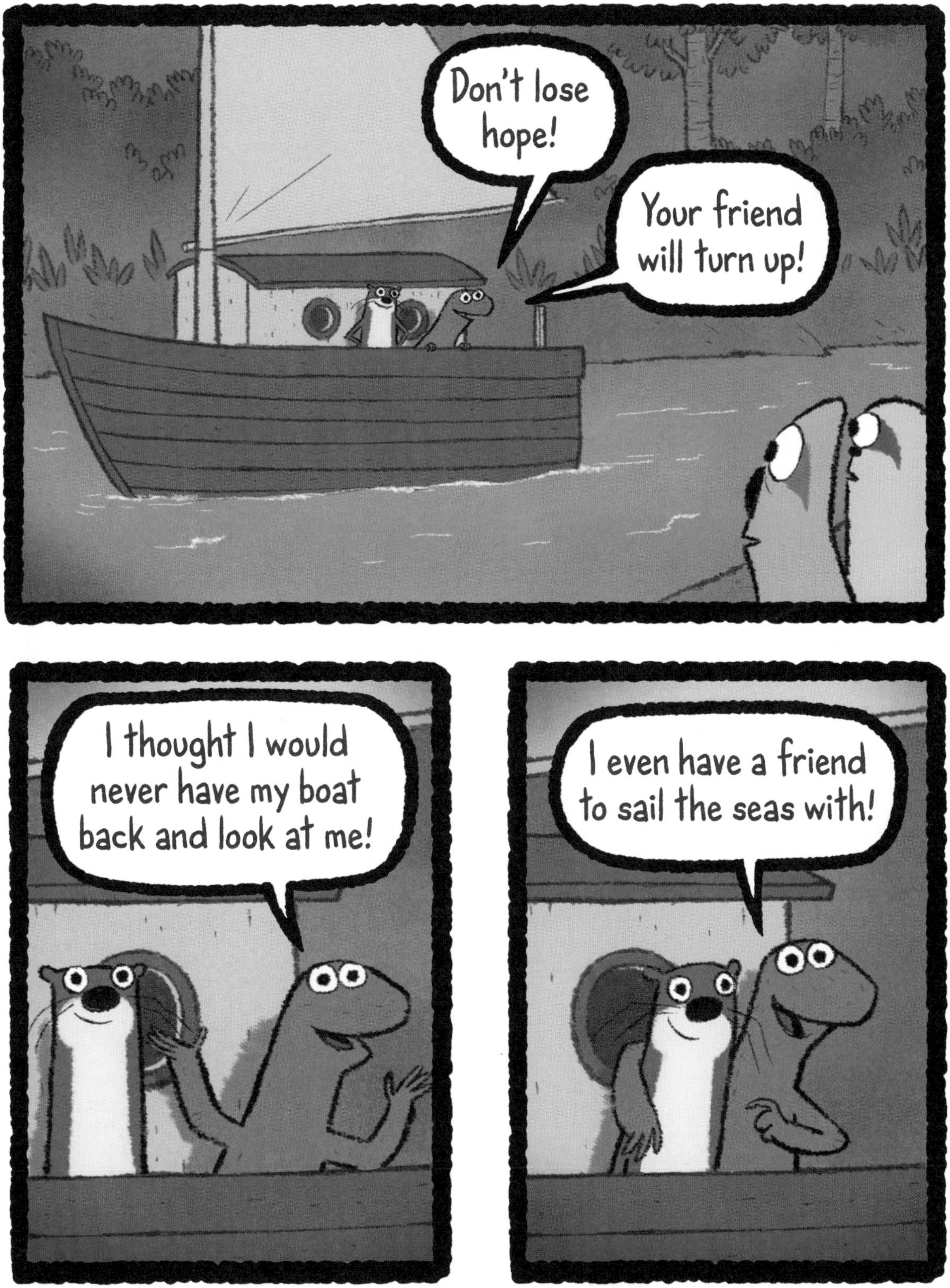
Don't lose hope!
Your friend will turn up!
I thought I would never have my boat back and look at me!
I even have a friend to sail the seas with!

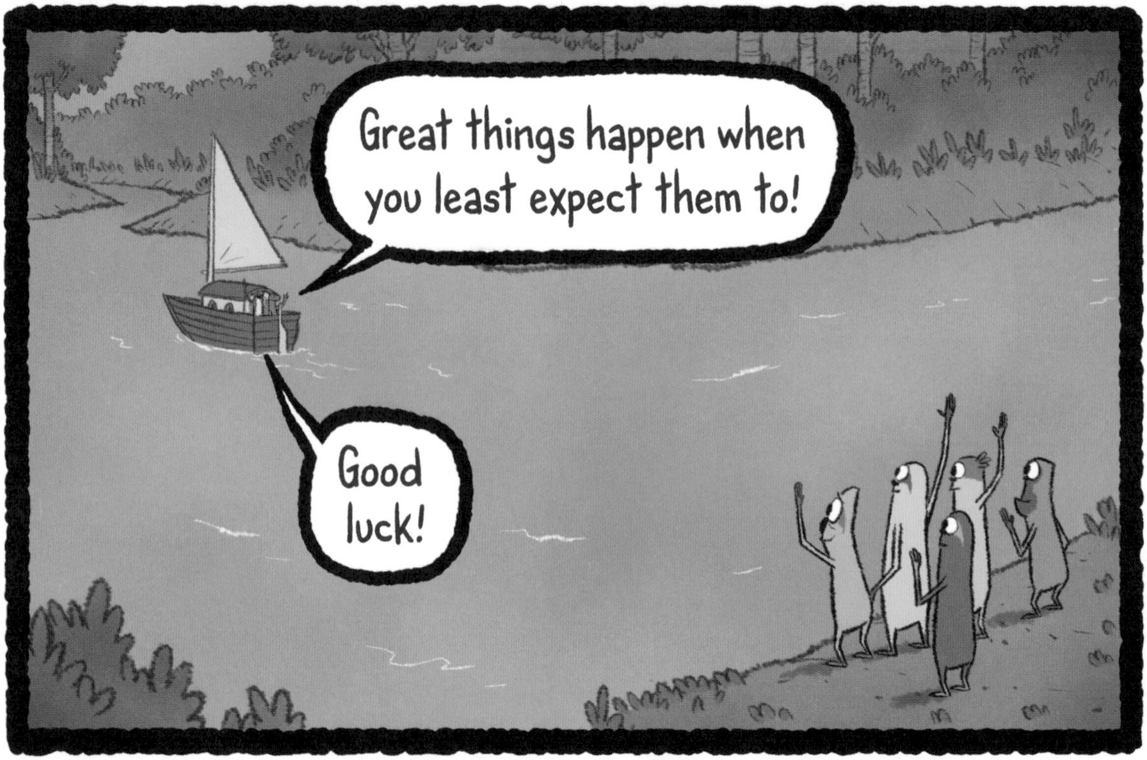
Great things happen when you least expect them to!
Good luck!

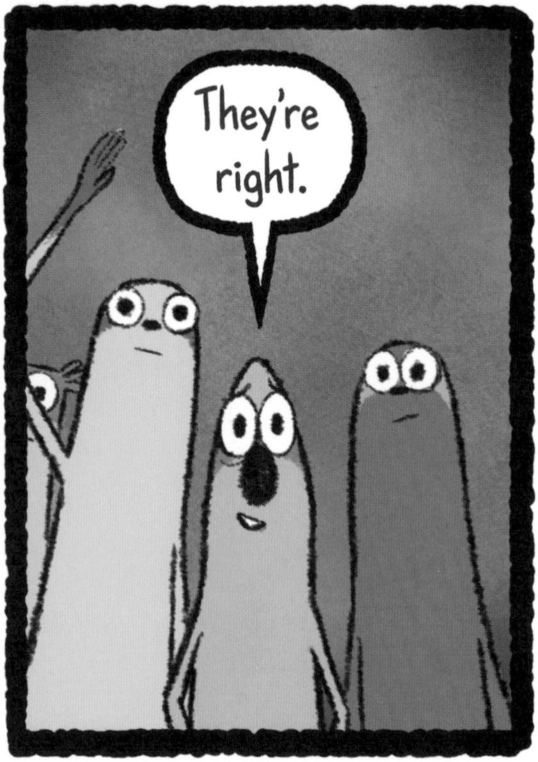
They're right.

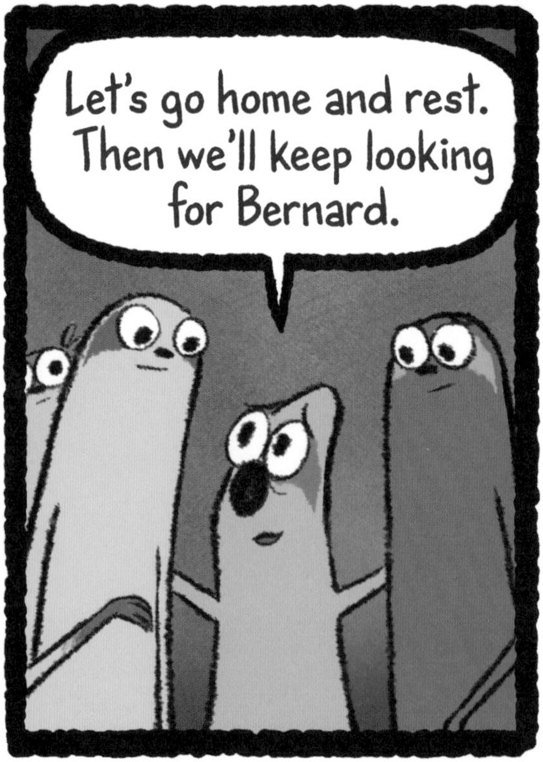
Let's go home and rest. Then we'll keep looking for Bernard.

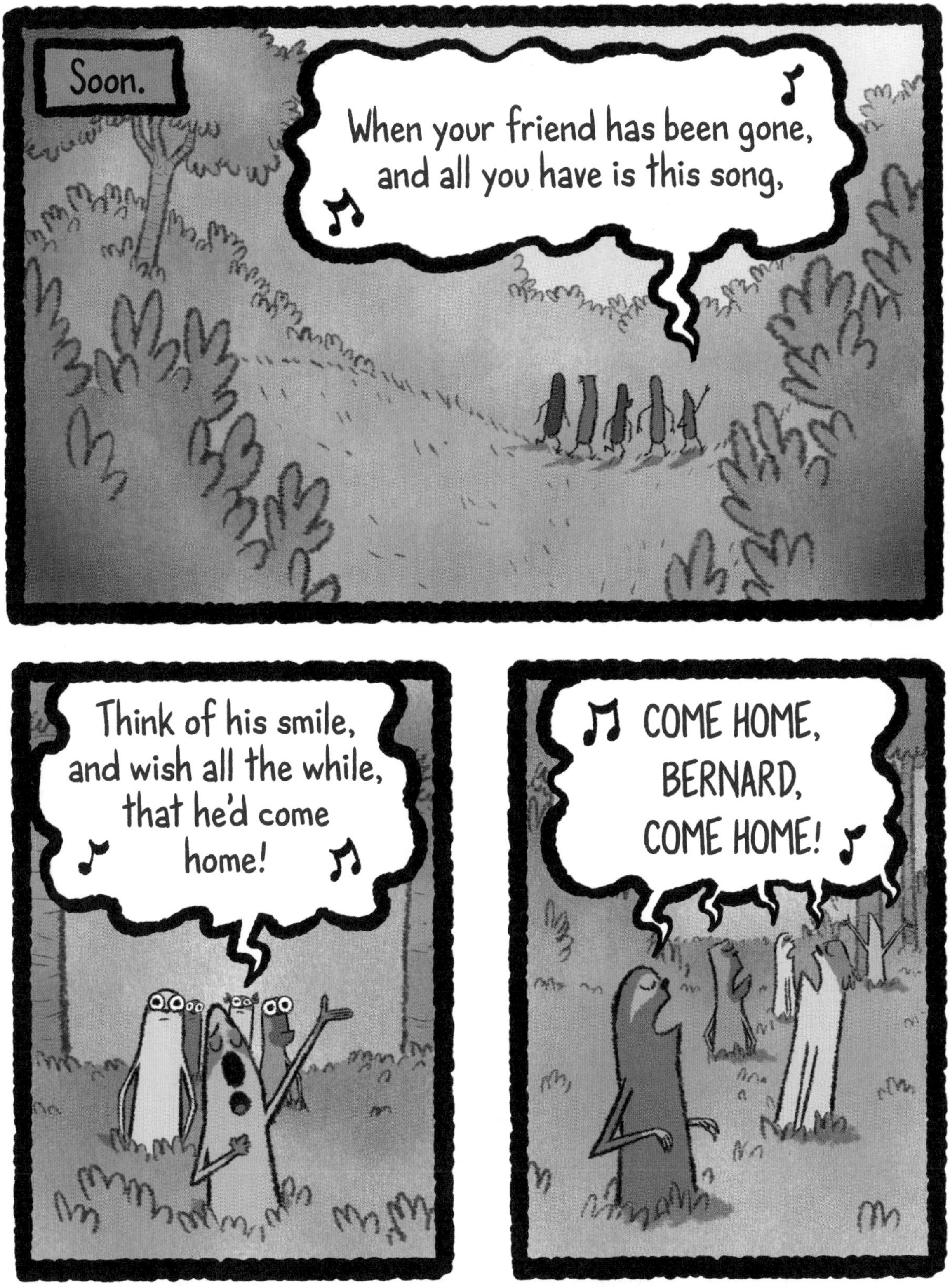
Soon.
When your friend has been gone, and all you have is this song,
Think of his smile, and wish all the while, that he'd come home!
COME HOME, BERNARD, COME HOME!

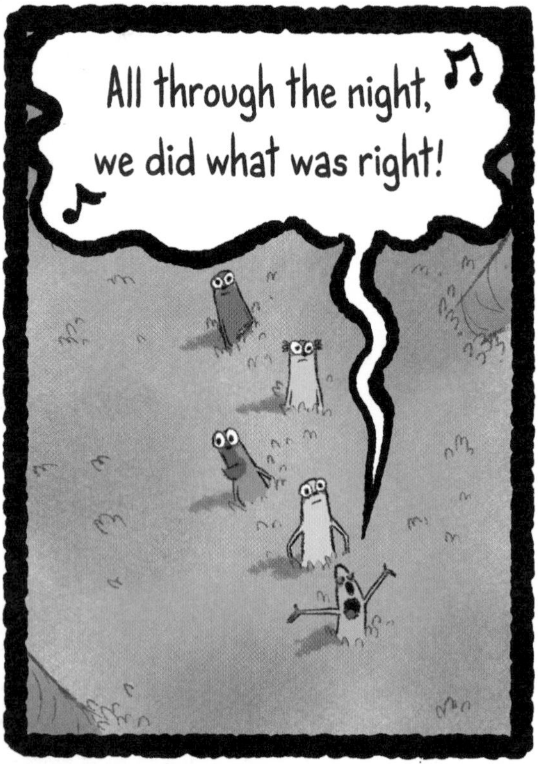
All through the night, we did what was right!

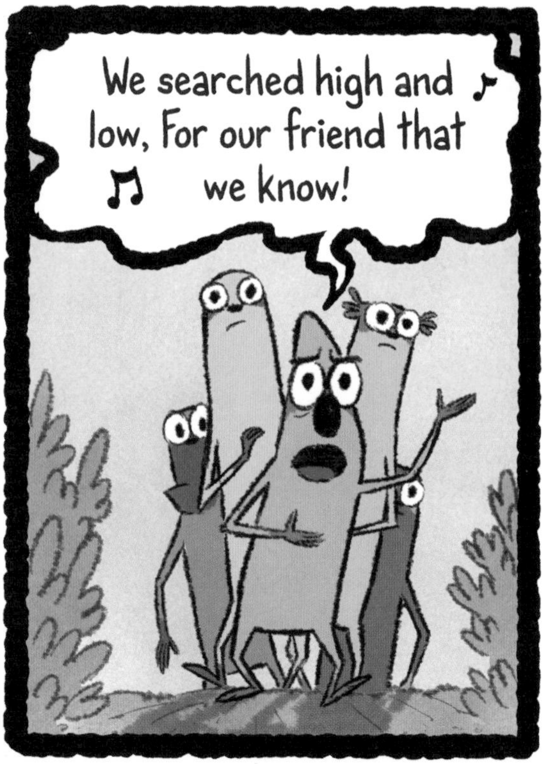
We searched high and low, For our friend that we know!

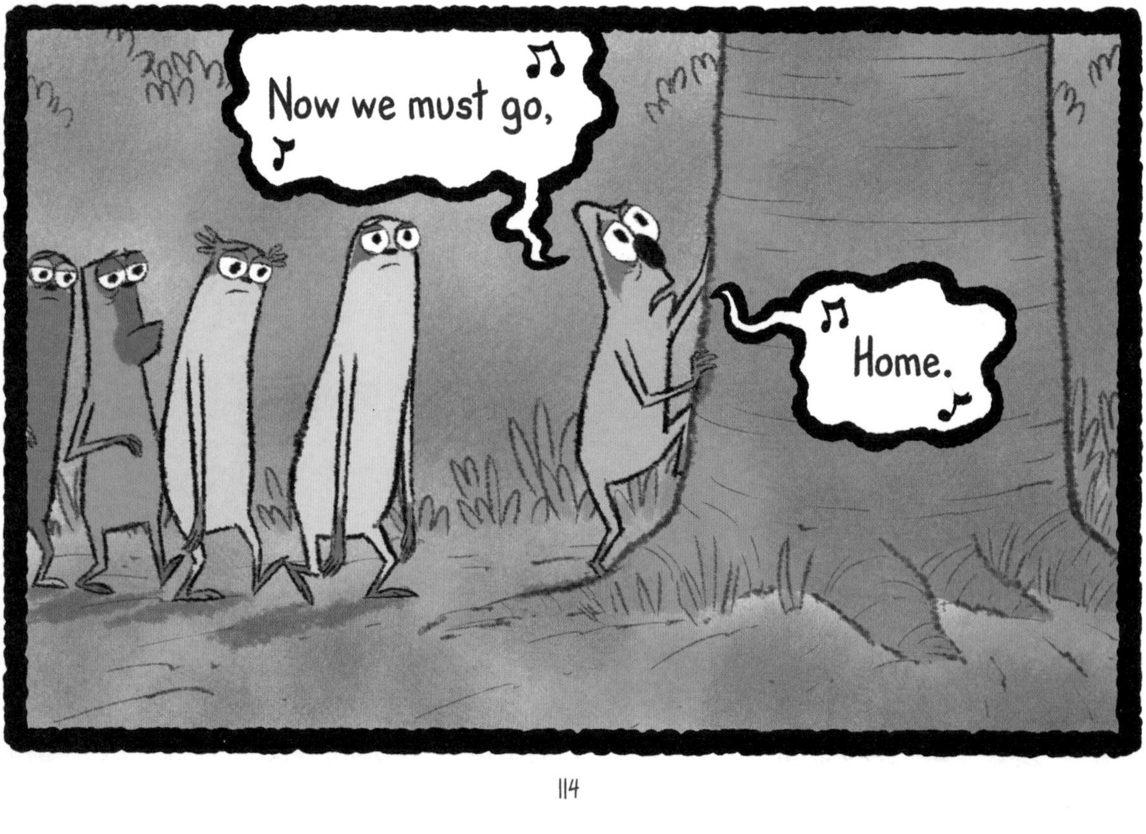
Now we must go,
Home.

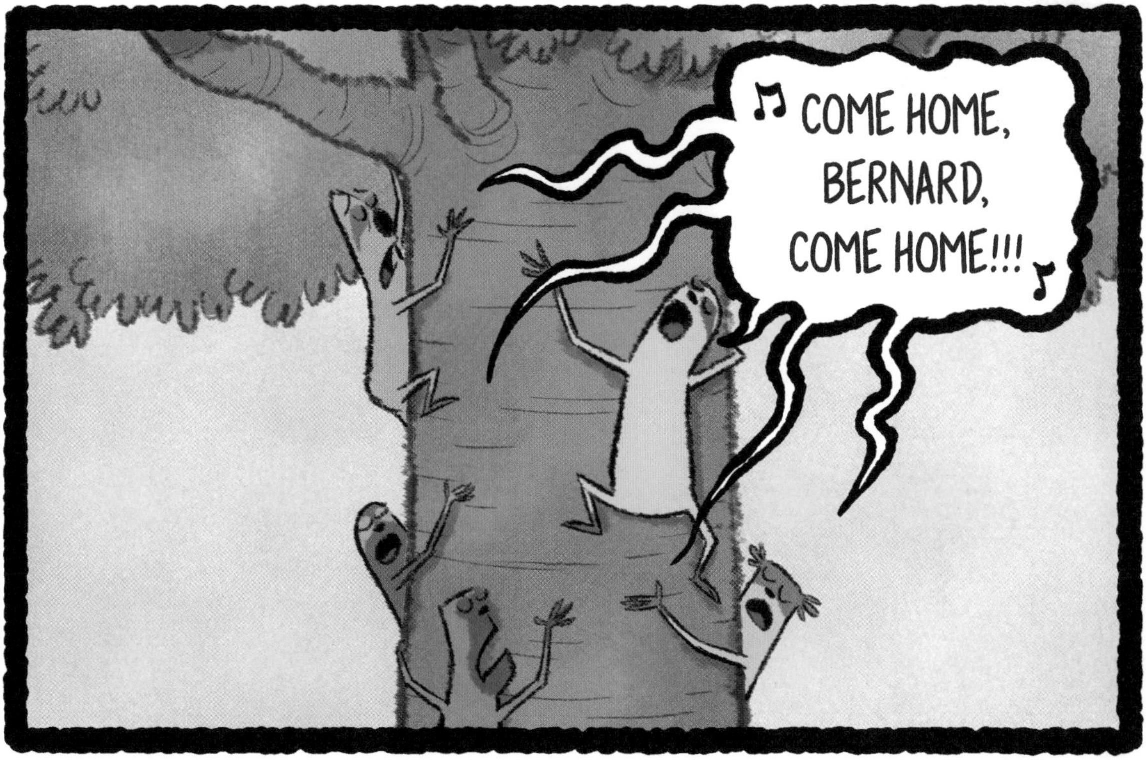
COME HOME, BERNARD, COME HOME!!!

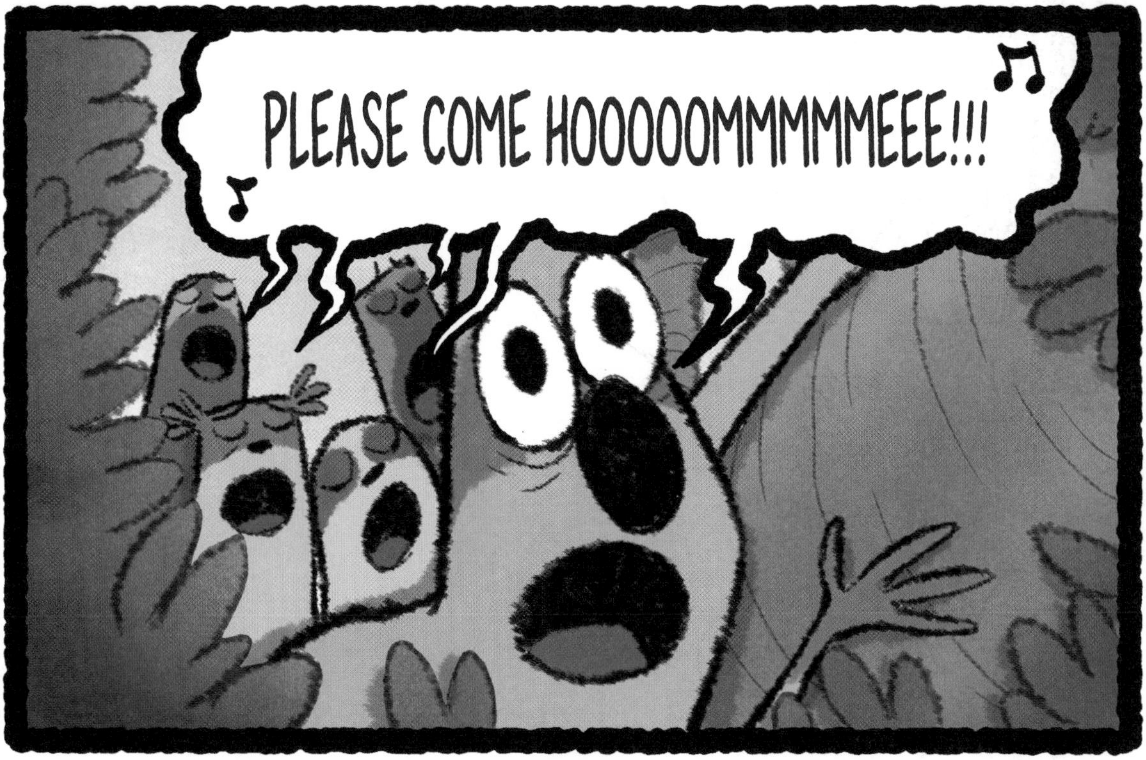
PLEASE COME HOOOOOMMMMMEEE!!!

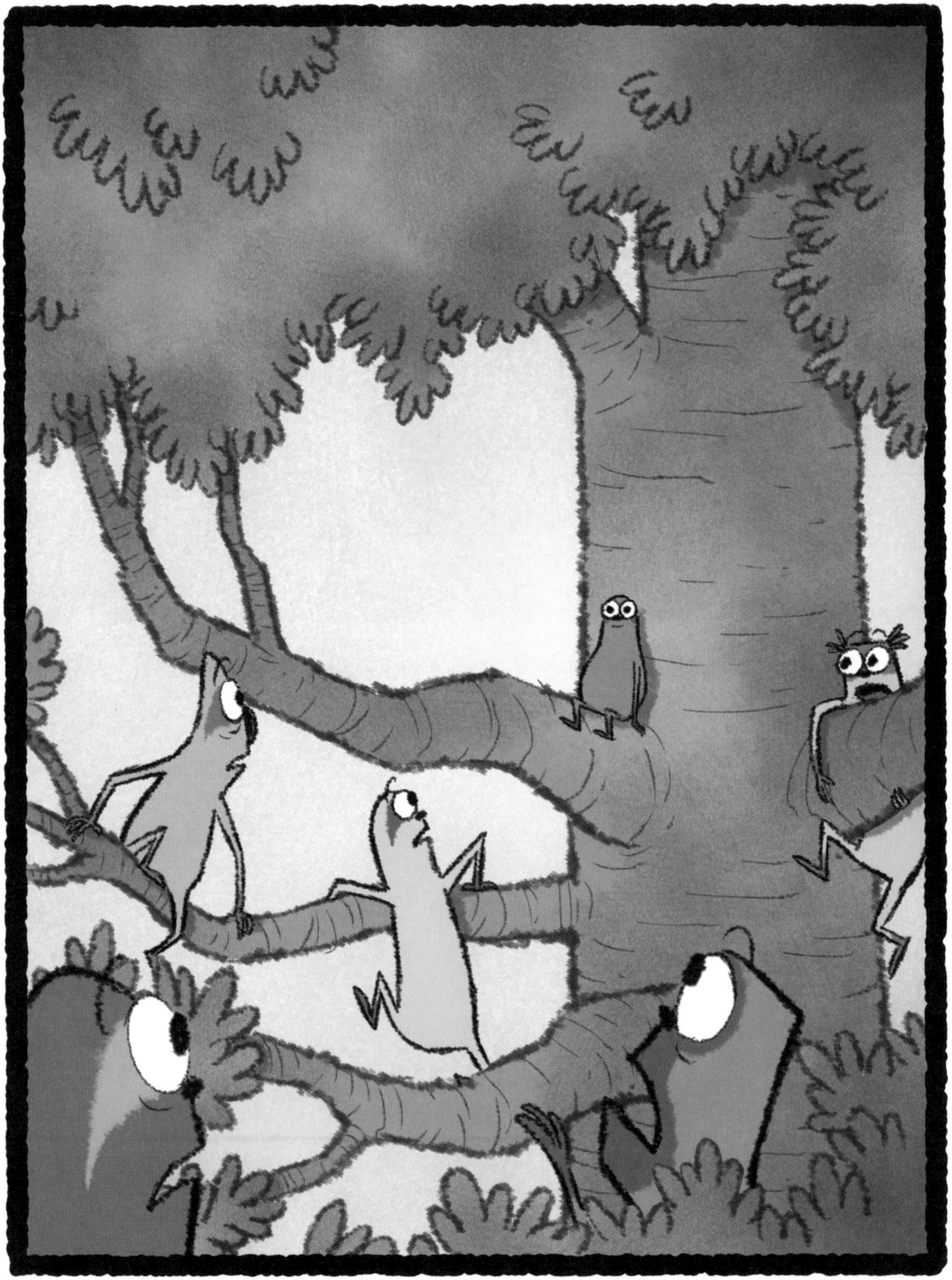

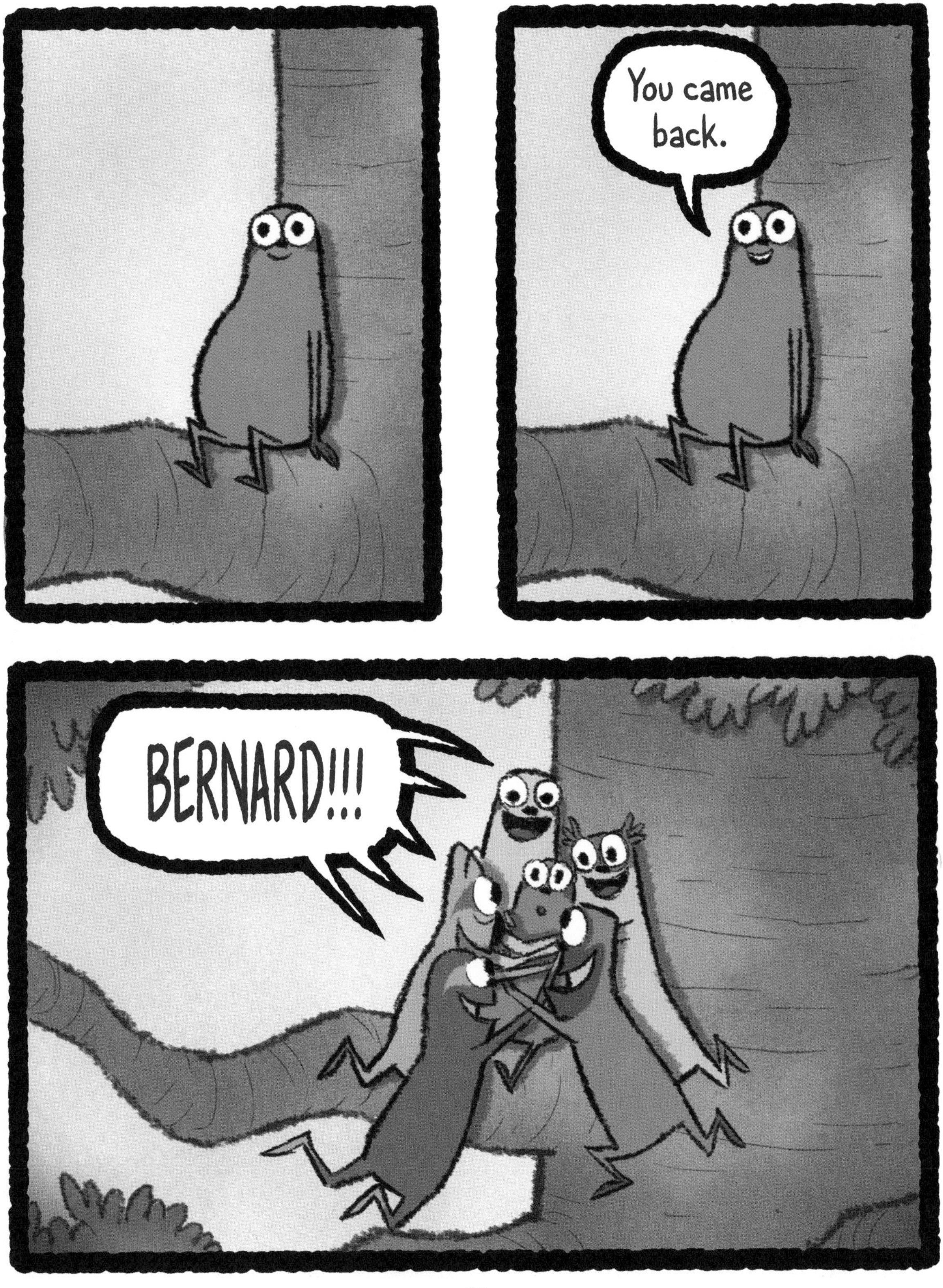
You came back.
BERNARD!!!

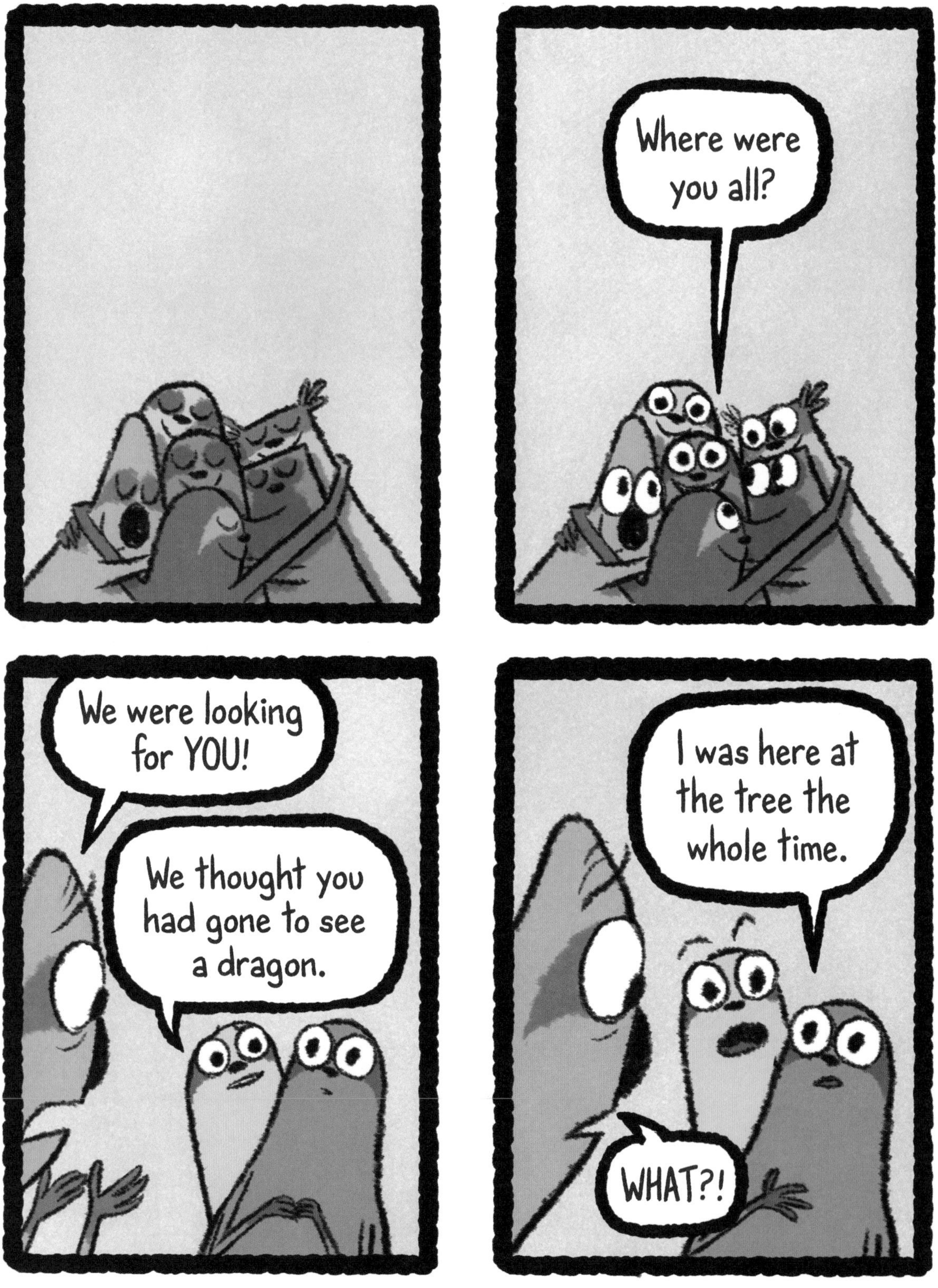

Where were you all?
We were looking for YOU!
We thought you had gone to see a dragon.
I was here at the tree the whole time.
WHAT?!

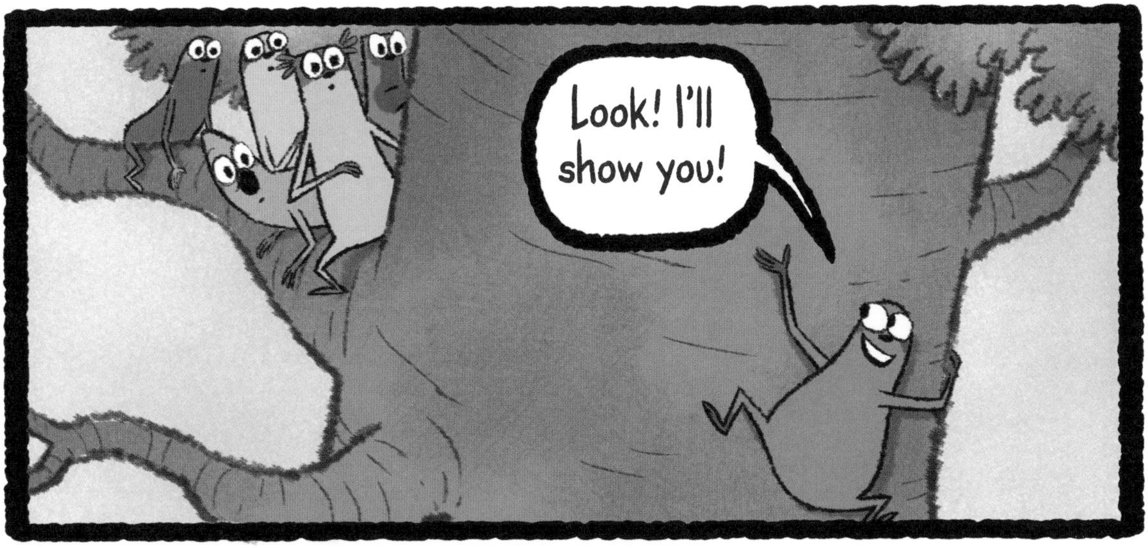
Look! I'll show you!

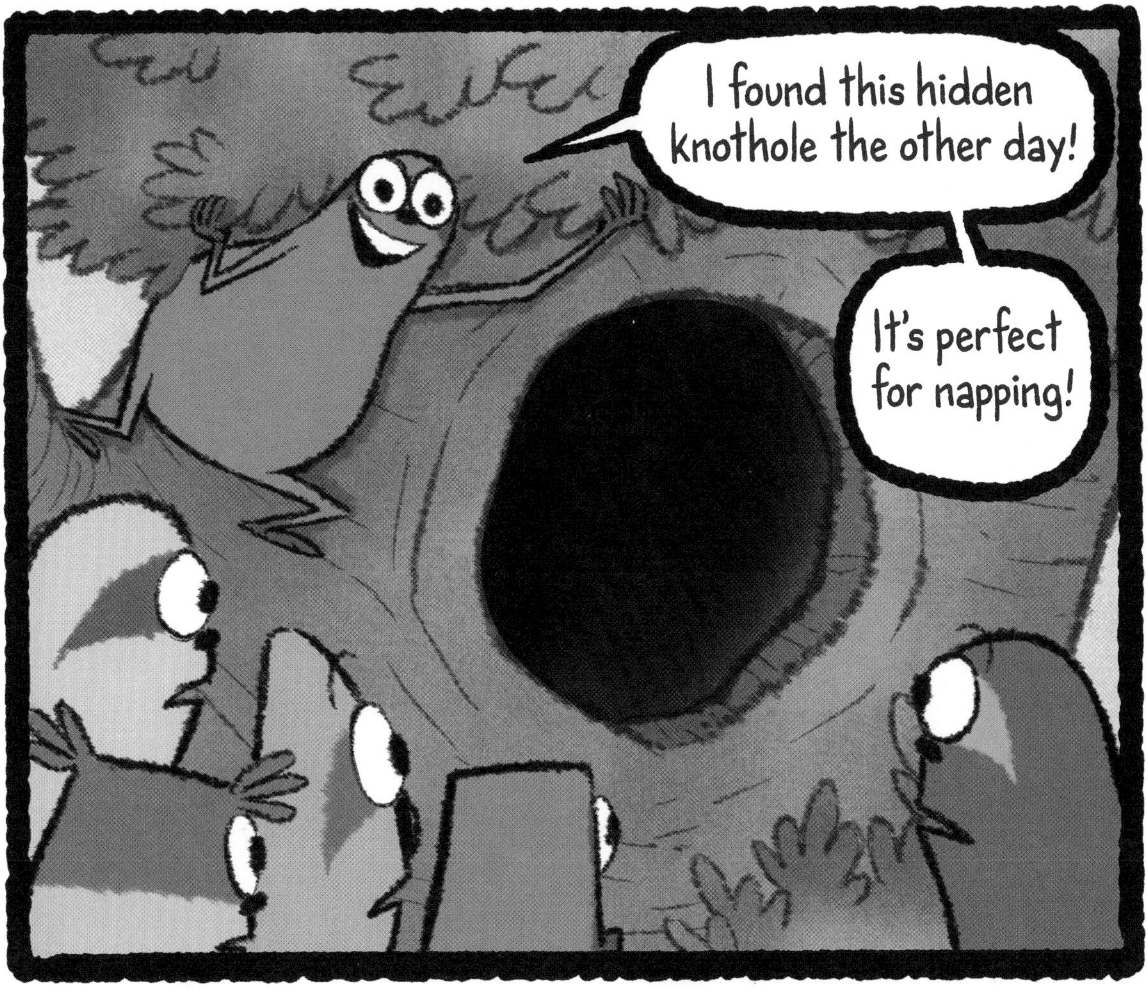
I found this hidden knothole the other day!
It's perfect for napping!

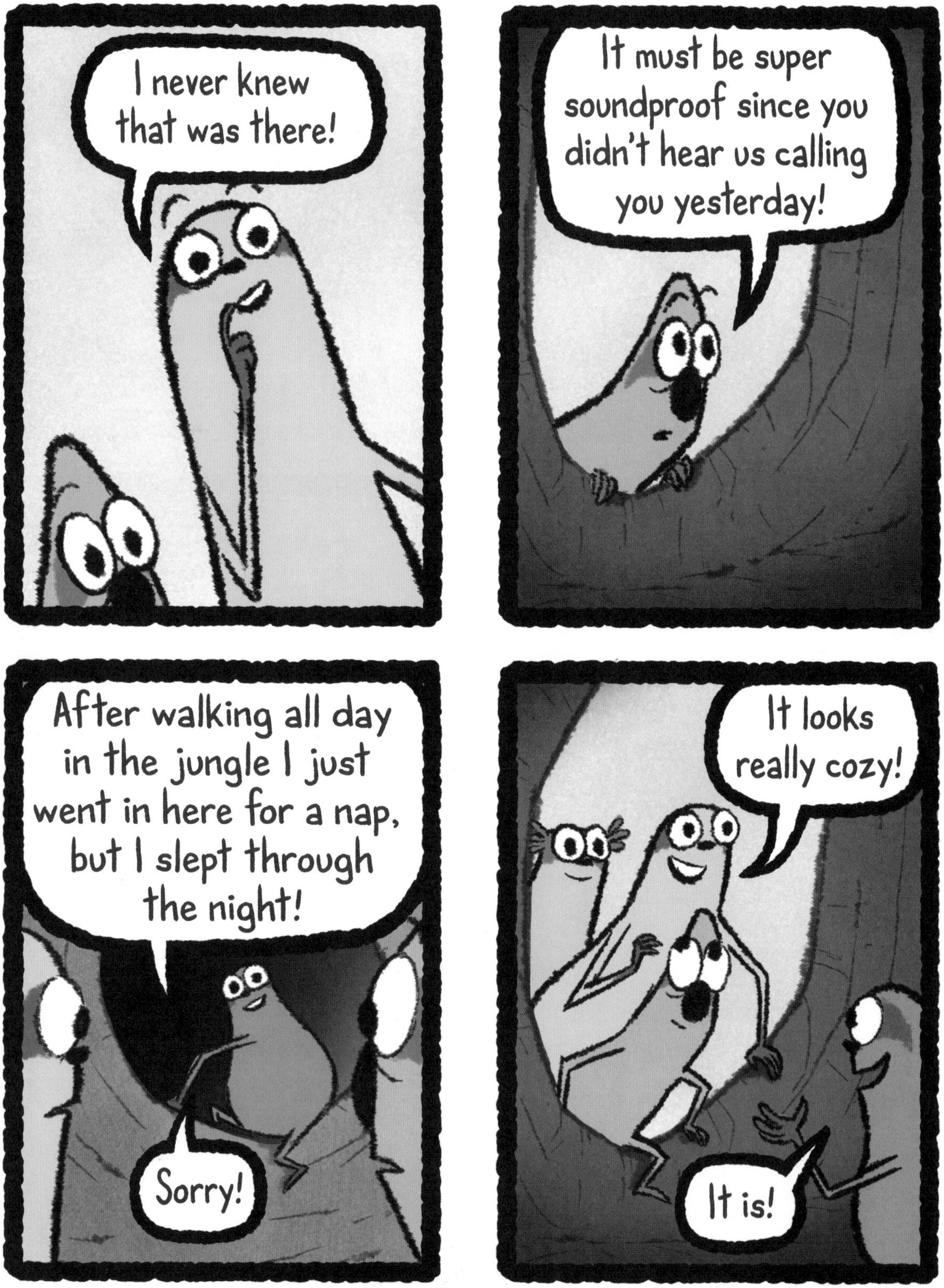
I never knew that was there!
It must be super soundproof since you didn't hear us calling you yesterday!
After walking all day in the jungle I just went in here for a nap, but I slept through the night!
Sorry!
It looks really cozy!
It is!

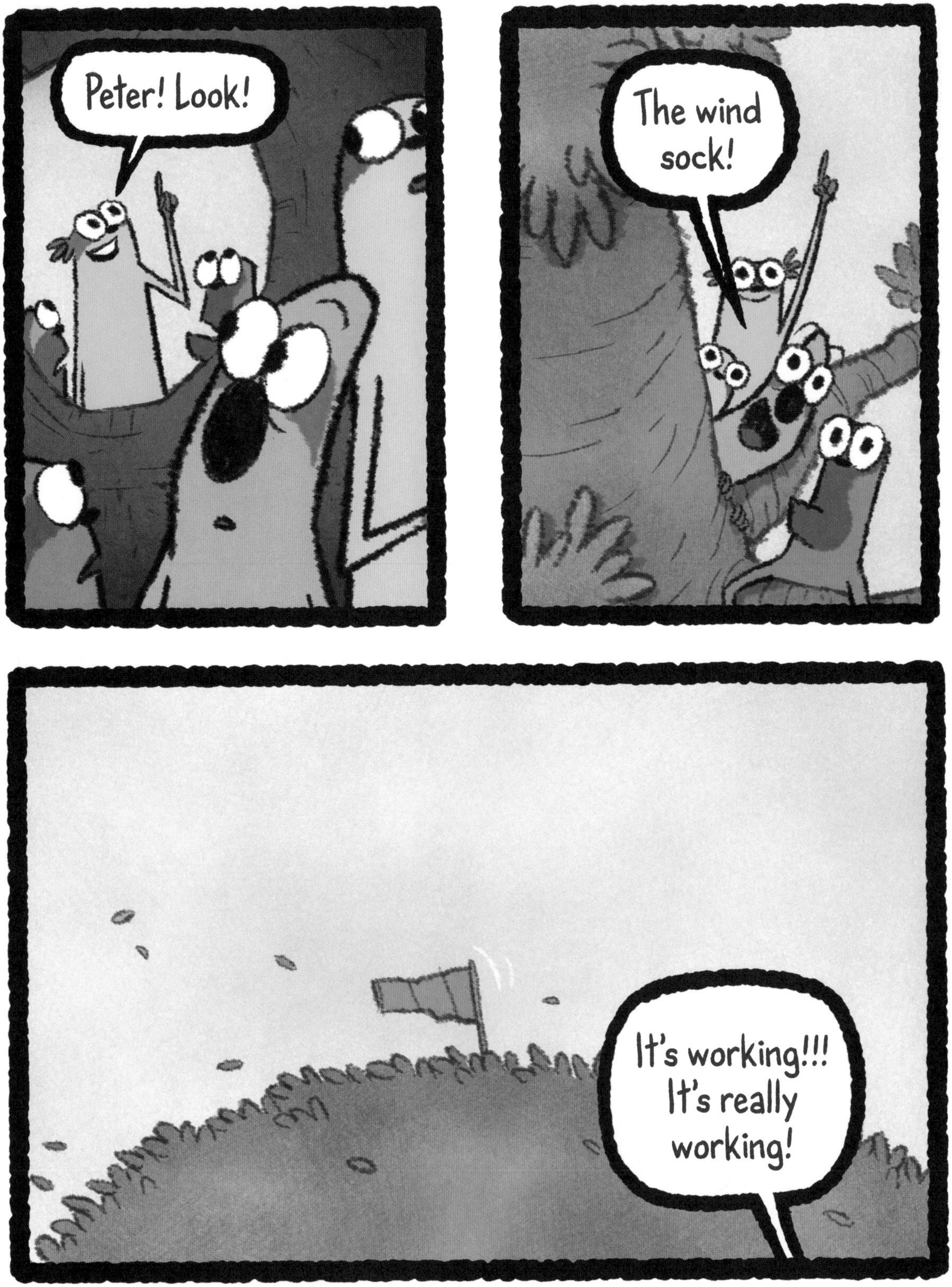
Peter! Look!
The wind sock!
It's working!!! It's really working!

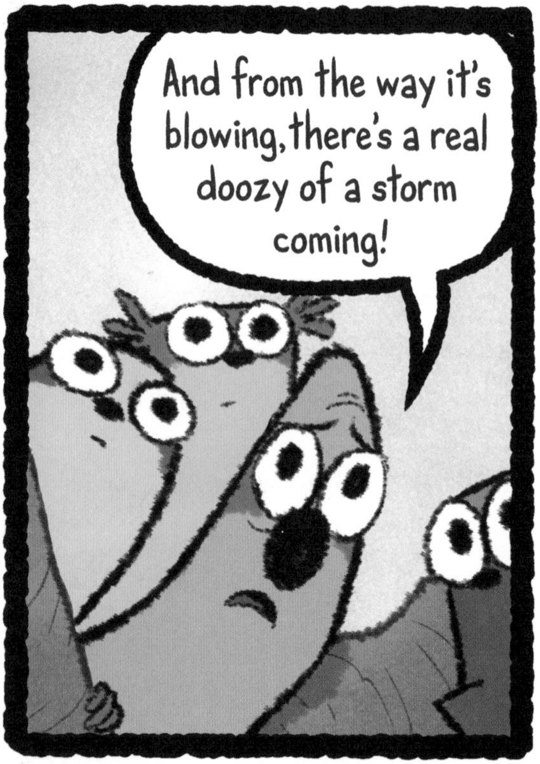
And from the way it's blowing, there's a real doozy of a storm coming!

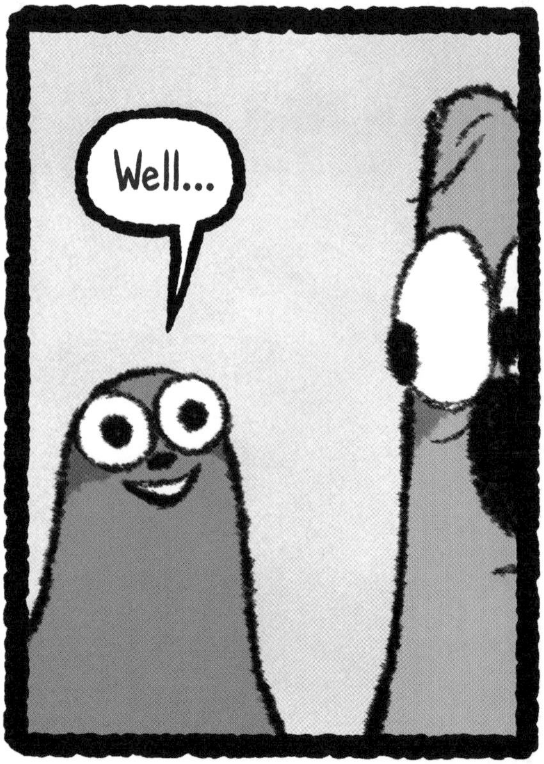
Well...

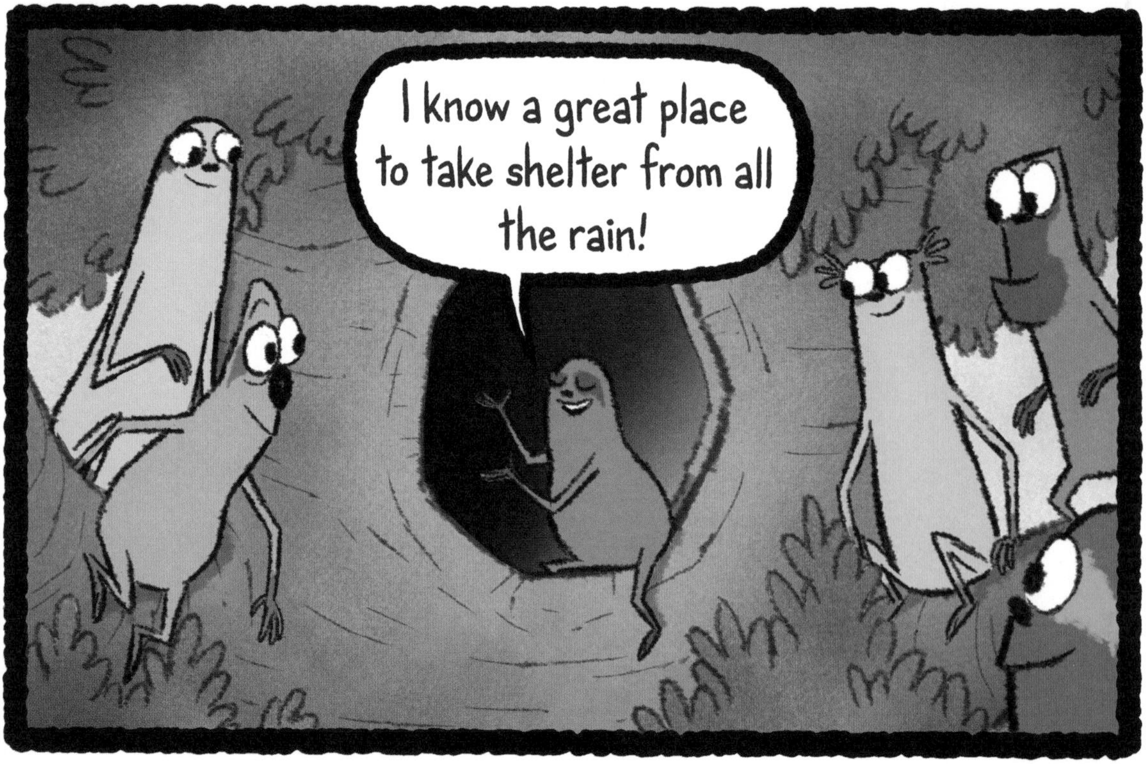
I know a great place to take shelter from all the rain!

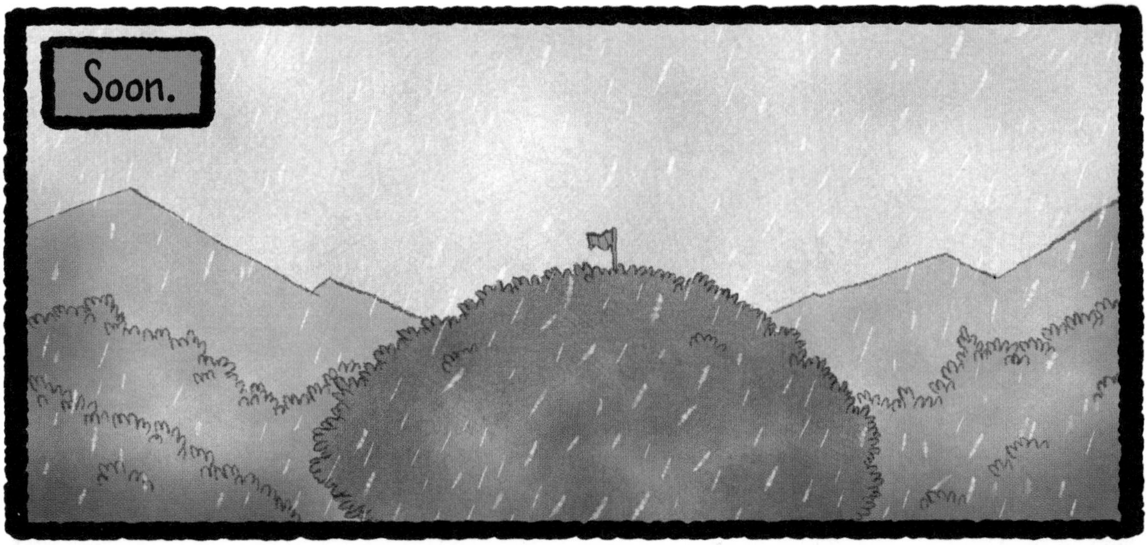
Soon.

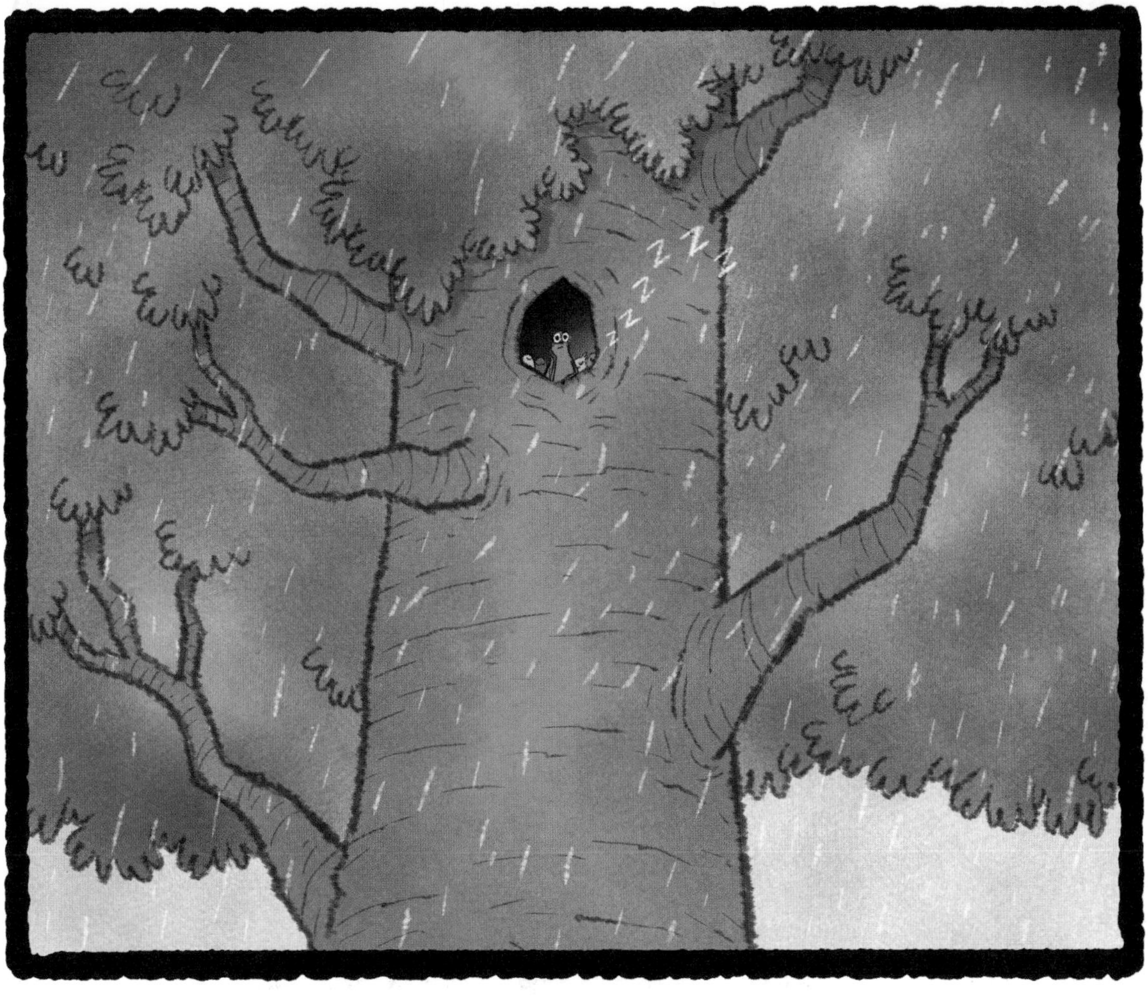
Z Z Z Z Z Z Z

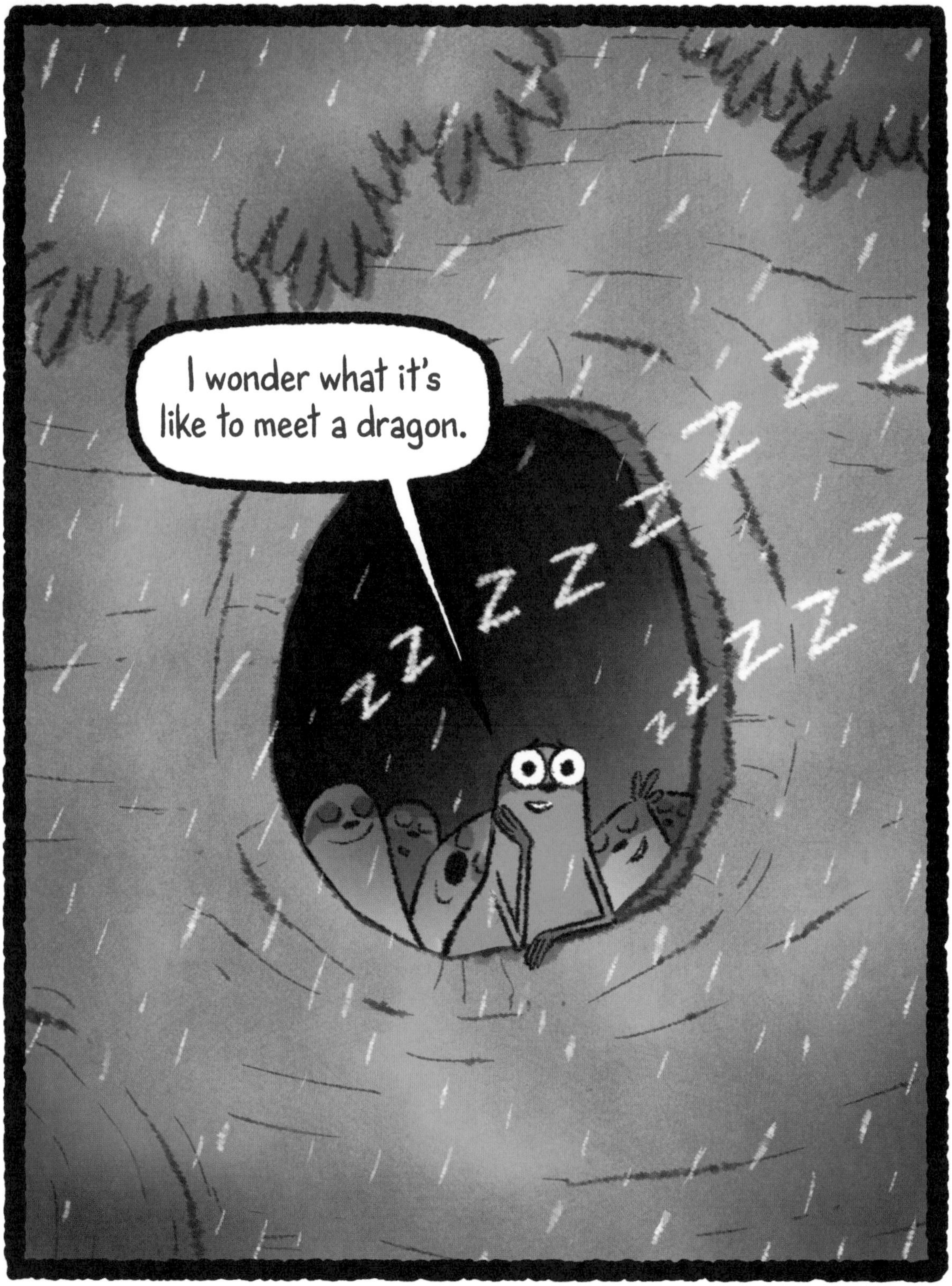
I wonder what it's like to meet a dragon.

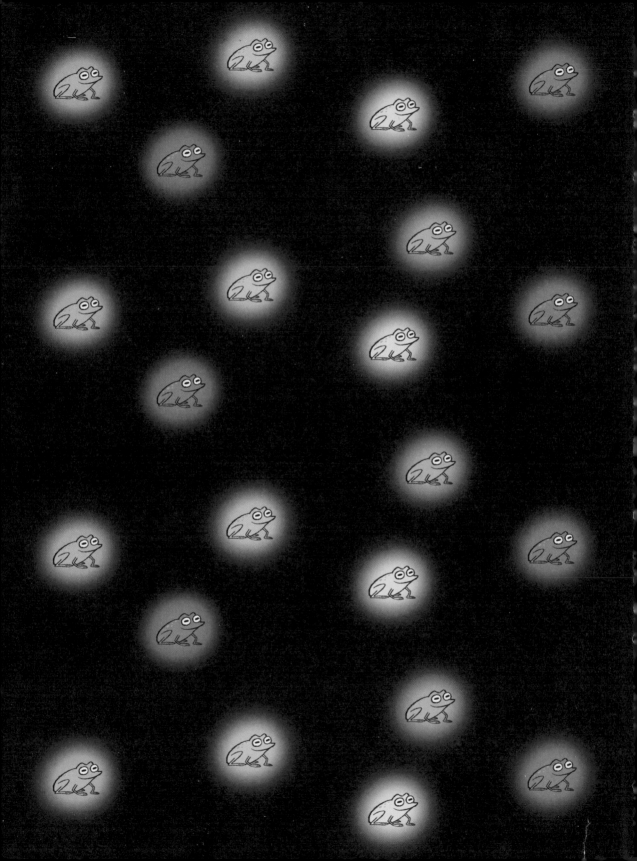